THE BLACK MASK LIBRARY

THE EARLY YEARS (1920–26)

The Man in the Shadows: The Complete Black Mask Cases of Terry Mack *by Carroll John Daly*

Zigzags of Treachery: The Complete Black Mask Cases of the Continental Op, Volume 1 *by Dashiell Hammett*

THE SHAW YEARS (1926–36)

Blood on the Curb *by Joseph T. Shaw*

Black Harvest: The Complete Black Mask Cases of Jules Tremaine *by Norvell W. Page*

Boomerang Dice: The Complete Black Mask Cases of Johnny Hi Gear *by Stewart Sterling*

The Case-Hardened Samaritan: The Complete Black Mask Cases of Dal Prentice, Volume 1 *by Roger Torrey*

Dead Evidence: The Complete Black Mask Cases of Harrigan *by Ed Lybeck*

Laughing Death *by Raoul Whitfield*

Luck: The Complete Black Mask Cases of Oscar Sail *by Lester Dent*

Murder Maze: The Complete Black Mask Cases of Jerry Tracy, Volume 2 *by Theodore A. Tinsley*

The Price of a Dime: The Complete Black Mask Cases of Ben Shaley *by Norbert Davis*

Somewhere in Mexico: The Complete Black Mask Cases of Jerry Frost, Volume 1 *by Horace McCoy*

South Wind: The Complete Black Mask Cases of Jerry Tracy, Volume 1 *by Theodore A. Tinsley*

That's Hollywood: The Complete Black Mask Cases of Bill Lennox, Volume 1 *by W.T. Ballard*

White Talons: The Complete Black Mask Cases of Tex of the Border Service *by Katherine Brocklebank*

THE LATER YEARS (1936–51)

Dead and Done For: The Complete Black Mask Cases of Cellini Smith, Volume 1 *by Robert Reeves*

Dog Eat Dog: The Complete Black Mask Cases of Cellini Smith, Volume 2 *by Robert Reeves*

The Hound with the Golden Eye: The Complete Black Mask Cases of Luther McGavock, Volume 2 *by Merle Constiner*

It Happened at the Lake *by Joseph T. Shaw*

Let the Dead Alone: The Complete Black Mask Cases of Luther McGavock, Volume 1 *by Merle Constiner*

Murder Costs Money: The Complete Black Mask Cases of Rex Sackler, Volume 1 *by D.L. Champion*

Murder on the Midway: The Complete Black Mask Cases of the Human Encyclopedia, Volume 1 *by Frank Gruber*

Murder Pays 7 to 1: The Complete Black Mask Cases of Rex Sackler, Volume 2 *by D.L. Champion*

THE HOUND WITH THE GOLDEN EYE

The Complete

Cases of Luther McGavock

1943–45

MERLE CONSTINER

illustrations by Peter Kuhlhoff

cover by Rafael de Soto

BLACK MASK
2023

"Kill One, Skip One" originally appeared in the November 1943 issue of *Black Mask* magazine (Vol. 26, No. 3). Copyright © 1943 by Popular Publications, Inc. Copyright renewed © 1970 and assigned to Steeger Properties, LLC. All rights reserved.

"The Hound with the Golden Eye" originally appeared in the May 1944 issue of *Black Mask* magazine (Vol. 26, No. 6). Copyright © 1944 by Popular Publications, Inc. Copyright renewed © 1971 and assigned to Steeger Properties, LLC. All rights reserved.

"Killer Stay 'Way from My Door" originally appeared in the November 1944 issue of *Black Mask* magazine (Vol. 26, No. 9). Copyright © 1944 by Popular Publications, Inc. Copyright renewed © 1971 and assigned to Steeger Properties, LLC. All rights reserved.

"Until the Undertaker Comes" originally appeared in the March 1945 issue of *Black Mask* magazine (Vol. 26, No. 11). Copyright © 1945 by Popular Publications, Inc. Copyright renewed © 1972 and assigned to Steeger Properties, LLC. All rights reserved.

Visit STEEGERBOOKS.COM for more books like this.

Table of Contents

Kill One, Skip One

Stolen hot biscuits, a nut who collects cats, and a phony medium—a happy threesome to start McGavock off in the sleepy little town of Archersburg where nothing ever happens—except two bludgeonings, two murders and a cat that skipped a death dance at the scene of the crimes.

1

Cat Mystery

THE DAY WAS oppressively hot, sultry. McGavock, in his shirtsleeves, his cuffs rolled back on his forearms, was standing at the window, staring at the heat waves shimmering from the tarred rooftops, when Miss Ollinger bore down on him. The secretary minced across the floor as though she had buckshot in her shoes. Pinched distastefully between her thumb and forefinger was his tropic-weight coat. "This goes back on, if you please!" She leered stiffly. "The staff must be fully garbed at all times. That's our rule here, you know, Mr. McGavock!"

He purpled. With trembling fingers, he took the jacket from her hand, fought his way savagely into it. "Is this a detective agency or a dancing academy?"

"We've no time for banter." She arched her pigeon chest. "Mr. Browne wishes to see you. And he means right now!"

McGavock strode angrily into the chief's sanctum. Old Atherton Browne was enjoying himself in a condition of supreme ease. His shoes were off, and so were his coat and shirt. He was sitting in a baggy mesh singlet, a coffee mug in one hand and a pitcher of ice water in the other. On the battered desk in front of him was a sheaf of effervescent fruit powders in little envelopes. Penny packets produced for the moppet trade—lime, raspberry, cherry, and so forth. The old man filled the mug with ice water, slit an envelope marked ORANGE, and tapped out the powder. The mug erupted in a poisonous-looking salmon colored froth. The oldster gulped noisily, set the empty mug on the blotter. "Yah!" he gasped with relish.

McGavock exploded. "Put on those shoes! Put on that coat and shirt! You know the house rule!"

The old man smiled sadly. "I'm a disgusting sight. I guess I'm just eccentric—eccentric and comfortable." He added mildly: "That's just one of the griefs a boss must endure—he can do as he pleases. What did you want, Luther?"

"What do I want?" McGavock was acid. "You sent for me, didn't you?"

The oldster studied him with bloodshot, mucous-rimmed eyes. "No, Luther, I didn't."

"Didn't you tell Miss Ollinger to hustle me in here?"

Atherton Browne looked embarrassed. "There's been a mistake, she must have misunderstood me. A rather peculiar case has broken for us back at Archersburg but it's hardly in your line. Jokingly, I asked Miss Ollinger to send me in my mediocre detective—those were my words. I meant Pete Coyle." He coughed politely. "She just got things twisted. You're not mediocre, you're my ace!"

"Baloney!" McGavock placed his hand flatly on the desktop, leaned forward. "You're trying to wheedle me into something. I don't know what it is and I don't want to know. I'm not interested." His face flushed with self pity. "I'm just heeltaps around here. If I'm so good why don't you give me a decent contract?"

McGavock was a small man, wiry and tough, with a touch of salt-and-pepper gray over his temples. He had a jangling, irritating quality about him that aroused instant animal antagonism in total strangers. He'd worked in most of the major agencies in the country, and was a genius at getting results but he was a hard man to take. Never, until he'd hit this Memphis berth, had he actually found a home.

His employer liked what he brought in but didn't want to know too much about his methods. He worked under a sort of roving license that the agency could repudiate at the drop of a hat—if things got too hot. This unilateral contract was a source of constant inflammation to him. He asked warily: "What's this business about Archersburg?"

Old Atherton Browne produced a yellow telegraph flimsy, handed it across the blotter. McGavock took it, read—

ATHERTON BROWNE DETECTIVE AGENCY MEMPHIS
I AM NO CRANK AND THIS IS WORTH TWO THOUSAND DOLLARS TO YOU IF YOU PLAY IT THROUGH. SOMEONE HAS BEEN STEALING MY HOT BISCUITS. I WANT THIS INVESTIGATED.

PERCY RAMSBAUGH MILBURN
ARCHERSBURG, TENNESSEE

IT WAS DATED that morning. McGavock perused the text moodily. It didn't strike him as funny. As a veteran, he'd learned long ago that grotesquerie in a criminal case could pack some mighty grisly background. He said under his breath: "Archersburg, Archersburg. Somehow that name rings familiar. . . ."

The oldster belittled it. "Just a tank town in the hills over near the Alabama line. Too trivial for you to waste your time on. Now Pete Coyle—"

McGavock grunted. "I make it now. It's at Archersburg where they've been having those bludgeonings. Two killings in three days!"

Huge footprints, rubber boots, coming and going... and Bellew's sly, cruel eyes staring lifelessly out into the valley.

"Is that so? I don't recall, Luther. Now, as I say, this is Pete Coyle's style. It's just a routine checkup. Who'd pay two grand to apprehend a pastry thief? Just because the man says he's no crank certainly doesn't make such the case. It sounds loony to me!"

"Hush-hush!" McGavock frowned. "I've got it snagged now. There was a feature story in last Sunday's paper. *Village in the Grip of Nameless Terror!* Stuff like that. A couple of guys have been mauled to death on the streets at night. Yassuh. It all

comes back to me now. Archersburg is where the catman is!"

"Luther, you're being absurd."

"Don't try to sidetrack me. There's a nut in that little town, a big-hearted crackpot, who buys stray cats from kids. He takes these cats up in the hills and releases them. He claims that cats revert quickly and that when they live the undomesticated life of their ancestors, they're happier and healthier. And this man's name is Percy Ramsbaugh Milburn!"

"Gracious. It that so? Then he is crazy, isn't he?"

McGavock brooded. "I'm not so sure. I believe there's eighty thousand bucks involved in some way."

"Well, son, Pete Coyle will soon find out."

"Phooey on Pete Coyle. I'll take it myself. Adios." He slammed out.

Ten minutes later, when the spinsterly secretary fluttered into the office with a letter to be signed, the oldster beckoned to her. "Get that file, the old one, down from the shelf in the closet. I want letter *M*."

Miss Ollinger looked bewildered. "I don't know of any file in the closet."

"It's there." He was impatient. "I haven't had it out for fifteen years—it's back there under that pile of unwashed socks."

She rummaged around, located it. A cardboard box. The old man lifted the cover, sorted through a stack of yellowed newspaper clippings. "It's here," he muttered. "It has to be. Ah!"

He clipped a pair of smudged glasses onto the bridge of his bony nose and scanned the faded column-length item.

> New Orleans, May 11—Percy Ramsbaugh Milburn, grocery-clerk turned robber and killer, met his death last night beneath a hail of police bullets as he resisted arrest in a shabby waterfront hotel.
>
> Milburn, aged 59, a bachelor, was wanted in six states. For eight years, he had cut a swathe of homicide and larceny.
>
> His career of violence over, and positively identified from fingerprint records on file at police headquarters, a résumé of his record shows him to have been a desperado of the worst type, cunning, daring, and merciless....

The oldster laid away the item. Penciled on the margin was the annotation: May 11, 1919.

Atherton Browne did a bit of silent calculation. Say it wasn't Milburn that the police had slain. Say that somehow the fingerprints had got mixed up. If Milburn had been fifty-nine at the time that would make him eighty-three now—a fantastic age. Atherton Browne shook his head. He, too, had seen the feature story to which McGavock had referred. And the photo of Archersburg's benevolent catman pictured him as in his late forties. No, it wouldn't work. This old clipping was correct. This 1919 Milburn, the real Milburn, was dead.

What was it all about? The only possible conclusion was that for some outlandish reason, someone had deliberately assumed a dangerously notorious name. You couldn't get around it—there simply couldn't be two Percy Ramsbaugh Milburns!

It was a tough problem. The oldster's eyes glinted sensuously, visualizing the tangle that McGavock was up against. He sighed happily, filled his mug with ice water, and poured in a strawberry fruit powder.

HIS WRISTWATCH SAID five after eleven that night when McGavock swung down from the train steps onto the station platform. It had been a slow trip from the city with many changes and much shuttling. Archersburg was buried in a hinterland of wild, wooded hills. He'd arrived at the tail end of a summer storm. The rain had ceased but spasmodic lightning slashed the overcast sky and thunder skirled among the distant hilltops. McGavock picked up his over-sized Gladstone, circled the dingy unlighted depot, and headed for Main Street.

The pavements were deserted. A typical little southern town, quaint and peaceful, it was the sort of place that McGavock knew well—and liked. The fresh-washed air fanned his cheek with an earthy cleanness. Puddles of water in the gutter, motionless now after the gale, caught the feeble street lights in a plating of new silver. In the center of the business district was a court square—telling McGavock that the village was a county seat—and from the vine-hung pillars of the old courthouse came the spicy, sweet fragrance of wet honeysuckle. A night-singing mockingbird tried out his throat from a tall red-oak. McGavock glanced about him at the lifeless sidewalks, said under his breath: "What an idyllic spot to be bludgeoned to death. We shall see what we shall see."

He walked along the row of darkened store fronts, swinging his Gladstone at his knee. He'd traversed about half the line of small shops and was crossing the mouth of an alley when a beam of light burst in his eyes. A shrewish female voice said: "Stand right thur 'til I git a look at you!" He set the bag on the sidewalk between his feet and waited.

The withered crone that emerged cautiously from the alley came about to his shoulder. She was stooped with age and her face was wrinkled to an almost sexless quality. She carried a seven-cell, coonhunting flashlight and, to McGavock's amazement, she was dressed like a highschool girl and literally plastered with tawdry jewelry. McGavock said: "Go back and come out different. You scare me that way. Who are you?"

She clamped shut turtle jaws. "Never you mind who I am. I'll ask all the questions. What you got in that thur satchel? I'm Mrs. Deppity Oglesby."

"The law? Excuse me, I didn't recognize the uniform."

"Never you mind the smart alecky remarks. Sandy, that's my man, he's sick to bed. I'm doin' Sandy's round. They's been too many killin's hereabouts. I'm dressed up this way because I'm jest a-comin' home from a pie-supper at the Kind Hearts and Nimble Fingers Quiltin' Club. What you got in that satchel, stranger?"

"A miscellaneous assortment of heterogeneous impedimenta—think nothing of it. Tell me, how do I get to the hotel?"

"Should I tell you, you'd never forgive me." The beldame fired up. "The feller that runs hit hain't moral. Hit's called the Butler House and hit's a block down the street. You jest walk straight by hit and you'll come to a watering trough in front of the undertaker's. Turn left there—you're on Elm Avenue. Keep goin' 'til you git to the end of the pavement. The big house up on the hillside is Acacia Gardens. They advertise in northern newspapers sayin' come to Archersburg and put up at Acacia Gardens and git you a whift of the ole south. They got a prissy little cotton patch in back to prove to guests that they're in Dixie. The food's bad, the prices are high, but Mr. Baylor that runs it, is a—"

"Is a moral man? Thanks and good night."

THE BUTLER HOUSE was a shabby old brick structure crammed between a two story department store and an ancient office building. There was a monkscloth curtain in the window and a vase of dusty palm leaves. In front of the window, along the sidewalk, was a decrepit church pew within spitting distance of the curb, for those of the hotel's guests who might wish to sit in the sunshine and watch the race of man drift by. A dull gleam of light came through the grimy window pane. McGavock opened the door and entered.

The lobby was stale smelling, musty. A six inch tooth of faded purple wallpaper drooped from the water stained ceiling. A half dozen rocking chairs were scattered about the worn carpet. An anemic, elfish fellow with pale yellow gabled eyebrows sat behind the desk paring his fingernails with a rusty razor-blade. He greeted McGavock with intimate enthusiasm. "Well, friend, you finally got here, eh?"

McGavock looked jolted. "What does that crack add up to?"

"I never go to bed until the last train gets in. Now I can hit the hay. I'm Butler, by the way. This ain't the best hotel in the world but we struggle along. My grandfather built this hive, he kicked it off to my dad who wished it off on me. You have to take your bag up yourself. It's what I call the Butler plan. No service, cheap prices, and good food. Your room is number seven—up at the top of the stairs."

McGavock got mad, choked, found himself laughing. "O.K." He signed the register, set his bag inside the corner of the desk. "I won't be turning in for a while. I guess I'd better take my key along with me. Thanks." He hesitated. "Do you know a man in town named Percy Ramsbaugh Milburn?"

Butler stared. "Yes, I know him. You can have him—I don't want him. He stays at that other hotel, that ritzy tourist dead-fall. He's a resident there." He inspected his trimmed finger-nails, added casually: "Know what I think?"

McGavock looked bored. "What do you think?"

"This man Milburn's a spooky character, in my civic opinion. He's been putting out the word that he wants to buy stray cats. He declares that he's taking them out to the country and releasing them. That doesn't sound like Milburn—if you'd ever met him, you'd see my point. He's no humanitarian. He gives me the creeps! I think he's a maniac. I think he buys those cats from kids, butchers them for their hides or something, and then burns the carcasses up in his kiln."

"In his what?"

"His kiln." Butler's eyes boggled. "It's a horrible thought but I can't get it out of my mind. He came to town about a month ago, leased that abandoned clay mine out at the end of Main Street, and built himself a small kiln. He's a kind of a sculptor—supplies museums with lowgrade facsimiles of ancient ceramics. That's his livelihood. No matter what he claims, he couldn't take those cats out in the hills—he doesn't own a car! And if he doesn't take them out in the hills, what does he do with them?"

McGavock shrugged, said, "I wouldn't know." He sauntered across the lobby, stepped out into the night.

2

The Dapper Looking Corpse

GRADUALLY THE LAST vestige of the storm was disappearing. Great curd-like clouds were splitting before the moon, withdrawing to the hilltopped horizons, exposing a luminous cobalt sky. The night was aromatic, fetid. At one end of Main Street was Archersburg's dilapidated depot, at the other, McGavock reasoned, he'd find a situation worth looking into. He wanted to give this abandoned clay mine a quick once-over. He thumbed the brim of his hat back from his forehead and set off at a brisk walk. The business district gave way to a scattered residential neighborhood and that, in turn, thinned out to fields and weedy commons. Suddenly, at the exact edge of town, the asphalt street went into a rutted red-clay county road.

A quarter of a mile beyond the city limits the road forked, running in two tines up into the hills. At the point of confluence was a weathered, eight-foot wooden gate bearing the almost obliterated sign: STAR CLAY MINE—*No Admittance.* And underneath, in bright new paint was printed: *And This Means You!* PERCY RAMSBAUGH MILBURN. The gate was ajar—an expensive padlock hung hooked in the open hasp. McGavock pulled down the corners of his mouth, ambled inside.

He peered into the shifting shadows. The side of the slope seemed to be enclosed in a high board fence. The mine would be back there on the hillside. About halfway between the gate and a small domed structure—the kiln—was a ramshackle building. The kiln, he decided, could be passed up for the present. He turned his attention to the sagging structure. Hooding his flash with his hand, he looked about him. It was an old warehouse, completely unroofed by the ravages of time, its windows broken to ragged shards. Next to this hulking shell, and built directly onto the side of the old wreck, was a small neat shanty. The shanty was constructed of new lumber, with new window sash and a strong, new door. A large cardboard placard was thumbtacked to the door. It said: ARTIST'S STUDIO.

McGavock grinned. This was the first artist that McGavock had run into for a long time that called himself an artist. Most artists recoiled from the term, preferred to be called painters, sculptors, musicians. McGavock tried the knob—the door was locked.

The third key on his ring did the trick. He listened a moment, heard no sound, and entered. He took his cupped hand from the flashlight lens.

It was the strangest sculptor's studio he'd ever seen and by far the most interesting. The room was small and perfectly bare of professional equipment. No work bench, no half finished masterpieces, no tools. Just the bare walls and floor and three articles of furniture—a footstool, an easy chair, and a smoking stand. Just these—and a corpse.

The body was lolling in a roly-poly position on the chair and McGavock knew as soon as he laid eyes on him that the dead man, the catman, whose picture he had seen in the news story, and his client were one and the same. This was the lad with the tricycle name: Percy Ramsbaugh Milburn.

And he made a vicious, nasty-looking little corpse. He was dapper, pint-sized, and he wore a wispy, reddish Vandyke. This Vandyke was the sole feature about him that was at all suggestive of an aesthete. He was garbed in checked trousers, a horse-blanket sport coat, and fancy perforated shoes. Blank out the beard and you had a typical petty confidence man, or maybe a race track tout. McGavock studied him in bleak silence—the sly heavy lidded eyes, the cruel, greedy mouth. Percy Ramsbaugh Milburn's necktie was powder-burned, there were three bullet holes in his chest.

FOR A LONG moment, McGavock gazed at the body. At last he spoke. "I won't work for you," he exclaimed aloud. "I don't like you! You go your way and I'll go mine. Get another detective. I'm going to get another client. And that's final." He paused dramatically, asked: "Any objections? O.K. That's that. Pardon me while I—"

He bent over the corpse, began a thorough search of the dead man's clothes.

Milburn's pockets were strangely empty. Generally a man carries something somewhere about his person but Milburn was clean. Not a match or a penny or even a key. It was the absence of a key that told McGavock that the killer had beat him to the search. Milburn had to possess a key to get him through the front gate—and there was no key. The way McGavock put the picture together was this way: the murderer had slain his man and rifled his pockets of everything, down to the lint, in a super-cautious effort to leave no clue.

That was the situation. Yet somehow it seemed a bit askew.

Put it this way, instead. Milburn spelled slicker from haircut to shoes, yet he'd allowed someone to walk in on him, lay a gun against his necktie and blast him out of this world. This simply couldn't jibe with the man's character as McGavock reconstructed it. Milburn wasn't the sort of man to be taken by surprise. It was more likely that he met his slayer in some sort of off-color rendezvous.

If this was true, Milburn must have distrusted his accomplice, and if he distrusted the man he met, it was quite possible that he, Milburn, had emptied his own pockets in advance, in anticipation of some unpleasant strongarm circumstance arising at the meeting. He must have had something on him that he wished to keep in his possession.

There was a kerosene lamp on the smoking stand. McGavock lit it—the chimney was still warm. He gazed broodingly about him. A bare room has few hiding places. He inspected the footstool, the easy chair, and the smoking stand, and found just what he expected—nothing. The floorboards were sound, and so were the walls.

Milburn's hiding place was beneath the window sash. The bottom plank, at the base of the trim, came out and in the crevice between the frame and the wall was a folded handkerchief. McGavock took the handkerchief from the aperture, held it beneath the lamp. It contained four dollars and twenty-seven cents, in change and bills, a fountain pen, a key pad, and a small powder-blue envelope about two and a half by four inches square.

The address on the envelope, in a meticulous backhand, read: *P.R. Milburn, Esq., Acacia Gardens, City.* On the reverse, the return address said simply: *Cahill, 811 Spring Street.* He slipped the letter from the flap, scanned it hastily:

Dear Mr. Yancey,

I must again turn down your persistent request for a seance to be held in our attic. My personal opinion is that you are a faker, but faker or not, I wouldn't give a dime a dozen to see all the ghosts you could muster, playing pingpong and dressed in Indian war bonnets. In other words, if you'll permit me to repeat, I'm not at all interested.

(signed) G.C.

Stolen hot biscuits, a man who collected cats—and now Milburn pops up in the role of a phony medium! And what did that Yancey business blurb mean? The envelope addressed to one man, the letter to another!

McGavock dropped the key-case in his pocket, replaced the other articles in the cavity beneath the sill, refitted the board. He blew out the lamp and left the shack.

LOCATING THE EXCLUSIVE tourist hostelry which labeled itself Acacia Gardens was easy. McGavock, following the directions of Mrs. Deputy Oglesby, retraced his steps to the center of town, turned at the watering trough before the undertaker's shop, and proceeded out Elm Avenue until the pavement ended. The old mansion sat a hundred yards or so up on the hillside. Shadowed by a grove of locusts, it was hard to discern. McGavock got the impression of two-story verandas, of tall pillars, of a bulky, crazy angled roof against the faint moon. The place was completely dark but for a single golden window pane on the ground floor—most likely the foyer light.

McGavock wandered up the gravel-stone drive. The entire lower front porch, he observed, was screened. He ascended four stone steps, swung open the screen-door and stepped onto the veranda. A thin, reedy voice came out of the spongy blackness beside him. It sang: "*There was an old man came riding in, and the seat of his britches was lined with tin!* Heh-heh-heh!"

Then McGavock saw the glow of the pipe He stopped dead-still, asked sweetly: "Is someone back there speaking to me?"

The reedy voice said: "Heh-heh-heh! *And the seat of his britches was lined with tin!*"

McGavock blew up. "Listen, friend. I don't have the slightest idea what you're talking about, but I don't want any more of it. I'm not in the mood for wisecracks. I—"

"I wasn't talking about you." The reedy voice seemed genuinely embarrassed. "That's just an old folk-song I discovered today. I saw you coming up the drive there and something about you, the way you walked, I mean—"

McGavock said venomously: "Don't explain, it just gets worse. Who are you?"

Surprisingly, there was a click and the far end of the porch was flooded with a little spot of rosy light. On a wicker taboret was a boudoir lamp, pink-shaded and frilly with lace and ribbons. Next to the lamp, in a big fanback rattan chair, was a blubberous fat man. He was dressed in a baggy green tweed suit. And never had McGavock seen such ultra-tweed as this. It was super rough, it looked like it had bark and twigs woven into it. The fat man was smoking a big-bowled French briar. He grinned fatuously, wobbled his flabby jowls, lifted the pipe to his nose and gave it a polishing on the side of his nostril. "This is no way to start a friendship—I'm a sociable man." He was conciliatory, almost fawning. "I just said...."

"Who are you?"

"I'm Fortunatus Duff!" He said it gently, as if McGavock might be knocked down by the disclosure.

"You're who? Repeat that, please, and slower. It somehow leaves me cold."

"Don't tell me you've never heard of Fortunatus Duff?" The fat man was sympathetic. "I'm the greatest student of folk-lore and primitive customs alive in America today. I'm affiliated with a certain northern university which shall remain nameless. I'm down here in the southland collecting historical idiom and ballads."

McGavock looked puzzled. "Why did you ever leave the college campus? If you're interested in primitive customs, I'd think you'd find about all you could handle—"

Click! The light went out. Duff's reedy voice came again out of the spongy blackness. It sounded petulant, offended. "You have an irritating personality, sir. Be good enough to leave me alone. I'm trying to analyze this tune: 'There was an old man came riding in, and the seat of his britches was lined with—' "

"With college diplomas?" McGavock turned roughly on his heel, strode into the building.

THE OLD MANSION'S living room had been converted into a semi-public half-foyer, half-parlor. It was a large, high ceilinged room cluttered with odds and ends of domestic furniture. There was clean, new matting on the floor and the tall windows were hung with canary drapes. The stairway was at the rear, and at the right of the newelpost was a small, U-shaped counter, the manager's desk. A crooknecked student's lamp, with a reflector, burned on the desk, and next to the lamp was a tap-bell. McGavock held his finger over the bell, tapped out: *shave and a haircut—bay rum!*

He waited a moment. The portieres at the back of the desk parted and a gaunt man in a candlewick bathrobe answered his ring. He had a quiet, reserved face, and eyes like frosted slate. He asked: "Are you to be a guest at this modest domicile, suh? Are you from the north? Did you come to Archersburg to luxuriate in the blessed bounties of this Dixie paradise? Twenty dollars per week—board, room, and fresh air!"

McGavock peeled three twenties from a gambler's roll, signed the register card. The manager said: "I'm Mr. Baylor, Mr. McGavock. I don't seem to see your bag."

McGavock screwed up his face. "I'm a nervous wreck. I just got away from it all as fast as I could—traveling bags annoy me." He paused. "I want to stay three weeks, I want to build myself up. I'm edgy. If I should go off the deep end and break anything up, I'll pay for it."

Baylor didn't turn a hair. "That's all right, suh," he said calmly. "We've had high-spirited folks before. May I show you to your room?" He took a key from the desk drawer, lifted a flap in the counter, and without another word started up the stairs. McGavock followed him.

He led McGavock to the end of the upstairs hall, put the key in the escutcheon. "These are your quarters, suh. Bathroom's yonder. Breakfast at ten. I hope you're comfortable."

"One thing more." McGavock hesitated. "I hope this place is quiet. How many guests do you have? Someone was saying that there's a man here that keeps cats in his room, hundreds of them."

Mr. Baylor looked mildly irritated. "They were referring to Mr. Milburn." His eyes involuntarily flicked to a door across the hall. "Mr. Milburn has caused quite a sensation in the press, along with those two unfortunate deaths you've no doubt heard about. No. Mr. Milburn doesn't keep cats in his room. As a matter of fact, if you need rest you've come at a mighty good time. We're in a lull between seasons. There are just three residents at the present: yourself, Mr. Duff, a gentleman from the north, and Mr. Milburn." He bowed. "Good night, suh."

"Two unfortunate deaths? What do you mean?"

"Two citizens were slain on the streets at night last week. More than that, I can't tell you. I never read the newspapers and never listen to gossip. Forget it. You're perfectly secure here at Acacia Gardens. Should we have a prowler—ahem—I think that I can take care of him." He said it humbly, but his eyes were little granite blobs. "Again, good night."

McGavock rattled his doorknob, stood silently in the dark hall. He heard Mr. Baylor's footsteps padding down the stairs. A moment later he heard the counterflap drop, heard the portiere rings tinkle. The manager was back in his hole.

McGavock crossed the corridor. He produced Milburn's key-case, selected a key that matched his own, and opened the dead man's door.

He eased the panel shut behind him, flipped on the wall switch.

No light came on.

He took three steps sidewise softly along the wall and dropped to his hunkers. For a good two minutes he sat there on heels, against the baseboard—listening. It was like staring into a curtain of velvet. There must be a bed in here, he thought, and a bureau, and chairs. He could see nothing. Nothing but the long, faint oblong of the window and the gray-blue night outside. The window interested him. It was about seven feet high and faced the second-story veranda. It was a new type of window to him. Where most windows were composed of two large panes, or several small panes, this window seemed to have six panes. The funny part about it was that the panes were different widths. There were three upper panes and three lower and they graduated in size, from left to right. And suddenly he solved it. The window swung on hinges from its side. It was partly open. He was looking at it from a foreshortened angle. What he'd taken to be the cross-bar of the sash was in reality the banister of the veranda beyond. He had company—there was someone else in this room of death.

Somewhere in this dark room Milburn's killer was crouching, listening, just as McGavock was.

It didn't take much logic to figure out the sequence of events. The slayer had hastened from the scene of the crime to search Milburn's effects. He was looking for something. McGavock had surprised him in the act.

McGavock's jaw set. He took a penny from his pocket, and bracing himself for action, tossed the copper toward a far corner of the room.

Things happened fast.

In the first place, McGavock's ear was involuntarily set with the wrong timing. He'd expected the penny to make its parabola through the air and strike the far wall. The penny struck the floor, all right, it struck it almost instantly—almost as soon as he released it!

The killer was standing in the center of the carpet. *He'd hit the killer with the coin!*

The shots came instantly. Four of them. They cut loose in a deafening, reverberating volley, handrunning. McGavock, on his heels, winced. His eardrums rang with the detonations. There was a vacuum of silence. The door to the corridor opened and shut. His assailant had left the room, had fled *into* the old mansion.

McGavock put his hand to his shoulder. He could feel the powder of dry plaster on the cloth. He stood up, groped along the wall behind him with his fingertips, and located the bullet holes, four of them, in a line. Just about on the level of a man's chest.

He said grimly to himself: "Have your fling, chum. Gather ye rosebuds while you may. You're just making it tougher on yourself. I'm in this business to the bitter end, now. You're looking a pair of handcuffs in the face—and don't know it. Give me twenty-four hours and I'll have the old butterfly net over you."

He crossed the room, stepped from the open window onto the veranda. In the murky moonglow, he walked along the veranda to the back of the building, past a row of darkened, untenanted bedrooms. At the rear of the porch there was a small gate in the banister. He descended a flight of outside stairs to the lawn, skirted the old mansion at a cautious distance, and noticed that the lower floor was now completely blacked out. Mr. Fortunatus Duff had evidently retired—as had Mr. Baylor of the frosty eyes.

McGavock set off down the shadowed pavement toward town. Interlocking elms arched in a vault of leafy foliage above his head. He said reproachfully to himself: "Why can't I learn to carry my gun! Now maybe it'll be months before I'll need it again. Doggone!"

3

A Chat With $80,000

NUMBER 811 SPRING STREET was a friendly little white-brick cottage set in a bower of flowering shrubs. A serpentine flagstone walk led from the street to the tiny thumbnail porch. McGavock ignored the path, headed directly across the close-clipped lawn for the front door. It was 12:07 by his wristwatch, yet the place was blazing with lighted windows. He pressed the buzzer on the door jamb and waited.

A girl answered his summons. She whipped the door open in his face like he was a peddler. She was a pretty little thing, about eighteen, McGavock judged. She had ash-blonde hair and baby blue eyes. Her short skirted frock was a clean starched blue cotton print. She was bare legged and wore spike heeled blue pumps. If you examined her in isolated detail—the modest gingham dress, those childlike eyes—she seemed just another naive country lass, but put them all together and they spelled bother. She was sizzling mad. She said loudly: "This is the last straw! I positively refuse to spend the night under the same roof with you!"

McGavock bowed stiffly. "If that's the way you feel about it, give me back my letters and ring."

She explained furiously: "I'm not talking to you, I'm talking to my husband."

A man's face appeared over her shoulder, said: "Come in, sir. Be good enough to overlook this passage at arms. We go through it every night—been at it since nine o'clock. I'm Georgie Cahill, did you want to see me? What a foolish question. You certainly didn't want to see Lucinda—that's inconceivable! Come in."

McGavock followed them into a cozy, comfortable little parlor. There was a small fireplace with a brace of crossed sabers above it. Casually, the detective invoiced the furniture. Furniture, McGavock had long since discovered, is a fairly reliable index to the occupant's financial status. The furniture here was an assortment from a dozen different periods, ranging from *ante bellum* to the present and every piece, from the antique love seat to the modern radio, was a good, sound expensive stick of wood. These people, McGavock decided, had lineage—and money—and the family had had it for a mighty long time. The little blonde gave him a hard hostile stare, turned to her husband. "What does this person want, Georgie?"

Cahill was a rangy, almost gawkish chap in his early fifties. His clothes, like his wife's, were unpretentious. He had a rugged, homely face and quick, squirrel-like eyes embedded in puffy eye-sockets. All of his face with the exception of his eyes was deadpan—but his eyes were lively, merry, and seemed constantly to be having the time of their life. "I don't know what the gentleman wants, Lucinda. But I'm going to find out." He leaned forward, asked in a conspiratorial whisper: "What do you want, sir, beer, whiskey, or buttermilk?"

McGavock sat down on the love seat, hung his hat on his knee. "The buttermilk had maybe better wait. When you hear what I have to say, you might not feel so chummy toward me. My name's McGavock. I'm a detective."

Cahill nodded. "Fine. That's what Archersburg needs—a

detective. We'll have a campaign: McGavock for Detective!" He paused. "Don't tell me you've come here detecting?"

"No," McGavock answered blandly. "I've come here for information. "I'm from Memphis. I'm working on those two killings you've had here recently. I could go to the sheriff, but after all it's not the official point of view I'm after. I want to get the thing lined up from the townsman's angle. You were recommended to me. Will you let me ask you a few questions?"

"Who recommended us?"

"A charming harridan with a coonhunting flashlight, a Mrs. Deputy Oglesby."

The little blonde said ferociously: "Tell him to get out, Georgie!"

Cahill ignored her. "O.K., shoot."

"Those two murders here, two bludgeonings. I'd like to have the background on them."

Cahill nodded. "Wouldn't we all!" He frowned, got organized. "They were, as you've no doubt been informed, my uncles." McGavock looked wise. Cahill continued: "Uncle Mort and Uncle Nelson. They were retired lumbermen, lived with Baylor at his hotel. The Acacia Gardens—a horrible name, that—is the old Cahill homeplace. Don't look so astounded. This cottage is my wife's home, and don't think she doesn't throw it up to me! As I was saying, my uncles sold out to Baylor and moved in as residents. They were getting along in age and found hotel service more convenient than the labors of keeping up a home of their own. Uncle Mort was slain two weeks ago, in the alley behind the courthouse. He'd just spent the evening with my wife and myself. Uncle Nelson was murdered the following night."

"Returning from, a visit with your wife and yourself?"

"That's right. He'd been here consulting us on Uncle Mort's funeral arrangements."

"I saw a feature story in a Sunday paper." McGavock was thoughtful. "I don't recall your name. There was, however, the vague mention of about eighty thousand bucks."

"That's right. Eighty thousand dollars. You're not going to make me tell that story over again, are you? I blush when I think of it. Well, here goes. Mort and Nelson had a joint capital of eighty thousand dollars. They had duplicate wills—one was to inherit from the other—and the last one alive was to leave his property to me." He grimaced. "Do you want to hear the rest?"

"If I can stand it."

"You asked for it. I was to inherit the full eighty thousand on the day of my second marriage."

McGAVOCK BLINKED. "THAT'S something a bit novel, isn't it?"

"It's not only novel, it's illegal. The courts were eager to set the point aside. It's against public good, or something like that, to insert such a stipulation in a last will and testament. You see, I'm getting along in age—I'm over forty-five."

The blond Mrs. Cahill guffawed. "You're fifty-one!"

Cahill grinned. "I keep forgetting. As I was saying, I'm middle-aged. My uncles strongly disapproved of my marrying so young a wife. It must have been her youth they objected to—it couldn't have been her sweet disposition. To put it mildly, they loathed her. They couldn't drive her out of the family by snubbing us, so they danced this lure in my face, trying to tempt me to divorce her and remarry." He looked sad. "Now I've got the money and the wife, too. I'm in a mess."

McGavock gave a forced laugh. "Think of me. I don't have either! I'm in a mess too." He got up. "Thanks. I'll be getting along. I'm staying at Acacia Gardens. By the way, isn't that where Milburn, the catman, lives?"

"Yes. And let me warn you. I can't quite figure that fellow but he's up to no good. He's been writing me letters. He says his real name is Yancey and that he's a medium of some kind. He wants to come around and hold a seance in our little half-story attic. He claims he can materialize Uncle Mort and find out who murdered him."

"Why not give him a try?"

Cahill's little squirrel-like eyes went serious for the first time. "He doesn't give a hoot for Uncle Mort. I can't explain it—it's just a sensation—but I have the eerie feeling that Milburn-Yancey and *somebody else* is after my eighty thousand. I've got the strange impression that they've been after this money all along. That I'm somehow a cog in their scheme. They couldn't get it from Uncle Mort, so they killed him—they couldn't get it from Uncle Nelson, so they killed him, too. They figured out some way to get it from me. They wanted me to inherit. Their deviltry, whatever it is, is running along like clockwork." His eyes twinkled again. "Well, that's fine. I'm enjoying it. I think I can take care of myself. I'm a natural born sportsman!"

Mrs. Cahill pursed her pretty lips. "Mr. McGavock, you say you're a detective. That, I can believe. You say you've come from Memphis to Archersburg to solve these deaths. I've heard of private detectives—they always work for fees. Now, who is hiring you? My husband is the only logical person. Georgie, have you retained this man?"

Cahill looked stunned. "I hadn't thought of it that way. No, dear, it's all a puzzle to me." He showed traces of sudden worry. "Mr. McGavock, just who is your client?"

A cat walked across the carpet. A big, furry, tortoise tomcat. It came from behind the couch, and in a queer rolling motion, limped out of the room into the hallway. McGavock asked tensely: "Is that cat sick?"

Cahill shook his head. "No, just crippled. That's Old Ninety-Seven—we named him when he was a kitten because he howled like a freight. He was run over by an auto and his leg set crooked. It looks tragic but it really doesn't bother him anymore." The lanky man seemed unguardedly human. "Do you like cats?"

"I can take them or leave them alone."

Together, husband and wife, they paraded him to the front door. McGavock paused on the threshold, said: "You're going to have a little trouble swallowing this, but it's the absolute truth. I came to town to help a certain party find out who was swiping his hot biscuits. It appears as though I'm going to have to solve your uncle's murders as a side-dish in order to get to my objective. Now my original proposition with my client was two thousand dollars. I'm not sure that he'll ever pay me. I'll toss him over and tie up with you people for the same price—if you just say the word."

Cahill pondered. "Talk to me tomorrow. Give me a little time to figure this out."

The pretty little blonde said sarcastically: "And have a better story. Who ever heard of anybody stealing hot biscuits!"

Cahill said gravely: "Shush, Lucinda. The light's beginning to dawn. I think the man's sticking to actual facts. Good night, sir."

Main Street was like a graveyard when McGavock returned to the business district. The great courthouse clock bonged out the hour of one as he stepped from the pavement into the lobby of the Butler House. The place was deserted. He took his Gladstone from behind the desk, ascended the stairs, found his room—number seven—at the right of the landing. He flicked on the light, examined his quarters. They weren't bad at all, a little monastic, perhaps, but clean and sweet-smelling. An iron bed, a single chair, and a washstand with a pitcher and bowl. He stripped to the waist, gave himself a brisk sponge bath. He wasn't tired or drowsy—he wanted to get out on the street and do things. But there was nothing else to do tonight. He'd better not rush things any farther, he'd better let the dead sleep for one more night.

He opened his traveling bag, took out his pajamas. In the breast pocket of the coat was a folded paper, a sheet of the Butler House stationery. He straightened out the sheet. A lazy scrawl said:

> I know this is going to burn you up, my getting into your luggage like this, but I wanted to put this where you'd see it before you retired. Baylor, at the Acacia Gardens, phoned me and asked me if you were putting up here. I told him no. I always tell Baylor a lie if I possibly can. I think he believed me. Shortly afterward, another man called up and asked the same thing. This fellow pretended to be Percy Ramsbaugh Milburn—he wasn't. I gave him the same discouraging answer. Telling lies about guests is what I call the

Butler plan. Have a good night's rest and if you feel anyone beating you to death with a club, it's only the Phantom Killer of Archersburg. Think nothing of it—and please don't ring for room service.

Sam Butler, Prop.

McGavock grinned. He took his gun from his bag, put it under his pillow, and climbed into bed. In three minutes he was sound asleep.

WHEN McGAVOCK CAME down in search of breakfast next morning the lobby was empty. He prowled around a bit, located the hotel dining room down a dark corridor just aft of the desk, and had a fine day-opener of fried chicken and giblet gravy, cornbread, sliced peaches and thick, yellow cream. He was feeling placid when he hit the streets. Already, at nine o'clock, the big thermometer in front of the drugstore had climbed to eighty-six. Hillmen, come to town for a day's trading, hitched their tattered surries and mud-caked buggies to the rail behind the courthouse, their shaggy ponies lustrous-eyed and doleful beneath the impact of the fiery sun. Small white and yellow butterflies flickered in clouds above the rotted, mossy wood of the old watering trough by the undertaker's shop. The day had started hot and was going to get plenty hotter before sundown.

Now was a good time, McGavock decided, to make his purchase. There was no office-supply store in the village, so he tried a hardware emporium.

He found a squalid little shop with a peeling brick veneer front which seemed to fill the bill. He thumbed down the brass latch and stepped inside. An emaciated, studious-looking clerk was fiddling around at a counter at the back of the store. He had a pair of large bone dice in the jaws of a vise and was boring into the spots with a tiny drill. McGavock approached soft-footed, surprised him.

The clerk covered the vise hastily with a gunny sack, said: "Good-morning. Ahem-ahem. I was just doing a little repair job for a friend. You see—"

McGavock clasped his hands piously. "I understand, brother. First one bores out the spot and then one pounds in a small buckshot and paints it over with black enamel. It takes the game out of the field of luck and puts it into the realm of higher mathematics. Ah, yes. Well, brother, I won't detain you from your handiwork. I feel in the mood to buy a pair of cheap scissors and, oh—well, say a typewriter ribbon, standard size for an Upright."

The clerk produced the articles, wrapped them up. McGavock paid him, said greedily: "A pair of scissors—just what I've always wanted to own! And a real, genuine typewriter ribbon. I'll just carry it with me so if someone should give me a typewriter some time I'll be all fixed. Pretty smart, don't you think?"

The clerk-looked a little frightened. He remarked timidly: "Most folks usually get the typewriter *first!*" Then curiously: "Who are you, if I may be so rude to ask?"

"Oh, that's all right." McGavock smiled, started for the street. "I've often asked myself the same question." He eased the door shut behind him and headed for the courthouse.

THE FROSTED GLASS pane said in big, black letters: ORRIE NORTHRUP, OFFICE OF THE SHERIFF. McGavock hesitated a split second in the hall—a sheriff's office was like a bowl of vegetable soup, each establishment had its own particular formula for the magic variety of ingredients. You could never be certain just what was going to pop up.

He crossed his fingers, grasped the doorknob and entered.

A man in painter's overalls was down on his hands and knees touching up the radiator with silverish paint. He laid the brush on the can as McGavock advanced on him, got stiffly to his feet. He started talking at once, as though he were resuming some sort of a monologue. "And that's the way it goes. Today it's the radiators needs a new coat. Yesterday it was patching up rat holes with tin cans. The day before it was putting a new gooseneck in the public toilet. It hain't hardly worth the salary, now is it?"

"No it isn't," McGavock declared. "I'd secede. Where can I find Sheriff Northrup?"

The man laughed hollowly. "I'm Sheriff Northrup, but you wouldn't know it, would you? I'm jest a ole yaller houn'-dog to be booted around by the citizens of the county." He relaxed in the swivel chair behind the desk, took a generous pinch of brittle, homegrown tobacco and a scrap of butcher's paper from his pocket, rolled himself a cigarette. "What do you want with the sheriff, son? Don't tell me you want some plumbing or paintin' done!"

Sheriff Northrup didn't fool McGavock. He was a perpetual griper—he probably groused this way from morning to night—but he was as sharp as a fishhook. His weathered cheeks were lean and dolorous but his steel-blue eyes were calm and penetrating. On one hand, he could be a lot of help, or he could be double-trouble, whichever way the notion struck him.

McGavock said: "Sheriff Northrup, I'm going to take a

chance on you. I'm going to be perfectly honest with you. If it misfires and puts me in a cell, well, I'll just charge it up to experience and never tell the truth again as long as I live. Now grab hold of the arms of that chair and brace yourself. I'm going to tell you where you can find a stale corpse."

McGavock gave it to him straight, the whole thing. He recounted in detail everything that had happened to him from the moment he swung down from the train the night before, up to the present moment. He only omitted three items: the episode of the shooting in Milburn's room, the fact that he was registered at both hotels—and his recent purchase at the hardware store. Sheriff Northrup listened dreamily.

Finally, the sheriff spoke. "So this feller that called himself Milburn is went and got himse'f destroyed! Ding-dang it! And here I been a-layin' fer him ever sinst he first showed up in town. You claim he's out to the ole clay mine, eh? I'll try to get out and bring him when I git this durn radiator painted."

"That's right, don't rush yourself." McGavock was genial. "He's all stretched out in an easy chair. He wont mind waiting."

There was a long period of silence between them.

McGavock said, "Well?"

Sheriff Northrup looked pained. "Well, what, son?"

"You know what." Venom crept into McGavock's voice. "I've come here to co-operate, you've accepted my assistance—yet you're deliberately holding out on me. You say that you've had your eye on Milburn. I'd like to hear just what you mean by that!"

Sheriff Northrup sighed. "I guess my mouth run away with me fer a second. Milburn never done nothing out of the way, he allus acted perfect. But he was a phony—even his name was fishy. You see, son, the real Percy Ramsbaugh Milburn was a ole time desperado. He was kilt by the law down in N'Orleans, in 1919, as I recall. The real Milburn would be at least eighty year old by now!"

McGavock was stunned. "Are you telling me that a man voluntarily assumed the name of a notorious criminal?"

"That's what I'm tellin' you. But I ain't tellin' you why, 'cause I don't know why. I been tryin' to figger hit out myse'f ever sinst."

A blank look came into McGavock's eyes—he was floored. He said: "Well, I'll be getting along—"

"Where are you puttin' up, son?"

"At Acacia Gardens. Drop around some evening and bring the Kind Hearts and Nimble Fingers Sewing Club." McGavock waved a hasty farewell and left the room. Sheriff Northrup picked up his paint brush.

4

Lead Pipe

THE NIGHT BEFORE, in the faint moonlight, the old mansion so euphoniously christened Acacia Gardens had looked like a great black granite tombstone. Now, in the broad daylight, as McGavock ambled up the gravelstone drive, he decided it looked more like an abandoned asylum. It was big and rambling—but it was a wreck. The clapboard was warped from the siding, the eaves sagged, and the tin down-spouts were rusted from their bracings and lay askew like jackstraws. Slats had rotted from the pretentious pillars leaving the weathered, two-story columns with gaping vertical slots. The lawn had fallen into a wild, primitive state, Bermuda and prickly pear had pushed out the blue grass, and the hillside was an eyesore of eroded red clay.

The detective stepped through the screen door, crossed the porch, and entered the building. The gilt clock with the little cupids above the manager's desk said seven minutes after ten. According to Mr. Baylor's injunction, he was seven minutes late for breakfast.

He found the proprietor and his guest from the north, Mr. Fortunatus Duff, in the dining room. They were seated at a table in the corner. The fat man had a soup bowl before him, on the tablecloth were the shells of six softboiled eggs, and at Duff's elbow was a stack of toast eight inches high. He walled his eyes at the detective as McGavock pulled out a chair and joined the group. "Go right ahead," McGavock said pleasantly. "Pour it in. It'll be two long hours before lunch."

"You must like our beds," the manager said amiably. "I see you overslept."

McGavock shook his head. "Not me. I've been up for hours. I don't eat breakfast. I've a theory that the more you eat, the fatter you get. I live on vitamin pills and weak lemonade. When I need roughage, I'll eat a head or so of lettuce to make up for the deficiency." Mr. Duff gagged. McGavock went on sociably: "Where's Milburn, the catman? Won't he eat with the help?"

Baylor flushed. "If you're referring to me, sir, I'm not the help, as you term it. I am Acacia Gardens in person." His old, icy poise came back. "Mr. Milburn appears to have spent the night out." He smiled vaguely.

McGavock pushed back his chair. "I think I'll mosey up to my room and maybe take a nap." He got to his feet. "Well, Mr. Duff, how's the folklore going? Discovered any brand new old ballads today?"

The fat man appeared flattered. He pursed his blubberous lips, said: "I haven't done any field work as yet. I've just arisen. I...."

McGavock lost interest, he started to leave, stopped. "Mr. Baylor," he remarked casually. "Last night, just before I went to sleep, I had a funny sensation. I thought I heard some one bursting paper bags. It sounded like pistol shots, but you told me that you wouldn't ever allow anything fractious to go on around here. Now, why would anyone burst paper—?"

Baylor's hand shook in cold rage. "Mr. McGavock, you're the most antagonizing person I ever talked to. You know, as the whole town knows by now, that those were pistol shots you heard. Mr. Milburn came home long enough last night to shoot my wall full of holes—and then departed. I can see you are getting ready to ask me why he should do this. Please don't. I don't think I could answer you in a gentlemanly manner. I haven't the slightest idea." He reached for his teacup, spilled it before he could get it to his mouth.

McGavock gazed at him in paternal solicitude. "Mr. Baylor," he said unctuously, "your nerves are giving away on you. You're edgy. You need a rest. Why don't you pack up your bags and move over to the Butler House for a few days? Get out of the routine, enjoy yourself."

Baylor choked. "Will you leave us alone, will you go away!"

McGavock looked hurt. "If you feel that way about it." He turned on his heel, walked stiffly from the dining room.

THE UPSTAIRS HALLWAY was deserted. McGavock took his key-ring from his pocket, selected a skeleton key, and methodically, went down the row of rooms, opening and shutting the doors. The first three were vacant, the fourth had a big photograph of Fortunatus Duff on the dresser. McGavock gave a silent raspberry, retreated. Next in line, two more empty chambers—and then the room he was seeking.

He knew it was the right place as soon as he saw it. The room which had been occupied by the elderly Cahill brothers, Mort and Nelson. Logic told him that he would find it, that things moved slowly at Acacia Gardens and that the frosty Mr. Baylor would be likely to leave it alone, pretty much as it was when murder struck down its occupants, until he should need it.

McGavock entered, slipped the bolt shut behind him. It was a large, sunny room, really two rooms with a partition removed.

It was one of the strangest set-ups he ever ran into—everything was twinned. Just like an imaginary-mirror bisected the chamber. You stood in the center of the rug and gazed at the two facing walls and they seemed almost reflections of each other. On the left and right hand, the furniture was gathered in two absolutely identical groups. Over here was a bed and under the bed was a pair of red carpet slippers, over there was a bed and under the bed was a similar pair of slippers. The same with the bureaus, the toilet accessories, magazine racks, reading lamps. Uncle Nelson and Uncle Mort had certainly been parallelists.

Five minutes of intensive search uncovered absolutely nothing of interest. Papers, clothing, all personal effects had been cleaned out. Cleaned out, no doubt, and burned by Nephew Georgie Cahill.

Suddenly, out of his subconscious, an inspiration struck him. The hunch was immeasurably foolish, and yet he couldn't resist the impulse. He went to the window, fiddled with the plank beneath the base of the trim. It came out in his hands. Just like the hiding place of Milburn's at the shack by the old clay mine. McGavock leaned down, stared into the crevice between the sash and the laths.

The aperture contained a piece of lead pipe.

McGavock took it from its resting place and examined it.

It was about eighteen inches long, and surprisingly heavy. The hollow tube had been filled with a core of solder, and one end was wrapped with tire-tape. McGavock knew it for what it was—the murder weapon. As vicious an implement of death as he had ever had in his hands. This was undoubtedly the mace that had slain first Mort Cahill, and then, in turn, his brother

Nelson. McGavock restored it to its hiding place, refitted the board. He stood for a moment lost in dark, moody thought.

He said: "Riddle for young children: when is a piece of pipe not a pipe of peace?" So wrapped in meditation was he, that he hardly realized he was speaking.

He left the room, strolled down the length of the corridor, let himself into his own quarters.

His bedroom, he observed, was just about like the others he had inspected, no better, no worse, just as rundown and morbid. There was the same carved-oak bed and bureau, the same hinged window leading out onto the upstairs veranda.

McGavock went to the bed, stirred up the covers. He dragged a chair up to the marble-topped table, took out the package he had purchased at the hardware store. He took the typewriter ribbon from the box, unrolled about six feet from the spool, cut it off. With his scissors, he pried the small metal end-clamps from the cut-off section, fastened them to ribbon on the spool, and rewound it. He whistled to himself as he worked.

When he had finished, he put the ribbon back in the box, the box back in his pocket. He felt better already. He shed his coat and shoes, stretched out on the bed and grinned. He waited fifteen minutes, and then came the knock on his door.

HE'D HAVE LAID a ten to one wager that his visitor was Georgie Cahill—and lost. His caller was the obese Mr. Duff. The fat man edged through the half-open door with surprising agility. McGavock studied him with obvious distaste. Mr. Fortunatus Duff was childishly happy. He practically quivered with uncontrolled pleasure. He wiggled his fingers commandingly, said urgently:

"Put on your shoes, get your hat. We're off. I think I've struck pure gold."

McGavock waited. The fat man explained. "You've kept quizzing me and pestering me about how a folklore expert works. Well, now I'm going to show you. I'm going to let you witness it, with your own eyes, from the inside. I'm going to take you along with me on a field trip!"

"Not me," McGavock said coldly. "I got bunions."

"A field trip doesn't mean we walk through fields. It's just our expression for an interview. Old Chappie, you just can't afford to miss this." He thrust out his bread basket, assumed a professional air. "I suppose you're familiar with the interesting genesis of folk ballads. One school holds that they're of communal creation, but that's pish-posh. Folk ballads are made by individuals. The type of inspiration for these untutored songs varies. They may be inspired by a famous train robber, like Jesse James, or by, say, a railroad wreck, or maybe a grisly crime."

McGavock looked bored. Duff went on: "The folk ballads being made today, by untutored mountainmen, are every bit as authentic and as valuable as those sung in the sixteenth century in the highlands of Scotland. Now brace yourself—here comes the surprise! I've located a man right here in Archersburg, a hillman, who is in the actual process of composing such a song. It deals with a series of recent murderous crimes and is called *The Death of the Two Brothers.* It's about a Mr. Mort and Mr. Nelson Cahill, who...."

McGavock laughed. "Why leave the house? Just sit down on the bed and I'll fix you up a little ballad myself. According to your lecture, it's just as good no matter who composes it. Let's see. *'Twas on a Tuesday night, the evening it was late, when the older brother, Uncle Mort, went out and met his fate.* Yow! I didn't know I had it in me."

Duff was horrified. "That's sacrilegious. That's a rank parody. You have to be untutored to compose a genuine ballad. This man I'm talking about, this Foss Bellew, who lives out beyond the cemetery in that shanty under the bridge—this man is almost primitive. His guitar and his fiddle are well known back in the hills."

Duff was enthusiastic. "I think he really knows something about these homicides. The sheriff's had him in for questioning but Bellew's a hillman and the law's just wasting its time. He doesn't want to get involved and he's clamming up."

McGavock looked scared. "Is that so! Well, I'm glad you told me. I don't want to get involved either. If you take my advice, you'll stay clear of this stuff yourself. It doesn't pay to mess around in anything as serious as a chain of murders!"

Duff faltered, attempted to assume a devil-may-care attitude. "You have to take risks in my profession. Yessiree! You have to be reckless!" He said good-by, left the room. McGavock watched his enormous back float down the corridor. Mr. Fortunatus Duff didn't seem any too sure of himself.

McGavock dressed, waited ten minutes, giving Duff time to clear the premises, and sauntered downstairs.

LUCINDA CAHILL WAS in the foyer. The supple little blonde was draped across the manager's desk, chatting with Mr. Baylor. She was dressed in a perky rose-lavender linen frock, was still bare-legged, and wore spike-heeled snub nosed play-pumps of lavender cloth to match her dress. She was a gorgeous, refreshing picture. And she appeared to be on fairly intimate terms with the hotelman. McGavock tossed his key on the blotter, said: "Luxuriating in the blessed bounties of ole Dixie, I see, Mr. Baylor. Why good morning, Mrs. Cahill. How's Old Ninety-Seven this nice hot morning?"

The girl gave him a sultry smile. "Oh, hello, there. I want to talk with you."

"No soap." McGavock accelerated his walking. "You leave me alone!" She caught up with him, followed him out the door, onto the porch. McGavock drew down the corner of his lip, said softly: "Disperse, disperse. This is no good." She trailed him through the screendoor, down the gravelstone drive to the sidewalk. He completely ignored her. He could hear her high heels clicking placidly behind him.

A block from the tourist home, in the lee of a great cavern of flowering hydrangeas, she grasped his elbow, swung him about to face her. All traces of her previous coquetry had vanished, her cheeks were stiff with rage, her little-girl eyes were narrowed, hard. "Don't ever put me through a routine like that again," she ground out. "I don't like chasing men." She got her breath. "Last night you offered us your services. All right. I want to retain you."

"You?" McGavock frowned. "Let's get this straight. Who has the moola in your family? You or your husband?"

She was speechless with anger. "Was that necessary? My husband has the money, of course. Is that a novel situation in your experience? But he sent me to you. It's perfectly legal, if that's what's bothering you."

McGavock considered. "So he sent you to me, eh? Well, I sent you right back. Tell Mr. Cahill that I won't work for you, or for him, but that I'll work for you both—jointly. It makes for domestic tranquillity. Tell him to hang around the house. I'll look him up later this morning."

She stood frozen, rigid. "So that's it! You don't trust me. You've been listening to the rumors someone is spreading about me!"

McGavock looked wise. "We won't go into that here. Tell Georgie that I'll see him in an hour—and that I want to see him alone. No females fluttering around." He watched her fume, asked obliquely: "Who is this Foss Bellew?"

She tried desperately to be casual. "Just riffraff, just scum. Why?"

"For once our opinions coincide." McGavock was deliberately vague. He lifted his hat straight up from his head, nodded farewell, swung away from her, down a backstreet.

He had been in town twelve hours, and he hadn't until now begun to get his teeth into anything. It had been an uncomfortable sensation, running into a lot of cockeyed clues, having people shoot at you in dark rooms, paying a double hotel bill—and not being able to get started. Now that was over, now things were beginning to roll. From the minute that he'd seen that lunatic telegram in the old man's office back in Memphis, that message about the stolen biscuits, he'd realized that this business would pan out plenty mean. There'd been plenty of clues and they'd all seemed so absurd. But in the last analysis, they didn't lead to anything—and that indicated he was up against grade-A brains.

Add them all up: Milburn-Yancey's fake name, his hobby for collecting and releasing cats, his stolen biscuits, add them all up and they appeared to be a slew of red herrings. But McGavock knew that this wasn't so, he knew deep in his heart that everything he'd uncovered, as ridiculous as it seemed on the face of it, was a practical and functional part of some diabolical scheme. And now, finally, he was beginning to get the drift. Things were beginning to shape up.

He'd been pushed around. Now he was getting in position to do a little shoving, himself.

5

The Dancing Cat

HIDDEN IN A grove of walnut trees at the edge of town was the cabin. It was a small, neat cabin of new logs, efficiently notched and chinked, and roofed with velvety rose-colored cedar shingles. Built in the manner of mountain cabins, it was composed of two solid little buildings about eight feet apart, the space between the two buildings sheltered over. A man sat in the enclosure, or "dog-run." He was an old man, and barefooted. His brogans, their laces tied together, hung from a horseshoe nail by his shoulder. He lolled on a thong-bottomed rocker, his froglike feet plastered flat to the floor. He was carving an ox from a block of white pine with a Barlow knife. McGavock was astonished at the grace and power of the carved figure. Little chips of yellow wood lay about the floor like curls of golden butter. The old man lifted kindly, preoccupied eyes on McGavock as he approached, said: "If yo're one of the fellers from a burial society, we'uns has done took care of ourse'ves on that point."

McGavock settled himself on the edge of the porch. "I've got the right place, haven't I? You're Deputy Sandy Oglesby?"

"Yes, I am. She ain't here," the old man said.

"How's that again, please?"

"I see yo're a stranger hereabouts. I'm the Deppity but I seldom work at it. When there's something to be did, the woman, she takes keer of it. I'm ailin'—I think."

"You hope."

His eyes crinkled at the corners. "Yes, sir—I hope. Howsomever, I'll do my best to he'p you. If hit's walkin' or movin' around, you'll have to wait for my wife to git back, if hit's talkin', let 'er go Gallagher, I'm at yore service."

McGavock said sociably: "I made the acquaintance of your wife on Main Street last night. She threw a flashlight in my face and wanted to search my traveling bag. What a woman! She's truly a blessed jewel in the crown of something or other." The introduction over with, he declared candidly: "I'm a detective from Memphis. I'm here to solve, among other things, the murder of Nelson and Mort Cahill. I met your eminent sheriff earlier this morning, offered to co-operate with him. He treated me like I was a long lost son—but I have the feeling that he gave me the brush off."

Mr. Oglesby took a little brown, glass jar from his overall pocket, laid a pinch of snuff on his tongue. "That's like little Orrie," he agreed. "The sheriff, he used to be a stock dealer and he figgers he's got to beat ever'body down on whatever they offer him. I kin solve more durn crimes jest a-whittlin' here on my porch than he kin flyin' around actin' hateful. What do you want to know, friend? You want to know who killed the Cahill boys, or you want to know why? Jest ast me."

"Oh, I couldn't do that!" McGavock exclaimed politely. "I'm getting paid money for this and if you'd clear everything up for me at this stage in the game it would make it too easy for me. Ahem!" He cleared his throat. "If you insist—"

Mr. Oglesby tested the knife's keenness on the ball of his thumb. "Wal, here's how she lays. Yo're a-wastin' yore time, Orris Northrup, he's a-wastin' his time. The way I see hit, cain't nobuddy never make no arrests. These killin's is soopernatteral! Mort and Nelson was destroyed by a ghost!"

McGavock agreed sagely. "Now, that's the best opinion I've heard. It fits all known facts. What was this ghost's name?"

"I cain't personate him, friend. But this I kin tell you—he wears boots."

"He wears boots?"

"That's right. Big, ole gum boots." The old man laid his carving on his kneecap. "As I said, Sheriff Northrup, he don't gossip much. They's things about these two slayin's that he's keeping under that black Stetson. My woman, she knows about 'em and she passes 'em on to me. I jest sit and think about 'em."

McGavock twitched. "Sure-sure. Now, for Gawd's sake, get to the point!"

Mr. Oglesby looked ruffled. "That's what I'm a-doin', hain't I? I'm referrin' to the tracks. Those killin's both happened on rainy nights. Ghosts fancy rainy nights. First, Mort Cahill was slew. It was did in the alley behind the co'thouse. He was found layin' by Widder Higgen's flower bed and they were soopernatteral tracks in that-there flower bed!"

He watched McGavock to see how he was taking it. McGavock said blandly, "Go on."

"The next night Nels Cahill was murdered. Nels was did away with out on Elm Avenue, by the parsonage. Preacher Wallam was trying to raise a stand of new grass on his lawn. He'd sowed seed and had laid burlap over it. The destroyer kilt Nelson and then run acrost this-here burlap. He left more tracks."

"And these tracks," McGavock prompted, "were big rubber-boot tracks?"

“The biggest my woman ever seed!”

“It was the killer, all right,” McGavock agreed. “But what makes you think it was a ghost?”

“In both places, in Widder Higgen’s flower bed and Parson Wallam’s new lawn, they were *cat tracks running right along aside of the boot tracks.* Now cats lives, as everybody knows, half in this world and half in the evil world. They consorts with ghosts and traffiicks with the unholy. They was a cat looked on whilst the Cahill boys was being murdered. This cat looked on and danced.”

The bright sunlight fell through the walnut trees. High above McGavock’s head two blue jays were scolding their noisy fledglings. McGavock moistened his lips, said hoarsely: “What do you mean, *danced?* How could they tell the cat danced?”

“If Sheriff Northrup says hit danced, that’s enought for me. He’s done a heap of trappin’ in his day and kin reely read tracks.” Mr. Oglesby waggled his head. “You cain’t git around it. This cat was doing funny steps. The little prints was all sprangled and helter-skelter—like the cat was drunk.”

McGavock looked suddenly pleased. He got up, laid a five dollar bill in the shavings between the old man’s feet. “Give this to your favorite charity.”

The old man picked the bill up with prehensile toes. “Thanks. I shore will. My woman, she’s my favorite charity. Good day, to you, and come agin!”

GEORGE CAHILL WAS out on his lawn, plucking plant lice from a scrawny rosebush, when McGavock arrived at the cottage. He meandered up the flagstone walk, called a cheery greeting. The lanky man acknowledged his salutation morosely. McGavock sensed that he had caught his client at an unguarded moment. Gone was that veil of forced jocularity. Deliberately, as though he could turn it on and off like an electric switch, deliberately and instantly the rangy Mr. Cahill became lively and merry. He said drolly: "You're a befuddling critter, Mr. McGavock. Lucinda came home a little while ago with some sort of confused report from you. The gist was, as I made it out, that you're now working for the two of us."

"That's the gist, Mr. Cahill."

Cahill went deadpan. "You're afraid of us separately, eh? But you figure you're safe as long as you parlay us. H-m-m. You're a mighty smart detective, McGavock. But confess—you're just playing hunches, aren't you?"

"I'm just a pilgrim from the outer world. There's nothing soopernatteral about the way I work. Something tells me to be cagey with you folks, that's all."

Cahill came to a decision. "You're a deep one. Somehow, I can't pigeonhole you. I guess I'll have to tell you about the hats and stay on the safe side." He turned abruptly on his heel, said: "Come with me."

McGavock followed his host around the side of the house, stopping at the back porch. There was a small backyard with a vegetable garden and woodshed, beyond these was an old combination barn-and-carriage house peeling in red paint of past decades. Immediately behind the barn, rose the scrubby eroded brushland. It was a beautiful old barn, corniced in wooden gingerbread and built, in two levels, up onto the hillside. Because of the rolling hills, the barn and the woodshed and the little vegetable garden seemed all jammed up against the tiny back porch.

About two feet from the corner of the barn, between the barn and the woodshed, was a low platform of half-rotted planks. It was perhaps five feet square and sat flush in the packed, grassless earth. Cahill paused here, indicated it. "That," he said carelessly, "is the cistern. More about that later. Let's go into the barn."

He led McGavock through the creaking door into that part of the building which, in times long past, had been the carriage room. There was the musty, not unpleasant smell of harness oil, dry aromatic hay. In the dim light, McGavock could see that the great room was empty, could make out the outline of a work bench along one wall. Cahill threw open a hinged board window, and sunlight cascaded in upon them. The lanky man said casually: "Take a look at these!"

There were two straw hats on the workbench. Men's hats. They were soaking wet and almost shapeless. McGavock examined them. They were the same size—7 ¼—the same model, they'd been sold by the same dealer. Only in one detail were they different. The gold stamped initials on the sweatband of one read *M C,* on the other, *N C.*

McGavock whistled softly to himself. Finally, he spoke. "Uncle Mort and Uncle Nelson. Don't tell me the old gentlemen willed these to you, along with the eighty thousand."

Cahill closed the window. The room went dim again. McGavock sensed that his host was torn in the stress of a violent emotional strain, realized, too, that somehow it was physically impossible for the rangy, poker-faced man to release his tongue in the revealing glare of the hot morning sunshine.

Cahill began to talk. At first his words came stumblingly, and then, hypnotized by what he was saying, his voice slipped into a low, regulated monotone. "That's correct. My uncles were wearing these hats when last I saw them alive, when, one by one, I said good night to them on my threshold and they went out into the darkness to their bloody deaths. When the bodies were found, the hats were missing."

"And they showed up here, eh?"

"Not exactly here. In the cistern. Last night, when Lucinda was away, while she was at the meeting of the sewing club, I found them."

McGavock said blandly: "So now she was away at the Kind Hearts and Nimble Fingers! Last night you told me that you two had spent the evening together squabbling with each other."

"I lied. I was fussed. This is the truth." Cahill got organized. "I was sitting in the parlor reading, outside it was raining. Finally, the rain stopped. I stepped out on the backporch to get a breath of bedtime air. I turned on the porchlight. I happened to look at the cistern—it was overflowing, you know, water was coming up and running out the top between the planks. Hardly realizing what I was doing, I went out and lifted the trap to see what it was all about. It was full to the brim, the water level was clear up to the ground level, and rising fast. Bobbing around, just inside, were these two hats. I didn't know what they were at first, I took them out and examined them. When their significance struck me, I was appalled!"

"No kidding?" McGavock sighed. "I hate to do this, but for the record let's have a little routine cross-questioning. *In primo,* how could a cistern overflow? Cisterns are of two types. They're either filled with water from tin down-spouts or from seepage. When I saw the one outside, I thought it was a well—I didn't see any down-spout."

"There isn't any. There used to be, but it's gone. I guess the reason the cistern overflowed was because of the terrific cloud burst!"

"Mayhap, mayhap. But I don't seem to be able to visualize it. So you actually saw this water bubbling up?"

"I thought I did. Of course my eyes were a little strained from reading. The important thing is that I found the hats."

"Found them on a night when your wife was away."

Cahill missed the irony. "Precisely. I see you get the idea." His voice shook. "You get the implications, don't you? It's terrible, isn't it?"

"Implications?" McGavock sounded puzzled. "They're just a couple of wet hats as far as I'm concerned."

Cahill said lifelessly: "It's getting me down. Who brought these hats here and put them in the cistern? My wife—there's no other answer. Where did she get them? She had to get them from the dead bodies of my uncles."

McGavock snorted. "And why would she do this?"

Cahill ignored him. "Lucinda," he whispered, "must be protected from herself. You and I, McGavock, will team up together. We will shield the irresponsible child from a misunderstanding world."

McGavock guffawed, said: "Hoopla, Mr. Cahill, hoopla!" He walked vigorously across the rickety floor, stepped out into the steaming, saffron sunlight.

OVER A QUICK lunch at the Butler House, McGavock chatted with the proprietor. The elfin-faced Mr. Butler was dumping new ice in the battered water-cooler. He elevated his yellow eyebrows with pleasure at the sight of his guest, said: "Good morning, officer. Caught any felons this beautiful summer day?"

McGavock scowled. "They all know it, eh? I never saw such a town. I might as well be wearing puttees and a tunic."

Sam Butler grinned. "It's the sheriff. He's putting out the word, careless-like. I think he's trying to cramp your style. It's bitter to the salivary glands to have a city smart aleck come in and show you up."

McGavock glowered. "He's just cutting his own throat. I'm trying to help him. Oh, well. This isn't the first time I've had to solve a sheriff before I solved the crime." He added with relish: "Those are mighty good biscuits your cook dishes up. And by the way, I've been intending to ask you. When I checked in last night, you said that Milburn had leased the old clay mine. Who did he lease it from?"

"He leased it from me," Butler answered. "It's part of the unprofitable flotsam that my kinfolks left me." The elfish hotelman arched his pale eyebrows pedantically. "I'm glad you enjoyed our pastries. Don't call them biscuits, however. That's a misnomer."

"They sure looked like biscuits to me. They tasted like—"

"I know, I know. Millions and millions of people make the same error. They call them biscuits when they're not."

"I see. Everybody's wrong but you," McGavock said dryly.

"Exactly." Butler was enjoying himself. He launched into his proof. "The word comes from the Latin *bis,* meaning twice, and *coctus,* meaning cooked. Hundreds of years ago, the Romans had a little cracker that they baked twice. That's how the word biscuit came into being. What you fallaciously refer to as a biscuit is only cooked once." He looked smug. "A biscuit is something entirely different."

McGavock perked up. "Pardon?"

"I say a biscuit is something entirely different. It's a term used in ceramics. You know, in pottery-making and so forth. When I was a kid and the old clay mine was working, I was literally raised on the terminology. Here's the procedure in ceramics. Say you're making a plate or a figurine or a jug, or whatever. First it's shaped in the clay, then this shaped-clay object is fired. If it's delicate, it's placed in a fire-clay box known as a sagger and fired—if not, it's just fired. The object is then glazed and fired long and hot in the grand fire. That sets the glaze. The unglazed pottery, after the first firing, but before the second, is known as the biscuit. That's where we get the word bisque—bisque is a corruption of biscuit. Do I win my argument?"

McGavock spoke emphatically. "You surely do! Those are golden words you're uttering, if you only realized it." He started to leave, hesitated. "Can you lend me something and keep it a secret? Fine. I'd like to borrow a folding carpenter's rule and a small brown paper sack. If I don't return the rule you can put it on my bill."

Butler nodded. He disappeared in a back room, came out a few minutes later with the articles McGavock had mentioned. The detective stowed them away about his person. "Thanks," he said. "I'm sorry I can't let you in on this. It's going to be a kick in the pants. You're a man with a good sense of humor—it's right down your alley. See you later. Oh, yes. One thing more." He glanced at his wristwatch. "In precisely one hour call Sheriff Northrup. Disguise your voice. Tell him that someone's out at the old clay mine, prowling around. You'll be telling the truth, it'll be me."

"The clay mine?" Butler grew concerned. "That's where they found the corpse of Percy Ramsbaugh Milburn! Found him out there this morning. Three bullet holes in his chest—"

"Save it for later." McGavock smiled. "I'm in a hurry."

6

Kiln: Pronounced Kill

MARKET STREET BEGAN at court square and bore, north by west, directly toward the finger of flat, lush bottomland that touched the town on its outer perimeter. The village corporation line, in this neighborhood, was a broad ravine, a jagged chasm-like strip of badland. In the old days, when Market Street had left the town's borders and emerged in a county pike, the unsightly gulch had been spanned by a gangling wooden bridge. Times had changed things. A new state highway four hundred yards or so to the south had left the old bridge and the rutted county-road practically abandoned. The gulch was a vile, swampy cesspool. A lethargic, scummy stream fed tangled elderberry and hazel and giant hairy marshweeds.

There was a faint path at the foot of the old bridge, looping a few feet down the bank and under. McGavock descended.

The shack of Foss Bellew was malarial, evil looking. It sat back under the bridge beams, in the crotch where the hill-slope met the overhead timbers. No sunlight reached it. It was a foul, one-room structure of tarpaper and scantlings, and lay back in a nest of shadowed vines and green, moist brush. The air was laden with milling mosquitoes. They left the underside of dock and mullen as McGavock advanced, circled in swarms before his eyes. A few paces from the shanty McGavock halted, called out: "Foss Bellew! Are you there?"

The door opened and a man came out into the dappled shadows. The door was narrow and low and the man was forced to stoop as he emerged. He straightened, tried to adjust his eyes to the daylight. "Who is it? Who's a-wantin' me?"

Bellew had a cruel, sly animal face. Rarely had McGavock seen features so devoid of the every-day influence of human relationship. This man's face was the face of a brutal, cunning swamp creature, small, bleak eyes, thin lips grinning constantly in an involuntary, mirthless gash. He wore a filthy white shirt with rosetted sleeve-garters, his greasy clay-caked overalls were stuffed into cheap, imitation cowboy boots. McGavock said: "I want to talk with you for ten minutes—at one dollar per minute. Yes or no?"

Without a word, the man turned, crept back into his den. His voice came out through the dark doorway: "Come and set." There was the faint flicker of light from within as Bellew lit a kerosene lamp. McGavock entered.

The place was almost like a cave. The lamp stood on a nail keg, there was a pallet in the corner, two small boxes served as chairs—the sum total of Bellew's furniture. Standing against the wall, just inside the door, was a brand new, flat-top Spanish guitar. McGavock produced a ten dollar note, handed it to the ballad-singer. Bellew took it, thrust it into the watch pocket of his overalls, waited.

McGavock perched himself on the edge of a box. Bellew sat himself facing the detective, his guitar resting on his knees. "I reckon you want me to sing you my new song, I reckon that's why yo're here."

"For ten bucks?" McGavock gave a nasty laugh. "No, Brother, not at those prices." He said slowly, and insinuatingly: "Don't put me in the same class with that fatso, Fortunatus Duff."

Bellew answered in ugly braggadocio. "Mr. Duff, he's a gentleman. He claims I'm historical. Hain't everbuddy kin make up a song like I kin. I'm a wanderin' minstrel, I'm a sur-vival of the Golden Age o' Bonnie Queen Bess! They hain't many like me left no more. Some fellers sings other folks' songs—I just strum my ole git-tar and make up my own." He said it in one big breath. It was almost a recital.

McGAVOCK LISTENED WITH interest. "Think of that! Now how do you get the ideas for these songs?"

"I get 'em different ways." Bellew leered. "Now you take the feller that fixed up the songs about Jesse James, or Barbara Allen, or any o' them people. I betcha them ballad-singers never even seen the person they was singing about. Me, I never fool round with nary a thing I hain't seed with my own two eyes. That's why my songs is the best. That's why gentlemen like Mr. Duff comes clear down from the no'th jest to talk with me! Fellers like Mr. Duff and you—yo're a Yankee, too."

McGavock passed that one by. "So you never sing about anything you haven't seen with your own eyes, eh? Now that's interesting. Duff tells me your current masterpiece concerns the Cahill boys. Don't tell me you were in on the kill!"

Cruel lines etched themselves at the corners of Bellew's bestial mouth. "I didn't do hit, if that's what you mean. But I'm a great night-roamer. I like the moonlight. When other folks is sleepin', I stroll aroun' and take my ease. If you walk reel quiet and don't make no show of yourself, you shorely see some peculiar sights. And I don't mean mebbe!"

"Let me get this straight." McGavock flattened his lips against his teeth. "Are you telling me that you were prowling around and happened to witness the murders of Nelson and Mort Cahill?"

"That's whut the law was a-wantin' to find out. I went deef and dumb on 'em. The law hit don't like me and I don't keer much fer hit! I hain't gonna testify and git no nice woman hanged! I tole 'em that at the garage and I tole 'em that at the barbershop—and I durn well mean hit!"

McGavock said quietly: "What's this song about? I'd like to hear the words."

Foss Bellew shrugged. "Hit's a long baby, so I won't bother you with the words. I'll tell you the story. It starts off, it's a dark night, I'm a-roamin' down the alley behind the co'thouse. The moon comes out from behind a cloud. I see a pretty blonde gal a bending over a corpse. She's wearing boots and she's got a club in her lily white hand. They's a tortoise cat frolicking about her feet. She hears me and takes out on the run. That's the first part of the song. The second part's jest like the first. It's the follering night, I'm strollin' out by Preacher Wallam's on Elm Avenue. The moon comes out from behind a cloud. I see a woman a-bendin' over a body, the moonlight's shinin' on her yaller hair. They's a cat—"

"I get the drift." McGavock cut him off. "Did you ever sing this song for Mr. Fortunatus Duff?"

"No, I hain't. I hain't quite got 'er the way I want 'er yit. Mr. Duff comes and talks to me, jist like yo're a-doin', and pays me jist to hear me talk. He says I'm a sur-vival of the Golden Age o' Bonnie Queen Bess, I'm a wanderin' minstrel, an' that I should be in some museum, somers."

"So I believe you mentioned." McGavock got up. "I've got another ten dollars. I've changed my mind. This extra ten's yours, too, if you just run over the melody and lyrics of that ballad. You've worked up a craving in me. I understand that you haven't got the job finished yet, but I'd like to hear just as much as you've got."

Bellew nodded. He put his fingers on the strings of the guitar, opened his mouth, closed it. "Doggone!" he exclaimed. "I cain't sing today. I done forgot—I got a sore throat."

McGavock said softly, "Just pick out the melody on your instrument."

Foss Bellew stood the instrument against the wall. "You'll have to come back later. My git-tar's broke. They was a bad rain last night and hit done warped hit. The bridge is jipper-jawed out o' line, the strings is buckled, and the F-holes is out o' order."

McGavock said: "You're no ballad-singer. You don't know a guitar from a monkey wrench. This guitar here is a flat-top Spanish. It doesn't have any F-holes. And if it did, they couldn't get out of order."

Bellew's eyes got clammy. The cords of his neck inflated, grew rigid in suppressed rage. McGavock added slurringly: "To tot it up, my friend, you're a damn liar and I give it back to you in your dirty face."

Bellew made a desperate effort to control himself. "Not so fast." His voice was hoarse, wheedling. "You got me all wrong. O.K., I cain't play, I cain't sing. What of it? If I take a city feller like Duff fer a few frogskins, what's it to you? Take back yore ten dollars and git t'hell out'n here!"

"Keep the ten dollars," McGavock said calmly. "You're about to earn it. No, Bellew, it isn't as simple as you present it. This ballad-composing hocus-pocus is no petty gyp. If you can pick up a few dollars here and there you're perfectly willing to do it—but there's more behind it than that. You're about the lowest vermin I ever wasted time on. You're in the employ of someone and I'm getting a good idea who that someone is. I'm a detective from Memphis. You know it, you've known it all along. The whole town knows it. You've been going about the village, in your sly underhanded way, trying to poison the minds of the townsmen, trying to blacken the character of Mrs. Lucinda Cahill. God forgive me for mentioning her name in this rat hole. You're working for someone who can't see anything but eighty thousand dollars."

Saliva gathered at the corners of Bellew's mouth. He said coarsely: "If you've came here lookin' fer trouble, I've got some. I tole you to git out and I mean hit. I'm speakin' the truth. I saw the gal hunkered over the bodies. The moon cleared a cloud and hit was Lucinda Cahill—"

McGavock slapped him three times. He slapped him openhand and backhand, hard punishing blows that cracked like railroad torpedoes. Bellew went back against the wall, attempted to catch his balance, stumbled to one knee. From his half-prostrate position, he reached for his pallet on the earth floor. McGavock stepped forward, kicked into the tangle of filthy bedclothes. A pistol, a long barreled .38 Special, slithered out onto the packed dirt. McGavock gave it a second deft kick, sent it spinning through the doorway, said: "A wicket for our side!" He waited a second, but nothing further happened. He left the shanty and started back to town.

It was important that he get to the old clay mine before Sheriff Northrup arrived.

THE HIGH WOODEN gate at the Star Mine was padlocked. The dolorous sheriff had evidently followed McGavock's tip long enough to lay aside his paint brush and collect the corpse of Percy Ramsbaugh Milburn. The dead wagon had come and gone and the law had chained the portals. McGavock took out his keyring, picked the massive padlock. "Breaking and entering," he reflected. "If there's a slip I'll be building county roads for ten years." He entered the premises, shoved the gate shut behind him.

This was the first time McGavock had observed the place in daylight. He looked about him in keen attention. Back on the hillside was the mouth of the derelict mine with a few sheds clustered around the opening. To the left of the sheds was a big heap of dirt, a sort of dump. It was this dump that he was particularly interested in. One glance confirmed his suspicions. All along, when he'd thought of the clay mine, he'd just naturally visualized a pottery, or kaolin clay mine. This, however, didn't tie in with facts. He noticed, with relief, that embedded in the ancient dump were shards of reddish material—*The Star* was a brick-clay mine. That was better, that was the way facts had indicated all along.

He strolled to the kiln, peeked inside, found it empty. That didn't surprise him. It had served its purpose.

He walked to the dump, poked around in the old debris. He knew exactly what he was searching for. It had to be here, he told himself. This pottery job was done under the press of urgency—there had to be a few imperfect specimens, a few discards.

He located them on the far side of the dump, under a covering of dead grass. About half a bushel of broken, red-clay fragments. Just as they had come from the kiln.

McGavock then set up his plant. His wristwatch told him he had just sixteen minutes before Sam Butler would be calling the sheriff.

He selected several of the largest shards, those which most completely preserved their original shape, and carried them to the old warehouse by Milburn's "Studio."

As he had perceived last night in the moonglow, the old warehouse was just about a total wreck. Just a roofless shell of weathered siding. He entered the sagging door. The planking on the floor was rotted, littered with refuse. With a piece of the soft clay shard, he made a big red cross on the inside of the door's lintel. He then got out his typewriter ribbon, unwound it, and using it as sort of a tape-measure, he laid it along the base of the wall. It reached the width of one wall and part of the next. Where the ribbon ended, he thrust the pottery shards beneath the decaying floorboards.

He then rewound the ribbon and returned to the cross-mark on the lintel. He produced his carpenter's rule and went again through the same routine, this time using the rule in lieu of the ribbon. The rule took him about six feet beyond the crevice where he had concealed the shards. Here, he placed the ribbon beneath the floor. He stood up and grinned. "Just like Cap'n Kidd, by golly!"

McGavock then left the warehouse and entered the little shanty, the so-called "Artist's Studio," where he had discovered his client's body just after his arrival in town the previous night. Working quickly and efficiently, he removed the bottom board from the window-trim. Milburn's little cache of personal effects were just as he had left them. McGavock sorted through them, put the Yancey letter in his wallet. He produced the brown paper bag given him by Sam Butler, turned it inside out and with a hard lead pencil scrawled a faint, irregular message. He then restored the sack to its original condition, so that the writing was on the inside, lifted Milburn's belongings from the hiding place, dropped them in the bag—added the carpenter's rule—and replaced the window-trim.

He heard the crunch of brogans on gravel outside the door. His watch told him it was the sheriff. He turned his back to the door, began rapping the walls with his knuckles, listening.

Sheriff Northrup's outraged voice bellowed at him from behind. "Mr. McGavock, you stop that, suh. I hereby arrest you for trespassin', tamperin', and meddlin'. Put up your hands!"

McGavock ignored him. He continued his methodical sounding of the walls. He tapped the bottom of the window-trim, said exultingly: "Hah! Eureka! At last!"

Sheriff Northrup asked uneasily: "What do you mean, at last?"

McGavock greeted him stiffly: "Oh, it's a sheriff. Did you want to see me? Let's go outside where we can talk."

Sheriff Northrup said suspiciously: "Why you so anxious to get me outside? No, 'y doggies, we can do our talkin' right here! What are you lookin' for? What did you find?"

McGAVOCK BLEW UP. "What I find is my own business. For Gawd's sake! I never saw such a town as this, or such a sheriff as you are! I come here, out of the generosity of my heart, and try to get you people out of a mess you've gotten yourselves into. Does Archersburg thank me? Does its sheriff grasp me by the hand, look into my eye and say: 'Much obliged, old pal, this fiesta is too much for me—I admit it.'

Does he? Don't make me laugh. The sheriff's got ants in his pants thinking about re-election. He'd rather have a multiple killer lay doggo, rather have these homicides stay unsolved, than to have an outsider solve them." McGavock spat. "I come to you in your office, I take you into my confidence. What do you do? You sneak around town, wising the citizens to keep mum around me, warning them that I'm a big city detective. Now, believe it or not, you're all set to arrest me. What a farce!"

The sheriff's tanned face flushed angrily, dark blood surged to the network of capillaries across his gaunt cheekbones. "Don't you stand there and throw off on me thataway!" He became defensive. "You hain't no one to talk. You hain't got no record to be proud of, yourself. You come to town and right off you find a corpse. The next morning you manage to get around to reporting it. You break in places, you trespass. And that hain't all by a long shot. I've jest found out that durn if'n you hain't registered at both hotels. They's something might shady about that!"

"Shady, phooey! I did it to save my life last night. I was afraid to put myself under the protection of Archersburg law and order. If you couldn't stop the wave of murder up to now, I wasn't going to be the lad to break the ice." He lowered. "Get out your handcuffs. I'll go along with you. I got a special delivery letter to write and I can do it in a cell as well as anywhere else."

Sheriff Northrup's curiosity got the best of him. "Letter to who?"

"To Memphis, a report to my chief. While you were flying around, attempting to derail me, I finally managed to crack this case."

Sheriff Northrup laughed. The laugh was plenty hollow—the sheriff couldn't seem to put much life in it. He said: "You're jest idle-talkin' me! If you're so doggone smart, who's the guilty party?"

"That end can wait." McGavock pursed his lips. "I've been interviewing a charming associate of yours," he lied. "A Mrs. Deppity Oglesby. She informs me that when you got Milburn down to the undertaker's, you found his pockets as clean as a hound's tooth. Now, a man usually totes something around with him. Now—"

"Double-doggone Sarah Oglesby and her gossip." The sheriff nodded reluctantly. "Hit's the truth, though. The killer robbed the body afore he left it."

"A wonderful theory." McGavock seemed thoughtful. "You stick to it. I've got a slightly different opinion." He rapped the window-trim again, removed the board, revealed the hiding place. Sheriff Northrup's birdlike body flicked between him and his "find." For a split second, the sheriff's dolorous pose vanished. He spluttered with excitement. "My Redeemer! Look what we done discovered!" He craned his neck down, and forward. "I do believe to my soul that this here's a clue." He fished around in his pocket, produced a pair of steel-rimmed spectacles, set them carefully on the bridge of his nose. He took the sack from the hole, poured the contents into his hat, examined the miscellany with trembling fingers. He listed the items verbally: "A fountain pen and one, three, four dollars and twenty, twenty seven cents, and a hankercheef. *And a carpenter's rule!*"

"Milburn put it there before he was murdered," McGavock said patronizingly. "Here's the way I figure it—"

"You get yourself some hushmouth and leave me figger hit out myself." Sheriff Northrup shouldered him away. He studied the paper sack, said: "Now maybe we can trace this here. For Heaven's sakes—they's something wrote inside!" He turned the bag inside out, read aloud in a nervous, faltering voice:

> "To whom it may concern:
>
> I, P.R. Milburn, am directly involved in the slaying of Mort and Nelson Cahill. Another brain, however, has laid the plot and controlled me. I meet this arch-murderer here tonight. I fear for my life.
>
> Should my employer slay me, here is the evidence which can hang this killer:
>
> Take this carpenter's rule, go to the old warehouse, measure six lengths from the door, south and east. I hear someone outside—sorry haven't time to finish this, will finish later—"

McGavock looked wise. "Now that's really something, isn't it? H-m-m! Here's the way I interpret it—"

"Be quiet. You bother me. I kin read cain't I?" The sheriff started, hotfoot, for the ramshackle warehouse.

7

Old Ninety-Seven

IT DIDN'T TAKE Sheriff Northrup long to locate McGavock's red chalk-mark on the lintel. He unfolded the rule, laid it out along the wall. "Hit comes to here." The sheriff thought out loud. "They hain't nothing here but wall. Hit must be buried, hit must be right here under the floor."

He got down on hands and knees, groped about under the rotted planking, came out with the little tin typewriter ribbon box. McGavock stood humbly by.

The sheriff got to his feet, opened the box, took off the cellophane, and stared. McGavock said helpfully: "It's a typewriter ribbon, a new one."

"Of course it is!" The sheriff stormed. "I got eyes, hain't I!" He wavered, completely befuddled. Inspired, he got down again on his knees, groped again beneath the floor. Baffled, he gave it up. "That's all they is, just this durn ribbon."

McGavock shifted restlessly. "Well, let's be getting downtown to jail."

Sheriff Northrup hardly heard him. "This little ribbon must mean something."

McGavock yawned. "Doubtless, doubtless."

"You got any idee?"

"Let's get jailhouse-bound. I have to write an important letter."

"Now, Mr. McGavock," the sheriff reproved him, "that hain't

no way to ack. You're a-sulkin' on me. You been beggin' me to cooperate and, like now, when I want to do it, you git selfish. We're in this thing together, you and me is working in the same harness. I'd shore be obliged to hear any opinions you got. I want to be your friend, put 'er here." He thrust out his hand, McGavock gave it an enthusiastic pumping.

"That's fine." McGavock glowed. "I've always wanted a friend like you. But before I express myself, I'd like a little token of your esteem." He went back on his heels. "When I visited you in your office this morning, you informed me that Percy Ramsbaugh Milburn was an assumed name, that the real Milburn was slain years ago in a duel with the police in New Orleans. You spotted him as a phony because you remembered the name. Now you're a comparatively smart man, Sheriff Northrup, it's only realistic to assume that you made inquiry through law enforcement channels. I'd like to hear just what you learned."

The sheriff braced himself—it was just like pulling teeth. "Wal, Mr. McGavock, I guess you're right, at that. I did send a few telegrams to police departments here and yander, in the big cities. It 'pears that our man was reely a certain Gus Yancey. This Yancey is knowed throughout the South as a petty con man. He wasn't considered as dangerous. He was from East Liverpool, Ohio."

"Oh." McGavock looked pleased. "Now we're getting some place. That's where he learned the pottery trade. East Liverpool is a big pottery center."

The sheriff came back to the point, said petulantly: "I tole you about Yancey, now you explain this ding-dang ribbon."

McGavock pondered. "First we've got to bisect Yancey's

brain, we've got to apply what the college professors call posthumous, neo-cerebellum analysis. What do we know about Yancey's thought habits? We know he was sly, subtle. Now if he wanted to hide something important, he wouldn't just hide it—that would be too simple for him. He would likely *double-hide* it. Let's unwind this ribbon and use it as a tape, let's measure all over again, beginning from the red chalkmark."

Sheriff Northrup surprised McGavock. He seemed doubtful. He said slowly: "I ain't sure you're right. This here is a standard ribbon fer a upright typewriter, the customary len'th fer sich is thutty-six foot. We done measured exactly thutty-six foot with the rule. It'll come out the same place!"

"Maybe," McGavock suggested, "maybe he cut some off the end of the ribbon!"

The sheriff measured, found the shards of fired-red crockery. He was speechless with amazement. "All that foolishness and this is what we git! I do declare, I believe that Yancey man was crack-skulled. Take a common, everyday mess o' junk like this and then hide it with all that fumadoodle! He's been prankin' us."

McGavock said seriously: "It's no joke. This is the biggest clue we've yet uncovered. Sheriff, you're now looking at one of the wickedest criminal implements that the mind of man ever constructed. It's the answer to why Milburn bought cats to release in the woods, why Mort and Nelson Cahill were bludgeoned to death, why Yancey-Milburn was himself murdered by his killer-employer!"

"I cain't believe it." The sheriff was skeptical. "I've seed hunnerts of farmers use this stuff, it's jest ordinary—"

"I know, I know." McGavock was bleak. "Let's get going, Sheriff. There's nothing more here for us."

They were silent on the way back to town. At the courthouse steps, they separated. McGavock said: "It's all over now, Sheriff. All over but a few details. Meet me tonight at Acacia Gardens. Bring George Cahill and that firebrand wife of his. I'll have an interesting story to tell."

Sheriff Northrup was impressed. He said: "Mr. McGavock I wanta apologize—you're shorely a wizard! See you tonight, suh!"

IT WAS JUST about suppertime when McGavock returned to the cottage of George and Lucinda Cahill, and this time he came upon the little residence from the rear. After leaving the sheriff by the courthouse, he strolled out Spring Street to the six hundred block. Two squares short of his destination he turned to the left and almost instantly found himself at the foot of the rolling uplands that rimmed the south side of town.

He began a steep climb to the hillock's crest. The going was laborious. Underfoot, the washed clay was treacherous, insecure. The brush was matted, almost impenetrable. Three times he thought he'd reached the ridge only to find that he'd conquered a knobby, steplike foothill, and that the real ridge lay beyond. Finally, he accomplished the topmost rim. Below him lay the quaint, sleepy town—a maze of jumbled roofs in the slanting, coral sunlight. Just beneath him, in the near foreground, was the objective for which his eye had been searching, the cluster of small buildings which comprised the dwelling lot of his clients. There, beyond the tops of the young cedars, was the small white cottage in its velvety green yard and behind the cottage was the woodshed, the vegetable garden, and the cumbersome old barn built right up onto the hill's slope.

McGavock started his descent. Almost immediately he was engulfed in the scrub and brush. The panorama of motley rooftops was obliterated by foliage. McGavock kept his course as nearly as possible in a tangent directed toward the back of the Cahill barn. This face of the hill, just behind the Cahill stable, was eroded badlands—red clay washed into gullied dunes and covered with scraggly evergreens and holly. He'd descended within fifty or so yards of the barn before he found what he was looking for. And it was almost exactly as he had imagined it. He spotted it as soon as he saw it. He had let the topography lead him to it—he knew he couldn't very well miss it. He'd followed a shallow gully down the slope, the gully had gone into a ravine and the ravine, in turn, had branched into a dry gulch.

He stood moodily in the hot sunlight, studying the prospect as it lay about him. Here, the gully formed a small oval basin of sun-dried clay and shaley outcrop. At the lower end of the basin was a pile of twigs and branches. The branches had been cut within the last few weeks, the thick sprays of dead leaves were just beginning to curl and discolor.

McGavock was grim. "I wish I'd brought my camera. What a charming scene for my photo album! *How to Make Eighty Thousand Dollars in One Easy Lesson.*" He cast a farewell glance at the innocent looking mound of twigs and resumed his descent of the slope.

He pushed through a thicket, came out onto a faint trail. A few paces and the path forked. He passed the fork, retraced, and investigated. The side path led to an abandoned log springhouse in a tiny glade of moss and fern. The earth about the little building was miry and soft, and fairly trampled with gigantic footprints. Huge footprints, rubber boots, coming and going, criss-crossing.

He circled to the front of the structure, started to enter, froze in startled horror.

Foss Bellew was sitting in the doorway. He was sitting just inside in the half-light of shadows, on an old wagon seat. His grimy hand, resting on his overalled knee, grasped a pair of powerful field glasses. His sly, cruel eyes stared lifelessly out into the valley. His stubbled chin lolled in the hollow of his shoulder, his forehead was a shattered mass of bone and flesh. The lead pipe, the pipe that McGavock had last seen in the bedroom at the Acacia Gardens, lay in the muck by his feet.

McGavock turned, lined himself up with the doorway, attempted to reconstruct the range of vision that Bellew had controlled at the moment of his death. The detective found himself looking through a gap in the foliage, down onto the roof of the Cahill barn, directly into the Cahill backyard.

"In spite of the binocular," McGavock said, "in spite of the binocular, the setup smells. It's impossible. Death by bludgeoning is violent—he would have been knocked from his seat. No, it won't work. He was killed and arranged. It all fits in." He considered the corpse a moment in preoccupied distaste, said absently: "Well, Bellew, you had it coming. Play with murder and murder will play with you."

Things were heading up—and fast. You could expect anything now, the killer was getting panicky. He was being cornered and he knew it. McGavock's jaw hardened. From now on, this business was going to be plenty touchy. The slayer had jumped his trolley. He'd laid a careful, devilish plan, had started it in motion, had backtracked and covered every possible trail—yet his scheme was crumbling. He was losing his sense of logic, he was stampeding, butchering his associates. First Milburn-Yancey and now Bellew.

McGavock was all set for the crackdown and now, at the last moment, the killer was blowing his top, running amuck.

McGavock didn't like it.

LUCINDA CAHILL WAS in the side yard, transplanting a bed of iris. McGavock came around the corner of the cottage and she waved a trowel at him in silent, sulky greeting. He approached, sat down on an old hitching block and watched her as she worked. If you could just overlook her hateful disposition, McGavock decided, she was attractive enough for any man. She wore a lavender, broad-brimmed garden hat which cast delicate, prismatic shadows along the column of her milky throat. After her initial greeting, she promptly disregarded his presence. She moved from flower bed to flower bed, back and forth, in supple, graceful strides.

And then McGavock noticed the cat.

Old Ninety-Seven was enjoying himself on the lawn, in the evening sunlight, with his mistress. The great tortoise-shell was acting more like a playful puppy than a cat. As the blonde walked across the lawn, the cat followed her—as she halted to dig rhizomes, the cat paused—as she returned, the cat wheeled and galloped along beside her. It was always at her heels, capering in that queer, crippled rolling gait.

McGavock said blandly: "Old Ninety-Seven seems to fancy your company."

The blonde showed annoyance. "He's always been that way. I despise him but he's infatuated with me." She pointed to the rear of the cottage. "Ninety-Seven, get out of here, go to your basket on the backporch. You're getting on my nerves!"

To McGavock's amazement, the cat limped down the walk, around the building, out of sight. "Now that's something to charge admission to see. I never knew cats to obey like that!"

"Old Ninety-Seven's no fool. He knows I've got a temper, he knows I mean what I say!"

"Oh, sure!" McGavock nodded. "You're dynamite, you admit it." He ogled her maliciously, asked: "How come you and Brother Baylor of the tourist hotel are on such intimate terms? When I came downstairs this morning, you were leaning over the counter chatting with him like you were counting the dandruff on his lapels. What were you talking about and how did you get to be such pals?"

"I shouldn't answer you—but I will." She gave him a baby stare. "We lived at the Acacia Gardens just after we were married. Just before we got my little house here all fixed up. That's how I got to know him. As to what we were talking about, believe it or not, we were trading recipes. I was giving him my lemon meringue pie and he was telling me how to fix clam chowder."

McGavock hooted. He sobered suddenly. "And this Fortunatus Duff. Was he staying at the hotel when you and Georgie were there? What do you know about him?"

"No, he wasn't there when we were there. He's only been around town for a short time. I don't know anything about him except that I see him on the streets and consider him rather handsome in a—"

"In an inflated sort of way."

"In a distinguished sort of way. Don't finish my sentences

for me." She bit her lip. "There's something about you that burns me up!"

He seemed pleased. "No kidding? Now, here's one question more—and brace yourself for a shock. Here's a question I have to ask you when we're alone. Your husband says you people spend your time quarreling. Is this true?"

"It's George that does the quarreling, not me."

"Just one thing more—and be honest. The whole case swings on this point. *Down deep, you really love your husband, don't you?*"

She looked nauseated.

He said: "That's all I want to know. You do love him. You don't deceive me one bit. From now on, this business is in the bag. You had me worried."

He turned to leave. She stood in the turbulent sunset, her face contorted with anger. When she spoke, her voice was honied, cutting. "You've been in town almost twenty-four hours, Mr. McGavock. You've been hustling around, acting important. You simply must have discovered something, you can't be a perfect washout. I'm your employer, don't you remember? Would you care to confide in me?"

McGavock said doubtfully: "It's about Mr. Fortunatus Duff. Can you keep a secret?"

She almost fell over herself in excitement, her eyes got big. McGavock said: "You know those super-rough tweed suits he wears?" She nodded. "Well," McGavock whispered, "he makes them himself. He weaves them out of old cigarette butts! Think of that!"

She cursed him.

8

Murder, Hit and Miss

THE THREE MEN—MR. BAYLOR, Fortunatus Duff, and McGavock—sat on the screened veranda of the old mansion and watched dusk-dark creep down from the purple hillsides. Gradually, the gloaming clouded Elm Avenue, softened the barred pattern of gray tree boles. The harsh noises of the summer's afternoon, the chattering of blue jays, the skirling of the jar-fly, faded in the twilight. Night sounds rose up around them, the muted piping of the treefrog, the mellow flute-call of the owl. The obese Mr. Duff leaned back in his wicker chair, clasped his hands beneath his bulging stomach. "Ah, sweet eventide! 'Tis at vespers, truly, when the soul drinks in the rich elixir of life!"

Mr. Baylor applauded. "Very nicely put, sir. We can see that you're an individual of sensitive and cultivated tastes. Blessed Dixie! The Elysium of aesthetes!"

McGavock agreed in heavy confidence. "It's very pretty but it's too warm. I don't know about you gentlemen, but I'm sweating like a blue mule at a weight-pulling contest. What I'm trying to say is—"

The hotelman said stiffly: "I think you've made yourself perfectly clear."

There was a long, pained silence.

"O.K.," McGavock declared at last. "I'm a sociable man. If you folks don't want to talk about sunsets, let's talk about murder."

Duff clicked on his little table lamp, dispelling the shadowy gloom. Baylor said: "Some other time, some other place, please, Mr. McGavock. This is such a peaceful period of the day. Frankly, we're not interested in murder."

"Well, you should be!" McGavock swung into his subject. "There have been a slew of killings hereabouts in the past few weeks, and if you've ever stopped to think about it—good old Acacia Gardens seems to be the focal point for all of them!"

Mr. Duff appeared highly agitated. "Goodness Gracious! I never thought of it that way. You see it was going on long before I arrived in town."

"So I understand." McGavock was laconic. "The point I'm making is this. Here's Archersburg, a town of about two thousand. It has quite a quota of residences, yet everyone that gets himself killed seems to be associated some way with this old mansion. There's Mort and Nelson Cahill, and Mr. P.R. Milburn, and so on. They were all guests of Mr. Baylor, here."

Duff seemed impressed. "I hadn't thought of it that way." He puffed. "You're just trying to frighten me. It's simply sophistry—there's nothing to it." He got out his big briar pipe.

Baylor said angrily: "Mr. McGavock I'll need your room tonight. Consider your stay under my roof terminated. You're deliberately introducing an element of friction in my household. Stop at the desk as you leave and collect the return rent due you. I—"

McGavock chuckled. Three figures took shape in the opaque twilight, advanced across the lawn. "It looks like we have company," McGavock observed. "Don't tell me it's a meeting of the Kind Hearts and Nimble Fingers! Oh, I see. It's the high-sheriff and a few friends."

Sheriff Orrie Northrup opened the screen door, bowed Mrs. Cahill and her husband in before him. The sheriff was dressed for a fish fry. It was evident to McGavock that the officer was making a gala occasion of the evening. McGavock had told him earlier that he would make an arrest and it was obvious from his complacent bearing that it hadn't occurred to him to doubt McGavock's words. His shoes were shined and he was wearing some sort of tonsorial parlor perfume. He was all set for headlines. He saluted the company cheerily. Before anyone realized what he was doing, he stepped into the house, flicked on the porch light and reappeared. "I like plenty light," he explained succinctly. He added elegantly: "And Miss Lucinda she's a lady and no doubt wants all these gentlemen to look on her and find her good."

The little blonde took the sheriff's gallantry coldly. Her husband pivoted his deadpan face about the assembly, said: "Howdy all! What's what?"

The newcomers pulled up chairs, sat down. McGavock said genially: "Well, Sheriff, it's all over. I've got your killer. But before you drag out your manacles, maybe I'd best sketch in the background for you. This is a strange crime, one of the cruelist I've ever bumped into."

Cahill cleared his throat. "Murder's always bad."

"But this is worse than murder." McGavock spoke rapidly, woodenly. "Two elderly brothers, Mort and Nelson Cahill, have retired on eighty thousand dollars. A certain party works out a scheme to transfer that eighty thousand from one bank account—bingo!—right into another bank account. It was a cunning scheme, it seemed foolproof, and it almost came off. It was Milburn and his hot biscuits that threw it out of joint."

Lucinda Cahill got into the picture. "What kind of a crime could be worse than murder? I don't understand."

"You will, my dear, you will." McGavock chose his words carefully. "This person had no more right to the money than, oh, say, Duff over there. The unholy plot that this party concocted required a middleman who could double as a specialist in pottery, so Milburn was imported. With Milburn established in town, the plot got under way. The two old men were eliminated, the money began its journey." He paused, turned to Georgie Cahill. "Just to keep the record straight—where did this money go?"

Cahill said lifelessly: "It was left to me under an illegal stipulation. Under the stipulation that I remarry. The courts overrode the ridiculous restraint. As I told you last night, the money went to me."

"So it went to you—check. My next question is, how much of that moola do you still have in your possession?"

Cahill began to tremble. "You're being rather personal. I can't see—"

McGavock said kindly: "Don't be afraid. Everything's under control. Tell the truth."

"I've still got forty thousand dollars."

McGavock sighed. "Half gone already, eh? You'd have been as clean as a hound's tooth in another week." His face was tired, drawn, beneath the harsh overhead light. He said softly: "That does it, Baylor. I charge you with multiple murder. Now's the time for those handcuffs, Sheriff."

DUFF'S EYES BUGGED. The little blonde's mouth dropped open. Cahill went as white as a sheet. He spoke and his words were strained, hushed. "Mr. McGavock, you're wrong. I've been paying the money to Mr. Baylor, all right, but he's not the killer. Let's not go into this any further."

McGavock studied Cahill with quiet respect. "Brother," he declared, "you're really a sportsman, and I don't mean maybe. Your sense of fair play won't let you stand by and see me hook the wrong party, will it? Well, don't worry. Baylor's our man—no matter what you think. He killed your uncles, he killed Milburn-Yancey, he killed Foss Bellew. Don't interrupt me. I'll tell this my own way."

Baylor grinned, said: "And then I'll tell it my way. I'll rip this town wide open."

McGavock ignored him. "It's a strange crime, as I said, a crime that's little short of ghoulish. This man Baylor is certainly a felon straight out of hell. I don't know where he came from—I imagine that Sheriff Northrup will find that he has a long record. What brought him to Archersburg, I don't know. Maybe he was hiding out. He came to Archersburg, bought the old mansion, and set up his hotel. His first two guests were Mort and Nelson Cahill. He then heard about the eighty thousand dollars. Later, Georgie, here, and his wife Lucinda moved in until they could get their cottage fixed up. The uncles must have treated Mrs. Cahill pretty rough, and Georgie, a damn loyal chap, stood by her."

The blonde said quietly: "George's uncles weren't very nice. They tried to pry us apart."

"That," McGavock said, "was the situation. Baylor mulled it over in that warped brain of his and saw how he could touch it up a little and make it pay off to the tune of eighty thousand bucks."

Fortunatus Duff boggled. Sheriff Northrup said happily: "Mr. McGavock, I'd shore cherish to hear the rest o' this."

"And that you shall." McGavock went on: "You've got the picture—everybody alive and circulating, and the old men with a fortune in their kicks. How to get this money? Not from the oldsters, surely. And not from Lucinda Cahill, not even if she had it, no sir, not from that gal—not in a thousand years! That leaves Georgie."

Baylor scoffed, exclaimed: "Balderdash! How—"

"Just sit steady in the boat, my friend. That's the nub. I'm about to tell you how. And that's an education in personality. Georgie, he's the soft spot. To get the money in Georgie's hands, Baylor went through an ordinary murder progression. Uncle Mort is eliminated, he leaves the money to Nelson. Nelson is slain and George inherits. That's the first step. The first step is easy—the second step is the critical one and it has to be fancy."

McGavock paused, continued: "The problem is to drive George half crazy with the suspicion that his wife killed the uncles to get the dough. Now, get this clear. It's not to frame the wife in the eyes of the law—that would nullify Baylor's scheme. It's just to convince one man, George Cahill, of the gal's guilt."

Cahill said gravely: "Even if you don't prove your point, McGavock, you're doing some sweet talking—and that's already earned your fee."

"That's the way he worked it," McGavock declared. "Kill one, skip one. Get the dough from the oldsters to George, and from George to Baylor. To bring about the second step, he imported a petty crook, a man who knew how to fire clay. This man was named Yancey and was from the North. Baylor renamed him Percy Ramsbaugh Milburn. Yancey no doubt thought this was just a funny name, but Baylor knew that any Southern law officer would recognize it. That was a loophole for Baylor. If thing's should go askew, which they did, he could knock off Yancey, which he did, and everyone would say: 'Milburn Yancey's a mighty suspicious character'—which they did."

George Cahill said: "I never liked that man Milburn. What did he have to do with this?"

"Well may you ask! He was in town for the sole purpose of wrecking your life. Of convincing you that your wife was a murderess. He made three attempts, two successful, to excite you. The unsuccessful try was the attempt to get into your house to plant evidence against Lucinda. You remember how he nagged at you to let him hold a seance in your attic? His two triumphs were the cats and the hats—if you'll excuse a bit of rhyme."

Baylor asked haughtily: "What cats? I don't know what you're talking about."

"Lucinda Cahill has an extraordinary pet feline, Old Ninety-Seven. It walks with a limp, it's well known in town. Milburn put out a goofy story that he'd purchase stray cats, that he wanted to take them out into the hills and release them. He knew kids. They began bringing in cats of all kinds, pets as well as strays. Milburn sat and waited. One day a gamin showed up with Old Ninety-Seven. He made plaster of Paris prints of Ninety-Seven's tracks and released him. It was these prints, of course, along with the boot prints that were found by the bodies of Mort and Nelson."

SHERIFF NORTHRUP NODDED. "I knowed something was wrong. Take those prints out at the Parson's. They was made *through* burlap. Can't nary a cat walk down that heavy!"

McGavock said: "It was evidence that wouldn't stand up in a court of law but it would alarm Cahill when he learned of it. The hats gag, however, was Baylor's masterpiece. It ruined him, too, by the way. It brought me in from Memphis." He looked grim. "Baylor laid tiles, ordinary drainage tiles, from the hillside behind Cahill's, down under the barn floor, *into his cistern.* He damned up a gully on the slope. He did all this long in advance of the actual murders. He probably had a sneak named Foss Bellew to do the actual labor for him. Then after he'd slain the brothers, he took their hats and placed them in Cahill's cistern. All he had to wait for then was for a flash rain to come and flood the reservoir. Which event occurred last night. It was a spectacular and devilish way to weaken his victim."

Cahill frowned. "Last night you mentioned something about stolen biscuits—"

"Hot biscuits, yes. We'll never know just what slipped up on Baylor, but here's how I'd reconstruct it. He was afraid to buy tile, afraid he'd tip his hand. There was an old clay mine and kiln here already to use, so he imported Yancey. Yancey baked the tile for him. I'd say that Baylor never completely took Yancey into his confidence, that when the tiles came out of the kiln, Baylor sent Bellew around that night to filch them. That would give Baylor an out if Yancey ever talked. Yancey-Milburn saw these tiles disappearing and wired us to catch the thief. He offered a big fee and did so with tongue in his cheek. He didn't intend to pay us a dime. These fresh baked tiles, of course, were the 'hot biscuits'."

Baylor said earnestly: "Let's argue. The best you've made out against me is a blackmail case. My defense against murder is that all this stuff happened in town and I just took the opportunity to turn a penny. I'll pay back the—"

"You can't buy your way out of four killings, Baylor. You made one bad blunder. I can identify you with that tile scheme. Now who but the actual killer had the chance to get possession of those hats!"

Sheriff Northrup snapped on the handcuffs, said: "I'd shore like to watch the faces of a hill-jury when the prosecutor waves around Mr. Cahill's cancelled check for fo'ty thousand dollars!"

Mr. Duff coughed gently, asked: "Please, Mr. McGavock. What about this Foss Bellew?"

"Bellew was a phony from the word go. Baylor sent you to him, didn't he? I thought so. Bellew's job was to spread harmful rumors through the community. He claimed to have witnessed the murders. He was Baylor's lever in extracting the money from Cahill."

The sheriff and his prisoner left the porch, disappeared in the darkness. Cahill and his wife loitered a moment. The little blonde seemed embarrassed. She said: "I want to thank you, Mr. McGavock. You know what you said this afternoon? Well, you were correct."

"Sure-sure." McGavock waved them away. "Where you see the smoke of domestic battle you see the fire of love. Or words to that effect."

They, too, vanished into the night.

For a long solemn interval, Mr. Fortunatus Duff and McGavock sat in tomblike silence. The fat man seemed badly worried.

At last he spoke. "So my ballad-maker was a fake! That's awful! You don't realize what that does to me. I'd already written back to the university telling them of my discovery, of finding a completely original folk-song. There'll be nothing for me but sneers and jeers when I return to the campus." He meditated. "Comes to my mind your little imitation: *'Twas on a Tuesday night, the evening it was late, when the elder brother, Uncle Mort, went out and met his fate!* Heh-heh-heh. Very good." He made a puffy O of his lips. "Now this might seem dishonest to you, but don't, I pray, misunderstand me. It's just that I don't want to let my colleagues down. Do you think, do you think—er—that you could, say, finish up that interesting opus as well as you started?"

McGavock grinned. "Sure. Why not? Go get a pencil and some paper."

The Hound with the Golden Eye

"Have reason to believe bad crime in town. Am forwarding bottle of sawdust to be analyzed by you," read the cryptic little note which dispatched McGavock posthaste to Kempton, Tenn. Delightful place—with "you-all's" thick on everyone's lips and the town's two murders on everyone's mind—on McGavock's particularly!

1

The Sawdust Trail

THE APRIL MORNING was leaden, dreary. The tall windows of the old office were closed against the river fog and the feeble nightlight, hanging from the grimy ceiling, burned with a coppery tinsel glow. McGavock leaned back in his swivel chair, said persuasively: "When this ladies' club meets at your house tonight, tell them about it. It's a game and everybody likes a game."

Miss Ollinger, the Old Man's spinsterish secretary, was skeptical. "How is it played?"

"Generally with a mallet, a meatsaw and an indeterminate number of candy buckets." McGavock warmed up. "However, you can just imagine that part. Here's the way you do it. Select a member—say Madam President—sit her in the center of the floor, and have the others stare at her. The trick is to estimate how many buckets you'd need to ship her to Denver, postage paid. And how much it would cost. There are postal rates to calculate, poundage, and so forth. The game's called 'Let's Dismember the Member' and I guarantee—"

Miss Ollinger's pigeon chest quivered in horror. "I've never heard anything so repulsive—"

A great hammering came from beyond the frosted glass partition. The secretary jumped, started across the floor in a hurry. A moment later, she was back. "Mr. Browne wishes to see you—and he means now!"

THE CHIEF'S SANCTUM was foul with the stench of assorted medicines. McGavock strode roughly through the door, stood stock-still on the threshold.

The oldster was a pitiful spectacle. He sat slumped behind his bird's-eye maple desk, his ancient, dew-lapped face twisted in agony. On the desktop before him was a box of aspirin, a bottle of clove oil, a matchstick with a little cotton swab on it. He turned watery, pain-racked eyes on his ace detective. "For once, Luther, we won't argue, will we? We won't yell at each other. I'm half crazy. Got an abscessed molar thumping around in my skull—"

McGavock waited dourly.

Old Atherton Browne spoke with difficulty. "Son, there's something cooking at Kempton—that's a small town in the eastern part of the state, in the hoot owl and possum country. It sounds mighty like murder. I'd appreciate it if you'd give it the once-over-lightly."

McGavock began to shout. "Send Pete Coyle—he's your pet! And don't screw up your face! Toothache, malarkey. You haven't had a natural tooth in your jaw for forty years, since some drunken dentist went berserk in your mouth with a pair of lineman's pliers! You're not fooling me—" He suddenly lowered his voice evilly: "Sure, on second thought, I'll take it. If you sign a contract with me."

The Old Man gazed at him fondly, through scaly, mucous-rimmed eyelids. "I always do right by you, Luther, don't I?"

McGavock glared. He was a small man, wiry and tough, with

a touch of salt and pepper at his temples. There was a taunting quality about him that aroused instant animal antagonism in perfect strangers. He was a genius at getting results, but he was a hard man to take. He'd worked in every major agency in the country but never until he'd hit this Memphis outfit had he found a real home.

He had no contract and this was a sore point. His superiors liked what he brought in, but didn't want to know too much about his methods. He functioned under a sort of roving commission that the agency could repudiate with alacrity if he got into hot water. He asked savagely: "What about this homicide at Kempton?"

The Old Man smiled pathetically. "I did not say homicide. I said it had the earmarks. Go 'way and leave me alone. I'm sick. I want to see Pete Coyle."

McGavock faltered. "You're sucking me in and I know it. Be that as it may, what about this—"

Wordlessly, the chief produced an envelope from the desk drawer, handed it across the blotter. It was dated a week previous. McGavock slipped out two pages of cheap stationery, each letterheaded in job printing: *J.R. Gatch, South Market Street, Kempton, Tennessee.* The script was in a big flowing hand, without salutation or signature, and the message extended from the top of the first sheet to the bottom of the second.

> Have reason to believe bad crime here in town. Am forwarding under separate cover bottle of sawdust to be analyzed by you. Please return laboratory results to me in custody your best detective.

That was all. McGavock returned the letter to the Old Man,

asked: "Does he mean analyzed for blood?"

"I don't know. Could be."

"This note was mailed a week ago. Why are we just getting on it?"

Atherton Browne looked grim. "I've been waiting for the sawdust. It never came."

"Oh." McGavock pulled moodily at his lower lip. "Like that, eh? Well, it sounds like a mare's-nest, but I'll take a flyer." He started for the outer office, stopped abruptly. "No monkey business? This is on the level?"

The oldster looked hurt. "Why, son, I always—"

McGavock slammed the door behind him. Alone, the Old Man took out a third sheet of stationery. It matched the other two. Placidly, he arranged them on the desk so that they formed a long, continuous sheet.

> ... Please return laboratory results to me in custody your best detective.
>
> If you don't receive the sample within the week, forget it. The whole thing might well be a figment of my imagination.
>
> I reside at my cousin's home and should you contact me, it might be well to remember that he does not know I have written you.
>
> Yours respectfully,
>
> Cortland Kincaid Endicott.

Atherton Browne closed his eyes in happy reverie. There was no doubt about it—Luther McGavock was the best operative he'd ever had on his payroll. But he worked best under pressure. He was dynamite, but you had to manipulate him.

THE CONNECTIONS WERE good and it was about nine that evening when the train pounded up to the little station at Kempton. McGavock was the only passenger to alight and hardly had his luggage hit the platform when the locomotive hissed off again into the darkness. He underwent the definite sensation of having been deposited abruptly from one world into another. The spring night was clear and mild, heavy with the scent of honeysuckle and swelling magnolia blooms.

The depot was deserted but for the stationmaster, squatting on his hunkers in the light of a lantern, feeding raw peanuts to a pet raccoon. McGavock came up behind him, said enviously: "I declare! That's a fine beast. He's twice as pretty as mine—and twice as smart!"

The stationmaster was overcome with pride. He gave the animal a rough slap, to cover his embarrassment, mumbled, "Aw!"

"No kiddin'." McGavock nodded vigorously. "By the way, I'm a stranger. I might be here for a couple of days. Where's a good place to stay—and I mean good?"

His companion pondered. "They's a hotel, but you go and put up thur an' the mice'll have nests in yore shoes afore you kin git 'em off'n yore feet!" He pursed his lips. "Then thur's Miss Grinnell out on Plum Srreet. She'll take you in. You married or single?"

"Single as of this moment. Why?"

"You steer shy o' Miss Blanche then—she's hell on wheels. You'd best stick it out at the hotel. I'm shore sorry."

McGavock picked up his bag. "Thanks."

The crowds were thinning out as McGavock swung his

Gladstone along the row of dingy storefronts. Here and there were little flurries of horseplay and banter as Kempton's citizenry broke up for the evening, the menfolk ambling in direction of home and bed, their women and children lagging a pace or so behind. Everywhere was good feeling and friendship. Clean overalls and washpants, cotton print and ribbons. This was the sort of small, southern town McGavock knew so well, these were the kind of people he liked.

A chuckleheaded youngster gave the information he needed. The village was larger than he'd anticipated, with a population of maybe a thousand. He passed the courthouse, with its scraggly, eroded lawn and weathered park benches, turned from the business section and strolled down a sidestreet. The great maples arching above his head were in new leaf and the bright moon threw their star-shaped patterns on the white pavement before him.

The house was a pleasant little one-story cottage, set back from the street in a thicket of syringas. McGavock took a glazed brick walk across the grass, passed a small sign nailed on a cedar tree, ROOMS, and stepped up onto the diminutive porch enclosed in vine-hung latticework. His hand had hardly touched the bell-pull lever when the door opened and he found himself facing a plump female. He said politely: "Miss Grinnell? I'd like to take lodging with you." Ceremoniously, she led him into the living room.

Miss Blanche was fortyish, dressed in a voluminous lace blouse and a blushingly skin-tight skirt. She gave McGavock a quick inspection that priced his ties, suit and shoes, guessed his age and income. She wasn't any too sure about him.

There was a vase of cattails in the corner of the room, a

bowl of violets on the piano, and a garland of withered leaves along the mantelpiece. On a rosewood stand was a kerosene lamp with forget-me-nots and pansies painted on its shade, and beside the lamp was an open copybook. McGavock glanced down, noticed that it contained verses of some sort. He exclaimed extravagantly: "Miss Grinnell, you're a poet! I'll just go on to the hotel. I'm interrupting the Muse!"

That did it. She said artificially: "A very paltry one, I fear, though the Kempton *Journal* does refer to me as the Sweet Singer of Lunken County." She beamed on him. "I can readily see you're a human with a soul. You don't go to any old hotel—you stay right here where I can take care of you!" She paused. "Don't think me rude, but just as a matter of form, who are you and what is your business?"

"I'm Luther McGavock. I'm a sweet potato inoculator."

She looked confused. "A sweet potato inoc—I don't believe I ever..." Miss Blanche proffered a key. "It'll be a dollar a night. Your room is at the end of the hall."

McGavock lingered. "I'm not going to bed just now. It's a beautiful evening. I'm going out and walk a little while under the wonderful stars."

She took a big breath, looked dreamy. McGavock said: "So you're the Sweet Singer of Lunken County! They told me it was a man named J.R. Gatch who lives on South Market."

She had a little trouble straightening it out. Finally she retorted: "If Jim Gatch writes poetry, I never heard of it. All he's interested in is making money. And the South Market Street place isn't his home—that's his shop. He lives in a brick house out on Old Church with his cousin, Cort Endicott. Maybe Cort composes verse. I shouldn't be surprised—he's a cultivated gentleman of the old school."

McGavock walked to the front door. He stopped a moment, his hand on the knob, ogling her. She enjoyed it. He said sanctimoniously: "Endicott? Don't tell me that's Endicott I've been hearing the scandal about!"

"Not scandal—just gossip. And it's not Cortland. It's his brother, Scully. The Scully Endicotts live in the big house, out by the water tower. They say since Scully inherited all that money he's gone conceited and won't even speak to Cort. He's suddenly decided that Cortland's not a real blood-tie because he's merely a half-brother." She was talking but she was not thinking about what she was saying.

Her eyes were lit up with a female, predatory look. She touched him on the elbow, said slowly: "I'm so glad to have you in my home, Mr. McGavock." McGavock opened the door. She said self-consciously: "Kempton's so lovely in the spring. Why didn't you bring Mrs. McGavock along with you?"

Her voice was flat. This is it, McGavock decided—ten minutes and she wants to marry me. She was sounding him out.

He looked indescribably sad, said: "I wanted to bring Mrs. McGavock. But I didn't dare. She's got a trick of slipping her chains and—presto!—she's off and away!" He tucked his chin into the hollow of his shoulder, stepped out into the night.

McGAVOCK HAD HIS own particular system for breaking stubborn cases. Gather in the tag ends, he reasoned, get them under control, and the big business will fall apart in your lap. Strictly speaking, there was no actual case. Just something indefinite about some sawdust—that was all. But the detective was a veteran at his trade and ever since he'd put his bag down at the station he'd had a chill at the nape of his neck. He split it two ways—he was either wasting his time on a fiasco, or he was up against something pretty sinister.

He figured it might be a good idea to have a short talk with this new heir, this hoity-toity half-brother, Scully Endicott. He was looking forward to the interview. New heirs were always interesting specimens, especially when prosperity floored them.

He had no trouble locating the place. The water tower against the sky was his guide.

The great pillared mansion lay some distance back from the sidewalk on a hillside, in a sort of private park. The premises were sheltered from the street by an eight-foot lilac hedge. The ornamental wrought iron gates were flung wide open. McGavock passed through the portals, stood a moment in the shadows to get his bearings. The enormous Georgian house, with its fluted pillars and double-decked verandas, was white and shimmering in the moonlight. McGavock mumbled to himself. The edifice was much too showy to suit his taste.

The house was dark from attic to basement. Off to one side of the main building, however, a floodlight burned on a gooseneck above the garage. The occupants were away for the evening, and they'd left a light to welcome them on their return.

As he gazed at the pretentious layout, he felt in his bones that whatever the crime, if any, this great house—and the money which lay behind it—could most certainly provide sufficient motive. He chewed the corner of his lip in dark speculation. Finally, after a second's hesitation, he sauntered up the crushed stone drive, climbed the broad steps to the veranda and rang the doorbell.

There was no answer. He expected none. He hammered peremptorily, waited. No response. Here goes, he thought. Breaking and entering. Long live the glory of Atherton Browne the Great, long live the memory of his myrmidons! He tested the doorknob. To his surprise he found it unlocked. He entered, closed the massive panel behind him.

He got out his pencil flash, hooded it with his handkerchief. Good old Dixie, he reflected. At least one pistol per every home-owner—what am I doing? Wow!

The lofty hall was sumptuous in waxed walnut wainscoting. He flipped his beam into a luxurious parlor, dazzling in gilt furniture and brocade drapes, glanced into the elaborate dining room resplendent in silver plate and crystal candlesticks, came to the library.

Here, he decided to take a look-see. He swung the diffused glow of his torch over the book-lined walls, across the comfortable overstuffed chairs. He wandered into the center of the room. Suddenly, he flicked off his flash, froze in the darkness.

The big bay windows of the library faced the garage. A man on a bicycle came pedaling up the gravel drive into the pool of silver shed by the floodlight. He was a little fellow, well set up. McGavock could make out the glint of spectacles beneath a sloppy, black felt hat. The fellow dismounted energetically, whipped down the bicycle stand, took the clip off his trouser cuff.

He then started in a stiff stride across the lawn towards the house. McGavock waited tensely. If this was Master Scully returning, McGavock had his plan of exit all worked out. He'd listen for the door, front or back, and then simply step through the window bay out onto the lawn.

Brin-n-n-ng! The doorbell rang. The man was a visitor. That was better. McGavock relaxed. In a moment the caller would go away.

For about two minutes McGavock waited, his eyes on the bicycle by the garage.

Then it happened. So quickly that it caught him flatfooted. The man's head appeared at the window pane, staring into the room. McGavock knew that he was invisible in the spongy darkness, yet he held his breath. From the faint aura of the floodlight, McGavock could make out the black hat, the squarish face, the clipped mustache, the blank octagonal spectacle lenses, the blocky shoulders protruding from the shroud of shrubbery.

The man turned, strode back across the lawn. He slapped up his bicycle stand, put on his trouser clip, mounted, and pedaled off. And that was that. McGavock heaved a sigh of relief.

There was nothing of interest in Scully Endicott's library. A painstaking examination of the desk offered little beyond the fact that the Endicotts, man and wife, lived expensively and paid their bills.

He made a casual circuit of the rest of the ground floor, ascended to the second story.

It was upstairs he found the corpse.

2

Friend is Dog's Best Man

MASTER AND LADY, he discovered, had separate bedrooms. He passed by Mrs. Scully's dainty boudoir, entered her husband's mannish quarters. In the far wall, between a huge maple bed and an oversized chest of drawers, was a small door which he assumed led into a closet. Investigation proved differently. Beyond Scully Endicott's sleeping quarters, adjoining it, and with no apparent entrance but through the bedroom itself, was the master's den.

McGavock's inquiring beam cut into the cubbyhole, across the deep-napped Chinese rug, came to a full rest on the dead man in the chair.

He was an oldish, horse-faced chap with a protruding chin and blue eyes. His lower lip hung loosely in a V-shaped grin and his old-style goatee was neatly trimmed and tapered to an elfish point. His oily gray hair was combed back from his forehead in a country-gentleman pompadour. He'd been strangled with a four-foot length of heavy fishline.

The den's single window was heavily curtained. McGavock reached for a bridge lamp. His hand touched the metal bracket—*it was still warm.* He hesitated, clicked on the switch, listened intently. The house was tomb-silent.

The killer hadn't been gone long. He'd almost caught him red-handed.

The little room was intimate, cozy, and reeked with wealth. A brace of fine, gold-chased English shotguns was crossed over a mounted, leering bobcat on a shelf by the telephone. There was a red leather couch with an end table holding a manicure set and a musty book entitled, *Genealogy of Meggs County, Alabama, Gatch Family—1790–1890.* A label inside the cover said, *From the Library of James Robert Gatch.*

McGavock turned his attention again to the body. The old man's blue serge coat was shiny at the seams, his elastic-sided gaiters run-down at the heels. McGavock slipped a cumbersome old-fashioned timepiece from the oldster's vest, opened the case. Engraving in the watch read, *To Our Inspiring Sunday School Teacher, Cortland Kincaid Endicott. From a Grateful Class, June 12, 1911.*

So this was the cultivated Copland, Scully's half-brother.

McGavock moved—and moved fast. He produced his pocket comb, parted the old man's pompadour, combed the oily gray locks down on each side, gathered them back over each ear. He studied his handiwork with smug satisfaction. The effect was ghastly—that staring horseface looked the same, yet somehow it didn't.

Thoughtfully, he lifted the receiver of the French phone, called the sheriff. When he got his connection, he reported the murder, describing the location of the little den. He spoke in a throaty voice, larding his speech with "you-all's." Grinning, he hung up on a spluttering wire.

He switched off the light, went to the curtained window. The tall sash opened out onto an upstairs veranda. He wasn't surprised—it had to be this way. This was the route by which the killer had made his escape.

McGavock stepped through the window, onto the porch,

walked to the rear, and descended the stairway to the ground. A few moments later, he was off the premises and headed for Old Church Street.

It was high time he had a session with this J.R. Gatch.

WHEN McGAVOCK'S LANDLADY had said that the house on Old Church Street was brick, the detective had visualized something ancient and weathered and friendly, with moss-laden shingles, set perhaps in a grove of romantic magnolias.

Jim Gatch's bungalow was brick, all right, garish new yellow brick, built smack in the center of an ugly knob of bare red clay. Puny saplings, as big as a man's finger, had been planted here and there about the yard in an attempt to landscape it and burlap sacks had been spread to force a stand of grass. It was the kind of a house a man with a little money and no particular pleasure in living would select. McGavock sauntered up the cement walk, rapped on the door.

The man that answered the summons was a little fellow with a husky build. He wore octagonal spectacles and had a clipped black mustache. He was the man on the bicycle, the lad who had stared in the bay window. All he needed was the black Stetson. McGavock said silkily: "I'm the detective from Memphis. The one you retained. Lute McGavock's the name."

Gatch took out a gold and ivory toothpick, raised his lip and systematically began scraping the interstices of his large white teeth. Finally he spat, put the toothpick away. He stepped back, said: "Come in, suh."

McGavock followed his host into the parlor. The inside of the house gave the detective the same feeling that the yellow brick had given him—the impression of cold newness. The bright oak floor, the harsh plastered walls, everything was bandbox new. Gatch asked his guest to sit down, perched himself on the edge of a chair, facing him. He said: "So you're the detective I sent to Memphis for?"

McGavock gave him a careful scrutiny. He didn't look any better in the light than he had peeping through that window. His square face was solid, with meaty, muscular cheeks and behind the sheen of those octagonal lenses his little eyes, encased in sacs of wrinkled skin, were as hard as blue quartz.

McGavock nodded affably. "Yea, verily, I am he. Tell papa. What's troubling you?"

Gatch screwed up his mouth, declared worriedly: "I'm sure glad you came, suh. Cousin Scully wouldn't bring in help, so I took it on myself. They're logging Cousin Scully's land out at Snake Ridge. I want you to stop it. I'm prepared to pay two thousand dollars for the arrest and conviction of the lowdown culprits!"

"It's a lead pipe cinch!" McGavock smiled. "And then what else?"

"That's all, and, I might add, it'll be no easy matter. Log thieves in these hills are a heap sight more desperate than 'shiners. They shoot on sight—and they don't miss."

McGavock said genially: "We'll see what we will see. Now, one thing more. I've worked these small towns before. The local law isn't going to cherish the idea of an outsider taking over. I'll need a letter of endorsement." He groped for his wallet, located a small white card, handed it to his host. The card said:

> This is to introduce Luther McGavock
>
> (Signed)....

The stocky man unscrewed his pen cap, wrote *James Robert Gatch* in the blank, returned the pasteboard. "You'll have no difficulty with the local law, suh. I stand mighty well—"

The signature was written in minute, mechanically perfect script. McGavock tore the card into quarters, tossed it in the fire-place. He said petulantly: "What goes on here?"

Gatch elevated his coarse eyebrows. "I fail to understand, suh, just what you mean."

"I mean you're lying by the clock." McGavock flushed angrily. "Always I get cases with hocus-pocus! Just once, why can't I get a routine job! You're not our client. He used your letter-head, but the handwriting's different. Who is he? And who the hell are you?"

Gatch looked owlish. "That was just a little test. You're a man after my heart, McGavock. Not gullible. I like a smart man. You'll do, suh!" He cleared his throat. "If your client used my stationery, he must be the gentleman who shares my roof, Cousin Cortland Endicott. Now, I wonder why he would be employing a detective. He doesn't need one. I do."

"Where is this Endicott now?"

"Taking a bit of an airing, I presume. He'll be in later. There's no reason you can't have two clients, is there? I was perfectly sincere when I asked you to stop those timber thieves. What do you say?"

McGavock hedged. "You want their arrest and conviction? Maybe yes, maybe no. I got other work to do. But this I will promise—I'll stop the filching. Take it or leave it."

"I take it." Gatch seemed satisfied. His hard blue eyes bored into McGavock's. "I didn't quite get why you said Cortland wrote you."

McGavock reached for his hat, arose. "I didn't say. We'll discuss it tomorrow, after I've had a talk with him. After all, he's client number one. He has a list of grievances as long as your arm. Let him tell you about them. This I will say, though—he claims his life is in danger, and he wants us to analyze a sample of sawdust for him."

Gatch looked puzzled.

He led McGavock to the door. On the front porch, McGavock said conversationally: "I'm a Yankee. To most Yankees all Southerners sound alike. I like the accent, it's music to me. I've listened and I've learned. A Texan doesn't sound like a Georgian, and a Carolinian talks differently from a Kentuckian. You're not from Tennessee—you sound like Alabama."

Gatch listened intently. "You've got a good ear. An uncanny one, as a matter of fact. I was born in Meggs County, Alabama, but I left there when I was fourteen years old. For the last thirty years I've lived here and yonder about the Southland, mainly in Louisiana. So I still have that Alabama broad-talk! Think of that! Good night, suh."

McGavock pushed his hat on his head, strode hard-heeled down the cement walk.

KEMPTON'S COMMERCIAL THOROUGHFARE, Market Street, began back of the courthouse, by the jail, and extended south to the cotton gin at the edge of town. Beyond the cotton gin stretched the lush, marshy bottomlands. The street started off respectably enough, in small shops and tradesmen's quarters but soon slipped into ramshackle squalor. A few blocks and the sidewalk stopped. From here on, the buildings were on but one side of the street, and spaced hit and miss, with patches of barren meadow between them. Almost at the end of the line was the establishment of Mr. James Robert Gatch. McGavock drew up in the shadows and gave it the once-over.

A high board fence enclosed a sizable lot and the detective could make out the roofs of several weathered buildings. Above the big gate a new sign said:

GRAIN — FEED
LUMBER
COAL — MONUMENTS
J.R. GATCH, PROP.

Miss Grinnell had been right. It appeared that Mr. Gatch was a man of many trades and all trails led to the dollar.

The tall board fence was stark and black in the moonlight, ominous. The gates were crudely locked—a length of rusty chain was passed through two holes and secured with a cheap padlock. McGavock took out his key-ring, had the shackle from its case on the second try. He swung open the gate, stepped inside.

He found himself in an aisle, perhaps two wagon-widths in breadth, which wound between great stacks of lumber three feet and more above his head. Every so often, as he advanced, side passages branched off from the feeder lane in alleys of pitch darkness. He stayed in the center of the road and kept an alert eye cocked at these shadowy channel-mouths. After a little, he emerged from the maze and came out into the open.

In the hard earth yard were several sheds and, directly facing him, a large, rambling clapboard structure. This main building was T-shaped and above a door at the rear was lettered, OFFICE.

He considered a moment, passed the office by, skirted the corner of the building and went down the far side, trying the windows. About half of them were unfastened. There wasn't much to steal evidently, and little precaution was taken. He slid up a sash and climbed over the sill.

The sweet, aromatic scent of baled hay came to his nostrils. He switched on his flash and saw that he was in a feed storage room. He made his way to the office, a bare cubbyhole with a littered desk, a dented spittoon and a rush-seated rocking chair. A quick search revealed nothing of interest here. He retraced his way through the feed room, came to the low-ceilinged annex, the T-bar to the building proper.

This was the monument workshop. There was a strong narrow bench with equipment for cutting and polishing stone. Against the wall were the compressed air tools for lettering the inscriptions. To one side was a row of tombstone blanks, in red granite and black, in white marble—quite an assortment—just waiting for the finger of death to beckon.

McGavock examined the bench. He gave its surface a painstaking scrutiny, dropped to his haunches and inspected the floor beneath. He arose, brushed the pinkish dust from his trousers, stood a long moment in moody concentration. It was then he observed the burlap-covered object behind the door. He walked over, lifted the sacking. He stared down in amazement.

He'd uncovered a midget tombstone, about the size of a shoebox, made from the finest marble. At first he figured it to be an infant's stone and then he read the inscription.

Here Lies
RUFUS THE RED
Gallant, Faithful
Dog Is Man's Best Friend

HE REPLACED THE sacking, tucking in the corners carefully as he'd found them. He began talking to himself, softly, absently, his mind miles away. He said: "Always the same thing—dog is man's best friend. Why don't they give it a twist: man is dog's best friend, friend is dog's best man!" He sighed, returned to the window through which he'd made his entry, and left the building.

He was beginning to get a faint glimmer of just why the late Cortland Kincaid Endicott had posted that red-hot note to the Memphis agency. It was just a glimmer, not even a good sound hunch, but it didn't sit too well on his stomach. One thing he knew, he was mixed up in a pretty foul mess.

He crossed the open court, stepped into the engulfing shadows of the lumber yard, and headed for the gate. Two people he wanted to see, Cousin Scully and the timber thief who was logging his land back on Snake Ridge. The moon was high and white in the spring sky and laid a blue-and-silver strip of illumination in the center of the path between the high-stacked lumber. McGavock had progressed about half the distance to the fence when he heard the rattle.

He was just passing the mouth of one of those narrow side-alleys that led off from the main feeder lane. He pulled up to a silent stop and listened.

The rattling noise was repeated, back in the entrails of the dark alley. And suddenly there was a *plop!* A queer sound like the gunshot of a light caliber pistol muted and muffled by a blanket.

McGavock flattened himself around the corner, out of range, against the piled planking, and thought it over. *If he expects me to come in there after him,* he decided, *he's crazy.*

All at once, he straightened it out. He'd been foxed. The rattle had been a handful of gravel. And the *plop* had been nothing more than a tossed light bulb! His eyes roved out to the strip of moonlight in the middle of the road. There, at the edge of the lip of shadow cast by the stacked lumber, was the elongated silhouette of a hatless man. The strange illusion produced the split-second sensation that the fellow was as far away as his shadow.

Things happened fast.

McGavock threw himself into a protective crouch and the man came hurtling down the brief three feet, from directly above the detective's head, smashing him to his knee. In a threshing frenzy, the man struck at McGavock with a heavy pipe wrench and the detective, off balance, fended the blow, wrist crossed to wrist with his attacker, so that the brutal impact was diverted to his hip. His thigh was numbed beneath the crushing steel and for an instant he thought his leg was paralyzed. He reared forward and up, and cut loose with both fists. He heard the wrench clatter to the ground.

The man was on him now, panting, rigid fingers clawing at his throat. McGavock put his weight into a haymaker, felt his assailant sag. The dark form reeled, hesitated spread-eagled against the lumber—and then he was gone. Just that vague impression of a featureless face thrust into an upturned coat collar and it was all over.

McGavock could hear him scurrying away, in and out of the labyrinth of alleys. The detective picked up his hat, whipped it against his calf, thrust it on the back of his head. He said venomously to the empty night: "What's the hurry? Let's try that again."

3

The Corpse With the Fancy Hair-Do

MAIN STREET WAS deserted. Long ago, the merchants had closed their shops. Here and there some extravagant tradesman had left a feeble nightlight at the rear of his store, but for the most part the dusty windows were completely dark. McGavock came out from behind the courthouse, angled across the sterile square, proceeded down Main until he came to a watering trough at the curb before the hardware shop. Here he took off his coat, rolled up his sleeves and rinsed his forehead and neck from the cool stream flowing from the iron pipe. It was like strong medicine. He dried himself with his handkerchief, tossed the handkerchief out into the street. Now he was all set. He knew what was next on the list—and he thought he knew how to handle it. He put on his coat and started out to reconnoiter the general business section.

In a small country town like Kempton, he'd observed, the shop lights usually went out in the order of their respectability—the most reputable first, the least reputable last.

It took him some time to find the place he was searching for, and he almost passed it up. He found it by a hitching lot behind the row of brick stores at the end of the street. He was looking for a small restaurant, or maybe a poolroom. He almost passed this place up because it was a house.

A grotesque gray clapboard house, narrow—not much more than ten feet across the front—two-storied. It was built after the manner of rural river homes, on stilts. The clapboard had rotted and warped from the siding, the panes were gone from the upstairs windows. A light shone from the front window on the lower floor. His ear caught the strains of fiddle music, lowdown, brooding. He crossed the hitching lot, picking his way through the filth and dung, ascended the crude steps and opened the door.

There were six or seven men in the room, gathered about kitchen tables, and they stopped talking the second he made his appearance. The walls were papered in old newspapers, there was a short counter at the back, bare except for a pair of coal-oil lamps, and above it was hung the room's sole effort at ornamentation—an old chromo picturing a little girl in a nightgown wandering through the woods in a snowstorm, with the legend, *Prof. Mortimer's Juniper Salve.* On the tables were half-empty bottles of lemon pop, chasers, and while no whiskey was in sight the air was heavy with its fumes.

The customers were the lowest sort of riffraff. Renegade hillmen and the dregs of the town. A squint-eyed youth in a greasy apron laid a violin on a bench and came forward. He was about the dirtiest human that McGavock had ever stared at. His throat and wrists were unwashed and scaly and he had pallid Vs of fish-white skin between his fingers in contrast to his mottled, crusty hands. McGavock recoiled in disgust, said severely: "Bear this in mind, son. Grime doesn't pay!"

The boy fastened his lizard eyes on McGavock's tie, asked coldly: "What you want?"

McGavock could feel the pressure of the deadly silence about him. He took off his hat, held it stiffly before him at arm's length, and bawled: "Hooray for Roseville, Indiana! We can 'em, you eat 'em!"

The tension relaxed. Someone snickered. The boy said quietly: "Back up and pull out, friend. I'm afeard you done got yourese'f too much drunk fer me. We're law-abidin'. So-long."

McGavock smiled amiably. "I'm stone sober, son. He spoke calmly, managed to put a faint tone of condescension into his speech. "I'm just proud of my home town, that's all. You don't hold that against a fellow, do you? Let me tell you, Roseville's wonderful. Should I paint all its sweet charms, I swear you'd pack up your straw suitcase and catch the next train north. It's heaven on earth, a Garden of Eden—"

"I'm shore it must be." The boy was laconic. "If it's so durn perfeck, how come you to leave it? I wouldn't think—"

"I'm down here on—er—business. I'm secretary of the Roseville Cannery. Tomatoes, pumpkin, beans. We can 'em, you eat 'em." McGavock paused. "We're getting big, expanding. Now a growing cannery needs plenty warehouse space. That's why I'm down here. I'm in the market."

"You'unses come clean to Kempton to buy a warehouse?"

"To buy the lumber for one, yes."

The boy shook his head. "Don't y'all have no lumber back no'th?"

"Lumber we have, but it's expensive." McGavock lowered his eyelid, said slyly: "I'm after good stuff—and cheap. And I'll pay cash."

The youth went deadpan, said woodenly: "Well, I hope you get it. Good night, suh."

A customer alone at a table in the corner began thumping his pop bottle on the board for service. The boy hurried over. McGavock swept his glance casually in the direction of the clamor.

The man causing the ruckus was one tough baby. He was dressed like a mixture of the hills and the town. He wore corduroy pants stuffed into knee-length moccasin boots, a blue serge coat, and a jug-shaped, uncreased, western-style hat. He had the face of a ferret, vicious, predatory eyes and thin, cruel lips. As the boy in the apron approached him, he fumbled his change, dropped it on the floor. He bent forward and helped the youth retrieve it. For an instant, their heads were close together.

The man then got to his feet, yawned, and left the building. The boy came back to McGavock. He lowered his voice to a lifeless whisper, said: "I been thinkin'. They's a feller in town kin git you about what you want. Mebbe iff'n you was to be sittin' in Co't Square tomorrer mornin' at eleven o'clock, mebbe—"

McGavock nodded. He yawned in exact imitation of the man in the moccasin boots, followed him through the door.

Outside, the man was gone.

COUSIN SCULLY ENDICOTT'S great pillared mansion was lighted up like Saturday night at the carnival. Every window from basement to attic seemed to be blazing. The law had come and gone, the undertaker had come and gone, and the big house was still vibrating. McGavock strolled through the wrought-iron portals, sauntered over the park-like lawn, and climbed the broad steps to the front veranda. He lolled against the door jamb, rammed his thumb into the push button. He heard the bell ring deep within the house and almost instantly his summons was answered.

The lad that stepped out onto the flagstones of the lighted porch pretty well fulfilled McGavock's mental image of him.

He was middle-aged and chubby and dressed in the height of fashion—the fashion of the Nineteen Twenties. He wore a pin-stripe suit, tight around the buttocks and flaring at the ankles, his shoes were needle sharp and fancy with punched work, his vest was piped with silver braid. He had a big, fleshy head with tiny protruding eyes, and a hateful spoiled-child pucker about his mouth. He drew up in front of McGavock, tilted his body back as though the detective were emanating a vile stench, said haughtily: "Tragedy has descended upon this household, sir. Anything you have to say at this time will, frankly, be considered an annoyance."

McGavock looked miserable. He exclaimed wretchedly: "Mr. Endicott, I'm the detective you wrote to Memphis for. Golly, I'm all balled up. I can't find any clues. Just give me a starter, hey?"

Endicott blinked. "What's this, what's this?"

"Aren't you the right party?" McGavock faltered. "Endicott was the name, as I recall it." He looked embarrassed. "My memory's kinda weak, but I'm pretty sure the name was Endi—"

The pudgy man was doing some quick thinking. He came to a decision, said insolently: "Just step inside, fellow. We'll see what this is all about."

McGavock bobbed his head, groveled. "Thanks, Cap'n. All I need is a hint or a clue or something. Once I get rolling I'm a whiz."

"Sure, sure." Endicott appeared preoccupied. He led his guest down the parqueted hall, veered him off into the library.

The pudgy man selected the most comfortable chair, eased himself into it. He ordered curtly: "Sit down."

McGavock ignored him, remained standing. He quartered the room with a casual glance. The deep-napped rug, the bookshelves, everything was just about as he'd left it earlier in the evening. Two points of interest, however, caught his attention. In the small alcove between the bookcases were three staggered shelves—the top shelf held a mounted flying squirrel, the bottom, a hawk with a field mouse in its beak. The center shelf was empty. McGavock remembered the bobcat upstairs in the den. This wild life had been here on his former trip, he'd had a vague sensation to that effect. But the rolled blueprint on the desk was something new. It had made its appearance in the interim.

Endicott selected a juicy cigar from a rosewood humidor, said arrogantly: "Let's have it again, please. What's all the fuss and feathers? You say you're a sort of detective, and that someone named Endicott sent to Memphis for you? Now that's very strange. It wasn't I, sir, nor was it Linda, my wife." He puffed the cigar smoke outward in a succession of little balls, added thoughtfully: "It must have been my brother. Was it Cortland?"

McGavock nodded enthusiastically. "That's the gentleman! Where—"

Endicott cleared his throat pompously. "Tonight, by the hand of a foul murderer, Brother Cortland passed the Last Divide." He paused a moment in silent reverence, demanded: "What did Brother Cortland want with you?"

McGavock looked shocked. "My client's dead?" He cringed. "I daren't go back without a fee. They'll horsewhip me! What'll I do?"

"I'm your new client," Endicott purred. "We'll get along famously. If Brother Cortland had worries I want them cleared up. Why did you say he—"

McGavock was servilely coquettish. "I don't know should I tell you. It's a secret. I like you, but we're strangers!"

ENDICOTT'S HEAVY JOWLS purpled, his hand trembled in apoplectic rage. He began to mutter, his voice taut and incoherent. "I've never been subjected to such stupidity. Are all detectives— No, it's incredible. This man's a freak unto himself." He leaned forward, said loudly: "I can't stand you. Not with all I've been through tonight. Get out of my house. Out, sir!"

McGavock beamed placidly. "I place you now. You're the guy I was supposed to investigate. Think of that! Now you're my new boss! Well, boss, Cortland, as I recall, wanted two little mysteries solved." He pointed to the racks between the bookcases. "He wanted to know how come that shelf's empty."

Endicott took it quite seriously. "It isn't like Cortland to meddle in other folks' business. Maybe Linda's behind this after all. It was a little squabble between the two of us—nothing to call a detective over. Linda has a friend in town, a Mr. Gatch, who's rabid about outdoor life, hunting, trapping, and the like. He's constantly working on my wife, trying to sell her on the joys of the wide open spaces. Every once in a while he gives her a trophy, squirrels, hawks, and so forth. I put them on those shelves and Linda promptly carts them off and distributes them out of sight, about the house. She replaces them with vases, which I, in turn, dispose of—"

"Why?"

"Mr. Gatch is an important citizen and a frequent visitor at our home. There's no sense in offending him."

"That's what I always say," McGavock agreed heartily. "Never offend anyone! It's mighty nice of Mr. Gatch. I'm wild about outdoor life myself." He paused, declared humbly: "The feeling's coming over me that your brother was a trouble-maker, with a touch of the crackpot about him. Trying to break up a happy pair of turtle doves like you and your wife! And he claimed there was something sinister going on! Nuts! Take the way he was all steamed up over the sawdust!"

"Sawdust! What sawdust?"

"I haven't the slightest idea."

Endicott sunk back in the cushions, closed his eyes. After a moment he opened them, said smugly: "Well, it's been a brief and confusing relationship we've enjoyed, hasn't it, sir? I trust you can find your way to the door."

He figured he'd pumped McGavock dry, and now it was the brushoff. Hired and fired in ten minutes! The pudgy man dug into his vest, came out with a nickel. "Here, fellow, buy yourself a cigar."

McGavock gestured to the rosewood humidor of fifty-centers. "I'll just take one of these."

Endicott said icily: "Those are especially imported and—er—are heavily medicated. They'd be too rich for your blood, heh-heh-heh."

McGavock smiled oafishly, nodded good night.

Alone, in the hall, the detective studied the front door. The trim seemed to be O.K. He opened the door, ran his fingertips up and down the inside surface of the jamb. It was smooth, in good order. He found what he was looking for in the mortised slot which held the spring latch of the knob when the panel was closed. Within this slot his fingers encountered a small metal obstruction.

He stepped out onto the front porch, shut the massive door behind him. The spring night was clear and sweet and full of the soft musical cadences of the hill-country. Tree frogs were skirling with their rhythmless seesaw squeaks and whippoorwills were talking, flutelike and mellow. He was suddenly very tired.

He headed for Miss Grinnell's pleasant little one-story cottage—and bed.

IT WAS ABOUT nine, next morning, when McGavock awoke. The April sun was beating through the window pane, churning the little room in flashing gold. McGavock squinted, rolled over and sat up on the edge of the bed. He got his first good look at his surroundings. The bedroom was fastidiously clean. There was straw matting on the floor and the walls were painted baby-blue. And Miss Blanche, the Sweet Singer of Lunken County, had really gone to town on the decorations. Picture frames were gilded, the curtains were frilled and ruffled like the froth on a bucket of milk, big bows of ribbon were tied around the bedposts. McGavock splayed his hands before his face, let his eyes become gradually accustomed to so much female elegance.

That was when he saw the breakfast tray on the chair. Fried catfish, a pot of coffee, toast and homemade blackberry jam. There were two china cups, one filled with water with a rosebud floating in it. On a fold of note paper was written in lavender ink, *Eat hearty, dear man. Lunch at one-thirty. Blanche.*

He pulled the tray up to the bed, got to work. The food was fine. He stripped off his pajamas, took a quick sponge at the big bowl on the washstand, dressed, and set out for town.

The local law was quartered on the ground floor of the old courthouse, at the rear of the dank, dusky corridor. The black lettering on the frosted glass said, OFFICE OF SHERIFF—Pence Turley. McGavock palmed the knob, entered.

It was a pleasant office, bright and airy, with its white walls and two great windows looking out onto the courthouse lawn. A big battered desk and a steel filing cabinet were the only pieces of furniture. Sheriff Turley was standing on the desk. He was a scrawny, emaciated man in a cheap Sunday store-suit and clay-caked hightop shoes. The sheriff had a vacuum cleaner in his hands and was sucking drowsy flies off of the ceiling. When he saw he had a visitor, he descended to the floor, patted the cleaner bag, said proudly: "By doggies, machinery's wonderful! This durn thingam-a-bob is worth a thousan' fly swatters! It jest swoops them in and that's all they is to that." He laid the vacuum in the corner, added beligerently: "I cain't stand a bluebottle, durn 'em. They come in on a feller like the curse o' the Pharaohs and— Hello, thur. What you want?"

"I want the party that murdered Cortland Kincaid Endicott!"

"You and me both." Sheriff Turley sauntered behind his desk, lowered his lanky form lazily into his broken-down swivel chair. "Yo're Luther McGavock, that big city private detective. Ever'whur I go, 'y grannies, you been thur first. I'm right glad to git this chanct to talk with you." He burned in self-pity, said hostilely: "I hain't needin' no pardner in this. It's shore a mess, but lemme me alone—I'll wrassle 'er out."

"I'm sure you will," McGavock agreed smoothly. "I'm not after your star. I just want to see justice done, I'm funny that way." There was a long silence. McGavock said finally: "Well, what about it? Is it every man for himself?"

Sheriff Turley began to gripe: "Don't rush me. That hain't no way to make a deal. Feller usually bargains fer a while first. What you want out'n me?"

"Among your many friends and constituents," McGavock inquired, "did you ever happen to number a dog named Rufus the Red?" The sheriff looked angry. McGavock said hastily: "I'm perfectly serious. Let's hear all about him."

" 'Course I knowed Rufus. He was the meanest watchdog in three counties. He was a nacheral killer. He had mismatched eyes, one brown and one yaller—and that's poison in a hound. He was breeded and trained by a farmer back in the bottoms. Ever'body knowed about him—he was called Ole Red." The sheriff warmed up. "Ugh! He was big and bad. Last month, when Scully heired all that money and got married, he went and bought Ole Red. Changed his name to Rufus and kept him in a big pen back of the house. He had the dog about a week and then someone shot him."

"Shot him?"

"Yep. Shot him at night with a high-velocity rifle bullet." The sheriff fidgeted. "I thought you was interested in Cort's demise."

McGavock said vaguely: "I am. Let's hear about it."

"Last night someone kilt Cortland and toted his pore body over to Mr. Scully's, whilst folks was away." Sheriff Turley looked bothered. "Kempton ain't never had no murders before. Killin's, o' course we've had—shootin's and cuttin's and maybe a farmboy hits his ole man with the axe—but never no genuwine murders. Man, this has me plenty sprangled! Last night I was sittin' here candlin' eggs for my depity's wife when the phone ringed. It was a feller reporting Cort's murder, just like you'd call up and order a slab o' fat-meat at the grocery!"

"Who was it?—that's mighty important. And what did he say?"

"I can't seem to place him. He didn't seem half-bright. He kep' mutterin' you-all this and you-all that. Finally, I got out'n him what he was tryin' to say. I guess he was skeert. He'd just found Cort's remains. He tole me how to locate 'em."

"You went out?"

"I went right out." Sheriff Turley became confidential. "Rich people is strange critters. Lute. They has a special room fer ever'thin'. A parlor for their parlorin', a bedroom for each member of the fambly, liberries and so on. Scully Endicott even has a little extra sleepin' and readin' room off'n his main bedroom. That's where we found Cort. Strangled."

McGavock pressed him. "Then what? Were there any clues?"

Sheriff Turley lied blandly. "No, Lute. No clues. Just pore ole Cort, a-settin' thur—"

THE DETECTIVE SEEMED disappointed. He came in on an angle, said: "What's this about Scully inheriting money?"

"Now, Lute, Scully Endicott's as hateful as a stump-chewin' mule, and lower'n a chicken-eatin' hawg, but he hain't no murderer. He got his money according to law and order—through the courts. Iff'n he's guilty of anythin', hit's bein' a big-mouth, and they hain't no statute agin that, I'm shore sorry to say. Scully and Cortland were half-brothers. Old Mrs. Gatch—she lived in that fancy place whur Scully stays now—Old Mrs. Gatch died about three months ago. She was the richest mortal hereabouts. When she first died it 'peared like shc didn't leave no heirs. Then the lawyers got onto it and began trackin' it down. They found that Scully was a fifth cousin. That dumped it on him—he was next of kin. We never knowed they was related, it was so fur apart. Cort and Scully had the same father, different mothers. Scully heired on his mother's side. That left Cortland out—"

McGavock perked up. "You say the old lady's name was Gatch? Any relation to J.R. Gatch?"

"None whatsoever! They jest happen to have the same names. Jim's from out of town." Sheriff Turley threw a loop in his lower lip, dropped in a pinch of snuff. "We're a-tacklin' this hindside-before. Like I done said, Cort's body was toted thur. They's outside stairs at the back of the house. The corpse was carried up to the veranda and in through a window."

McGavock scoffed. "I don't believe it. Is that all?"

"That's all. Hain't it enough?"

They stared at each other.

McGavock said frigidly: "Okey-doke. How can I help you if you won't cooperate? All you give me is theories. I want something definite, something I can get my teeth into. You go your way, I'll go mine. Good-by. I think I'll pay the undertaker a visit. Maybe he—"

Sheriff Turley's face lit up. "Durn it, Lute, now you mention the undertaker, I 'member somethin' that slipped my mind." He cleared his throat innocently. "By doggies. I bet it's somethin' you'll be interested in. I cain't make no sense out'n hit, but maybe you kin. It's this. When we found pore Cort, up in Scully's den, he had his hair fixed different."

McGavock looked blank. Sheriff Turley amplified: "What I mean, he always wore his long white hair in a kinda pompadour. When we found him, his hair was parted in the middle and combed back over his ears. My, my, he was ugly thataway! Now, why—"

McGavock pretended to ponder. He struck his fist into his palm, said exultingly: "I've solved it! That was the clue we needed!"

Sheriff Turley boggled. McGavock said tensely: "I want to look at the hat. Trot out the hat."

"What hat?"

"Cort Endicott's hat. The one you found with the body."

A gleam of anxiety lit up the sheriff's small triangular eyes. He began to sweat. "I swear, they wasn't no—"

"An oldster of Cortland's age wouldn't go out into the night air without his skimmer. Now we're getting some place." McGavock started to talk fast. "It comes to me all at once. I get the whole picture. Old Cortland is lured to Scully's home, he's taken upstairs and slain. He leaves his hat downstairs, on the hatrack. Maybe the killer didn't intend to strangle him at first. When he did it, he got excited. He had to get the corpse out of the house. He'd use the outside stairs, back of the veranda, and quick. He'd take the body out some place, any place, and lay it down, maybe on a front lawn. But Cort would have to have a hat. The killer was rushed, afraid to get the hat from the hatrack. He'd use his own. Did Cortland have a big head?"

Sheriff Turley was fascinated. He nodded mutely, caught his breath, said: "Shore did. Big as a bull. Why?"

"That was the how come of the parted hair, to cut down the size of the head. The killer was going to use his own hat. He'd obliterate all identity by taking out the sweatband—that would help, too, in making the hat larger. Cort's real hat downstairs in the hall wouldn't make any difference. The killer would let Scully do the explaining for that, when he discovered it."

Sheriff Turley nodded reluctantly. "Sounds reasonable, but what does it prove?"

"That nutty hair-dress of Cort's proves they were getting ready to move him. That indicates he was slain right there. They certainly wouldn't move him in, and then out again."

Sheriff Turley was impressed. "Friend, you really push out the sweet-talk." He added bewilderedly: "Maybe I been a mite wrong, maybe Scully's mixed in this after all. It was his house, wasn't it?"

McGavock said cheerily: "I hope I've been of help to you. Well, I'll be seeing you."

4

The Hound that Couldn't Die

JIM GATCH WAS sitting on the cement porchstep of his garish yellow brick bungalow. He was in his pajamas and dressing-robe, basking in the warm sun. He was a man of business and of pleasure.

He'd hitched up the garden hose to the outside faucet and was spraying the sterile, burlap-covered, red clay yard. He got out his gold and ivory toothpick with his free hand and began to work on his big horse-teeth as McGavock ambled up the walk.

Gatch had changed considerably since the night before. His stolid, meaty face with its severe, close-clipped mustache seemed definitely on the haggard side. And those bleak, slaty eyes behind their octagonal lenses were certainly nervous. He put away his toothpick and cut loose with a blast of complaints. "What the hell kind of a detective are you, anyway? Did you hear about it? They've killed Cortland, killed him right under your nose! Last night you were here with me, hotshotting all over the place, throwing your weight around in a bucket, and that very minute they were murdering him! I do declare—"

McGavock flagged him to silence, said: "Get up. Let's go inside. I want to give his room a quick once-over." Gatch got to his feet, cut the nozzle on the hose. They went into the house.

McGavock asked: "How is it that the late Cortland K. Endicott put up here with you, by the way? As I understand it, he was some kind of kin, maybe a cousin. Was he a sociable house-guest?"

Gatch led his guest down the hall. "Scarcely. I despised him. He was always meddling in other folks' personal affairs. I just took him in because he hadn't anywhere else to go. That's the way it generally is—here I'm a stranger in town and I'm the one that has to dole out the charity."

Cortland Endicott's room was quite nicely furnished. Death, McGavock decided, had cheated the oldster out of comfortable quarters. There was a low, clean bed with a candlewick spread, a roomy bureau, generous overstuffed chairs. A game of solitaire was laid out on a card table and beside it was a wine glass and a half-empty bottle of excellent sherry. Gatch inquired curiously: "What are we searching for?"

"Anything we can find." Methodically McGavock went through the room. He took out the bureau drawers, examined them, examined the interspaces between them. He turned to the bed, said: "You have something of a rep about town as an outdoor-man. Ah, the wide open spaces!" Out of the corner of his eye he saw Gatch expand his stocky chest, heard him thump it.

"You can't beat it," Gatch declaimed. "Nature is a man's natural habitat. A walk in the woods hardens the tendons. Berries and bark, hah, that's the stuff to develop the teeth! What do you have there? Say! I was looking for those!"

McGavock came out from under the bed with a pair of shiny, elastic-sided gaiters. "They were way back against the wall."

Gatch reached for them. "Those are Cortland's Sunday kicks. The undertaker will want them for the burial. Thanks." He reached for them. McGavock whisked the gaiters deftly out of his grasp, probed inside them with his forefinger. He grinned, shook a small glass bottle out on the bedspread.

It was a four-ounce medicine bottle and was filled with dry, reddish granules. "You take the gunboats," McGavock said pleasantly. "I'll take this."

"What—what—"

"I couldn't say for sure, but my guess is that this is Cortland's sawdust, the item he wanted us to analyze." McGavock held the vial to the light. "Red. It looks like cedar. Is there valuable cedar up on Snake Ridge?"

"There's a little cedar, but it's hardly marketable. The good timber there is mainly oak and pine. Which reminds me—I retained you to stop that filching. Have you made any headway on that? Who's the logger? Why are you fiddling around here when you could be—"

McGavock thrust the bottle in his pocket. "That's all here. Let's go."

Outside, they stood for a moment on the front porch. Neither had much of anything to say. McGavock stared dreamily at the barren lawn with its puny saplings, its covering of burlap sacking, the eroded clay terrace. After a bit, he spoke. "Gatch, I'm the sort of guy that goes nuts when there's more ties on one side of the tie rack than on the other. Always I got to have my handkerchief folded just right when I stick it in my pocket."

"A tidy nature, suh."

"Heck, no. It's just nerves. A curse to happiness. I've always been that way."

Gatch, bored, clicked his tongue. McGavock went on: "I've got a kind of inner eye like the poet sayeth. Take those strips of gunny sacking out there. You see that little tree? Last night when I was here those sacks were laid in an L, around the sapling. Now they're a sort of T. There's been a new sack added. Did you do it?"

The sunlight reflected from Gatch's glasses. He said calmly: "I don't think so."

"Moreover, I observed that when you were sprinkling you passed that extra sack up. It's quite dry, isn't it?"

"Hose won't reach that far from the porch."

McGavock strolled down the walk, crossed over into the yard. Gatch followed him. They stopped by the little tree. The detective stooped, folded back the corner of the burlap. There, in a shallow hollow scooped in the clayey ground, was an old pigskin wallet. Gatch said: "Good Lord, That's Cortland's billfold!"

"What's it doing here? Did he carry it with him?"

Gatch shook his head. "No, he didn't carry it. He always left it in his room. He never—ahem—had much use for a wallet. Who hid it there?"

"Did you?"

Gatch's face twisted in excitement. His first impulse was to deny it vehemently. For some reason, he changed his mind. He said silkily: "To be perfectly honest, I don't know. I've been working too hard. I've got a bad case of what the medicos call cerebropathy, brain fag, to you and me. I have lapses."

McGavock grunted. He placed the wallet in his breast pocket beside the bottle of sawdust. Without a word, he turned on his heel and walked away.

McGAVOCK STOOD ON the hillside, with Kempton's water tower at his back. His wristwatch said ten twenty-seven.

Twice he'd been an unwelcome visitor to Scully Endicott's big house, and each trip he'd somehow managed to miss the lady of the manor. The idea occurred to him that perhaps if he'd drop in unconventionally, via the rear, the results might prove interesting.

He skirted the corporation line and circled in from the back. Down the bare slope lay the estate. Sheriff Pence Turley had certainly been right. There was no doubt about it—Old Lady Gatch had really been wealthy. It would take plenty kale just to keep up the grounds and buildings. In the center of the velvety lawn was the great white-pillared mansion. From back here, you could see the upstairs veranda and the back steps leading down from it. To the right of the house, was the garage—this was where the floodlight had been last night, where Jim Gatch had come pedaling in on his bicycle. Some distance behind the garage was a huge white barn and between the two buildings was a small nook sheltered on two sides by the outbuildings, on the rear by the tall lilac hedge, and from the front by a dense, flowering rose trellis.

Back in this pleasant shady bower, curtained from sight, was a gal. He'd never have spotted her at all if he hadn't been up on the hillside. She was seated in a huge fan-back wicker chair, bent over a typewriter which rested on a campstool between her knees. McGavock descended the slope, rounded the corner of the barn, parted the hedge, and came into the enclosure from the offside.

The girl was dressed in a short, green linen frock and she had a supple, youthful figure. She was blindfolded, with a silk scarf tied about her head, and was slapping the typewriter keyboard with vigorous, energetic fingers. McGavock approached within a few feet of her, said: "Good morning, Mrs. Endicott."

She took off the scarf. She was a brunette and plenty pretty—he judged her age to be about nineteen. She ignored him completely, stared angrily at the paper in the typewriter. "Mistakes, mistakes, mistakes!" she said hoarsely. "Now is the time for all blah-blah!" She reached forward with strong hands, ripped the paper from the platen, tore the ribbon from its spools, heaved the snarled mess into the shrubbery.

McGavock remarked patronizingly: "Mastering the touch system, eh?"

"Blast Gutenberg, Caxton and their diabolical works. I'm through. I want to do something worth while. I tried a sewing machine, no good. I tried cooking, horrible!" She suddenly focused on McGavock. "So you've finally come, Prince Charming. I've been warned about you. The sheriff and my husband and Mr. Gatch have all tipped me off. They say you're a very bad form of publicity."

"What do you mean, publicity? A corpse was found in your home last night. Is that good?"

"In Kempton, it's just unfortunate. Our friends feel sorry for us."

"I don't." McGavock glowered. "Where were you yesterday evening, by the way, when—"

"Now there's a novel question." She leaned back in the chair, folded her arms behind her head, and studied him with sultry eyes. "I was wandering the streets, chatting with anyone I happened to encounter. And Scully was engaged in a similar manner. In Kempton, that's a substitute for café society."

"An ironclad alibi!" McGavock was scathing. He set himself, asked rudely: "Do you want to help me?" She nodded indolently. He asked: "Just who is this J.R. Gatch? What brought him to town? Let's hear all about him."

"He's a friend of my husband's. I hardly know him by sight. He came to Kempton several months ago—"

"About the time Scully inherited?"

"No. I'd say a month or six weeks later. Well, he set himself up in business. He seems to be prospering. He's got a finger in everything."

"You can say that again, sister." McGavock frowned, declared slowly: "When I was gabbing with your husband last night in the library, I saw a blueprint, all rolled up, on the desk. What's it for?"

She laughed. "Don't tell me he's got that thing out again!" The girl tucked her legs up under, clasped her hands in her lap. "That's quite a story. Some weeks ago Scully received this blueprint in the mail—from Nashville. Along with it came a note from some starving architect who said that he was a genius but down and out, that he was trying this mail order method of digging up customers. Scully wrote him later but got no answer. We figure he must have—"

"What, I'm asking you, is the—"

"Don't hurry me, I'm getting to it. It's plans for a hunting lodge. Scully keeps toying with the idea of erecting such a one out at the Dillon place. The plan is all made up as though it had been ordered. Down at the bottom in big fancy letters it says, *Quailhurst, Scully Endicott, Owner.* And such a lodge! It's a pipedream. The plans call for a kitchen as large as a hotel, five bathrooms, and a refrigerator the size of a country schoolhouse to preserve the game in! It's just foolish enough to appeal to Scully. What with his name on it and all, his eyes stick out on stems whenever he peruses it. Some day I'm going to destroy it."

"Aren't you happy with your husband?" he asked her.

"Frankly, no. But I wouldn't want it broadcast, of course." Mrs. Endicott grew intense. "He married me for my money. Don't look so startled. When we were married last year I had a few thousand dollars—that was a fortune to him. Now I've got nothing and he's filthy with it."

"Ah, me." McGavock sighed. "Life is quite a prankster!"

"That's why I want to be useful. I might have to support myself sometime." Linda Endicott's hazel eyes clouded, her pretty lower lip trembled. "I've tried everything. Sewing and cooking and—"

McGavock smiled maliciously. "This is where I came in. I shall now make my exit. But first—"

HE WALKED TO the shrubbery, thrust his arm into the foliage, and retrieved the ball of paper the girl had thrown away. "You weren't learning the touch system," he said gently. "You already know it. I saw the way you played that typewriter."

Mrs. Endicott came out of the chair in a scramble of fury. "Put that down! Hand that to me this instant!"

McGavock continued sardonically: "You were sitting back here, doing a bit of highly personal typing. Coming up behind the hedge, I was almost on you before you realized it. You heard me, slipped your neckerchief from your throat up over your eyes, and gave me that 'now is the time for all good men' stuff. When a person is caught with a half-written page in the typewriter it's mighty hard to hide, isn't it? You really put out some quick thinking. I hate to do this—" He chuckled, unfolded the page. It ran:

Jim Gatch:

The person writing this is a complete stranger to you. Get out of town and I mean now or

"Or what?" McGavock grinned gapingly. "Or you'll put delphinium seeds in his cookies? Now this is a surprise. Would you like to explain it?"

The brunette's eyes widened. When she spoke, her voice was a weak, faltering whisper. "I told you I don't know him, and that's substantially the truth. I have seen him here and about. He scares me. There's something menacing in the way he ogles you through those thick lenses. Down in my heart I feel he's behind this slaying. I want to frighten him away, so there'll be no more—"

McGavock listened stoically. "You know, Mrs. Endicott," he said familiarly, "you know, there's a peculiar thing about that note. Maybe, like you say, it's a threat, an attempt to stampede him. But there's another way of reading it. Could be that Gatch was a mighty close friend, that you knew he was in danger and were advising him to scram before—"

She cast her eyes down demurely, said sadly: "Mr. McGavock, I expected so much of you, and now you're failing me. Alas, to whom shall I turn in this hour of need!"

McGavock cleared his throat with a hacking sound. He handed her the little ball of crumpled paper, said: "Mail it this way, in a little box—it'll be more mysterious!" and left the shady bower. Behind him, he heard her panting in rage.

THE PARK-LIKE PREMISES seemed deserted. Scully, no doubt, was down at the undertaker's haggling over a rock-bottom job of embalming. The detective strolled through the backyard, rounded the side of the great mansion, and took the gravelstone path to the street. Just inside the gate a gnarled and weathered man in faded overalls was planting gladiola bulbs. McGavock slowed up, dipped his chin in greeting.

"Howdy." The gardener was inclined to be sociable. "I'm a-gittin' these-here in the ground whilst the moon's right. We want 'em to grow up, not down."

He was a gnomish little fellow with crinkled, sunburned skin and bushy, dry eye-brows. McGavock said absently: "Planting, planting, planting. Always somebody planting something. Today, it's glad bulbs, tomorrow it'll be Cortland Endicott. Next week it might be you or me."

This was the kind of discussion the gardener enjoyed. He nodded sagely, said: "Them's true words, brother."

"Talking about planting," McGavock remarked casually, "Sheriff Turley tells me that you folks lost a watchdog a few weeks past. Who planted Rufus the Red?"

"I did, brother." The gardener got out an althea twig, began to masticate it. "I buried Ole Red, that's what we called him, an' I don't never want nothin' like that agin! It had me readin' my Bible ever' night fer two weeks!"

McGavock looked pleasantly interested. The gardener was glad to talk about it. "It was on a Tuesday morning. I was out in the toolshed puttin' a new edge on the lawnmower. Mr. Scully had been back in the pen to feed Ole Red—they never left nobuddy but the family do it, which is right an' proper with a watchdog. Wal, all at once he come flyin' in to me, white as a sheet, sayin': 'Willie, some'un's kilt him! He's been shot in the night!' I got my shovel an' went along. And, friend, he had!"

"So you buried him?"

"He was a-layin' thur in his pen, as stiff as a poker. His mean ole two-color eyes was open and he was a horrible sight! He was dead and yet somehow he couldn't seem to die. He was stiff and cold and yet that yaller eye of his'n, that devil-eye, bored into us with all the hate and evil I ever seen in man or beast." The gardener was entranced by the memory.

"So you buried him?"

"Yep. We takened him out behind the barn and put him four foot under. Mr. Scully's a-buyin' him a tombstone."

"Think of that! Was his master fond of him?"

"Red was Miss Linda's dog. Mr. Scully got him for her. He said he wanted her to allus take him out with her when she promenaded at night. Miss Linda, though, she just laughed an' said she didn't want no part of a dog. I guess Ole Red didn't have no happy life. Mr. Scully got so he despised him, too."

McGavock said vaguely: "Well, Willie, I'm keeping you from your work. 'By."

Two blocks away, he stopped in the lee of a forsythia bush and took Cortland Endicott's wallet from his pocket. Now was a good time to give it a thorough checking.

The pigskin was old, worn and frayed. Inside, in faint letters, was stamped C.K.E. The wallet was the folder-type, with two large compartments—in one section was a glassine envelope, in the other a small card. The card was pale tan with gilt edges, the printing on its face said, *Frontiersman's Club—Nashville.* At the bottom was typed, *Member No. 17, Daniel Boone.* McGavock chewed the corner of his lip, said: "Isn't that awful! Now it gives me Daniel Boone!"

He inspected the transparent envelope. It contained a pinch

of a darkish powder, something that looked like gray flour. He took a bit of the dust in his fingers, smelled it, tasted it warily. Suddenly, he looked pleased.

His wrist watch told him it was three minutes to eleven. He was due for his appointment.

All at once he remembered something—the bottle of sawdust he'd found at Gatch's bungalow. He groped in his pocket, located it. For a moment he held it in his palm and then, after a brief consideration, he tossed it into the gutter. It had served its purpose. He wouldn't be needing it from here on in.

5

Squire Weller's Apparition

SATURDAY MORNING KEMPTON was really astir. Blue riding mules and shaggy saddle horses were tied to the hitching racks, buggies and clay-smeared surreys were parked along the curbs. Folks were busy with their week-end trading. Hillman and townsman mingled on the narrow pavements, townsman a little supercilious to his country neighbor, hillman distrustful and cagey about the flashy lures of the sinful city. There'd be strange things bought and sold this day—pocket knives for fighting, bed sheeting for underclothes, canning sugar which would wind up in glass jars, all right, but in liquid form. The warm sun was gay and festive, mockingbirds warbled from the chinaberry trees. McGavock sat on a green painted bench in Court Square, beneath a magnolia—and waited.

The big clock above him bonged out the last stroke of the hour and hardly had the deep-throated vibrations dissipated themselves against the cloudless sky when the detective saw his man, the fellow who had dropped his change on the floor in the ginmill the night before. Blue serge coat, cowboy hat, moccasin boots, he suddenly appeared in an alley-mouth. McGavock diverted his gaze. The man crossed the street in an indolent, loose-jointed stride, entered the square. Casually, he shared McGavock's bench with him.

Daylight didn't add to his charms. McGavock knew he had been right in his snap appraisal of the fellow—he was one mighty hard baby. He held a greasy, nickel fried-pie in his calloused hand, munching it leisurely. His cruel ferret face showed no gustatory enjoyment whatever. Finally, he turned slowly, asked: "You the gentleman from Indiana? Was you lookin' for me?"

McGavock inquired curtly: "Who are you? What's your name?"

The man in the cowboy hat didn't like it. He said evasively: "I cain't see how personalizin' me is gonna help us—"

"What's your name? That's the way I do business."

He tussled with it, decided to play along. "I'm Todd Bailey. We ain't gittin' off to no friendly start. You say you want to buy good lumber cheap. I got it. How much and what kind?"

McGavock gave a nasty, jeering laugh. "I don't need any of your stolen timber, chum. I'm a detective. I've come to Kempton to stop the man that's doing that illegal logging back at Snake Ridge. So you're the fellow, eh? And your name is Todd Bailey."

Bailey jammed the hunk of pie in his mouth, brushed off his fingers. He placed his hands on his kneecaps, stared with unseeing intensity at two irridescent pigeons strutting in the patched sunlight. This is it, McGavock realized. He's weighing it in his mind, trying to decide whether to go for his 32-.20.

McGavock said quietly: "This is kind of public for a shooting, isn't it, Todd?"

The mountainman spoke without moving his lips: "It wouldn't be the first gunfire in this ole Court Square. So help me, I don't much know what to do." He added simply: "I shore don't like that penitentiary—and hit don't keer none for me, neither."

"How's your word, Todd?"

The mountainman flushed. "My stealin' and my word is two different things. My word's as good as my daddy's was, or my granddaddy's. Why?"

"I'm just retained to stop the thieving," McGavock answered reasonably. "All I want is your promise you'll leave Snake Ridge alone."

Bailey's cheeks crinkled in a slow, friendly grin. "Yo're a hell of a detective. O.K., I'll leave hit be." He paused a moment in reverie, said: "Look at it one way, I guess yo're doin'me a favor. Yessirree! I guess I'm glad to get shet of Snake Ridge. They's trouble—trouble up in them hills!"

McGavock looked bored. Bailey got it off his chest. "The other day I found the trailer."

"Trailer? What do you mean?"

"Jest what I say. A automobile trailer, hid back in the muscadine vines. No car, jest the trailer. Now what's that a-doin' there?"

McGavock was polite. "I haven't the slightest idea. What's your opinion?"

The hillman frowned. "I cain't ezactly say. But I bet hit's mixed in that ungodly graveyard despoilin' over at Bear Holler."

"I wouldn't know. I never heard of Bear Hollow."

Todd Bailey got riled. " 'Course you never heered o' it. Hit's been reported to Shur'f Turley time an' agin, but them folks out yonder don't git no help a-tall. You see it's thisaway—I been doin' my loggin' at the east end of the ridge. At the west end, they's a little bitty church, knowed as Bear Holler. One night, some weeks ago, vandals got into the churchyard an' busted up a lot of tombstones with sledges. Who it was, and why, nobuddy knows. Shur'f Turley jest looks wise an' says:

'We'll see.' Bear Holler is gittin' out their deer-guns an' prayin' the vandals'll come back."

"And you think this automobile trailer has got something to do with those smashed tombstones?"

"Yo're the hotshot from the big city. What do you think?"

"I think you're right. Go back to your friends at Bear Hollow and carry this golden message: Verily, brethren, justice shall prevail!" McGavock got to his feet, nodded a brusque farewell.

McGAVOCK HAD HIS lunch with his landlady on the back porch of her cozy little cottage. A delightful spot, cool and sweet and hung with honeysuckle. Miss Blanche had got out her best eating equipment and despite eggshell china and souvenir silverware the detective made satisfactory headway against the great fragrant stacks of chicken and corn pones, garden salad and mashed potatoes. Always in the background, Miss Blanche was shoving platters over his shoulder, in front of his face, and the Sweet Singer of Lunken County, dressed in her finest, had enough sachet bags tucked here and there about her ample bosom to smoke a possum out of a hollow tree. McGavock, giddy from the smell of steaming coffee, giblet gravy and sachet, finished his meal, leaned back in his chair.

"Quite a repast, ma'am," he said in his best Texas drawl. "I sure bet the boys in the bunkhouse envy me, eatin' like this with the rancher's daughter!"

Miss Grinnell tittered confusedly. "You say so many things I don't seem to understand, Mr. McGavock." She flounced into a chair across from him, beamed. "You fooled me last night. You're actually a detective, aren't you?"

"That's the new-fangled term for it, ma'm. I'm a Bow Street

Runner. How well I mind the time when—"

Miss Blanche sighed. "Detectives are so romantic! They're so intellectual. They just love puzzles, and the more difficult the enigma, the more they enjoy it. Ah, me. That's what Squire Weller says. He's heard you're in town, been around three times this morning. He's got a riddle for you."

"I don't answer riddles."

Miss Blanche looked conspiratorial. "You'd better talk to him. This isn't exactly a riddle—it's more like an apparition. The squire lives in the old hotel."

"What do you mean, apparition?"

"I'd rather you hear it from him, though everyone in town knows about it by now. I'll give you a hint, though. It has fangs in it—and bloodcurdling screams."

"Nuts." McGavock looked sour, frowned, and said: "My wife's people came from this neck of the woods. She was a Dillon. I've often listened to her yawp about the old Dillon place. Maybe while I'm here. I can take a gander at it?"

Miss Grinnell pursed her lips. "The old Dillon place? Why, no one's lived there for sixty or eighty years! It's just a landmark. Dillon was an early settler who had a cabin back on Snake Ridge in the Bear Hollow neighborhood, but it burned down long before my memory. You say your wife—"

"Not her, her people. She'll only be seventy-four next August." He got to his feet. "Thanks for the fine lunch." He eyed her speculatively. "Do something for me? Fine. Now listen carefully. Contact Sheriff Pence Turley. Tell him to get in touch with Nashville and find out about a set-up called the Frontiersman's Club. Can you remember that? Swell. Then tell him I said to be in his office about three o'clock."

IN A MELLOW aura of post-digestive satisfaction, McGavock headed for town. Things were really clicking. He was near and yet so far from the answer. He knew he had all the essential facts and despite this, somehow, the key to the affair seemed to evade him. He knew that the murderer of Cortland Endicott had barely left the corpse last night when he arrived, it was that close! He knew who the killer was and how he'd worked it. He had a good idea why—but he wasn't sure. He understood about half of the sawdust mystery. Half was a good start, but it wouldn't hang a murderer. When things began to break open, they'd break fast. It was just a question of time now.

The detective had just rounded the corner of Plum, and turned down a back street, when he heard his name called, followed by a raucous clatter. He came to a stop, looked over his shoulder.

A half block behind him was Scully Endicott. The portly little man was hammering a telephone pole with his heavy cane, night-stick fashion. "McGavock, McGavock!" When he saw that he'd caught the detective's eye, he strutted forward pompously. "Are you deaf, man? I've been trying to catch up with—"

"What you want with me?" McGavock asked roughly. "Don't you recall? You paid me off with a five-cent cigar—we're finished!"

The chubby man placed his needle-pointed shoes at a fastidious angle, clasped his walking-stick to his chest. "Just a rib, Mr. McGavock. Haw-haw, don't tell me you took it seriously. No, by Jove, we're not finished. You and I are going to get along famously. How you making out with Cortland's demise?"

"O.K., I guess." McGavock was indifferent. "I've boiled the

killer down to one of four persons. You, or your wife, or Gatch, or Miss Blanche Grinnell."

Endicott gaped. "You're out of your mind! You don't know what you're saying!" He batted his eyes. "And Blanche Grinnell! Why do you include her?"

McGavock confided in him. "You folks are the only people I know in Kempton. That's logic—it must be one of you."

Endicott smiled slyly. "Oh, I see. For a moment, you almost had me bamboozled. You're trying the yokel act again. You deceived me on our last meeting with it, so now you're back into character. Let me tell you, sir, I've revised my opinions of you since last evening. I consider you very astute—very dangerous. I want you on my side."

McGavock said rudely: "Endicott, is your wife in love with Jim Gatch?"

He took it calmly, spoke deep in his chest: "Not at all, not at all." He showed no embarrassment or anger.

They strolled down the pavement together. McGavock asked: "Is it true that you fear for Mrs. Endicott? That you brought her a vicious watchdog?"

The pudgy man got cagy. "Coming in like you're doing, and attempting to pull rabbits out of your hat, is a little risky. An outsider, like yourself, sometimes comes to highly fallacious conclusions. Yes, I acquired a canine protector for Linda, but it's a long story."

"How about a thumbnail synopsis?"

"Gladly. Please don't misconstrue what I am about to tell you. When I married Linda last year everything went along famously at first. Then she began taking trips to Chattanooga every two or three months. She said she just liked to be alone once in a while. I thought it over and decided that there was something here in town that frightened her. I bought her a man-eating watchdog."

"Isn't it a fact," McGavock asked insolently, "that according to your story your wife has been taking these trips from the date of your wedding, yet you just bought the dog a month ago, since Gatch came to town?"

Scully shook his head benevolently. "You're back on that track again, eh? No, my friend, you're wrong. I bought the dog a month ago, but Gatch came several days *after* I acquired Old Rufus. I'd never seen Jim Gatch in my life—or heard of him. I didn't know he was going to grace our community with his energetic presence. How, then, could I have anticipated his arrival? No, Old Rufus wasn't an antidote to Jim Gatch. Preposterous! Jim and I are the best of chums. In a distant sort of way, of course."

McGavock changed the subject. "You say you want me on your side. I come high. What do you want me to do?"

The pudgy man rolled his eyes in painful meditation.

"I don't know just how to explain this. It's going to sound very peculiar but believe me, I'm perfectly justified in my request. There are some forged documents floating around town that may very well jeopardize my recent inheritance. I want you to promise me that if you run into them, you'll confiscate them and, on your honor, destroy them. I don't want to see them. I don't want to know who has them."

"What are these papers?"

"I haven't the slightest idea. Please, let's not talk about—"

"Who has them?"

"Please, Mr. McGavock!"

"How will I know them?"

"You'll know them, all right. And one more point. It's highly important that this party doesn't realize it's you who took them. Just mark their presence, return at night, and—"

"Rob the house, eh? A snap. O.K., it's a deal." McGavock slowed up at a corner, pointed down a sidestreet. "Good-by, old pal. Here's where we part. I'm mighty busy this afternoon, and I don't want anyone tagging along behind."

THE OLD HOTEL had, in its heyday, borne the glorious appellation of The Magnolia House. That was a long time ago. Time and the weather and the rough hand of fate had buffed it down to shabby squalor. It was now known to Kempton's citizenry simply as Joe Brant's. It stood, battered in roseate brick, in the old end of the business section flanked on either side by produce warehouses. To this neighborhood, hillboys brought their winter pelts, farmers' wives their chickens and eggs for trading.

On the single, narrow window, opaque with the grime of ages, the half obliterated letters said, LODGING. McGavock grasped the big brass doorknob, stepped from the dazzling sunlight into the gloomy interior. The lobby was larger than he'd expected. Through the gray murk he made out a fine old oak desk with a wicket, several rundown couches and easy chairs. An emaciated fellow in a mildewed alpaca jacket materialized from the shadows beside the desk. He was sucking a stick of peppermint-candy jammed into a lemon. He said amiably: "You're now facc to face with Joe Brant, owner, proprietor and number one janitor. What can I do for you?"

"Is there a gentleman here named Squire Weller?"

"That's right. A permanent resident, and I mean permanent. He's been here for the last hundred years and he'll be here for the next hundred. Second floor, last room at the end of the hall, on your left."

McGavock ascended the stairs, made his way down a musty, darkish corridor, rapped at a massive paneled door. A hacking, strident voice from inside bade him enter.

This time the detective stepped from darkness into light. Not sunlight, but lamplight. It was a great, tall-ceilinged room with a threadbare turkey-red carpet on the floor. Its three windows had been scrupulously shuttered and sealed against the outside light and air. The furnishings were of a forgotten era—a tester bed, a mahogany secretary, Windsor chairs with frayed brocade seats. Everywhere were kerosene lamps—McGavock counted six. The walls were hung with steel engravings of Confederate generals and victorious Southern battles in the war between the States. In the center of the room, surrounded by a cluster of lamps, was Squire Weller. He was about the fattest man McGavock had ever seen. He was seated on a specially constructed oversize throne consisting of a feather mattress draped across two ordinary chairs, their adjacent arms cut off and their legs lashed together with baling wire.

The squire had a merry, ruddy face with twinkling china-blue eyes. He held an old-time school slate on his spherical knees and was making cryptic lines on its surface. He said petulantly: "What was the matter with those gentlemen anyway? Sherman could have been stopped!"

McGavock nodded. "Afternoon, Squire. I'm the detective you've been searching for. I dropped in to hear about the riddle Miss Grinnell was mentioning."

For a long moment, the squire stared. Finally he pointed a banana-like forefinger at a chair, said: "Set. You'll do."

McGavock followed his injunction, waited. Squire Weller cleared his throat with dignity. "You want to hear about my apparition, I presume."

McGavock said politely: "If you don't mind, sir."

"Well, I'm a sick man, my boy. Been sick and ailing from childhood. The doctors, the insolent puppies, claim I'm afflicted with virulent laziness. I know different. It's my liver and lights, my boy. They're withered. I'm a man, horrible thought, with perished organs! Just visualize it! Doesn't it make you shiver? I'll wager if we could remove my lungs this instant and lay them there in your lap they'd resemble two small, soapy bath-sponges—baby size!"

McGavock winced despite himself. The squire observed the effect of his rhetoric with a glint of satisfaction, continued: "Always, as my narrative progresses, we must pay obeisance to my perished innards, for my tale hangs on them, so to speak. Please forgive the anatomical pun. It was mighty lucky the man had a pistol—even if it was filled with blank cartridges. What say you, my boy?"

McGavock was patient. The fat man sank deep in his feather mattress. "Three weeks ago last night, it was. I'd been off my oats all day and knew that perished liver of mine was acting up. Nowadays, you hear of vitamins this and that, but when I was a youngster it was mineral water. Mineral water, the elixir of life! Like I say, I began to feel queasy and decided to do what I generally do in such a case, pay a visit to the old sulphur spring out by the water tower—"

"On Scully Endicott's land?"

"No. Don't ask questions. There's Scully's place, and behind it the water tower. Down at the base of the slope, beyond the tower, is the spring. No one but me uses it any more. Now this spring is in an open meadow, in a dense clump of scrub. I'd just filled my collapsible aluminum cup and was about to drink, when the apparition came down on me. *Yugh!* It was a grisly thing to behold."

McGavock fidgeted. Squire Weller went calmly on: "There was a mackerel sky and in the faint moonlight I could barely make out what was going on. All at once a man came running wildly down the hillside, gibbering in terror. Then the hound came over the rise in pursuit of the running man. I heard a human scream and the huge beast was on his victim. Time and again, the man fired a pistol. The cartridges were blanks, such as animal trainers use. The dog wasn't fazed. I decamped."

"You what?"

"I made for home—and quick. Behind me I could hear those gurgling ferocious growls, as though the animal were devouring something, and the man's muted cries."

McGavock was silent. At last he said: "What makes you think they were blank cartridges?"

"Because the man didn't kill the dog."

"Did the dog kill the man?"

"No. That's the riddle! What were they doing, master and hound?"

McGavock looked grim. Squire Weller amplified: "The dog was Old Red, of that I'm sure. He lived on to be shot later in his pen. You're now about to ask me who the man was. In my considered opinion, the man was none other than Scully Endicott, himself, the hound's owner. What's your solution?"

McGavock arose. "I've got the solution, all right, sir," he declared gravely, "but this is not the place or time to divulge it. I'm sorry to disappoint you. One thing I will say, tomorrow—when the sheriff is ballyhooing around about how he broke the case—you can laugh up your sleeve. It's you, sir, who have solved the murder of Cortland Kincaid Endicott!"

6

Snake Ridge

DESCENDING THE STAIR-WAY down to the lobby, McGavock noticed that the proprietor was nowhere in sight, and his first impression was that the foyer was empty. Then he saw Linda Endicott. She was standing by the water cooler, waiting for him, and in the half light her pert stance and wide-eyed, little girl gaze made her seem scarcely more than a highschool kid. He tried to fluff her off and walk past her but her trim spike-heeled pumps clattered along behind him. He felt her hand on his elbow and stopped. She guided him through a curtained doorway into what had once been the old hotel's dining room.

McGavock expostulated. "What comes off? Stand back and let me out of here! How'd you find me, anyway?"

"Miss Blanche told me she'd sent you here." The girl was plenty scared. "There's been another murder. Todd Bailey's been killed. His body has just been found in the loft of the old livery stable! His head was all crushed—"

McGavock said blankly: "Who in the world is Todd Bailey?"

"A hillman from the Bear Hollow country. He's the logger that's been cutting Scully's timber back at Snake Ridge. Folks will think that we—"

"Hold on, hold on." McGavock tried to get organized. "You telling me that this Bailey is the fellow who was stealing your husband's timber—and your husband knew it? Why didn't he have it stopped?"

She spoke with annoyance. "That's just a detail. Of course he knew it. In a town like Kempton there are really no secrets—word gets around. Scully pretended ignorance. He said he didn't care, said that the trees weren't valuable and that Bailey needed the money worse than he did. And that he wanted the big stuff cleared off because he intended building a lodge there and that brush was better than timber for quail."

"Then why didn't he give it to Bailey outright?"

"Hillmen have funny ethics. Todd wouldn't be beholden to a city man."

"Gnats! This Todd Bailey must have been one tough lad. Could it be Husband Scully was afraid of him?"

She flared. "We Endicotts aren't afraid of anyone."

"You're not an Endicott, sister. And what are you trembling about?" He switched the subject. "I'm glad you looked me up after all. I want to ask you some questions. What about these trips solo to Chattanooga?"

The little brunette spoke bitterly. "So they're trying to make something out of that, are they? Simply and truthfully, I went there to get away from Kempton. When I first married Scully he was so different from what I'd expected—domineering and arrogant. Well, I'd stand as much as I could and when I'd reached the saturation point, I'd pack up my luggage and migrate for a while. I don't do that any more, by the way. I'm learning the technique of enduring him."

"I sure wish you'd teach it to me. How did Scully take these vacations of yours?

Linda Endicott looked genuinely bewildered. "He didn't seem to mind a bit, and yet, underneath, I think they drove him crazy." She suddenly remembered something. "And that reminds me. You're a detective—explain to me how my husband does that slick following trick of his!"

McGavock grinned. "O.K. Let's have it."

"It's no joke. It's downright creepy. You see there's so much difference in our ages that since we married we had a sort of unspoken agreement—he goes his way with his friends, and I go mine. That's the way it's supposed to be. He makes a great pretense of being entirely uninterested in what I do. I have my key and he has his. We come in at different times of the night.

"Let's hear about how he follows you."

"It's making me a nervous wreck!" She looked pitiful. "I'd give a lot of money just to know how he does it. I come in alone at night, say twelve or one o'clock. I unlock the front door and hang my hat on the rack. Well, I hardly take off my coat when he drifts in, too. He hangs his hat up beside mine and gives me a big wink. He always says the same thing: 'We had a pleasant evening, didn't we, Linda?' Then without another word he goes to bed. Every time I go out and stay late, some time durring the night he picks up my trail. I've tried all sorts of ways to throw him off the track, but he's a devil at keeping out of sight. He never refers to it again—just that fiendish trick of trailing me into the hall and winking at me!"

McGavock asked innocently: "And where do you spend these late evenings?"

"Golly, how should I know! Different places with different people. A girl my age has to have friends." She sounded desperate. "I'd go crazy if I didn't—"

"Old Red didn't trail you, did he?"

"That's ridiculous. Rufus wasn't a bloodhound, and besides, he was never allowed out of his pen."

McGavock pondered. "I can't quite get the idea in your coming to me this way. If Bailey's dead, I'd find it out mighty soon myself—the whole county must know it. Well, I've got to be getting along." He gave her a saccharine smile. "You stay here. Count to a hundred before you leave, please."

"Why should I—" she started to protest.

He was bland. "I'm sure it didn't occur to you, but if you and I should wander down Main Street, arm in arm—such a pretty little kid, and the detective in the case—what would the townsmen say? Would anyone ever believe any testimony I might have to offer at a later date? You didn't think of that, did you?"

"Gracious, no!" Her lips parted moistly and her eyes lighted up in admiration. "A detective has to be careful, doesn't he?"

IT WAS NEARLY mid-afternoon by the time McGavock returned to the lumber-and-coal yards on South Market. The sun was unseasonably hot and its impact had dried the barren meadows to a sterile, earthy crust. At the end of the cracked pavement was the high board fence which enclosed the varied businesses of client James Robert Gatch. The place looked as dreary in the daylight as it had last evening in the moonglow. McGavock entered the tall gates, passed through the high stacked lumber. It was here, last night, that he'd been attacked. With hardly a glance of interest he continued through the alley, came out into the clearing. He made directly for the big T-shaped building in the center of the yard—and for the door marked, OFFICE.

Jim Gatch was in his office. He was behind his desk, tilted back in his rush-seated rocking chair. He was obviously idling away the time and appeared glad to see McGavock.

He showed his big white teeth in friendly welcome, called: "Come in, McGavock. Take a load off your feet. Caught any felons recently?"

McGavock sank onto an old church pew along the wall. After a moment's consideration, he said: "No, not recently. Murder always gets them first. Take Todd Bailey. He's dead!"

"So I heard." Gatch was deadpan.

"Todd was the lad that was filching Scully's timber."

A little quirk gathered at the corners of Jim Gatch's steeltrap mouth. The quirk twisted itself into a grin. Gatch roared in laughter, unhooked his spectacles, wiped them, put them back on. "You do have bad luck, don't you? Last night Cortland, your client, died. But you had a second string to your bow—me. I retained you to stop the lumber-stealing up at Snake Ridge. Now again death has cheated you out of a fee."

McGavock said slowly: "Death hasn't cheated me out of anything as far as you're concerned. At eleven o'clock this morning I got Todd's word that he'd stop his depredations. I thus fulfilled my contract. You owe the Atherton Browne agency two thousand dollars. It's a bit high, I admit, but it was your own idea."

"You got Bailey's word, eh? And what did that amount to?" Gatch was enjoying himself. "And now you ask me to take yours, to boot. Oh, come now, be honest. You made the whole business up, didn't you?"

McGavock met his companion's hard eyes for a full instant, remarked placidly: "You're not the first tanktown chiseler who's tried to work on us. Brother, we'll go over you with a currycomb before this is finished." He half lowered his eyelids, said affably: "What the hell! I might as well start in right now. Say I'd want to get a little dope on your background, how'd I go about it? It strikes me mighty peculiar. You come to Kempton from nowhere and already you've got a flourishing business."

Gatch was unruffled. "It's pretty hard to explain. About my flourishing business—the answer is, I'm that kind of a man. A go-getter. I set up shop here on a shoe-string. I worked hard and I'm making it pay. About my background, I've spent my life here and there and have followed about every trade you can name. I'm a licensed veterinarian, among other things—which brings up a rather eerie fact. When I came to town, I brought with me a small travel-clinic which I'd built and designed. The first night in Kempton, it was stolen. I left it by the curb and the next morning was gone."

"What do you mean, clinic?"

"I'm referring to a trailer that I'd fixed up. Now who could possibly find any use for a veterinarian's workshop?"

So that was Todd Bailey's trailer! McGavock left the question unanswered, asked: "With the entire state of Tennessee beckoning for your services, how did you happen to wind up in Kempton? That, as I see it, is the catch. Everyone I talk to appears to think it only natural that a man named Gatch should blow in only a few weeks after a wealthy old lady named Gatch died. And to make the coincidence even harder to believe, the two of you are no kin whatever. Would you like to discuss this subject with me?"

The hard eyes behind the octagonal lenses wavered. "There has been a lot of hokum about coincidences. As a matter of fact, they're quite common—they happen every day, all around us. The human mind is very limited in its outlook and because of its inability to encompass the vast pattern of universal occurrence, it tends to interpret with incredulity such events as may—"

"For the last time—how did you happen to wind up in Kempton?"

Gatch licked his upper lip, said in a bluster of goodfellowship: "McGavock, you and I have had our little squabbles. But deep in our hearts we like each other. Let's let bygones be bygones. I'm in a hole. If I tell you about it, will you promise to be open-minded, even if you can't be sympathetic?"

"I promise nothing. To heck with you."

The stocky man got to his feet, his mighty cheeks chalky white. "You're going to hear something fantastic." He began to pace the room. "I was born in Meggs County, Alabama. I was raised in an orphanage. When I was fourteen, I cleared out. Just before I left, the superintendent called me to him. He gave me a bulky bundle that had been entrusted to him when I was brought in. At the institution I was known as William Jones. The superintendent declared my actual name was James Robert Gatch. From that moment, I assumed that name."

McGavock listened intently. "What was this bulky bundle?"

Gatch walked to a small safe in the corner, opened it. He came forward with a big family Bible, brassbound, covered with musty red plush. "Take a look at this." He turned the pages, located the section marked "Marriages." In faded brown ink was written, *James Robert Gatch and Cynthia Taulbee, Wedded this Day, May 3, 1889.*

Gatch said "Those must have been my parents." He flipped a few pages, stopped under the heading "Births." McGavock read the last entry: *"Born to Cynthia and James Robert Gatch, this Day, November 7, 1892, a Son, James Robert, Junior."*

McGavock asked: "And they gave you this when you left the orphanage?"

"Yes." Gatch replaced the Bible in the safe. "I got to wondering just who my people were. They were pretty hard to trace. I found only one living relative, Miss Bella Gatch, of Kempton. I was kind of a roustabout, so I stayed away not to embarrass her. When she died, I came to town to see what was what."

"Then, after all, you're a kinsman of Scully's, eh?"

"Distantly, perhaps, on a different branch. The interesting point is, however, that legally I'm an equal heir with Scully. We have precisely the same degree of consanguinity under the law."

McGavock got up, stretched lazily. "Then why don't you make him share the estate with you? There's plenty for two."

Gatch was taut, pale. "If I take it to court I'll find I'm not Gatch at all, but somebody named William Jones. I've spent too many years building up my self respect. I'm not going to take the chance. I can make my own money!"

CONTRASTING WITH SHERIFF Turley's usual attire, his gray coupé was sleek and shiny, with plenty horses under her hood. The sheriff eased her nose out of the alley behind the jail, circled the edge of the court square, and rolled her gently down Main Street. When he hit the blacktop at the corporation line, he gave her the gas. She jumped like a bee-stung whippet and McGavock, lolling deep in the comfortable cushions, almost threw his neck out of joint. For the next five miles they really barreled. The sheriff said: "I think yo're up the wrong tree, like I said. Hit's true they's been a bit o' graveyard trouble at Bear Holler but hit hain't nothing to do with our killings at Kempton. Hit's jest countryboys a-prankin' theirselves in drink."

McGavock held his silence.

The sumac and hazel along the road were hammering by as if on a rampage. All at once, the sheriff cut the wheel, the wheels screamed, and they were jogging down a red-clay fork. The car stopped, Pence Turley got out and opened a gate.

They jolted through a farmer's woodlot, past the curious glassy gaze of grizzled mules and feeding cows, forded a shallow branch, and hit the hillroad. From then on, they climbed.

The trail was little more than an old logroad. As the slope steepened, the scrub and second-growth gave way to ancient oaks and hickories. Puff adders whisked away through the dead leaves at their approach, blue jays scolded them severely from the high stagheads against the sky. At the crest, the hardwood went suddenly into pine. A great nocturnal stillness fell upon them as they entered the half-light of the forest. There was nothing here but the clean straight boles of the pines, and the interminable forest floor carpeted with its mat of pungent needles. They started their descent. After a period of turbulent rocking, the coupé pulled up in a grassy depression. Sheriff Turley opened the car door. "Wal, this-here's Bear Holler. What we do now? They hain't nothing to see."

The little saucer-shaped hollow was flanked on all sides by the dense, overhanging foliage. McGavock said: "Come on." They skirted the neat, whitewashed church, made for the burying ground behind it.

One look at the graveyard and McGavock knew that he was really back in the hinterlands. It was such a cemetery as few outlanders ever behold. Each small grave was decorated according to the taste of the bereaved—with odds and ends of broken china, with porcelain fruit jar-tops, cracked teacups. It was like a macabre children's playhouse. Some of the mounds were edged with amber snuff bottles buried bottom-up. Some were covered with a low roof or corrugated galvanized sheeting to keep the rain from the deceased. The tombstones were all types and sizes, from antique sandstone slabs to glistening mail-order granite.

Sheriff Turley said gruffly: "Here's one. And they's another. And, durn, they's the third!" He was pointing to the block pedestals at the head of three graves, pedestals minus their tombstones.

McGavock nodded. "So these are the graves that have been despoiled. Where are the stones?"

The sheriff beckoned, led his companion into the lip of brush. Just at the forest's rim, was a clear, shalely pool, maybe eight feet deep and fed cold crystal water by underground springs. At the bottom of the pool was an accumulation of litter—rotted leaves and chewing gum wrappers and beer bottle tops. In a heap in the center, where they'd been carelessly tossed, were the sandstone shards of shattered tombstones. They'd been smashed thoroughly—no single piece was larger than a flatiron.

Sheriff Turley indicated a handful of fragments on the bank. "They was busted here an' throwed in. Fellers that busted 'em musta used a twelve-pound sledge. Does hit make any sense to you?"

"Yeah man." McGavock smiled. "Just as a matter of routine, who's the sexton of this church? Does he live anywhere nearby?"

The sheriff was irritated. " 'Course he lives nearby. Or he wouldn't be sexton. Hit's Lace Kilgore, an' his cabin's yander, up the branch bed. We'd best leave our car here and walk, but

I'm a-tellin' you, he cain't he'p us none. An' he wouldn't iff'n he could."

THE TINY CABIN was in a shelf-like crotch on the hillside. The chinking was crumbling from its weathered cedar logs and the broad hand-split shingles of its roof of were rotting from the ridgepole. There was no one in sight as McGavock and the sheriff broke through the stiff undergrowth, but as they came into the open, a man appeared in the dog-run. He was barefoot, in ragged denims, a wisp of a fellow with a wry Celtic mouth and snapping black eyes. He said: "Howdy, Shur'f. Jest stand whur you are."

They came to a loitering stop. Kilgore said sardonically: "I gen'rally expect you after a rain, Shur'f. How come you honor me on such a bright, sunny day?"

McGavock got the allusion and began to feel at home. A good rain and you could smell whiskey mash for miles. That was when revenuers were busy. Sheriff Turley said cautiously: "I'm here on a friendly call, Lace. This is Mr. McGavock. We're here about that vandalism. Mr. McGavock wants to talk to you."

"I done lost the blessed gift o' speech."

A woman materialized beside the man. She was in an ankle-length calico dress and wore big, hard plow-shoes. She carried a double-bitted axe over her shoulder. The sheriff bowed gallantly, said: "Good evenin', Miz Kilgore. How's yore boils, ma'am?" She ignored him completely.

"I'm here," McGavock said quietly, "because I promised Todd Bailey I'd come. I was talking to him in Kempton a few hours before he was murdered."

They were thunderstruck. "Todd's dead?"

The sheriff said: "Yes, ma'am. I been aimin' to put the word out as soon as I git something to go on—"

McGavock wedged his way back into the conversation. "I understand he was well liked back here. Well, I'm all set to nab the party that killed him. How about it, do you folks want to help?"

They wavered. McGavock said: "I'll just put a few questions to you. If you think I'm overreaching myself, just clam up. That's fair enough, isn't it? O.K. First, Todd's death is directly connected with the vandalism in the churchyard. All right, Mr. Kilgore, I want you to tell me whose tombstones were destroyed."

"They was just tombstones. Nobuddy knows whose. All three of 'em was so old that they wasn't no writin' on 'em no more.

The sheriff was amazed. McGavock declared: "That fits in. Now this. Todd admitted to me that he was logging the old Dillon place. There's no gripe about that, it's over and done with. What I'd like to know is how he got his timber out. He certainly didn't bring his logs up and down these hills, past your cabin, did he?

Kilgore said carefully: "I hain't sayin' that Todd takened no logs nowhur. I will say that a feller could log Snake Ridge and haul 'em out over that dry creekbed. Hit goes a mile or so and jines up with the State Highway."

McGavock smiled cordially, said: "Thanks, good people. We'll have the slayer under arrest by midnight tonight." There was a general surge of relieved tension through the group. Mrs. Kilgore observed pleasantly: "My boils are a heap better. Shur'f, thank you. How is Miz Turley?"

McGavock remarked amiably: "I'm afraid we'll have to save the sociability for later. Sheriff, can you find that creekbed?"

"Why, shore. Hit's jest over the hill."

"Then let's start walking. That's where we'll find the trailer."

7

Exhume the Dog!

AND THAT WAS where they found it. Back a hundred feet or so from the gully, hidden in the woods, behind a tangle of wild grapevines, just as Todd Bailey had said. As trailers went, it was rather small. But it was compact and neat. Across its side was lettered, *DR. J.R. GATCH, Veterinarian.* Sheriff Turley felt the sudden impulse to argue. McGavock flagged him down. They opened the door and stepped inside.

The interior was immaculate. The cubbyhole was truly a miniature clinic. There was a folding cot and midget cookstove, but the greater part of the space was taken with racks of medical instruments, shelves of serum ampules, cases of gleaming hypodermic needles. As an itinerant veterinarian, Jim Gatch had been well equipped. In one corner hung a suit of modest tweed, and in a cloudy glass of water by the stove was a set of false teeth—uppers and lowers, big, white horseteeth. McGavock smiled. "Eating berries and bark, says Mr. Gatch, makes the teeth develop. Those flashy babies he's always picking are phonies!"

Sheriff Turley could control himself no longer. "What's this mean?" He demanded. "You knowd this was here, you said so. What's it mean?"

"This trailer belongs to Jim Gatch. It was stolen the night he came to Kempton and towed out here. This is going to come as a shock. Public opinion to the contrary, Jim is an equal heir to Old Lady Gatch's fortune. He bears the same relationship to her as Scully Endicott does."

"And that's what brought him to Kempton?"

"No doubt about it. His original idea was get what was coming to him." McGavock turned, descended the step into the open. "Now I want to take a quick look at the old Dillon place, and then we'll be getting back to town."

"Why, this-here's the old Dillon place. We're at the east end of Snake Ridge. That's the old Dillon place."

McGavock was patient. "I mean the house. Wasn't there a house here long ago—that burned down?"

"Why, certainly-shore. But how kin we see hit, iff'n hit's done burnt down?"

"Do what I say," McGavock instructed. "We're after a killer and we're behind schedule."

The old Dillon home had been built on a triangular plateau, high on the ridge's crest, overlooking the valley. Wild forest growth had practically reclaimed the tiny clearing, briars and prickly pears flourished in the washed earth and out-cropping shale lay bleached and rotting in the soft coral rays of the setting sun. "Watch out fer rattlers," the sheriff warned.

The relic stood in the center of the clearing. A fieldstone chimney, rising from the underbrush like a lonesome dolmen. That was all that remained of farmer Dillon's ancient homestead—just the chimney and the squat, open-mouthed fireplace. McGavock advanced, studied the ruins in scrutiny. He lowered his voice, said bleakly: "Well, here we are, Sheriff. The end of the trail. What do you think of it?"

Sheriff Turley bent forward, peered.

On the smooth, gray hearthstone was a queer little handful

of blackish, curled embers. McGavock broke off a small piece, allowed the sheriff to smell it. Sheriff Turley grimaced, said: "Pee-oo, What on earth—"

"It's felt. A felt hat. And it hasn't been here long, or the weather would have beaten it to dust. My guess is that we're gazing at the sad remains of Cortland Kincaid Endicott's skimmer."

Sheriff Turley glowered, "By doggies, we're dealin' with a lunatic! Why'd he bring hit clear out here and—"

"Our party was trying to be smart. The killer feared we'd find it. The idea is to misdirect us."

Sheriff Turley snorted. "That's foolish!"

"Not foolish," McGavock corrected. "It's very foxy indeed. Now I understand the sawdust. That's all here. Let's be getting back to Kempton."

THEY SAT IN silence, shrouded in their thoughts on the tedious drive back to town. The timberlands about them, struck for a harsh instant to copper-red in the sunset, faded to pearl in the afterlight, became flushed with straggling purple shadows. Sheriff Turley drove more slowly on the return. He appeared heavily preoccupied—and a little muddled. Finally, he spoke. "Now, Luther, hit's been a lifetime sinst I made a good friend so quick, like I done you. Friends shouldn't hold out on one another—"

McGavock said comfortably: "Everything I know about this mess, I had to dig out myself. It's you who have been holding out. You've been doing it all along!"

Sheriff Turley palavered. "Mebbe at first, I held out a little. You see, Luther, we was scarcely acquainted then, you might say. I'm a hard feller to git into," He gave a forced laugh. "But now that's all over and did with! We're podners, eh?" He paused, puckered his loose lips. "How do you figger all this? Is Jim Gatch gonna sue for his share of Scully's money?"

"No." McGavock was definite on this point. "Scully's got him hogtied."

"You was astin' this mornin' 'bout Ole Red, the hound with the mismatched eyes, Was you jokin'? What's Ole Red got to do with this?"

"Plenty. Find the party who killed the dog and you'll have the slayer who did away with Cort and Bailey." He hesitated, explained confidentially: "Say Cort Endicott was keeping company with his sister-in-law, Miss Linda—say Old Red found it out and started to blackmail Scully. That would give you a motive for the canine's murder!"

"But Ole Red was jest a hound. Dog's cain't blackmail nobuddy!"

McGavock looked frustrated. "By Golly, you're right! I never thought of that."

Twilight settled down over the countryside. The gray coupé left the red-clay trail, turned out onto the highway. As they approached the outskirts of the town, McGavock asked: "Did you get the word I sent you by Miss Blanche? Have you contacted Nashville for the dope on that so-called Frontiersman's Club?"

"I did, Luther. But the word hain't come through yet. I should hear about suppertime. An' that's another thing I want to know! What—"

The coupé rambled over the corporation line, past the cotton compress, onto South Market. McGavock said earnestly: "Just stick with me a little longer, Sheriff. Believe me, it's all over. Meet me about nine tonight at Scully Endicott's. Bring Jim Gatch. I promise to explain everything."

Sheriff Turley ruminated. "Yo're a funny feller, Luther. I cain't make up my mind whether yo're as sharp as a tack, or whether yo're jest all lungs and silver tongue. You keep promising this an' that, an' sayin' you unnerstan' this an' that, till you got my head in a whirl. Keer if I test you jest once?"

McGavock didn't like it. He said warily: "O.K. Shoot."

Sheriff Turley gave a lupine grin. "Here's a for-instance. Out at Bear Holler Cemetary you claimed you knowed how come those tombstones's in that water-pool. If you wasn't runnin' a bluff, I'd shore relish hearin' what you meant."

McGavock sighed with relief. "Oh, the tombstones. I was afraid you were going to ask me to name our killer. Here's the answer to that. Our slayer wanted a tombstone, and he didn't want anyone to suspect he possessed it. He worked out a neat trick to acquire it. He went to Bear Hollow, dismantled three stones. Two of them he smashed into bits and dumped in the pool, the third he carted away with him."

Sheriff Turley listened attentively. McGavock went on: "You expected to find three stones—so that was what you saw. That was why he broke them into pieces. The little pile of fragments and the refraction of the water made it difficult to estimate them. Now don't ask me what he did with the extra monument—because I'm not going to tell you until tonight."

THE ENDICOTTS DIDN'T appear precisely overjoyed at McGavock's unannounced visit. They received him hostilely, and with a feeble effort at formality in the mansion's big parlor.

The Endicott parlor was something to write to grandmother about. Its walls were gold and rose, its lofty ceiling was barrel-arched in floral molding, and the nap of the soft sand-colored Oriental rug came up to the top of McGavock's heels. They sat him on a loveseat, perched themselves on chairs, facing him at oblique angles—and waited for him to explain his appearance. Their stiff formality and the elegance of the parlor, he knew, were an attempt to bludgeon him into servile timidity. After a deliberate survey of his surroundings, he said affably: "Quite a place you've got here. There's floor space enough for at least ten pool tables and a bowling alley!"

Scully Endicott crossed his chubby legs, punched his cigar into the corner of his mouth. "What a vulgar remark. May I ask why you honor us with your presence? Mrs. Endicott and myself are—er—great homebodies. We—ahem—rarely entertain. If you get my point."

The kid, Linda, McGavock decided, was even prettier than he'd realized. Her little-girl figure was trim and pleasant in her short plum frock. She sat stiffly, her chest raised, and stared at him as though she had a bad case of myopia and someone had just whipped away her pince-nez.

The little French clock swarming with cupids and butterflies on the mantelshelf said three minutes to nine. McGavock began to talk. "To tell you the truth, folks, this is one of the most erratic cases I've ever tangled with."

Scully came out of his self-induced stupor. "That's been my impression, too. You're not getting anywhere, are you?"

"I don't mean that. I think I've got these murders solved. I'm talking about clients. People hire me and fire me until I hardly know where I stand. It's beginning to appear as though I've been working for the sheer joy of it. Last chance. Nothing sold after train leaves the station. Anyone want to get on with me?"

They gave him the old stony stare.

The doorbell rang. Mrs. Endicott arose, left the room. She returned with Sheriff Pence Turley and Jim Gatch. The sheriff looked uneasy, Gatch seemed to be eagerly curious. He said: "Good evening, Linda. Hello, Scully!"

Scully Endicott was swept with a sudden attack of apoplectic anger. He leaned forward, shook a trembling finger at the man with the clipped mustache. "I believe I spoke to you this afternoon, sir! You have the impertinence to cross my threshold after our conversation? I said it to you before, and I shall say it again in the presence of these persons—rather unpleasant rumors have come to me. To be brief, you are making a nuisance of yourself to my wife!"

Gatch grinned.

"Let's take this in an orderly fashion," McGavock ordered. "It'll all come out in the wash. And such a wash! We're after a triple killer. And Scully, I think, is our man."

THERE WAS AN instant of stunned silence. Sheriff Turley said weakly: "You think? You have to do better than that, Luther. I gotta perduce proof!"

Gatch chuckled. "We're free now, eh, Linda?"

The girl said helplessly: "I don't understand you, Mr. Gatch."

Scully began to shout: "Sheriff, get that Gatch man out of here—"

"Horsefeathers!" McGavock cut in genially. "Scully, you and your friend here are in this together—and equally guilty—though you did the actual killing. This jealousy act is just a rotten routine you put on, per agreement between you. You kick the gal around as a red herring. She doesn't even know what it's all about."

Gatch showed his big teeth. "Now it's me too, eh?"

"Why, certainly. It was Scully who knocked off Cortland. He lured him to the den last night and strangled him—which brings up two things simultaneously. How did Scully get out of that room so quickly last night, preventing me from catching him red-handed, and how does he trail his wife so mysteriously that she can never get a look at him? There's a tiny alarm contact in the front door slot. The door closes and rings a buzzer up in the den. You see he held frequent secret consultations there with his fellow pardner in crime. He didn't trail his wife—he'd be sitting in his den, hear the buzzer, grab his hat and come down the back veranda stairs and follow her in the house. The buzzer tipped him off when I entered last night, just as he was cooking Cortland's goose."

The chubby man smirked. "Why should I murder an old man like Cousin Cort?"

"Because of the sawdust. You stole a tombstone at Bear Hollow, took it to Gatch's monument works, probably at night, and cut off the rounded top-end. Cort was trying to get something on you. He saw the gray dust left by the saw—by the way, stonedust can be sawdust as well as wood—Cort saw this stonedust, suspected its source, and wired us in Memphis. I found Cort's evidence in a glassine envelope in his wallet. I found the wallet under the burlap in Gatch's lawn, where he'd planted it. And speaking of planting, Gatch tried to throw me off by substituting a bottle of cedar sawdust."

Linda asked: "But why should Scully kill Cortland? You haven't told us—"

"Because Cort had discovered about the hound with the golden eye. *Because he'd learned that Gatch wasn't Gatch!*"

The man in the octagonal glasses said jovially: "This is wonderful. And who, then am I?"

McGavock said coldly: "Frankly, I don't know—and it's not important. But we'll find out. Sheriff, what did you get on the Frontiersman's Club?"

"Hit's a gambling club in Nashville run by a feller named Bogart."

"You're Bogart," McGavock said quietly. "Now it finishes up. When Old Lady Gatch kicked off, Scully inherited. A distant kinsman, an itinerant veterinarian named James Robert Gatch, heard about it and came to town with a family Bible to prove his blood relationship. When Linda went to Chattanooga on her trips, Scully had been running down to Nashville, playing in your gaming house. The real Gatch appeared and had to be eliminated. Scully thought of you as a likely assistant. You, the two of you, did away with him and took his trailer out to Snake Ridge. Bogart, here, was smart. He hoped the trailer would never be found but left an out for himself should it ever be. He placed some of his clothes in the clinic, as well as a set of his spare false teeth. He had Gatch's Bible by now and figured he'd assumed a new identity—an identity, by the way, that could keep Scully in line. This, under the head of blackmail, explains Bogart-Gatch's sudden business prosperity." He paused. "It was Scully, by the way, who tried to smack in my skull in the lumberyard—just like he did to Todd Bailey. Todd was filching timber at Snake Ridge. The boys were scared he'd find the trailer. Scully wanted to let him alone, Gatch wanted him in jail. In the end they killed him."

SHERIFF TURLEY ASKED woodenly: "Whut about Ole Red, Luther. Tell me 'bout the hound."

"That man-eating beast almost got them into trouble. Scully set Old Red on the real Gatch—at night. Gatch got away and ran through the pasture behind the water tower. The hound caught up with him, bowled him over. Gatch shot the dog. Squire Weller thought the cartridges were blanks, but they were not. Scully and Bogart came up later and finished him. Finished both of them, as a matter of fact, the dog and the man. They were afraid to keep Old Red because he was wounded. They buried man and dog together. That was why—"

Linda objected. "But that must have been weeks ago. And Rufus the Red was in his pen until—"

"Not Rufus. Another red hound, But Rufus had mismatched eyes. Scully was the only person who saw the substitute and was in constant fear his deceit would be exposed. He solved it in a foxy way. He killed the new dog at night, he took out one of the dog's brown eyes and replaced it with a glass taxidermist's eye—a yellow eye he got from the stuffed bobcat in the library. He then took the mounted cat up to his den. If you don't believe me, go back of the barn and exhume the dog!" McGavock turned to the girl. "With so much murder flying about, you figured Gatch was responsible and wrote him a note warning him to get out of town."

Bogart said: "McGavock, I'm not much of a lawyer, but the way I see it is this. Nobody can prove anything at all about Cortland. You claim I'm not Jim Gatch and that Gatch is buried somewhere. Until you materialize this phantom cadaver, this other so-called heir, you're talking through your hat. Produce the corpse, my friend."

McGavock ignored him. "Take those blueprints for the hunting lodge. Scully had them drawn up to flash as an excuse whenever anyone should suggest that he get rid of the non-profitable Dillon place."

Sheriff Turley came in on the chorus. "Whur's the corpse, Luther?"

"It's under the hearthstone by the chimney—up on Snake Ridge." McGavock reached for his hat. "They needed a bigger hearthstone for their secret grave. So they used an old tombstone from Bear Hollow. They picked it because it was old looking and weathered. They made a mistake here. An old settler like Dillon wouldn't have had a dressed stone for his hearth. He'd have a piece of rough shale he'd pick up from the creekbed or hillside. Dig under that fireplace, Sheriff."

As McGavock made for the door, the girl headed him off. She placed her small white hand on his shoulder, said: "Good-by. You probably saved my life."

McGavock went back on his heels, glared at her. "Nonsense, nothing of the kind. But I did dump a fortune in your lap. As a consequence, I shouldn't be surprised if you'd be getting fan letters from a man named Atherton Browne in Memphis."

Killer Stay 'Way From My Door

"I've decided that Brother Lew was killed by balderdash and find myself suffering from a mild but irritating condition of abaction. I would appreciate it if you would send a man here to alleviate it," read Mark Thatcher's letter to the Atherton Browne agency. So McGavock became Ashton's prime alleviator—dividing his attentions between Ralph Gregory's acousma and the teetotaler who met his Maker with Boysenberry cordial on his breath. But even the Memphis shamus was powerless to prevent murder—until his victim's checkbook tied a noose around the killer's throat.

1

The Deadly Balderdash

THE GRIMY OLD office was golden in the autumn sunshine—golden and hot. McGavock, sprawled in his swivel chair, was whiling away the tedium composing a poem about a bizarre brazier in a Byzantine bazaar, and trying to work in a brassiere for luck, when a clamorous thumping came from behind the frosted glass partition.

McGavock got to his feet, strolled into the chief's sanctum. Old Atherton Browne was seated behind his battered bird's-eye maple desk, waiting.

This morning he seemed particularly ancient and weary. Before him was a small white enamel tray containing an open box of ampules and a four-ounce bottle of greenish liquid. His pitifully spare shoulders were hunched forlornly and his mucous-rimmed eyes, usually so malevolent and venomous, were veiled in gentle introspection. He gazed at his ace detective fondly, spoke in a quavering voice. "Luther, together we tread Life's highway. You are at the crest. But I'm an old man, at the end of the lane, groping in the dusk for the garden gate!"

McGavock was touched in spite of himself. He said brusquely: "I've told you before, and I repeat it, when you want me, send for me. Don't hammer on the floor as though I were a— What's this all about, anyway?"

"They're having a bit of difficulty up at Ashton, that's a cozy little village back in the hill-country. Maybe you'd like to knock off a couple of days and go up to Ashton to—"

"So that's it!" McGavock cleared his throat with a derisive, hacking sound. "Not me. Get Pete Coyle, he's your pet! I don't even have a decent contract with you." He leaned against the plasterboard wall and glowered.

HE WAS A little man, wiry and tough, with a tweedy touch of gray above his temples.

Through the years he'd worked in about every major agency in the country, but never until he'd tied up with this Memphis outfit had he found a real home. He was a genius at getting results—but a hard man to take.

Old Atherton Browne screwed up his face, thrust his fist into his vest against his chest. After a moment he said: "Don't worry about me, Luther. I'm all right." He pawed listlessly in the desk drawer, came out with a legal-sized envelope addressed to the agency. Inside this was yet another, note-sized. "A cagy customer," the old man explained. "He was afraid his message would be candled." From the smaller envelope, he took a folded sheet of paper, handed it to McGavock.

In neat, rounded script was written:

Atherton Browne Detective Agency

Memphis

Gentlemen:

To be perfectly frank, I'm worried. Things are happening here in Ashton that I don't seem to be able to grasp. Last week my brother Lewis died and while at the time we considered his passing normal, by Jove, I've been giving it some thought and have decided that he was killed by balderdash!

However, I must admit that the theory is merely conjecture. I'm writing you about a different matter. I find myself suffering from a mild but irritating condition of abaction and would appreciate it if you would send a man here to alleviate it.

I'd like a fairly good man and am disposed to offer him board and room here in my home and a generous wage of sixty-five cents an hour. Should he care to bring his wife and family with him while he is on his sojourn, they are, of course, welcome. In such instance, however, we would be forced to make just and amicable deductions in his remuneration.

Sincerely,
Marcus Kimberly Thatcher

McGavock roiled. "What a chiseler! Wants a detective with a wife and family, so he can take out a chattel mortgage on them. Wants to pay his fee by turning his home into a hotel. A crackpot if I ever—"

"He's no crackpot, Luther," the old man said patiently. "And he's well able to raise that sixty-five cent limit. I've heard of the Thatchers. They're a powerful and wealthy family back in that neck of the woods. I'm firmly convinced that you can go back there and dig up a case of homicide—"

"Brother Lewis killed by balderdash!" McGavock snorted. "That's not crackpot, is it! And wanting a man to alleviate his abaction! What is—"

The old man sighed. "Mr. Thatcher, as I said, is a wary human. He uses roundabout speech. Abaction had me stumped, too. I called up the public library. It simply means cattle stealing."

"So someone's been taking his cows. Why doesn't the local sheriff—"

Old Atherton Browne spoke quietly. "The local sheriff isn't quite up to this, Luther. It's my guess there's mighty bad business afoot back in those hills. There's an atmosphere of secrecy about this whole thing that I don't like. I want you to take a flyer on it, see what you can uncover, and I don't want you working for birdseed, either. How about it? This is no rustling

Golden Vevay's broken body was found at the bottom of Jackdaw Cliff. Four hundred dollars was pinned to her clothing and a traveling bag lay nearby.

case. Big stakes are involved."

"No soap," McGavock said dourly. "Send Pete Coyle. He'll make a better impression with the nobility than I will. He shaves three times a day and watches his whom's."

"Forget it, then. What with this other situation coming up, I'd just as soon have you around the office here. You're my backlog." With trembling hands he shifted the enamel tray on the desk top.

Curiously, McGavock asked: "What's that stuff?"

"Oh, just glucose and digitalis." The old man smiled bravely. "My heart is giving me a bit of trouble again. Doctor says I have to go home and stay in bed for a couple of days. That's why I can't send Pete, by the way. While I'm away from the office, he's going to be acting manager."

McGavock seethed. He said in a monotone: "I'm to be a big shot, the backlog, and Pete's to be the manager. I see. All I gotta do is be on hand so Coyle can order me around as if I were his personal lackey. I've changed my mind. How do I get to—"

"You get there by bus," the old man said mildly. "Good luck."

McGavock slammed out of the room.

A little later Miss Ollinger, the chief's secretary, entered. The old man was sitting alone, a dreamy, evil smile on his ancient face. He said: "That McGavock is the best man who ever drew my pay, but you've got to boot him into a job." He picked up the box of ampules, dropped it into the waste basket.

Miss Ollinger asked: "What's that? What are you throwing away?"

"How should I know?" the oldster answered, nettled. "It's just some junk I had sent up from the drugstore."

THE BUS ROUNDED the blacktop ridge-road and McGavock observed the little hamlet just below him, nested in the cup-like hollow. To either side, as far as the eye could see, great tumbling, wooded hills stretched to the horizon.

The town in the miniature valley was larger than he had expected. Maybe a population of, say, six hundred. There was a water-tower, a thriving business section, and the sun's rays glowed on a prosperous-looking cotton compress and warehouse.

The bus pulled up before a drugstore and McGavock got out. It was just at supper hour, Main Street was deserted. He saw the courthouse, a squat, stolid building of weathered stone centered in a patch of weedy, eroded lawn and knew that he'd hit a countyseat. The business section was built about Court Square in a rectangle. In the setting sun, the place seemed almost a memory of something else, abandoned, ghostlike.

McGavock located the hotel at the far, rear corner of the square. It practically took a detective to find it. About halfway down the block-long brick building, an entranceway between two dingy shops bore the information: HOTEL. At the bottom of the sign, beneath the lettering, a scabrous golden hand pointed vaguely up a flight of narrow steps.

McGavock stepped into the gloom, ascended the rickety staircase.

He came out into a small, cell-like lobby. The carpet on the floor was musty, the walls, in the dim light, appeared to be papered with great clusters of twining grapes and flying pheasants. There was an antique, built-in hotel desk, a marble-topped table, a few plush-bottomed chairs. There was no one behind the desk. McGavock set his luggage beside a spittoon, looked about him. At the front of the lobby, a tall casement window was opened wide to the stifling autumn evening. McGavock pushed through a rusty screen door, found himself on a thumbnail veranda.

This small upstairs porch was located, McGavock realized, directly above the sidewalk. From where he stood he could gaze down into Court Square, and beyond. As he turned to re-enter the building, he pretended to notice his companion for the first time. He asked gruffly: "You the manager here?"

The man was lolling just outside the window sill, his cane-bottomed chair tilted back against the clapboard siding. He was a big man, unhealthily fat, and dressed in dirty white flannels and white canvas sport shoes. The ribbon on his filthy sailor straw hat had been lost, and repainted on with liquid shoe polish. His cheeks were stubbled and unshaven and his jowls had been rubbed with talcum to hide this negligence. He was dangling a ready-made polka-dot bow tie on his knee and when McGavock addressed him he hastily donned it, said formally: "Good evening, suh. No, I am not the proprietor of this hospitable hospice. And while I'm on the subject, I may say—"

"Thanks," McGavock said curtly. "That's all I wanted to know."

The fat man cleared his throat, and said cordially: "Welcome to beautiful Ashton, suh! Didn't I, harrumph, just see you get off the Memphis bus?"

"You did."

"Permit me to introduce myself. I'm Jimmy Kitchell, ex-schoolteacher, ex-postmaster, ex-sheriff. An all-around ex-cellent fellow, ha-ha!" The fat man rolled his eyes at his own drollery. "What brings you to our lovely village?"

McGavock looked embarrassed. "You'll have to excuse me. It's a secret."

Mr. Kitchell went deadpan. He gazed far away at the circle of hilltops fading in the afterglow. "I certainly don't want to pry." His voice was bland. "But I have the inside track here in Ashton. Just what is this secret mission of yours, suh? Mayhap I can help you."

"Do you think so?" McGavock seemed doubtful. "O.K., then, I'll take a chance on you. It's snakeskins!"

Mr. Kitchell gaped. "What say? I don't quite grasp—"

McGavock's face became taut. He spoke softly, rapidly. "That's right, snakeskins. They're using them for everything nowadays, shoes, belts, billfolds. These hills are loaded with rattlers, black snakes, copperheads, and so on—all this fine stuff just going to waste. The way I do it, I go to country schools and offer the kids a prize for the biggest pelt. All skins become the property of the sponsor. Give me five years and I'll parley it into a monopoly! It'll be a gold mine!"

The fat man looked baffled, and a little nervous. He said: "What a remarkable idea." He got to his feet, wiped his perspiring jaw with a soiled handkerchief. "Well, I'll be getting on. Good luck to you, suh." He strolled through the casement window.

McGAVOCK WAITED UNTIL Mr. Kitchell's huge form appeared below him on the street, waddled out of sight around the corner. The detective then re-entered the lobby. He made straight for the phone on the desk. He got the local operator, asked for the railroad station. His connection made, he spoke in a neutral, colorless voice. "Stationmaster? This is Mr. Marcus Thatcher. I hate to bother you, but here is a minor detail that I overlooked. Just when did that wire come in? Two hours ago, eh? Fine. If you have it handy, would you mind reading it to me again?"

The stationmaster's voice squeaked tolerantly. "Be glad to oblige, Mr. Thatcher. She's addressed to you care of Barstowe's Hotel. I don't know why, but that's the way you wanted her. She says: '*Sorry, do not seem to comprehend the gist of your communication. Must be some mistake.*' She's signed, '*Atherton Browne, Memphis.*'"

Someone was coming up the stairs from the street. McGavock said, "Thanks," replaced the receiver on its bracket.

The hotel clerk appeared at the head of the landing, came forward to greet his guest. He said apologetically: "Sorry to keep you waiting. I was just around to see the preacher."

"You mean you've just been down the alley for a couple of snorts of beer." McGavock signed the register.

"Who's this Jimmy Kitchell?" he asked.

"So you know Mr. Kitchell?" The clerk spoke with respect. "He's a very brainy gentleman." He picked up a key. "May I show you to your room?"

"Not just now." McGavock rubbed his jaw thoughtfully. "I've got a good friend here in town. I think I'll drop in and surprise him. Maybe you can tell me where he lives—Lew Thatcher?"

The clerk's face expressed polite consolation. "Lew Thatcher passed away last week, heart trouble. Hadn't you heard? His brother Mark lives in that big brick house at the corner of Cherry and Elm. On the left. Lew lived diagonally across from Mark. The houses are sort of curiosities. They're exactly alike, and built facing each other thataway—"

McGavock nodded absently. "Who's the best doctor in town?"

"There ain't but one and he's jim-dandy, if you can catch him at home. Doc Powell. He's quite a card. Studied medicine all over the face of the earth and come back home to practice. He'll doctor you if you force him to it but his hobby is trading stock. And a mighty sorry swapper he is, too. I'll betcha right this minute he's in some farmer's barn lot trying to trade a buckskin mule for a run-down mare with a speck in her eye. I mind the time, like the feller says, when—"

McGavock chuckled heartily. "No kidding. Think of that. Well, I'll be seeing you."

He left the hotel. Dusk was darkening into night. McGavock stopped a passerby, inquired about a Dr. Powell.

The doctor's residence was on a lonely strip of hillside just outside of town. The cracked pavement came to an end. McGavock took a graveled drive through a grove of locust and came out on a weedy, unkempt lawn. The small, one-story house was flatish, with a peaked roof and a projecting, railed porch that enclosed all four sides of the structure. Like a summer lodge—or a makeshift sanatorium. The doctor's car a cumbersome, clay-smeared sedan, was parked by the front steps. A lighted window showed warm in the gloaming.

McGavock crossed the porch to the door. He was about to touch his thumb to the buzzer when he realized that the door was standing open. From his position on the threshold, he was looking down a short, dark hall, and beyond, into a brightly-lighted room.

It was then that he saw the corpse.

The head and shoulders of a man—a man twisted in death—lay on the apple-green carpet.

2

Cordially Yours

McGAVOCK ENTERED THE building. Softly and quickly, he walked down the hallway, stepped into the room at the rear.

It was a combination bedroom and study. The walls were lined with books. There was a small cot with a row of shoes beneath it, several comfortable overstuffed chairs, and a big rolltop desk. A frugal but somehow pleasant layout, the quarters of a man who knew what he wanted in life—solitude and leisure.

The body on the floor, McGavock decided, was Dr. Powell. He was plenty dead, shot through the temple. A large blue automatic lay under his buckled hip. He was a skinny, undersized little fellow, and he pretty well fitted the hotel clerk's intimations of eccentricity. He wore a stiffly-starched white dress-shirt with gold cufflinks, blue denim pants, and old-time leather motorcycle puttees. His legs were spread-eagled and his black horn-rimmed glasses, unhooked from one ear, lay askew across his mouth. He was a kindly man, you could tell that even in death—kindly and sensitive, and shrewd.

A blind mood of dark, angry resentment surged through McGavock. He dropped to his hunkers, went through the dead man's clothes. In one hip pocket was a key clip, a wallet containing a few bills, a driver's license, some loose change. In the other, wrapped in the doctor's handkerchief, was a large red candle, burned down to a half-inch stub. McGavock replaced the articles, stood up.

He sauntered to the big rolltop desk. On the blotter was a sheet of gray notepaper. A letter had been started on it. The script said:

> Dear Mrs. Gregory:
>
> In regards to your husband's acousma, I'm forced to consider it very gravely indeed! I've been doing a bit of extra curricular activity lately, buying cattle, etc., you know—fieldwork. I'm now in a position to inform you—believe me, this comes difficult to such a sweet child—that events occurred precisely as Ralph described them. He may never have the hallucination again but Rest assured that he is perfectly insane. It was, according to my medical opinion, dear girl, a most extraordinary incident and I don't feel that, all things considered, you should make it public, or as yet that I should release the full story.
>
> Sincerely,
>
> Michael Powell, M.D.
>
> P.S. I'm very tired tonight, and blue. I think I'll...

Here, at the end of the postscript, the writing fell into a scrawl. It was a weird document. McGavock shook his head in amazement, carefully reread it. After a moment's concentration, he left the study, began a painstaking search of the house.

It was in the third bedroom that he noticed something which interested him.

As he stood in the doorway, crisscrossing the cubbyhole with his flash, he felt that something was wrong. At first it was just a vague sensation. Cautiously, he made a mental invoice. The same straw matting on the floor, the same washstand, bedpan, and bed. But this bed was different—different in one minor detail. *It had no blue quilt on it.*

He stepped forward into the room—and the tornado hit him.

One second he was wrapped in meditation, the next he was fighting wildly for his life. He knew where the quilt was now. It was engulfing him!

Things happened, and fast. The coverlet fell in an enveloping tangle over the detective's head. McGavock clawed frantically to free himself, an arm from behind grappled him about his waist, twisted him roughly to one side, off balance. And then, in a flash of fear, McGavock realized his true peril, and went to work. He threw his body into a half turn, stepped directly into his assailant, and let loose with everything he had. He brought his right fist up in a haymaker from his belt, felt it crash into his attacker's cheek, followed it through, hit or miss, with three furious heart punches. His assailant stumbled. McGavock pushed his advantage, swung wildly, left and right, fanned the air.

Suddenly, he realized that he was alone.

He pawed the coverlet from his shoulders, stood panting against the door frame. After a moment, he groped about the floor, located his flashlight. He located something else, too. A vicious, wooden-handled pruning knife, its hooked blade whetted to a razor edge.

These folks in Ashton were playing for keeps.

DR. POWELL'S STUDY was just as McGavock had left it. With a bleak, sympathetic glance at the body on the rug, the detective walked to the bookcase. After a bit of searching, he found what he wanted, a dictionary. He'd been mulling over Client Mark Thatcher's vocabulary since he'd left Memphis. He reasoned this way—if Client Thatcher used "abaction" for cattle stealing, he must like big words with concealed meanings. Maybe "balderdash," too, had a hidden meaning. Deftly, he thumbed through the b's. Yep, here it was. There was the ordinary meaning—jumble, but the very first definition was something entirely different. The dictionary said: *1. Balderdash—A shabby concoction of liquors.*

That was more like it!

Out of sheer curiosity, he then looked up acousma and found it to be a medical term denoting an auditory hallucination, an imaginary sound.

He replaced the book on the shelf, sat down at Dr. Powell's big desk. He pulled the sheet of gray notepaper over in front of him, ran his eye carefully over it once again. The message was bogus, of course—that is, half true, half fake. It was written in big, round script, a handwriting easy to forge. The margins were wide, and originally the lines were widely spaced. Someone had simply supplied alternate, interlocking lines, new lines, to change the whole message. Lots of things about it indicated the alteration. The added lines contained so much unnecessary padding—"my dear girl," "you know," "in my medical opinion," and so on. But most of all, there were two little things that gave it away. One, the forger couldn't change; the other, he attempted to. The word "Rest" originally began a sentence, and as a consequence was a capital letter. The other was that absurd expression "perfectly insane." Originally, the word had been "sane." The meddler had simply prefixed it with "in."

McGavock, taking alternate lines, read Dr. Powell's last message to himself: "In regards to your husband's acousma, I've been doing a bit of extra curricular fieldwork. I'm now in a position to inform you that events occurred precisely as Ralph described them. Rest assured that he is perfectly sane. It was a most extraordinary incident and I don't feel as yet that I should release the full story."

The postscript, of course, was a phony to indicate suicide. "What the hell!" McGavock said sourly. "If this is a round robin, I think I'll join the party." Carefully, and in a remarkable imitation of the rest of the text, he expanded the postscript. When he finished, the garbled message read:

Dear Mrs. Gregory:

In regards to your husband's acousma, I'm forced to consider it very gravely indeed! I've been doing a bit of extra curricular activity lately, buying cattle, etc., you know—fieldwork. I'm now in a position to inform you—believe me, this comes difficult to such a sweet child—that events occurred precisely as Ralph described them. He may never have the hallucination again but Rest assured that he is perfectly insane. It was, according to my medical opinion, dear girl, a most extraordinary incident and I don't feel that, all things considered, you should make it public or as yet that I should release the full story.

Sincerely,

Michael Powell, M.D.

P.S. I'm very tired tonight, and blue. I think I'll have a tough time staying awake—and yet I must! *I know my life is in danger and have every reason to believe that before sun-up I shall be murdered!*

"That," McGavock murmured proudly, "puts the kibosh on the phony suicide picture. From now on, the killer's out in the open."

McGAVOCK RETURNED TO town, headed for the home of his client. This was mighty bad business. He didn't know what it was all about, but he intended to find out—and soon. There was a sly, ruthless killer walking Ashton's pleasant streets, mingling genially with its citizenry. A murderer who had killed twice—for Lew Thatcher's death had certainly been contrived.

The two big brick houses faced each other across the intersection of Cherry and Elm. In the luminous night, McGavock could see that, as the hotel clerk had said, they appeared to be identical in structure. From their slate roofs, silver-blue in the starlight, to the orderly black evergreens which edged the low stone wall along the pavement, in very detail they were identical.

In every detail except one. The late Lew Thatcher's residence was dark, while Brother Mark's was blazing light from every window.

McGavock strode across the flagstone porch, jangled the old-fashioned doorbell.

The door opened a couple of inches, a suspicious voice said through the crack: "Who's there? What do you want?"

"If you're Mark Thatcher, I'm Luther McGavock—the man from Memphis."

"Oh, splendid!" The door opened wide. "Come in. I have company but I can, ah, get rid of it."

Client Thatcher was a mighty seamy looking customer. He

had a bony forehead, a big bony nose, and tiny crescent eyes retracted in pouches of puckered skin. A dab of yellowish hair on his chin was trimmed vaguely in the general style of an imperial. His clothes were good, but threadbare. He said: "I never employ anyone at this hour of night. Therefore your time will start tomorrow morning, say at nine sharp. However, I'm delighted that you dropped by. Come in, we'll just, er, chat, hey?"

McGavock smiled blandly. "Sure, Mr. Thatcher. Anything you say."

The parlor was spacious, gloomy. High on the walls were a few primitive portraits of sallow, stern-eyed gentlemen and dainty apple-cheeked dames. There was a small, serviceable fireplace, some odds and ends of good furniture. There was a bay window with a built-in bench, and seated on this bench was Jimmy Kitchell, the fat man in dirty whites. He watched McGavock's arrival gravely, said: "Well I do declare! It's the snakeskin gentleman. Howdy, suh."

Mark Thatcher said: "I'm sorry, Jimmy, but this is personal. I'm going to have to ask you to leave us alone."

Kitchell got to his feet, ambled lugubriously toward the door.

McGavock ruminated a moment, said: "If I'm going to start to work tomorrow, I'd better get all lined up. Now your letter said you wanted me to find out about some stolen cattle, and investigate your brother's death—in that order of importance. We'll take the cattle first. What about them?"

THATCHER LOOKED BLANK. "I don't know what about them, and that's the God's truth. After Lew died last week, I was going through his papers, paying his debts and so forth, and I found this bill from Keenan's Feed Store. A milking stool and feed and other bovine impediments. Now Lew never owned any cows. I searched his stable to no avail. My first reaction was that there must be some kind of error. The story got around town and one day I got a phone call from Mrs. Vevay. She—"

"And who is Mrs. Vevay?"

"She's better known by her first name, Golden. She's not a person you'd be interested in, though. Well, Mrs. Vevay said she'd heard about my befuddlement and called to tell me it was really true. Lew had bought three Jersey cows over in Swanson county just before he died. Now here's the astounding thing. She claims that she herself conducted the deal, delivered the cows, according to Lew's direction, at his stable, in the dead of night, and that if they're not on hand, they've been stolen."

"Don't worry, we'll run this business down." McGavock smiled. "Mr. Mark, you are a man who enjoys the color of his money, as don't we all. I've got a bit of good news for you. While I'm here in Ashton, I'm working for you at half price!"

Thatcher's cheeks cupped greedily, his wispy goatee reared itself avidly. Then he looked a little worried. "What's the catch? Maybe the agency in Memphis just sent me a low-grade detective, is that it?"

"No," McGavock said. "I'm very high-grade. It's not that. It's just that Mr. Gregory and his wife are taking part of the financial burden from your shoulders. Yes, sir, they're sharing the expenses, fifty-fifty!"

Out popped Client Thatcher's cheeks. He boggled angrily. "None of that! No, sir, we'll have none of that!"

McGavock wheedled. "But they're good people, aren't they? What's your objection?"

"Ralph Gregory is a very sorry human indeed, as you will discover. Jenny, my niece, is a dear sweet child, a little highly seasoned perhaps, but I've taken care of her in the past and will continue to do so in the future."

"Hasn't her husband a job?"

"I'm referring to Jenny's own personal income. I don't care to go into the matter."

"Of course," McGavock said sanctimoniously. "Far be it from me to pry. You're interested in those three missing cows, Mr. Mark. To be honest, it's the death of your brother that intrigues me. There's something alluring about the idea of homicide, isn't there? You said in your letter that he was probably slain with balderdash. Now balderdash, as everyone knows, is a mixture of cheap liquors. Would you care to amplify?"

Thatcher was impressed. "You appear to be very astute, despite your irritating mannerisms. Yes, by balderdash, though I used the word loosely, I meant cordial."

McGavock waited. Thatcher said: "Lew had heart trouble, bad. That part of it was perfectly true. Medical charts from a dozen big-town specialists will bear that out. Well, not so long ago he had an attack and a few days later, last week, he had another. This second one was critical. He went around to Dr. Powell's little hospital. It cleared up, or appeared to, and at Lew's insistence he was allowed to come back home. The first night home, he died."

McGavock raised his eyebrows politely.

"He had no servants, and being worried about him being across the street there, all alone, I worked out a system of communication with him. His bedroom was upstairs, at the front, and his bed was by the window. If anything should go wrong, he was to hang his bedlight out the window by its cord.

I couldn't miss it. That very night, about eleven thirty, before I'd retired, he did it. I went flying over. He was there on the bed, almost in a coma. He talked though, a little."

"What did he say?"

Thatcher was somber. "He said he'd been killed by drink. That surprised me. Lew was always a militant teetotaler. Well, I gave him a good tongue lashing—"

"You scolded him?"

"Certainly. I knew he was dying so I told him it was a disgrace to meet his Maker with whiskey on his breath." Thatcher looked self-righteous. "Then he told me it wasn't whiskey he'd been drinking, but cordial. He said they'd given it to him and explained that it was good for his heart. Boysenberry cordial."

"Maybe he said poison berry?"

"No, I quizzed him on that. He was quite definite."

"Who gave the stuff to him?" McGavock looked at his wristwatch.

"I was so annoyed at what I thought was his moral lapse that I forgot to ask him. He slipped into an unconscious state and never came out of it. Dr. Powell attributed death to a bad heart. I think it was morphia."

"Why?" McGavock scowled. "Do you know more about medicine than this Powell?"

"No, I don't. But I do observe things. There was no glass in the room. If Lew was done away with, the murderer must have brought his own bottle of cordial, must have taken the glass downstairs, washed it and put it in the cupboard."

"Or taken it from the house with him." McGavock changed the subject. "This fat man, Jimmy Kitchell, is he a good friend of yours?"

"Quite to the contrary. I find him most revolting. He bested me in an important business deal some time ago. Since then he constantly comes around, trying to ingratiate himself back into my good graces. I despise him."

McGavock asked: "When you write letters, do you stick them in the mailbox by the gate for the postman to pick up?"

"That's right. I'm a man of habit. I always attend to my correspondence before I retire."

"Thanks," McGavock said. "Good night."

3

Mr. Gregory's Acousma

THE GREGORYS, McGAVOCK learned, lived on the south edge of town. He had no trouble at all in locating them.

The small stone cottage lay back in a crescent of neat lawn flanked by formal poplars, sepulchral and rigid in the moonlight.

The girl who answered his knock was a pretty little brunette in her early twenties.

McGavock said: "Mrs. Gregory? Fine. I'm a detective brought to town by your Uncle Mark. I'd like to talk a bit with you—confidentially. Is it possible?"

"It's possible," she said placidly. "Come in. I'll call Ralph, Mr. Gregory." She stepped back, showed him into a cozy living room, indicated a huge overstuffed chair. "Did you know we had another murder tonight? Dr. Powell has just been found dead, in his study. Sheriff Durbin got an anonymous telephone call and there he was—"

"Get Ralph," McGavock said pleasantly. We'll thrash this all out together."

She left the room. McGavock attempted to estimate the household's income. The furniture was fair enough, but inexpensive. The walls were tastefully hung with excellent water colors. He'd just finished his inspection when Jenny Gregory returned with her husband in tow.

Ralph Gregory was a youngish, slightly balding lad in

worn brown tweeds. He put out a good handshake, firm and calloused, and his tan, weathered face was creased about the corners of his eyes with a network of crow's-feet. He seemed highly interested in McGavock. "A detective, eh?" he said. "Brother, you've come to the right house. I'm in a jam."

"How so, friend, how so?" McGavock grinned.

"A mysterious female voice phoned me the other night. Jenny's burning. I thought I recognized this party, and yet I couldn't quite place her. It was some kind of joke. She wanted to sell me half interest in three Jersey cows."

Jenny Gregory flushed. "Cows? Malarkey!"

"I wouldn't stand for it a minute, Mrs. Gregory," McGavock said solemnly. "It might have been a wrong number, but I wouldn't stand for that either." He paused. "Uncle Mark feels that his brother Lew was deliberately eliminated. From the looks on your faces, the idea doesn't come as a surprise. Now before I start on a case, I always like to lay in a little background about my client. He tells me he doesn't care much for you, Ralph, but that in the past he's contributed to the upkeep of this beautiful niece of his. Just what does he mean by that?"

Ralph Gregory waggled his hand at his wife. "You take it from here, Jenny. It's too delicate a subject for me to tackle."

The little brunette nodded. "First we'll take Ralph. When I married him, my uncles put up an awful howl. He wasn't good enough for a Thatcher. He didn't know how to hold a salad fork—I taught him. Then it was his clothes. They said he dressed like a wild man. I taught him a little about clothes, how to tie his cravat, and so on. And still my uncles weren't pleased. By then we began to get the idea they simply didn't like him."

McGavock asked: "Does he have kale?"

"No," Gregory said, "no money, but a pure heart, a wholesome nature, and aspirations."

The girl ignored him, said throatily: "My uncles were all right, just misguided. All my life they've cared for me. About ten years ago my grandfather died. He was an exceedingly wealthy man. He left no will. My parents had both died previous to that. The only heirs were Uncle Mark and Uncle Lewis, with me coming in for a possible minor share. Well, they never settled the estate—"

McGavock coughed politely. She spoke quickly: "I know you think that sounds bad, but it's done every once in a while in families that get along all right together. Now listen to this. From the very moment that my grandfather died, they began dividing the income from the estate in three ways—a third for each of my uncles and a third for me. When I became of age, I got my third, no questions asked, and annually since then I get the same proportionate disbursement. I've no kick coming there, have I?"

McGAVOCK DIDN'T ANSWER. After a moment, he said: "Do you have any Boysenberry bushes?"

They chimed in together: "No."

Ralph then said: "I don't think there are any in town. Why?"

McGavock said intimately: "There's a fellow been pestering me since I hit Ashton. A Jimmy Kitchell. What do you know about him?"

They both laughed. Jenny said: "Don't tell me that Uncle Mark brought you here to pin something on Mr. Kitchell!" The two of them seemed to be enjoying some sort of secret joke.

McGavock looked attentive. "What's the gag? Let me in on it."

"It's Deacon Witherspoon," the girl answered. "Haven't you heard about him? Here's the story. A few years ago, Ashton put in a watertower. The engineers from the capital came out and looked over the land, trying to decide where to drill the well. They narrowed their selections down to two choices—Dowdell's Hollow, just north of town, and the meadow out by Sycamore School. They said there was a good pool under the ground in both places, and both were in easy piping distance of the hill where they were going to put the tank."

"So?"

"Dowdell's Hollow belongs to my grandfather's property. Uncle Mark tried to close the deal but failed. The town bought the Sycamore land—that's where the pump is now. The Sycamore meadow was owned by Jimmy Kitchell."

So that was the business deal Mark Thatcher had referred to. McGavock asked: "But it couldn't have brought much?"

"Only about five hundred dollars. But you evidently don't know Uncle Mark. Five hundred dollars is a staggering sum to him."

"Who," McGavock asked, "is this Witherspoon? How does he tie into the affair? Where does he live?"

"You'll have a pretty hard time locating him," Jenny Gregory answered. "I imagine he's disintegrated. He shuffled off this mortal coil about a hundred years ago. Why don't you ask Uncle Mark? He'll give you all the details."

"Phooey," McGavock said reprovingly. "You kids are just shoving me around because I'm a city slicker. You better watch out or I'll get mad and go back to Memphis. Then you'll be sorry. You need me." He stood up.

Ralph Gregory said quickly: "Don't pay any attention to

Jenny, Mr. McGavock. We'll help all we can. As a matter of fact, I'd like your professional advice myself. Have you ever heard of acousma?"

"Sure," McGavock retorted carelessly. "I guess everybody knows about good old acousmas. It's an auditory hallucination, an imaginary noise. What about it?"

"I'm subject to them. That's all. I'm daffy."

The girl began to look troubled. Gregory explained: "A couple of days after Lew Thatcher died, I was in his old house, seeing what was what. We've been toying with the idea of moving in the old place. It's a little Victorian, but much more roomy than where we are now. Uncle Mark wasn't enthusiastic about the plan, but he didn't say no, so I thought I'd give the joint a critical once-over. It was at night—"

McGavock asked: "Will this take long? Shall I sit down?"

"It was at night. I'd got the keys from Uncle Mark and had let myself in by the back door. I'd inspected the downstairs, had gone upstairs. I was in Uncle Lew's master bedroom when I heard the noise. This was the first time I'd ever been in the old mansion and I was so interested in gazing around that I hardly realized I'd heard anything. About five minutes later my brain registered it, in a kind of delayed response. There had been a low creaking sound, not like the noise made when someone steps on a floorboard, but as if two polished sticks had been rubbed together. It had come from the room directly across the hall. I went over and investigated."

"A very foolish thing to do. You should have hightailed."

"The room was empty except for an old broken-down sofa and one of those big, old-time wardrobes. I experimented with the sofa—no squeak. I swung open the doors of the wardrobe—no squeak there. On the way out, I even tried the door to the room, with the same negative result. You see, it was all in my mind. It worries me. I can still hear it just as plain—"

McGavock made gestures towards his head with his hat. "I'll be getting along. I imagine I'll be seeing you folks again."

THE COURTHOUSE WAS deserted. McGavock wandered through the corridors, looking for the sheriff. He found the sheriff's office, at the end of the hall, but the door was locked and there was no light. It was just as well, he reflected. He wasn't sure he was quite ready to talk to the local law. He sauntered out of the building, down the broad stone steps, and dropped onto a park bench in Court Square.

The air was balmy and pleasant. With night, a crisp, sweet breeze had come down from the hills. Though it was scarcely nine o'clock, the town was closing up for the night. A shaggy hill-nag pulled a solitary, rickety buggy down the uneven street, bound for the timber and home. The rectangle of dingy shops about the square was lonesome-looking, derelict of movement. Here and there a feeble night light burned in a store, but for the most part Main Street was blacker than the inside of a hoot owl's egg.

It wasn't long before McGavock noticed the little glow of red. Across the street, in an alley mouth, someone was smoking a cigar and watching him. This made him bull-mad. He controlled himself with difficulty. After a moment, a huge sloppy figure detached itself from the shadows, ambled awkwardly across the square toward him. Once more—Mr. Jimmy Kitchell.

Wordlessly, Kitchell seated himself on the bench beside

McGavock. He tossed the stub of his stogy into the dry magnolia leaves at his feet, produced another, struck it to flame. In the light of the match his stubbled, piggish jaw sparkled like tinsel. His eyes intent on the operation, he blew out the tiny bulb of flame, said vaguely: "Glad I ran into you. Ashton gets a might lonesome at night. Being an ex-chief of police, I can't sleep. Would you like to walk around while I point out the sights? It might be entertaining to you. I can show you where I arrested different fellers for doing different things. What do you say?"

McGavock was bleak. "I say get the hell out of here. When I want you, I'll send for you."

"Now what on earth do you mean by that?" The big man sucked and the cigar glowed. "You're just downright unsociable. Are you a F.A.T.U. man?"

"No. Don't tell me you're a bootlegger."

"Of course I'm no legger." Mr. Kitchell was highly indignant. "I'm just making sure before I offer you some Southern hospitality. I want you to meet a lady, a mighty fine, educated lady who enjoys the company of sporting gentlemen."

"Who is this lady?"

"Mrs. Golden Vevay. She runs a gambling and drinking establishment that caters to a very select and wealthy group of distinguished citizens. They ain't more than twenty fellers, all businessmen, who can get through her doors."

McGavock got up. "O.K. But I don't gamble. It always brings out the beast in me."

"Nobuddy's asking you to. This ain't the night that the club meets, anyway. I just want you to meet the lovely hostess, and maybe fight your way into a bottle of good red whiskey on the house."

About a quarter of a mile beyond the corporation line, a dirt pike forked off from the State Highway. In the crotch of these two roads was a small triangular yard, enclosed on all three sides by an eight-foot osage hedge. Trespassers were barred by a tall board gate that swung from timber gateposts.

The gates were chained. Kitchell thrust his hand through an aperture, dragged the chain forward so that a padlock came into view. He unlocked the padlock with a key from his watch pocket and they entered. Meticulously, the fat man relocked the gates behind him. McGavock said: "Don't tell me I'm a prisoner?" Kitchell chuckled tolerantly.

There was hardly a blade of grass on the lawn. The bare clay was rutted in the crisscross pattern of many automobile tracks. Directly in the center of the open space was a foul-looking stucco cottage which stood a couple of feet above the ground on log stilts. The steps to the front door were of new pine planking. In the moonlight, McGavock could see that the roof had been patched and repatched with many-toned tarpaper. The detective followed the fat man up the steps into the building.

They were in a small parlor. McGavock stared about him with interest. To his surprise, the place was scrupulously clean. Five chairs, of assorted ages and styles, were pulled up to an old-fashioned circular library table with a green felt cover. The floor was laid with red linoleum, the two windows shrouded with heavy lace curtains decorated with a froth of frills and appliqued pink silk butterflies. On the wall was a flowered motto which said, HOME SWEET HOME. Lined up on a little shelf above a cordwood heater-stove were two silk pillows, one saying DAD AND MOM, the other with the greeting,

Hello from Lookout Mountain! Impressed, McGavock took off his hat.

A woman came through a doorway at the rear. She was about forty years old, not much over five feet in height, and as plump as a partridge. She was dressed quietly, but expensively, and in the latest style. Her fine flaxen hair shimmered in highlights and, astonishingly, there was a tremulous sort of beauty in the doll-like delicacy of her chubby face. She smiled, said: "Good evening, James." She went to the table, drew out three chairs, arranged them in a sociable grouping. "Glad to see you. Sit down."

They followed her suggestion. Kitchell spoke formally. "Golden, this is a gentleman from out of town. He's got time on his hands. How about a drink?"

She gave McGavock a flash of white teeth. "Lots of us here in Ashton have time on our hands." She went to the stove, opened it, and came back with a quart of whiskey and a cruet of homemade catsup. At Kitchell's insistence, she tilted the bottle to her lips, took a quick swig of the catsup as a chaser, passed the paraphernalia to McGavock, who followed her example. The whiskey was red-hot popskull, but he was amazed at how pleasantly the catsup obliterated the gag. Kitchell took the bottles from his hands, joined in.

FOR ABOUT TEN minutes hardly anyone said anything. The two bottles went the rounds three times. Finally, McGavock broke the ice. "I'm Luther McGavock, a private detective," he said. "I'll tell you something if you guarantee it won't go any further—" They both nodded. "Good. It's this. I'm working for Mark Thatcher."

Mrs. Vevay made a maidenly gesture. "Maybe I'd better leave if you men want to talk."

"No, stay." McGavock went on seriously: "I'm here working on a murder case—that's one thing. The other is a cattle theft. Mrs. Vevay, they tell me you are the one who brought those cattle in from Swanson County. What became of them?"

She grimaced. "How should I know? The whole thing is mighty funny, if you ask me. Lew Thatcher, the skinflint, paid me fifty dollars to go for those cows. Why me, a woman? A man would have done it for less than half!" She suddenly frowned. "What was that? James, didn't I hear something outside in the yard?"

Kitchell shook his head disparagingly. "Not likely, Golden. That gate and chain will keep out prowlers."

They passed the whiskey and catsup around again. McGavock said: "Yes, sir. In Dixie land I'll take my stand. Whoof. What were we talking about? Mr. Kitchell, how did you flimflam the Thatcher brothers on that city pump deal? What's this about a Deacon Witherspoon?"

They were plenty taut. Mrs. Vevay held up her hand for silence. "There it is again. It was scratching at the door."

Kitchell grinned nervously. "You're on edge, Golden. Ain't nothing outside, honey. No, Mr. McGavock, I didn't flimflam anyone. Did old Mark Thatcher say—"

Mrs. Vevay arose unsteadily. She lowered her voice to a hoarse whisper. "You men listen to me. It's outside the window now. I know. I've got ears like a cat. We're being eavesdropped."

She walked to the row of silken pillows on the shelf, pawed behind them, came out with a blue steel .38 in a man's work sock. She took off the sock, held the gun, butt first, to McGavock who was across the room. "Just go out and look around, and I'll feel better."

Kitchell was between McGavock and the woman, a little to her left. He reached out an enormous hand for the pistol, said good-naturedly: "We'll go, honey, if it'll make you easier. But—"

McGavock said sharply: *"Don't touch that gun. Kitchell!"*

The big man froze. He blinked, said: "What's got into you, Luther?"

"Don't touch that gun," McGavock repeated, "until you hear what I have to say. If anything should happen to me, they wouldn't like it back in Memphis. They know a little about you, Kitchell, in Memphis. I've wired them some interesting lowdown."

The fat man looked hurt. "What you talking about, Luther? You drunk?"

"Maybe. I didn't hear anything outside any window, and neither did Sister Vevay here. Could be a knockoff, couldn't it? Could be you're the triggerman and I'm the goat."

Kitchell looked exasperated. "Don't get unreasonable, McGavock. We're all good friends. We just—"

"Jimmy, me boy," McGavock said genially, "let me tell you what they know about you in Memphis. Client Mark Thatcher wrote his letter to us at night before he turned in, and stuck it in the mailbox by the gate. You were snooping. You examined the letter, saw the Atherton Browne Agency address and figured he was bringing in a detective. That's what you figured, but you wanted to know for certain. You used the old tracer gag."

Golden Vevay said coldly: "Really, Mr. McGavock, I must

ask you to leave. I maintain a refined establishment and you're getting boisterous—"

McGavock ignored her. "You went to the hotel to wait for me. From the hotel you sent a wire to the agency, a phony tracer. You said something like 'Detective hasn't shown up yet—when can I expect him?' You signed Thatcher's name, gave the hotel as the return address, and loafed around on the veranda, waiting to make a rush to the telephone. But Old Atherton Browne was too smart for you. He wired back that he didn't know what you were referring to. Nevertheless, you stayed around and gave me a cross examination when I hove in on the bus."

Mrs. Vevay said: "James, you and your friend had better leave me. I'm getting a headache." Kitchell's cheeks sagged. He said hoarsely: "Even if it was true, they couldn't prove it."

"It isn't forged telegrams they're after in Memphis," McGavock declared. "It's homicide. If the lady doesn't want us around, I guess we'll mosey along back to town, eh?"

Kitchell nodded dumbly. "Sure," he mumbled. "That's what I say. Good night, honey."

4

Mrs. Gregory's Quandary

SHERIFF TREGO DURBIN was that variant from the species, a highly talkative hillman. He was dressed in a doggy suit of brown sharkskin and wore a big beryl ring on his little finger. His pants had been home-pressed and had several overlapping creases running down the front of each leg. His cheeks were weathered and hollow, his hands and chest were scrawny to the point of malnutrition, but he didn't fool McGavock one minute. Sheriff Durbin was as tough as whit leather and as smart as a hungry fox. He said: "That's the way hit stacks up. I shorely appreciate yore jedgment on hit."

McGavock took off his purple pajamas, put on his shorts and shirt. He said sleepily: "When I heard your knock on the door, I could hardly believe it. I thought it was the hotel clerk with my breakfast. See me later, after I've had some food." He reached for his socks. "I don't know anything about any murder."

"Come around to the house," the sheriff suggested, "an' leave my woman dump out some scrambled eggs fer you. We'll tell her yo're from Hollywood and she'll go hogwild a-layin' out her fanciest vittles."

"I'd like to," McGavock answered blandly, "but I'm not allowed to accept free meals while I'm on a job. I guess I'm awake now. Let's get this straightened out. What's troubling you?"

"You are, fer one thing. We had murder last night and doggone if you didn't come to town, with yore nice yaller travelin' bag, jest in time for hit. In the memory of man, this-here is the fust murder that Ashton's ever had."

McGavock looked mildly surprised. "That's quite a record, isn't it?"

"It shore is, an' we're all mighty proud of hit. We've had election shootin's, an' bushwhackin's, an' jealousy killin's, an' all them things, but we never had no genuwine murder like this Dr. Powell business. I got a anonymous letter in the mail this morning claiming you was a detective an' saying that you was out at the doctor's place at the time of the death. We figure he was slew about sundown. Where was you at sundown?"

"I was right here at the hotel, out front on the veranda. I was chatting with Jimmy Kitchell. He can alibi me."

"Kitchell?" The sheriff didn't like it. "You playin' around with him?"

"It's all over now. We're mad at each other." McGavock put on his tie and coat, sat on the edge of the bed. "Forget that anonymous letter. It was written by the killer—it had to be. Either the killer or some troublemaker. Listen, Sheriff, answer me this—is there any big gambling going on here?"

The sheriff looked offended. "O' course not! They may be some pastime gamblin' down at the poolroom—fellers bets on them little balls amongst theirselves and hit's hard to get to—but they hain't no bigtime stuff in Ashton. I wouldn't stand for hit. Why?"

"I just wondered. Do you recall the name Deacon Witherspoon?"

"Witherspoon? They hain't nobuddy in town named— Oh, I

recollect now. Deacon Witherspoon hain't no gambler. In fack he hain't alive. He's been dead a hunnert years." The sheriff's eyes crinkled in silent laughter but when he spoke his voice was level and polite. "Somebuddy's been prankin' you because you come from the city. Lemme tell you about the Deacon."

McGavock said impatiently: "Please do. That's what I'm trying to find out."

"HIT ALL GOES back a few years, when Ashton was puttin' in a waterworks with tower an' all." The sheriff indulged in a bit of chimneynook gossip. "The experts from Nashville come out and looked over the land. They picked two places to drill—Sycamore School which was owned by Jimmy Kitchell, and Dowdell's Hollow which was owned by the Thatchers. The Hollow was a little closer to where they was going to put up the tank an' the deal was about closed in favor of the Thatchers when this old guy Witherspoon popped up."

McGavock waited. The sheriff took out a toothpick, began to pick his molars. "Back yonder, afore the War Between the States, they was a small log church in Dowdell's Hollow. Along in the seventies, the church was moved into town. Not the church, o' course, jest the congregation. The old buildin' was left to rot away—I remember playin' around it when I was a little chucklehead. Well, they's a old lady back in the hills, a Miss Donovan, who owns the original record book, afore the church moved. Some o' her kin were preachers. While the water deal was pendin', the editor of the county paper got an idee that he could make a news story out of the history of the de-funct Dowdell church. He went out to look at Miss Donovan's record book."

"And he found Deacon Witherspoon, eh?"

"That's right. An' printed about him in the paper and there was hell to pay. They was just a little mention of him. The church secretary had wrote down that on so and so day they'd went and buried Deacon Witherspoon alongside his dearly beloveds, in the shadow of the chapel where he had so devotedly served. Well that did hit."

McGavock puzzled. "I don't quite get you."

"Ever'buddy in Ashton had heered about the old church, but nobuddy had knowed they was a ole churchyard buryin' ground alongside hit! Graveyard water shore don't make healthy drinkin'. Town Council changed hits mind an' went an' bought Kitchell's property instead. The Thatchers hollered their heads off!"

McGavock said calmly: "Well, Sheriff Durbin, you've come to the right man. I'd be glad to go along with you on this. Maybe the two of us can break it."

The sheriff said smoothly: "Now don't get me wrong. I like you. Hit's jest that the taxpayers would want me to keep hit in our fambly. I'm gonna have to turn you down. This I will do, though. I'll offer you the freedom of the city, as long as you mind yore own durn business. No hard feelin's, McGavock."

"Of course not," McGavock smiled bravely. "It's just the vicissitudes of the profession. You can tell me this, though—were there any clues to Dr. Powell's unhappy—"

"He left a goofy letter." Sheriff Durbin looked cornered. "I been a-studyin' hit but I cain't make too much sense out'n hit." He brought out a big wallet from his hip pocket and McGavock got a split glimpse of a gunbelt and a big walnut-handled revolver. "See. Here she is." He held out the paper, the round robin forgery that he'd left on the doctor's desk.

He bent forward to look at it, clasped his hands behind his back. "I won't touch it, fingerprints, you know." He stared for a moment at the script, his own among the others, said impressively: "H-m-m! Very interesting. That's the first one of those I've seen this year."

Sheriff Durbin reddened. "What in hell are you talkin' about? What do you mean by that nutty remark?"

"That letter has been tampered with. It's what we call an interliner alteration. The postscript looks authentic enough, but the remainder has been monkeyed with. Look, even that *in* has been added to *sane.*" He pursed his lips. "You just read every other line: In regards to your husband's acousma, I've been doing a bit of extra curricular fieldwork,' and so on. The killer added the rest to reverse the meaning. Dr. Powell was telling this Mrs. Gregory that her husband was sane, the forger switched it around so that it says just the opposite."

Thunderstruck, Sheriff Durbin glared at the paper. Finally he said: "McGavock, I apologize. I've shore had a change of heart. By golly, I want you on my side."

McGavock answered piously: "Thank you, Sheriff, it'll be a pleasure." They walked out into the lobby, down onto the street. As they parted, McGavock said: "I'll be seeing you in your office, say, about one o'clock. O.K.?"

"O.K., Luther. I'll shore be there!" The letter in his hand, the sheriff hurried away, in search of the mayor.

KEENAN'S FEED STORE was in the alley just back of Main Street. The management would buy, sell, or barter, as the occasion demanded. It catered to countryfolk. McGavock wove his way precariously through the crated chickens, stacked high in the entranceway, entered the cool interior, fragrant with the sweet yeasty smell of grain and clover, musky with the odor of raw smallgame hides. He passed through an aisle of bulging burlap bags and packing boxes, located a small office at the rear. The proprietor, a freckled little man in blue denim and plow shoes, was seated straddle-legged across a bench, fiddling with a fish-hook on a catgut leader. Before him on the benchtop was a collection of feathers, quail and rooster and guinea, to say nothing of a piece of red flannel underwear and an assortment of dimestore costume jewelry. He looked up, said: "Hidy, brother. I'm jest about to invent hit, the foolproof trout-fly!"

McGavock said: "Good morning. Mark Thatcher sent me around to talk with you."

"He still gripin' about that statement I sent him?" The man on the bench picked up a quail feather, snipped off a piece of the red flannel, gathered them in a sort of a little corsage about a glass emerald stickpin, tied the conglomeration onto the fish hook. "That should do hit," he said in critical admiration. "They hain't nary a trout in Letcher County kin resist hit!" Before McGavock could retort, he pointed over his shoulder to a canvas ledger on a littered desk. "See for yoreself, brother. Page 37, fifth item down."

McGavock opened the ledger. On page 37, fifth item down, the entry said that on the 17th of the month Lewis Thatcher had purchased a milking stool, a milk bucket, feed, and salt, to be charged and delivered. McGavock said: "What's the salt for? Don't tell me he was aiming to barbecue these mysterious cows!"

"I kin see you don't know much about farmin', brother. This

salt is block salt. Hit comes compressed in small bricks. Stock raisers leave 'em in the field fer the cattle to lick."

"How long does one last?"

"That varies accordin' to rainfall an' sech. Mebbe a season. They melt, but they don't melt as fast as table salt."

"Is it poison to humans?" McGavock asked.

"Lawsey no! I wouldn't want to eat hit, but hit wouldn't poison anybuddy. You go back an' tell Mark Thatcher what I done told him myself a dozen times. Lew called me on the telephone an' ordered that stuff. I even delivered hit jest like he wanted. I delivered hit at night. I put the milkin' stool an' feed, an' so on, in the barn. I carried the salt blocks out in the pasture behind the house and set them in the fence corners."

"I'll tell him," McGavock agreed. "But he's a hard man to convince."

The town was full of hillfolk in for Saturday excitement. Buggies and wagons lined the curb. A little knot of people had gathered in front of the post office and McGavock, curious, slowed up.

A hand-lettered sign in the post office window said, *SALE—Letcher County Ladies Uplift and Helping Hand Society.* So that was it, a country bazaar. Inside, he could see a plank trestle table loaded with pies and cakes and doughnuts, with canned fruit, with golden squash and watermelons and nosegays. It made him a little homesick for something he'd missed. He was standing there on the cracked pavement, indulging in a light recreational mood of self-pity when Jenny Gregory walked up behind him. She brushed his elbow with her hand, said in a whisper: "Follow me."

He caught her reflection in the grimy window, stood rigid until she had passed, and then dropped into step behind her.

She walked about five blocks, out of the business district, turned down a side street and stopped before a small boxlike frame building set flush to the pavement in a vacant lot.

Across the side of the building, in four-foot letters, was painted, THE ROSELAWN CAFE. Mrs. Gregory took a key from her purse, unlocked the door, and entered. McGavock lagged a moment, followed her inside. He shut the door behind him, said: "Nobody knows we're here—nobody but the whole town."

It had been a long time since the place had been used. There were several tables with wire-backed chairs, a counter, some empty shelves. Dust was an inch thick. The girl said: "This is one of the Uncle Thatcher enterprises that didn't pan out. If anyone catches us, we'll say that you are a barbecue tycoon with the impulse to expand. Pretty slick, hey?"

McGavock said venomously: "I won't bother to answer. What brings this on? This is bad business. Let's get it over."

SHE WAS PRETTY, all right, and trim and neat in that little-girl print frock. She studied him gravely with level hazel eyes. He wiped the dust from the seat of a chair with his handkerchief and she sat down. She placed her ankles and knees together, folded her hands in her lap, said: "I want to talk to you. I'm in a quandary. My husband and I love each other, but sometimes I think I'm just a trial and a tribulation to him. Is there an easy, non-scandalous way of getting a divorce that would protect him in the eyes of the public?"

"Why, sure," McGavock said heartily. "Just sneak back into the hills some night when he's asleep, crawl into a cave, live there for twenty years or so on earthworms and mushrooms—

and he can slap an Enoch Arden on you. Now I'll be getting along."

She flushed. "Don't you want to hear all about it? Such as why I'm a trial to him?" McGavock looked bored. She went on: "I'm very conservative, really, and domestic, but I somehow give him the impression of being flighty and too social-minded. Take that sale around at the post office. All the prominent ladies in town are connected with it. I'd like to be there right now."

"Then why aren't you?"

"I have a feeling Ralph wouldn't approve—because of the way he acted the last time."

"I'll bite," McGavock said. "How did he act?"

She smiled bravely. "It's so personal, I'll have to keep it locked in my bosom. Maybe when I get to know you better—"

McGavock said silkily: "Mrs. Gregory, what you need is financial advice. According to my talk with you last night, your husband's a pauper. Why don't you throw a little coin his way now and then? It might get that hunted look out of his eyes. Maybe even set him up in some small business. Give him a chance."

She looked hurt, but her jaw went granite hard. "Everything I have is his, and he knows it. We have a joint bank account. And he's perfectly welcome to draw on it if he should ever need anything. But what could he need? He can charge his clothes at the dry goods store, I feed him, and he can charge his tobacco at the grocery store. He can go in and get a coke whenever its real hot and I keep him supplied with razor blades. Good gracious, he's living in clover! I bet that even makes your mouth water, doesn't it?"

"It does at that. It makes me slaver."

Her voice icy, she added: "And he actually has an income of his own. Not large but appreciable. He owns fishing privileges in a small lake over in the other part of the state."

"Then why doesn't he buy his own tobacco?"

"I don't think you're being particularly sympathetic about this, but I'll answer you. I told you we had a joint account. He puts his money in with mine, as is obviously only fair."

"And you pay him off in cokes and merit badges. Was this Uncle Lew's idea?"

"It was. And everybody's happy. I think you're being difficult about it. How did we get on the subject anyway?"

"Would that give Husband Ralph a motive for murder?"

She cast down her eyes. "Yes. A motive, but—"

McGavock gave the conversation a twist. "I've been thinking about Ralph's strange experience in Uncle Lew's house, you know, the acousma. Have you seen the sheriff in the last hour? Has he showed you the proper way to read Dr. Powell's dying letter? The doctor was saying that your husband was perfectly sane."

"Yes. It was a little intricate, the way Sheriff Durbin explained it, but I certainly agree. Of course Ralph's sane. I have a personal theory that, looking at it one way, everyone in the whole world is actually sane. You see—"

"Oh, sure." McGavock flagged her down. "Now that we're taking down our hair, I'd like to find out a few things for myself. Ralph said last evening that he heard this noise while he was going over Lew's house with an eye to moving in. Now what happened that you people changed your minds on that score?"

"We haven't changed our minds. We're moving in as soon

as the place is redecorated. Uncle Mark wants to touch it up here and there with a bit of paint first. It may take a week, or six, but when he gets through we'll occupy—"

"Who's doing the painting for Uncle Mark?"

"Why, he's doing it himself. It's more economical that way."

"And pennies have a strange fascination for Uncle Mark." McGavock nodded. "However, there's something wrong with this picture. Here's the way you explained it last night. Your grandfather died and left a big estate. The settlement hung fire. There were three prospective heirs, your uncles and yourself, Your uncles divided the income and gave you a third. Right?"

"That's true. They were very scrupulous on that point."

"Now that Lew Thatcher is dead, you're in for a half. O.K. Now if Brother Mark, my client, is so—er—formal about cash on the barrelhead, how come he breaks down and offers you the place rent-free?"

"Oh, he doesn't. We couldn't expect that. We're to pay rent. He pays rent for his place, too."

"But look here. There are just two houses, and two heirs. The houses are exactly alike, have the same appraisal value. Why can't one heir take one house, and the other go and do likewise?"

She stood up. "It's not that simple, the way Uncle Mark explains it. I own half of his house and he owns half of mine. So we must each pay rent to keep the records straight. Uncle Mark is fanatic about records."

McGavock put his hat on his head with the flat of his palm. He said rudely: "I'm going now. Give me at least five minutes before you show. And don't waste my time like this again. I'm a busy man."

5

Golden Vevay Meets Her Maker

THE SMALL PASTURE behind the late Lew Thatcher's residence was bare with shale outcropping, starved looking. McGavock made a round of the fence corners. There was no sign of the salt blocks the man in Keenan's Feed Store had spoken of, and no sign of cattle dung, either. Just shale and Bermuda grass and prickly pear. He left the field and made for the rear of the big brick house. It was high time, he decided, that he have a look around the place for himself.

On the back porch were several buckets of paint and brushes. He glanced at them, tried the china knob, and found the door unlocked. He stepped into the kitchen, listened, heard no sound. Painter-client Mark Thatcher was evidently taking this day off. McGavock had decided to give the place a thorough searching, from roof to cellar, and the best way to do this, he felt, was to begin with the attic and work down. He took the back stairs to the second floor, located a second flight at the end of the upstairs hall.

The attic, itself, proved to be of little interest. It was a long, narrow, empty room which appeared to run the entire length of the building, just under the roof. A rough ladder, nailed to the south wall, led to the roof, dormer windows looked out over the street in front. The ceiling and walls were covered with stained, dank paper, the floor was tongue-and-groove planking. He had a feeling that there was something wrong here, but he couldn't place it. Finally he gave it up, dismissed his suspicions as being unfounded, and descended to the second story.

Here he found a big bathroom with a new bathtub, an unused bedroom, a sort of upstairs study, and at the front, just as Brother Mark had described, the master bedroom where Brother Lew had died. It was a creepy layout indeed with its mouldy red brocade drapes, its high tester bed, and ornate gilt bric-a-brac. There was nothing of importance here, either.

Across the hall, according to Ralph Gregory, was the room from which the acousma had originated. McGavock crossed the hall.

The room was precisely as Gregory had pictured it to him. Uncarpeted floor, empty but for a large old-fashioned wardrobe which stood between two tall windows, and reached from the baseboard almost to the ceiling. Gregory had said that the eerie noise sounded as if two sticks were being rubbed together, a squeak and yet not a squeak. McGavock swung the wardrobe door open on its hinges. It opened silently, closed silently.

There was no sense to it. The wardrobe was the only thing in the room, and yet it gave off no sound.

Suddenly the answer occurred to McGavock. The wardrobe was on casters. The entire closet had been moved. McGavock placed his shoulder against the wardrobe, swiveled it from the wall. The old casters gave off a rusty, ticking sound.

There was nothing whatever behind the wardrobe. If anything had ever been there, it had been moved.

McGavock shoved back the big cupboard, went down to the ground floor. He made a painstaking inspection of the dining room, kitchen, library and parlor, discovered nothing.

It was in the cellar that he made his big strike—the best break that had come his way since he'd been on the case.

As cellars go, it wasn't much. It was more of a hole under the kitchen. There was no light, so McGavock used his flash. Lacy tree roots had groped through the crevices in the stone walls, hung in the darkness like gnarled festoons. The dirt beneath McGavock's feet was hard-packed and dry, crusted with time. He played his torch about him. Nothing but the moist, white-washed walls, the raftered ceiling, the vile stench of long disuse. And then, from a far corner, his beam picked up a flickering, silver glint of reflected light. He walked over to investigate.

It was a new tin can. A can of white corn syrup, such as you put on pancakes, and it was almost full. Beside it, on the earth, were three splotches of candlegrease. McGavock remembered the candle-end in Dr. Powell's pocket.

The detective dropped to his haunches, sat on his heels, and studied the objects in brooding concentration. And then he noticed that the ground had been disturbed. He stirred the loose earth with his hand, uncovered a tiny bottle. The label had been scratched from it. Holding his flash behind it, he saw that it contained a bright red liquid, like red ink, or mercurochrome. He uncorked it, smelled it. It was odorless.

Grinning to himself, he laid it back in its hollow, smoothed the dirt. He was beginning to see the answer to a good many things. So that was the story behind this business!

It might prove fruitful, McGavock decided, to have a little talk with Mrs. Sheriff Durbin. Not with the sheriff this time, but with his good woman.

McGAVOCK LEFT THE house, as he had entered, by the rear. He'd circled the building, was going down the front walk, when he observed Client Thatcher across the street, fiddling around in his yard. Uncle Mark was down on his scrawny hands and knees, with a paring knife, cutting dandelions out of the lawn. When the detective hove into view, Thatcher jerked his goateed chin to one side, pretended not to notice. If he doesn't want to see me, McGavock decided, then I'd better see him.

He rounded the corner, advanced across the grass. He said loudly, jocularly: "Why, Mr. Thatcher, I'm surprised. Engaged in manual labor—a man of your great wealth and exalted position. You could get a smart chimpanzee to do that for you at ten cents an hour!"

Thatcher stood up with effort, brushed off his trousers, said severely: "Mr. McGavock, please don't yell at me. It's not in our contract. You're a little late, aren't you? Our appointment was for nine sharp." He reared back sternly. "You've committed a breach of agreement and I'm afraid I'll have to penalize you two dollars for your negligence. You see—"

McGavock spoke with adulation, said flatteringly: "Mr. Thatcher, you're the stingiest client I've ever had. I bet you didn't get that way overnight. I bet you learned it the hard way!"

"My boy," the old man answered, "I'm not stingy, I'm thrifty. I'm the custodian of a great estate. I owe it to my beloved father and my beloved brother to keep this accrued wealth intact. On sunny days I work about the yard. When the weather's inclement I retire indoors to paint and repair and polish. Every dandelion out of the lawn enhances the property, every bit of painting contributes to its value, every bit of carpenterwork increases—"

"Sho', sho'." McGavock nodded agreeably. "You make it sound attractive. I wish I had some property to slave over.

And while we're on the subject of interior decorating, I've just come from the house across the way. I was wondering why you started with the floor in your brother's bedroom. I see you've given it a shiny coat of nice black paint."

"Do you like it?" Thatcher seemed pleased. "That's just the beginning. I'm going to do that entire room over. Lew's gone and there's no sense grieving over him. That's the way he'd want it. Remembrances of death can be pretty trying. I'm going to—"

"I think I see your point. By the way, can you keep a secret?"

Mark Thatcher, for a moment, seemed almost human. The corners of his mouth quirked downwards, his eyes twinkled. "Indeed I can, sir. I've kept quite a few in my day. What is it you wish to confide?"

"It's this. I went out last night and did a little roaming around. I heard that this Golden Vevay, the gal who was mixed up in your brother's peculiar cattle deal, runs a ritzy gambling joint for Ashton's firebrand sportsmen. Is this news to you?"

Thatcher pursed his lips, pondered a moment. "Yes, it is news. I can hardly believe it. I'd heard nothing about it, and I'm pretty well informed about local activities."

"Jimmy Kitchell said so."

"Then it's certainly true. It's the sort of a project about which he'd be informed. I'm sorry to hear it. Ashton's such a lovely little paradise—"

McGavock spoke casually. "I was wondering if, say, Brother Lewis had acquired the habit. It's a vice that has a strange lure and reaches into some strange places."

"No." Mark Thatcher shook his head with finality. He showed no resentment whatever. "Lew wasn't a gambler. He couldn't have hidden it from me if he was. It would have cost him money, and I handle our account books. Any defalcations on his part would have been immediately apparent."

McGavock said obliquely: "Ralph Gregory, they tell me, has a small income. They say he owns fishing privileges on a lake somewhere in the other part of the State."

"So I've heard. It's a most peculiar way to earn a living, isn't it? However, if you're intimating that his income is derived from gaming, I must ask you to disabuse your mind of that idea. It isn't likely that Jenny would condone it."

"And Jenny's a Thatcher, and the Thatchers know everything, eh? Well, that's one way of looking at it."

McGavock's gaze traveled upward to the roof of Mark Thatcher's home, then turned and studied the roof across the street. They were identical, built in the style of the early 1900s—hipped, with a small platform at their peak, a platform surrounded with a little wrought-iron railing. The detective said: "Now here's a question for the grab-bag. Your house is like your brother's, isn't it?"

"In every detail, yes."

"Describe your attic."

"My attic? Why, it's empty."

"Describe it anyway."

Thatcher looked irritated. "That's rather foolish, it seems to me. However, if you say so." He closed his eyes. "Let's see. The floor is bare. The walls and ceiling are a patchwork of old wallpapers—you know, odds and ends left over from previous downstairs jobs. There's a ladder that leads to the roof and some dormer windows. Is that any help?"

"No. Frankly, it isn't. How do I get to Sheriff Durbin's from here?"

Thatcher told him, added: "I hope you're not in any sort of partnership with the sheriff in this sad affair. You may make discoveries of a highly confidential nature, and Durbin's a little too garrulous for my taste."

McGavock turned on his heel, started down the walk.

Angered at this abrupt rudeness, Thatcher called out: "You heard my warning. Stay away from Sheriff Durbin! He's a dunderheaded numbskull!"

McGavock stopped deadstill in his tracks. He leered, said blusteringly: "What did you call me?"

Thatcher was taken aback, answered nervously: "I didn't call you anything, Mr. McGavock. I was speaking of Sheriff Durbin. I said—"

McGavock made his face a mask of fury "You called me a dunderheaded numbskull. I'm forced to consider that a breach of agreement. I hereby penalize you two dollars and ten cents. You owe me a dime." He wheeled, headed down Cherry Street. He felt supremely happy.

IF SHERIFF DURBIN was wringing any graft from his fellow Letcher Countians, it didn't show up in his residence. The little white frame house was quaint, rural. A telephone wire ran to the gable but there was no electric wire. Evidently the Durbins preferred the good old-fashioned kerosene lamp. A grape arbor, lush and pleasant, afforded shade on the front porch, and another ran from the back doorstep to an outhouse. A gnomish-looking little woman in a voluminous apron and sunbonnet was drawing water into a cedar bucket at the well. McGavock took off his hat, said courteously: "May I assist you, ma'm?"

Mrs. Durbin said, "Thank you," handed him the pail. He carried it to the cool back porch. They seated themselves in hickory rockers. McGavock asked: "Is the man home?"

"No, sir. He's down to his office. Ashton's havin' itself some very bad trouble at the present an' the sheriff's got the runnin' fits. In, out, bing, bang. Kickin' the foot of his bed at night and yellin' out ballot counts. I do declare I sometimes wish I was back home in the hills where life is calm an' peaceful."

McGavock sighed sympathetically. "How true!" He watched the grape leaves in the breeze turning their smooth, silver-furred undersides this way and that. "The ladies are having a big sale at the post office this morning—"

"I know. I'm generally on hand. I shorely hate to miss—"

"Jenny Gregory was telling me she had a little difficulty with her husband the last time they—"

Mrs. Durbin looked indignant. "Why cain't menfolks leave us alone? Hit was a scandal an' a shame. Jenny's as sweet a child as ever was borned an' she's a-totin' a mighty heavy cross, a finicky husband. She baked a nice big layer cake with marshmaller icing. She'd hardly brought it in and went out when Ralph busted through the door, and bought it hi'self."

"Maybe he's got a weakness for marshmallow icing?"

"No. He cain't abide cake of any kind. I heard later, though I hain't know-ratin' no gossip, that he takened hit home and throwed hit out."

"That must have caused a fine domestic squabble."

"It hain't no jokin' matter." Mrs. Durbin looked outraged. "You know what we ladies think? We think he was ashamed of her cookin' 'cause she's so young. I swear, since that happened I cain't bear to gaze on Ralph Gregory!"

Her voice trembled with emotion. McGavock said: "It was just one of those things. I wouldn't get all het up over it."

"Oh, you wouldn't? Well, let me tell you somethin', young man, but keep hit under yore hat. Jenny Gregory cain't bake a cake. She can cook a mighty good meal, but cakes go flat on her. When she decided to give a cake to the sale, she brought the mixin's around an' asked me to do hit for her as a favor. They don't nobody know hit but the three of us, but I baked that cake! I get ribbons at the fairs for my cakes. I stood over a hot oven and then that Ralph Gregory—"

A grocery truck came rocketing around the corner. It made the turn on three wheels, bounced up over the curb and down, skidded to a stuttering stop in front of the house.

Sheriff Durbin piled out of the seat, came hurrying around the house. He was hatless, his hair was mussed, and he looked at McGavock with distraught, unseeing eyes. He brushed past them, into the kitchen, and reappeared with a big red-and-white checked tablecloth.

McGavock said: "Howdy, Sheriff. Don't tell me you're going on a picnic?"

The sheriff turned his head, spoke over his shoulder. "This hain't no picnic. They just found Golden Vevay's body at the bottom of a bluff jest south of town. I'm bringin' her to the undertaker—she's in the truck. I gotta cover her up. Hit's more decent thataway. You wanta come along with me?"

"No." McGavock answered grimly. "I've got other things to do."

6

The Mythical Deacon Witherspoon

THE DETECTIVE FOUND Ralph Gregory sitting on the front steps of his stone cottage. He was wearing an undershirt and a pair of baggy corduroy pants. On the lawn before him was a beautiful young Irish setter. The dog was frisking about in circles, watching Gregory's hands. Gregory heaved out a small block of wood, as large as a man's fist and studded with sharp brads. The dog raced after it, retrieved it. "He's just a pup," Ralph Gregory explained. "That teaches him to bite easy on birds. He likes it."

"Maybe so," McGavock answered doubtfully. "But I'm certainly glad I don't have to do it. My gums are tender. Is the wife in?"

"No, she isn't, McGavock. She's in town somewhere."

"Swell. Then we can talk. I've got personal questions to ask."

"Personal, eh?" Gregory's eyes crinkled thoughtfully at the corners. "I'm not so hot at answering stuff like that. I have a natural impulse to evade such issues. However, we'll see what we can do. Shoot."

"I'm going to put pressure on you," McGavock said amiably. "You'll see what I mean in a minute. First, we'll pick up a few tag-ends. Why did you gallop around to the ladies' sale some time back and buy up your wife's layer cake? That seems to trouble her a great deal."

"Man! When you detect, you really detect." He meditated

a moment. "Is that cake fracas tied up with this murder business?"

"You tell me."

"I'd say no. Nevertheless, here are the facts, just to be orderly. I'd heard that Uncle Lew Thatcher—he was alive at the time—was circulating around the village putting out the word that he was just a poor bachelor, cut off from his female kinfolk, meaning Jenny, and that whenever he wanted any of his niece's cooking he had to purchase it on the public market. He claimed he always bought Jenny's cakes. Well, my old pride rose up and I—"

"You're lying by the clock. And frankly, I haven't time to listen. Jenny doesn't bake cakes. She can't."

Gregory shrugged. "It's the best I can do on the spur of the moment."

McGavock said genially: "This isn't a parlor game, as you are about to find out, my boy. They tell me you have an income from some lake."

The young man looked nervous. He said rapidly: "It's nothing much, but in a way I'm pretty lucky. My folks, on my mother's side, owned some land and there was a lake—"

"Of course. What I want to know is where this lake is. What county, near what town—longitude and latitude. You're in a hole, son, and you'd better come clean."

"Oh." The young man studied the tips of his fingers. "I'm beginning to learn a little about big city detectives. So this is what you meant when you said you were going to apply pressure." His face looked strained, tired. "Presto, and it's all over, eh? You know, McGavock, you haven't been in town a day, and I think you've got me."

"O.K., then, I got you. Let's hear about that phantom income."

"McGavock, that income is blackmail!"

"Blackmail?"

"Yes, I'm pretty sure."

"You mean you're on the receiving end of a blackmail payoff and you still have doubts?"

Gregory took a deep breath. "To be charitable to myself, I like to think of it as involuntary blackmail, except for the obvious fact that I've been accepting it."

"Involuntary blackmail? I thought I'd heard of everything. Would you care to elucidate?"

"It started about a year ago, I guess, in a pretty devilish way." The young man's voice was low. "I got a letter from Nashville with a hundred-dollar cashier's check on a Nashville bank. The letter said that the money had been awarded to me because of my remarkable eyesight. That was all—just one little sentence signed with an illegible scrawl. Well, I was confused. I banked the draft for safekeeping and waited to hear further. Two weeks later I got another check, and this time the envelope was postmarked right here in Ashton. This letter was a different story."

"Let's have it."

"The letter said I was getting the money with the stipulation that I could forget anything and everything I might have witnessed between seven and eight, on the night of the 3rd. It said that from that letter on I would receive a check weekly, and that the payments would extend for one year."

"And that was a year ago?"

"Yes. I figure my next check will be the last."

McGavock said pointedly: "Now, I wouldn't want to ask you to break such a profitable arrangement, but would you consider—"

"You're wondering what happened on the evening of the 3rd? I'll be glad to tell you. If it looks like five thousand dollars a year to you, I wish you'd enlighten me. I was at Uncle Lew Thatcher's. In those days, Jenny was still attempting to placate the old gentleman and, shoes polished, hair neatly parted, I was on one of my periodic errands of humility. He let me in, in that grudging way of his, and we sat there in his study for an hour and chatted. He did the chatting, I did the listening. The conversation ran, as usual, to finances and family prestige, both of which I appear to lack."

"But what did you see?"

"I didn't see anything that I remember—until I got up to go. There was a folded newspaper on the desk and as I stood muttering my farewells, I happened to notice a sports item about a field trial for bird dogs. Without realizing what I was doing, I picked up the paper. When I started to replace it, I saw a dozen or so steel penpoints on the desktop, all laid out in a little row. Stub points, ball points, crow quills, all kinds. There was a small file there, too, and a piece of emery paper. I said: 'I never heard of filing down penpoints. And look, there's just about every style, too!' Lew passed it off with a shrug and said something about them belonging to Mark." Gregory paused. "From the way he said it, I had a feeling that he was lying."

McGavock frowned. "Did you say anything about it to anyone?"

"I think I mentioned it to Jenny when I came home, but she

wasn't interested." Gregory hesitated, asked quietly: "Would you like to hear my analysis of the thing?"

"Sure."

"It's simply that the whole affair's fantastic. Let's look at it logically. The only possible persons involved are Thatchers—one, two, or all, including Jenny. All right. For some reason, if that's true, they're buying me off at the rate of five thousand a year. Why? I'm in the family. The Thatcher clan is notoriously close-pursed and here they're tossing hundred-dollar bills into my lap like—"

"I hate to mention this," McGavock said, "but have you spent any of that kale? No? You banked it, but you've banked it in a joint account with Mrs. Gregory. If it's Thatcher dough, it's right back where it came from—if it's Thatcher dough, I say."

"If you're implying that I don't have the freedom of my own bank account, you're being just a little on the insolent side."

"And that's been said before, and better." McGavock smiled mirthlessly. "This is a bit more serious than you imagine. Say it was Uncle Lew who was sending those checks. Now he's dead, murdered in my book, and now, it just so happens, there'll be no more income. You said it was to last a year and the year's up. Do you see what this might mean?"

Gregory was ashen. "It gives me a motive for murder. It looks as though I had Lew in my talons and when he stopped paying off, I killed him to silence him! And it's all there, my deposits and everything, in the bank records."

McGavock said soberly: "How do I know that isn't exactly the case? In the meantime, don't tell anybody you've talked to me—and I mean *anybody!*"

SHERIFF TREGO DURBIN locked the door to his office, twisted the knob to test it, and started down the cool corridor at McGavock's side. They left the courthouse by the back, came out into a small combination hitching and parking lot. The sheriff reached languidly for a battered lard can, filled it at a cement watering trough and lugged it to the radiator of a powerful, gray coupé. Fastidiously, he carried the bucket back to the very spot on the dry earth from where he'd taken it, and joined McGavock on the car seat. He got the big job rolling, tooled it out of the narrow alley like an expert. McGavock sank back into the pneumatic leather cushions.

They rolled down Main Street, past the cotton compress, left the city limits. When they reached the tall osage hedge which enclosed Golden Vevay's yard, they turned from the State Highway, rambled onto the dirt fork.

McGavock sighed. "Good old Golden Vevay. What happened to her?"

"Was you acquainted with her?" The sheriff looked astonished. "Where'd you meet up with her?"

"I was a guest in her home last evening, suh. More about that later. What's the lowdown on—"

"Like I done tole you, we found her south of town, at the bottom of Jackdaw Cliff. Ever' bone in her pore body is busted som'eres. She was all dressed fer travelin'."

McGavock perked up. "No kidding?"

"That's right. Her little black bag was found a few feet from her corpse, with underclothes and stuff in hit."

"Was she carrying any money?"

"Yep. Had four hunnert dollars in big bills pinned under her arm. Does that make any sense to you?"

"It certainly does. Where is she now?"

"Where would she be? Why, at the undertakers. In the stockroom back of Lace Heppleman's general store. Lace is the Letcher County embalmer—"

The dirt road began a climb into the hills. They left the hickory and oak, turned left at a tiny frame school, and hit the ridge-road. They were in pine country now, sweet-smelling and silent. Finally, the timber broke and they could see a little hollow before them. Directly below them was a miniature cabin, its broad shingles weather-warped, the chinking crumbled from its rough log walls. The small, cupshaped depression was enfolded on all sides by the wild, steep hillsides. It was lonely, isolated, but the hollow and the cabin seemed somehow to McGavock to be proud and arrogant, sufficient unto itself. Sheriff Durbin said: "Put yore teeth in yore pocket, Luther. Here we go!"

He spun the wheel and the big coupé bucketed down the slope. McGavock's shoulders slapped against the back of the seat, his hat went over one eye. He grabbed blindly for anchorage, got a fuzzy prolonged impression of whipping brush and endless rose-and-silver sage and the car eased to a stop. "Here we are," Sheriff Durbin said calmly. "Get out."

Understandingly, the sheriff had pulled up a good fifty feet from the building. He called out: "Miz Donovan! Hit's me, Trego Durbin." There was no response. McGavock stared at the desolate, abandoned-looking little place, its one window webbed with cracks, vine tendrils prying loose mortar of the crude stone chimney.

The detective said: "Maybe she isn't at home?"

"Oh she's at home, all right, Luther," the sheriff insisted out of the side of his mouth. "She's jest a-doin' like she was brought up to do—hidin' from menfolks. A hill-lady always takes to the house when strange men come into view. They's city fellers that have drove all through the hills an' swear they hain't nothin' in the brush country but little boys an' men." He lowered his voice still further. "I see her now, dadrat her. She's a-peepin' out the corner of the window. I'll try once more." Woodenly, he yelled: "Oh, Miz Donovan! Hit's the Durbin boy. You recall me!"

A WOMAN APPEARED in the dog-run. Except for the fact that she wore a long cotton dress, you could hardly tell that she was a female. Her hair was done up on the top of her head under a knotted red handkerchief. She was gaunt-framed, with a long horse-face, lean and bronzed. She was bare-footed, and her feet, like her hands, were horny and knotted. She had an old Marlin .30-30 under her arm, and she held it just as politely as she could under the circumstances. She stared at the two men for a long moment, said at last: "I recall you now, Trego. Yo're from Two Chapel Hill. Yore mother was a Flannagan and yore pappy saw the light at the age of fo'ty-one. Come in an' set."

"Thank you, ma'm." The sheriff beamed.

"This is Mr. McGavock. He—"

"You mean McGannet, Trego, from over at Birdfoot Branch. I hain't laid eyes on a McGannet for years. When I was a girl, they was knowed as very trashy humans. But I'm not one to turn a leper from my door. Come in, come in."

The bedroom-parlor was feebly lighted, but clean. There were a few staunch chairs, a table, a pallet in the shadowed corner. Though the day was warm, a log smouldered in the fieldstone fireplace. The three of them seated themselves stiffly about the hearth. Sheriff Durbin said: "Miz Donovan, we come here to talk about that church record you've got. I've heerd about hit but I hain't never seen—"

For the first time, she smiled. "That book has give me a heap of bother lately. Yo're the second that's asked about hit in the last five year. Some time back the editor of the Letcher County *Journal* come out an' read it, an' went back an' printed all about hit in the newspaper. I've heered say hit caused quite a rumpus an' even had somethin' to do with Ashton's watertower. Shore, Trego, y'all can see hit."

There was a cabinet by the mantel, a cabinet filled with starfish and sea urchins and dusty, branching coral. She fumbled around in the gloom, came out with an old leather-bound book. McGavock took it from her hands, went to the window with it.

It was an authentic church record, that was certain, and an ancient one. One by one, he leafed through the dry pages of crisp, decaying paper, read the spidery brown script. For the most part the items were about church business—tithes, collections, births and christenings. Then he located the Witherspoon note. It said: *On this day, May 7th, 1847, we buried our good friend and brother, Deacon Witherspoon, beside his wife and loved ones, in the protecting shadow of the church he so devotedly served. Signed, P.K. Yarwood, Sec.*

It was the last inscription in the book. McGavock flipped back a few pages. It was a different secretary, too.

McGavock beckoned the sheriff to him, pointed out the page. "It's a forgery, Sheriff. He stuck it back at the end here since that was the only place he could sneak it in. He changed the secretary's name because, although he's a smooth penman, he didn't want to tackle all that fancy shaded script. Nope, Deacon Witherspoon never died—because he never lived. That's no obituary, anyway. An authentic record would say Deacon Tom, or John, Witherspoon."

Miss Donovan rose ghostlike from her chair. She took the book from their hands, restored it to its cabinet. "I didn't ask you-unses to come out here an' make light of my beloved relicks! That record has been in my fambly for nigh a hunnert year. If it sayeth Deacon Witherspoon died, then, 'y doggies, that's what he went an' did. An' no new-fangled smart alecks can change hit!"

The sheriff said hastily: "Jest a minute, Miz Donovan, jest a minute. What Mr. McGavock is tryin' to say is—"

Miss Donovan said coldly: "If yo're headin' back to town, don't leave me stop you."

As they climbed into the car, she said: "Yo're the sheriff, hain't you, Trego?"

"Yes, ma'm."

"Then why don't you keep yore own house in order? Why you meddlin' around back here where you hain't wanted?"

Sheriff Durbin was offended. "What you mean, ma'm, keep my own house in order? You referrin' to those killin's that—"

"No, I hain't referrin' to no killin's. I don't know nothin' 'bout no killin's, an' I don't want to. I'm referin' to that addle-pated courthouse you run. I been intendin' to call this to yore kind attention fer some time now. A while back I got a crazy letter from the courthouse at Ashton sayin' they was goin' to foreclose I my mortgage on a certain day. Well, I don't have nary a mortgage on nothin', as my Redeemer knoweth, so I walk to the State Highway an' ketch a bus on in. What do I find out? They hain't nobuddy at the courthouse wants to own up they sent that slanderous letter. I swear, I'm glad I don't live in the city where such goin's-on sap the very vitals o' them that—"

McGavock asked quietly: "Miss Donovan, when did you get this mortgage letter? Before or after the editor came out to see your record book?"

"I got hit about a week before, Mr. McGannet, if hit's any of yore business."

McGavock waved her good-by. He said: "O.K., Sheriff, get rolling. That does it."

THE DRIVE BACK to town started in a pained silence. Sheriff Durbin devoted his entire attention to handling his car. It was pretty plain that he was uncomfortable. After a while he spoke. "Durn them Donovans! The way they put on airs! They hain't one whit better than the Durbins, an' they ding-dang well know hit. I've heered my pappy say hit was a Donovan that stole the new window curtains back at Two Chapel when he was a young 'un. Yes, sir, a Donovan stole them nice new mail-order curtains to make his bride some petticoats. The secret come out when they had a fire an'—"

McGavock broke into the reverie. "I'd like to get back to Golden Vevay for a moment. Wasn't there anything in her overnight bag but clothes?"

"Nothin' but clothes, Luther."

"I see. Now what was in her purse?"

"Rouge an' lipstick an' cigarettes. Some small change an' a couple of one-dollar bills."

"That all?"

"Yep."

"Then there's something missing, something important." McGavock eyed his companion. "Aren't you all fired up over what we just discovered, over that Witherspoon forgery? You see what it means—"

Sheriff Durbin said reluctantly: "I hate to tell you, but I figger yo're all wrong on that. Witherspoon died a hunnert year ago. It's wrote there in the church book and church books are good enough for me."

"You better come in with me on this, if you want to catch your murderer. That item's a forgery, and a fluoroscope will show it up in a hurry. Here's the way our party worked it. He sent Miss Donovan a letter, just at the time they were deciding on the location for Ashton's water supply. The letter was phrased to make her mad, bring her flying into town—which it did. The forger stole into her house while she was away, and did his fancy penmanship."

"But why, Luther? Wait a minute, now. Kitchell had the Sycamore land an' the Thatchers had the Dowdell property. That fake entry condemned the Dowdell deal, and Kitchell sold his Sycamore place. You a-sayin' Jimmy Kitchell negotiated all that jest to make a little money?"

"There's more than a little money involved, Sheriff. But let's look at it another way. Maybe the Thatchers didn't want to sell."

"O' course they wanted to sell." The sheriff looked disgusted. "They was belly-achin' all over town when Kitchell beat them to it."

"You were here at the time, and know more about it than I do. But let me put it this way. Could the Thatchers really have sold?"

"Why not? They owned the Dowdell property, didn't they?"

"That's my point. Did they?"

"Sure they owned hit. Hit was part of the estate. O' course, they'd have to settle the estate to get a good negotiable title to it but—"

"That's all," McGavock said. "There's the solution to your case." He considered a moment. "When does Lace Heppleman, the undertaker, close shop?"

"Undertakin's jest pin money for him, a kinda hobby. He runs a general store. Locks up about nine. Why?"

"Meet me in the alley behind Lace Heppleman's at nine. And don't be late!"

7

Wired for Death

LUTHER McGAVOCK RETURNED to his hotel. He bathed, shaved, and put on clean underclothes. It had been a strenuous day and he was a little tired. The bath and shave picked him up considerably. He was alone in the hotel dining room, stowing away a succulent supper of black-eyed peas and stewed chicken, when Jimmy Kitchell came wandering in. The big man strolled over, pulled up a chair, and sat at McGavock's table, facing him.

McGavock first thought he was drunk, and then wondered if the man had been weeping. Kitchell spoke in a deep vibrant voice. "They've killed Golden Vevay, did you hear?"

"You mean the lady who put the bee on me last night? Yes, I heard."

"I'm not going to argue with you, McGavock. It may be that she really heard someone outside that window last night. It looks like it now, doesn't it?"

"Could be, I guess," McGavock replied.

"You bet. And you know what I think? I've got a hunch I'm next on the list!"

"Death has struck for the last time, Kitchell. Take my word for it."

Kitchell said heavily: "Golden Vevay never hurt anyone. She ran a gambling joint, but her games were square and she catered to a select clientele of respectable gentlemen. And they pushed her off a cliff. Ain't it awful?" His eyes filled up. "McGavock, I liked that woman mighty well. From the way I feel now, I guess I loved her. Yes, sir—"

McGavock said: "Tut-tut! Let's not—"

"I'm going to bury her out of my own pocket. I'm going to give her the best funeral that money can buy."

"I know she'd appreciate it, but why not let her pay her own way? She can afford it."

"You mean that four hundred dollars she had on her? Pshaw, that's not a drop in the bucket compared to what I aim to—"

"Listen, Kitchell," McGavock declared quietly. "You might have been in love with Vevay but you evidently didn't savvy her. She left plenty scratch."

Kitchell's liquid eyes searched McGavock's face. "I don't believe it!"

"I know what I'm talking about. I've just come from Lace Heppleman's back room. I've been going through Vevay's things. I found her bankbook. It was in her overnight bag, stuffed down in a toe of a shoe. She was filthy rich when she died."

"Baloney!" Kitchell smiled sadly. "Let's see it. I won't believe it, till I—"

"I don't have it with me. That Lace Heppleman's quite a character. I tried to swipe it, but he watched me like a hawk."

The big man looked puzzled. "Why swipe it?"

"I'm trying to beat Sheriff Durbin to the draw in this mess. I want to keep it out of his sight until I figure it out. That bankbook ties in with all these killings!"

Kitchell pushed back his chair, got to his feet. "Well, you can count on me. I won't tell the sheriff." He seemed dazed. "It's too much for me! I'm completely flabbergasted!"

McGavock nodded good-by. "Sure," he murmured sympathetically. "Sure."

IT WAS TWENTY minutes of nine when McGavock paid a second visit to the house in which Lew Thatcher had died. He'd seen something in that attic, something that didn't register. He decided to return and clear it up.

He crossed the lawn toward the dark building, tried the back door. A skeleton key from his keyring flipped the bolt in the mortise lock.

Hooding his flash with his hand, he made his way up the stairs to the attic.

Foot by foot, he inspected the empty room with his beam. Then he noticed it—the big stain on the ceiling, a large brownish blotch such as comes from a leaky roof. He walked to the ladder, played his flashlight up and down it. At the top of the ladder, set into the plaster of the ceiling, was a small trapdoor. He ascended, laid the flat of his hand against the door and lifted.

The trapdoor refused to budge.

He examined it. The beam of his torch caught flecks of silver in the yellow pine. It had been nailed, and recently, with new finishing nails.

He went back down to the kitchen, prowled around, located a flat-iron and a bath towel.

He turned to the attic, again ascended the ladder. He wrapped the towel around the iron to deaden the sound of the blows, and slammed into the trapdoor. The third stroke and the nails gave with a wrenching squeak.

He climbed upward, through the opening, and found himself

in a tiny garret, a small, cramped space between the attic ceiling below and raftered roof above.

And the first thing he saw was *starlight.*

Above his head was a second door that led out onto the roof. And this panel was open—about three inches.

He got his flashlight up where he could use it and cold sweat beaded itself along his jaw.

Three sticks of dynamite were neatly bracketed to an overhead timber by a leather strap.

With a steady hand, he disengaged the detonating cap. It was a tricky set-up—and mean. Wires ran from the dynamite to a copper plate on the doorsill. There was a companion plate on the trapdoor.

The trapdoor was propped open by a small white cube which McGavock first took to be chalk. Then he knew it wasn't chalk at all—it was a small block of salt. This was the end of the trail. Here was the cattle salt!

It was a simple device, and deadly. With rain and bad weather the salt would slowly dissolve, the trapdoor would drop closed, the circuit would be completed. And the force of dynamite, McGavock had always heard, drove downward.

McGavock left the house, crossed the street to the home of his client. It was almost all over now, and it might be a good idea to have Uncle Mark present at the showdown.

HUDDLED IN THE alley back of Main Street, McGavock and his client stood with the sheriff in the protecting shadow of a blacksmith's shop, their eyes fastened on the shabby row of stores across the rutted road. The rear of Main Street was actually one long brick facing, with a continuous, dilapidated loading platform a few feet from the ground, onto which the back doors of the shops opened. Singly, and almost in order, the window lights were going out.

Finally, after a hesitant interval, the window directly opposite them went black. "That's hit," the sheriff exclaimed. "Lace Heppleman's general store an' undertaking parlor. He's went."

McGavock asked: "You got the passkey from the marshal?" Durbin grunted.

They crossed the alley, ascended the platform. The sheriff produced a key, unlocked the door, and they entered an impenetrable blackness, smelling of harness oil and roofing paper. Sheriff Durbin turned on his big coon-hunter's flashlight.

It was a typical country store back room, topsy-turvy and littered with an assortment of odds and ends. Over in the corner, on a rough plank table, lay the body of Golden Vevay. The undertaker had given her an old style hair-do, the same that he'd been using for the last decade, had touched her up rather skillfully with rouge, and all in all, she appeared to be enjoying the experience of death.

Mark Thatcher's voice sounded querulous, reedlike, in the somber silence. "This, gentlemen, is scandalous. What are we doing here anyway? I demand—"

Sheriff Durbin threw his flashbeam on a shelf above a flat-topped desk. "Hit ought to be there. He puts their effects up yonder."

"You hold the light," McGavock ordered. "We've got to work fast." There was a pitiful little bundle of garments tied together with a string, the clothes she'd been wearing when she died. McGavock passed them up, turned to a large alligator pocketbook. Nothing there, other than the personal articles the sheriff had previously mentioned. He picked up the pigskin overnight bag. Here he found it—the bankbook—beneath the lining and fastened to the side of the case with adhesive tape. He ripped it out, opened it, ran down the column of figures. "We've got him now," McGavock grinned. "Our killer. He can't squirm out now."

Client Thatcher's blue-veined hand reached forward. "Oh, a bankbook. Let me see… Perhaps I may be of some assistance here. I'm something of an expert on finance—"

There was a sharp metallic clink out front. Sheriff Durbin switched off his light. McGavock said in a low voice: "Our company's arriving per schedule. He's forcing the front door. Quiet everybody. Are you ready, Sheriff?"

"I'm ready, Luther. I got hit out an' cocked."

After a moment, they caught the sound of cautious footsteps. The footsteps became clearer, less guarded. And now they knew it—the visitor was here in the backroom with them. McGavock said: "Now!" Sheriff Durbin flicked on his powerful flash.

Jimmy Kitchell stood centered in its beam. The big man was startled, slack-jawed. He held his hamlike hands before him, in a wrestler's position, fighting off the blinding glare. McGavock walked to the wall, turned on the ceiling light. Kitchell said stupidly: "What you folks doing here? I just want a peaceful minute with Golden before they—"

McGavock whispered in the sheriff's ear. Sheriff Durbin started for the back door. On the threshold, McGavock halted him, called out: "She's sitting in Court Square, according to agreement. She may give you trouble, but bring her along."

The sheriff nodded, then went out.

About three minutes went by, three minutes of tension.

And then, suddenly, there was a scuffle out front, out in the store. Sheriff Durbin appeared in the doorway, herding a handcuffed Ralph Gregory. Durbin looked grim. "Jest like you said, Luther. He was out there eavesdropping"

"Just one more mistake, Gregory," McGavock said calmly. "When Kitchell told you about the bankbook, you should have stayed clear. I see you've got him manacled, Sheriff. That's right. He's bad medicine—he's killed three times. He attacked me last night with a quilt and a knife."

GREGORY NARROWED HIS eyes. He spoke softly, viciously. "You'll pay for this, with your hides. You can't kick me around just because—"

Mark Thatcher cleared his throat. He said pompously: "Now, in my opinion—"

"Shut up," McGavock said roughly, "until you're called upon. Or I'll have to penalize you again! Any questions, Kitchell?"

"None, McGavock," the big man answered. "Except I don't want to get mixed up in this. I never killed anybody in my life."

"Well, just hang around. We can use you. Sheriff, since I hit town I've really been working for Dr. Powell. I liked the looks of that man, and I'm picking up where he left off. I've been working for Powell but Mark Thatcher's going to foot the bill. Ralph's first kill was Lew Thatcher. He went to his home just after the old man had come back from the hospital with a bad heart. While the oldster was upstairs in bed, he went to the cellar, lit a red candle, the one you found on Powell's person, and mixed up the Boysenberry cordial. He simply colored corn syrup with red cake coloring—and added a slug of poison. He called it Boysenberry because the old man had never tasted

Boysenberries, and couldn't spot the strange flavor. He got into a jam over the cake coloring, by the way. He had to recall a cake that his wife put on sale about that time to prevent the whole town from being poisoned. He thought he was being careful, but he just left a trail of indignation behind him. That was the way he got rid of Lew."

Gregory laughed. "I'd like to hear you tell that in court!"

McGavock went on: "He laid plans for Uncle Mark, too."

Mark Thatcher blinked. "Me? You mean—"

"Yeah man. He got some rock salt, rigged up a weather-trap in Lew's attic. He knew you dabbled around fixing up the house, painting, and so on, and he knew you always did this when the weather was inclement, rainy. His trap was set for a succession of rains. Of course it might be sprung at night, when you were at home, but he'd be far away and could afford to take the chance. What could he lose? That brought on Dr. Powell's murder."

Jimmy Kitchell looked disgusted. "Why should anyone want to kill Doc Powell? He had a heart as big as the Baptist church-bell!"

"That was another blunder he pulled, trying to be super-careful. He got the key from Mark to the house, pretending to look it over before he moved in. In reality, he was rigging up his trap in the attic. Now, he reasoned that Uncle Mark knew he was in the house, and if the dynamite should be discovered prematurely, suspicion would point to him. So he prowled around, learned that the wardrobe would squeak when it was moved, and put out the acousma story. He expected his family physician, Dr. Powell, would investigate and corroborate his story. That would imply that someone else, a mysterious nobody, was in the place at the same time he was. Powell solved the wardrobe puzzle—but he went further. In the cellar, he found the can of corn syrup and bottle of cake coloring. He found the candle, too, the candle with Ralph's fingerprints on its nice waxy surface."

"I know the candle you mean," Gregory responded readily. "He borrowed it from me some time ago. However, I don't know anything about any cellar or—"

Sheriff Durbin said: "So that's hit. He's been killin' off his wife's kinfolk, one by one, to inherit. I should've guessed."

Gregory smirked. "So now I have a motive, eh? Uncle Mark, tell them about the agreement I signed."

Mark Thatcher looked disturbed. "I hate to admit it, gentlemen, but he's clear of the charge you make. Lew and I wouldn't permit him to marry our niece until he, er, signed a legal paper forgoing any part of the principle of the estate." He frowned. "That seems harsh but the proviso was that if he passed his probation the paper would be destroyed."

"But," McGavock put in, "he shared a joint account with Jenny."

"That's true," the oldster confirmed. "He shared Jenny's income, not her principle. He certainly wouldn't sacrifice the ten or fifteen thousand in her account for the much larger amount they were slated for!"

THE DETECTIVE CORRECTED them. "Yet that's precisely what he did. He took big sums from the joint account. Has been doing so for some time. When Ashton decided to put up a water-tower, believe it or not, the project almost wrecked him. If Mark Thatcher had sold the Dowdell property to the town, the Thatchers would have had to settle the estate."

"We were ready to," the oldster said. "Lew and I should have settled it before, but we never got around to it."

"That's the picture," McGavock explained. "Who would suffer the most if the Thatcher estate were settled? Ralph, because there would naturally ensue a general over-all checking of family finances. And you could count on the penny-pinching uncles to discover that Ralph had been filching from his wife." McGavock paused. "So he forged the Witherspoon item. He's quite a forger, by the way. You should have heard the spiel he got off about Uncle Lew and his mythical assortment of penpoints. Lew, I might add, discovered the truth to this Witherspoon business and that set off the whole chain of deaths. He wasn't killing to eliminate the other heirs, he was killing to keep himself in good standing until the payoff."

Gregory said suavely: "But the opposite is true. Everyone knows I have an income of my own!"

"It's that income," McGavock declared, "that's going to hang you. You were, though you probably didn't know it until now, a victim of a swindle. You took your wife's money to finance Golden Vevay. You thought Vevay was running a gambling house. Actually, Kitchell, here, and the Vevay woman were running a confidence game on you. There was never any gambling at all done at that stucco cottage. You stayed away, by agreement, and poured in the capital. They pulled that ancient gag on you, gave you back part of your funds as profits. They milked you, friend."

Gregory's voice was gentle, deadly. "What do you say to that, Jimmy?"

McGavock continued relentlessly: "You went to Golden

Vevay this morning, tried to get back your kale. She brushed you off—you killed her. We've got her bankbook. It'll show deposits and withdrawals to correspond with the records at your bank."

Ralph Gregory wasn't listening. His reptilian eyes were fastened on the fat man in dirty whites. He said absently: "I should have known. I should have taken care of you, too."

Jimmy Kitchell said loudly: "Me, I'm a lawman at heart. I'm an ex-postmaster, ex-sheriff. You can count on me to cooperate, Sheriff Durbin. I'll take the stand for you!"

Mark Thatcher reached into his pocket, came out with a greasy, worn billfold. "McGavock," he said ceremoniously, "you've done a good day's work and it's a pleasure, sir, to pay you off. Let's see. Twelve hours at sixty-five cents an hour is—"

"You'll get a letter," McGavock said wryly, "from the chief in Memphis. He'll tell you all about it. We'll handle it that way."

Until the Undertaker Comes

"Let me warn you, sir. This is an unfriendly town and beastly things may be happening here," Dr. Rudd cautioned the Memphis shamus. As if McGavock had to be told! His first evening in Hetherton and already two deaths had occurred—with an elusive undertaker's apprentice on the prowl embalming the murder victims as fast as the killer could dispose of them!

1

Dr. Rudd's Dilemma

ONLY A SLIVER of chicken breast and a leaf of lettuce were on the plate. Miss Tincher folded the wisp of meat into the greenery, stuffed the morsel ravenously into her pouchy jowl. She was old and withered, her face coated with rice powder, and in the half light McGavock had the image of ruffled black satin and staring, hollow eyes.

Miss Tincher munched, swallowed, said: "Go 'way, young man. Leave me alone."

Soft dusk came into the bedroom, obliterated the crayon portraits on the walls, made a shadowy frame of the four poster in the corner. A small fire of green oak struggled in the grate, its gaseous flame spluttering against the damp chill of the winter evening.

"I don't need any detective," the old lady muttered angrily. "You know what I think? I think you're just a tramp. You know I live alone. Maybe you're going to rob me, maybe you're going to kill me. You get out of my house before I call Lace!"

McGavock repeated patiently: "This Atherton Browne I'm telling you about runs an agency in Memphis. He's my boss. He's a—well, we won't go into that. I'm finishing a case in Chattanooga when his telegram catches me. I'm to stop off here at Hetherton and look you up. If you'll just write out a simple statement saying there's been an error, I'll be on my way."

She wasn't paying any attention. She set the empty plate on the bureau. "I'm a sick woman. I'm diabetic."

"Who," McGavock asked, "is Lace?"

"My nephew. The best and truest nephew—" Her mind seemed to be on the subject of food. She began to complain. "I'm a heavy eater and they know it. Why do they give me a little dab of chicken breast? I asked them for a big bowl of rice pudding with raisins!"

"Folks with diabetes," McGavock explained helpfully, "should steer clear of rice pudding. You see—"

The old lady's words came with difficulty. "I always eat at six

McGavock's flash revealed Dr. Rudd standing midst the wreckage. "I was attacked," he said. "A man grabbed me and tried to choke me."

sharp and they make me wait till seven. They make me wait an hour, till I get starved, and then what do they feed me? A handful of bitter lettuce and—"

She stopped talking. As he sat there in the gathering darkness he had the impression that she was brooding in petulant self-pity. And then her dim figure seemed to be dozing.

Suddenly she collapsed, rolled headlong from the chair to the floor.

He got to his feet, found the wall switch, turned on the light. He left the bedroom, walked hard-heeled along the corridor and descended the stairs to the front hall. He'd seen a telephone on a stand by the hat tree.

McGAVOCK WAS A small man, wiry and tough, with a touch of gray about his temples. He was a genius at getting results but he was a hard man to take. He'd worked for about every agency in the country but he'd never had a real home until he'd tied up with old crotchety Atherton Browne.

He located the phone, lifted the receiver, and spoke crisply to the operator. "I want to talk to a doctor. And I mean quick!"

He got his connection with surprising alacrity. At the first ring, a gentle resonant voice came along the wire to him, said: "Dr. Rudd speaking. Yes?"

McGavock said quietly: "Grab a satchel of antidotes, Doctor, and hightail over to Miss Ella Tincher's. She's in a bad way."

The gentle baritone said: "I'll be right over. She's a patient of mine. She's diabetic." The voice hesitated. "Did you say something about antidotes?"

"I did. It doesn't look like diabetes to me, it looks like poison."

"Oh, so you've made a diagnosis. I didn't realize I was speaking to a fellow physician. I didn't catch your name, sir."

McGavock spoke through flattened lips. "I tell you the old woman is dying. This is no time to—"

Dr. Rudd cleared his throat. "Poisoned, eh? I'm very sorry indeed to hear it. You'll have to call Dr. Caffery."

"I want you," McGavock said venomously, "and now! What goes on here?"

"Oh, I'll come," the baritone said agreeably. "But I'll have to bring Dr. Caffery along to take charge. He handles cases of this sort, emergency stuff. You must be a stranger in town or you'd know about me. I'm rather expert with routine work but I have an embarrassing malady that unnerves me in the presence of death, or near-death. We'll be right over."

The sticks of heater-wood in the fireplace had burned to dusty flakes when McGavock returned to Miss Tincher's bedroom. It was a frugal, miserly setup—the sagging window blinds, the musty fetid air, the patched broken furniture.

Miss Tincher sprawled as he had left her, a mass of ruffles on the moldy carpet, face down, her bony arm curled beneath her forehead.

Then, in rapid succession, McGavock noticed three things: The supper plate was gone. Miss Tincher's baggy shoes were no longer on her feet but were paired neatly by the foot of the bed. And there was a small red smear, the size of a man's gloved thumb, on the white marble slab of the bureau.

McGavock dropped to his haunches, turned the body over. The old lady was dead but she had not died of diabetes. Nor had she died of poison. Her throat had been cut by an ivory-handled game knife which lay half concealed by her moist sleeve.

McGavock switched off the light and left the house.

The sky above the hills had deepened to indigo when McGavock passed the cotton compress and turned down Main Street. He'd disliked Hetherton from the moment he'd stepped off the train and now a close-up of the place merely confirmed his earlier opinion. It was a sullen town, shabby and hostile. The population, he judged, was maybe two thousand.

The business section was two blocks long, a ramshackel string of weathered, false-fronted stores, with the railroad running directly behind Main Street. A morbid, mean town, a town that was fighting hard for survival and showed it. As he strolled along the cracked sidewalk, through the golden oblongs of light thrown by the shops across the pavement, his nostrils caught the small-town smells of cheap eateries, of gasoline, of horse dung. And back of that was the faint sour stench of swampland. A loafer on a bench before a feedstore directed him to Lace Tincher's.

The yellow brick house was trim and modern-looking. It was better, more respectable than the neighboring residences, and had a small cement block annex, a sort of extra room, constructed at the rear. McGavock stepped on the porch. There were frothy, feminine curtains at the window and inside he could see a girl on a couch, with her legs tucked beneath her, reading a book. He laid his thumb on the buzzer and the girl got to her feet.

The porch light came on and the girl opened the door. McGavock said: "I'm Luther McGavock. You know, the man Mr. Tincher ordered from Memphis." He watched her face as he spoke.

She listened deadpan. She was perhaps eighteen years old with a lithe, supple figure. Her face was immobile, almost Indian with its high cheekbones, and Ketherton's hinterland beauty parlor had done its best to eliminate her youth with a coat of cosmetics and an ornate hair-do. She inspected him with lifeless black eyes. "Mr. Tincher isn't here. I'm his sister Judy. Won't you come in?"

He followed her into the house. Wordlessly, she led him down the hallway, into the kitchen where, on the far wall, a tongue-and-groove door had been set into the plaster. The girl lifted the latch and they descended two cement steps, came out into a boxlike room.

This was the annex he'd observed from the street. An office of some sort—a large flat-topped desk, several steel cabinets, a tiny but efficient safe. The walls were of new pine and the floor was covered with brightly-patterned linoleum. Judy Tincher seated herself in the swivel chair behind the desk, McGavock pulled up a cane-bottomed stool and faced her. The girl settled herself, asked stiffly: "You say you're the man from Memphis. Is it something in connection with the insurance policies?"

McGavock shook his head decisively. "I know nothing about any insurance policies." He pointed at the safe. "I'm here to fix that. Mr. Tincher wrote us that the combo's jammed."

She didn't answer.

The old-fashioned clock on the wall rattled and ticked. McGavock beamed. "Mayhap you'd like to hear about the time I missed a train and spent the night in Hollywood? Stars, bright lights, glamor?"

She looked at him blankly. He gave up.

The minute hand on the Seth Thomas had crawled eight spaces when there was the sound of footsteps outside and a little red bulb on the desk glowed suddenly red. The girl walked across the room and opened a door into the night. A man entered.

THE VISITOR WAS a vicious-looking man in his middle forties. His meaty jaw was grizzled and his eyes were steel splinters imbedded in puffy, dissolute eyelids. He wore a tattered black felt hat, a shiny serge coat, and filthy overalls stuffed into mud-caked cowboy boots. He gave McGavock a contemptuous glance, addressed the girl. "Mr. Lace here?" His thin, snuff-stained lips scarcely moved as he spoke.

She said: "He's out. Something's happened to Miss Ella. I can take care of you."

The man said: "Take keer of this other feller first. I'll wait."

McGavock smiled. "I'm waiting, too. Have a seat, brother."

The man faltered. After a moment, he made up his mind. He unbuttoned his coat, revealed a fine worked-leather shoulder holster. He broke a gun from the spring and handed it to the girl—a rusty-barreled .38 with a chipped mother of pearl grip. He said: "How about ten bucks, Miss Judy?"

She ejected the shells, twirled the cylinder, tried the trigger. "No soap. You can have five."

His gaze wavered. "I need cash an' need hit bad. O.K. Give me the fin."

She opened the safe, counted out five singles. The man took the money and departed.

The girl pulled out the desk drawer, laid the gun inside. McGavock got a glimpse of at least a dozen other guns, all styles and calibers. He asked dryly: "What kind of a dump is this?"

She smiled for the first time. "Years ago, before I was born, when Lace was a ridgeroad storekeeper back in the hills, he got in the habit of pawning things. Now he's a rich man, he owns about half of Hetherton, but he still enjoys it. It's a hobby with him, his rates are reasonable. Jewelry and guns are his weakness."

McGavock asked casually: "Who was that man who just left?"

"His name is Fannin. He's from back in the heart of the swamp country. He visits county seats on court days, performs a few rope tricks, does a little fancy shooting if they'll permit him, and passes the hat. Makes out that he's a Westerner. Lives here in town with his woman in a room over Lace's hardware store. I don't much care for him. He's seen the inside of too many jails."

"Did you know he slipped a fast one over on you?"

The corners of her eyes tightened. "You mean he tried to. It's an old gun but it's worth five dollars, easy."

"I don't mean that," McGavock said. "I mean he did something mighty funny. Something I don't relish thinking about." He changed the subject. "Who's this Ella Tincher and what happened to her?"

"She's my aunt. Word came through a little while ago that Dr. Rudd and Dr. Caffery answered an emergency call to her home and found her murdered." Her docile face was expressionless. "Dr. Rudd said that a stranger had phoned him. When he got there, the stranger had vanished. The sheriff isn't going to like that."

"I wonder why she was killed?"

The girl said dully: "I have a feeling she was murdered for my brother's money."

McGavock guffawed. "It's a nice trick if you can do it."

Her black eyes burned smokily. She offered no further explanation.

McGavock lowered his voice confidentially. "I don't want this to go any further. I'm a detective. By a strange twist of fate I happened to be on the death scene. I was with Miss Ella T. just before and after the tragedy. It has me completely baffled. I haven't the slightest idea how she was killed."

It was the opening she'd been waiting for. With great restraint, she said: "They tell me her throat was cut. Could that have been a contributing agent? Of course I'm no detective but—"

McGavock said graciously: "It's a pleasure to discuss such a bewildering affair with such a clear-thinker. I'd appreciate your opinion. She was eating her supper while I was chatting with her. All at once she rolled to the floor. Let me tell you, sister, I'm an old hand at this game and it had the earmarks of poison or drug. I left the room, and when I returned her jugular vein had been slit."

She was speechless. "That means two people tried to kill her at the same time—a poisoner and a knife wielder!"

"I don't believe it."

She tried again. "He poisoned her so when you left the room he could kill her completely with his knife!"

"Phooey. Once is enough. There'd be too much chance involved. And another thing—it was murder and robbery. When I first was with her, while she was alive, she had on her shoes. Afterwards, she was in her stocking feet. I bet she was killed for something she'd hidden in her shoe. Would you care to work up a little theory on that?"

Her face was masklike. "No I wouldn't. And I don't much care to listen to this. It's dangerous talk. Tell your story to the law. Why incriminate me by making me sit here and—"

"This is the proper procedure," McGavock declared mildly, "between client and detective. I'm just turning in my first report. You're the one who wrote us at Memphis, aren't you? You suggested to my chief that I call on Miss Ella and work into it from that end. Well, I'm here and there's been murder. Are you going to help me?"

"Absurd. I don't know what you're talking about!"

"It wasn't your brother, it was you who retained me. You're just cagy. You tried me out on that insurance policy gag to see if I was foxy. I came back with the broken safe business and you knew it was a lie—yet you took it poker-faced. Later you opened the safe to give me the sign that you were wise to me. By now, we were sitting pretty. You knew me and I knew you. Finally, you unload the big tip. *'My aunt was killed for my brother's dough!'* You'll have to do better than that, sister. What the hell is it all about?"

Judy Tincher got to her feet. "I guess Lace is going to be delayed. Good night." She showed him to the door. As he stepped into the damp, chill air, she said stolidly: "If you're going to be around town for a few days, I think you'll be comfortable at the Huston House."

THE COTTAGE WAS built on a shelf halfway up the bluff. Its lights were blazing away for fare-you-well and nestling as it did, in the scrub and bracken high on the cliffside, it seemed to McGavock, as he approached it along South Maple, to hang suspended in the night like a glittering golden tooth.

Where the street came to a dead end, he located a skeletal timber stairway and ascended, straight up, through winter brush and saplings, until he reached the small ledge. The town of Hetherton lay below him, a pleasant web of fairy lights, gold and rose, and he realized now that the man who had selected this site for a residence had a taste for beauty.

He saw, too, that the shelf was larger than had appeared. There was more than sufficient room for the tiny white clapboard building with its green shutters. He raised the brass griffin knocker on the door panel, snapped it sharply against its plate. He'd been hearing muted singing which he'd presumed was a radio. With the bang of the knocker, the singing ceased and the manner of its stopping, with a sort of hesitation, told him the singer was his host.

The door opened and Dr. Rudd invited him in.

Rudd was a youngish man, completely bald, with good shoulders and the stocky legs of an athlete. He was in his shirtsleeves and at first glance, he gave off the air of a prosperous businessman. Closer inspection, however, told another story. His cheap tweed pants were unnaturally shiny about the belt, an indication that the cloth had been turned English fashion, and his Scotch grain shoes had been resoled so many times that they had shrunk a good size-and-a-half. He said hospitably: "Sit down, sir. What can I do for you?"

That was it—the mellifluous baritone that McGavock had heard over the phone at Miss Tincher's. Dr. Rudd asked solicitously: "Are you ill?"

McGavock waved his hand about him, at the bare room with its cheap furniture, its simple but pleasant sporting prints. "Maybe I'm in the wrong place. I don't smell any ether."

Dr. Rudd said carefully: "Few patients ever come up here, the steep climb, you know. That's why I built here, so I could practice my music alone. Until recently, I reserved a small clinic down in the town. How did you say I could serve you? You don't look particularly sick."

"Well, I am. It's something I drank out of a fruit jar. And I don't mean fruit. All day it's been as if I were lost on a desert. Seeing mirages and craving good cool water. My fingers keep jerking and—"

Dr. Rudd said affably: "Frankly, sir, I don't have much sympathy for your predicament. Alcohol and nicotine are toxic and taken voluntarily. You wouldn't eat flypaper, would you? However, you didn't come here for a sermon. I think I can fix you up. Just a moment—"

His black doctor's kit was on the floor by his chair. He picked it up, set it on the wicker table. His brows were furrowed. "You know, I'm a singer. I have a good ear for voices. I'm annoyed by the sensation that I've heard your voice somewhere before."

McGavock nodded vigorously. "I had that impression, too. As soon as I saw you." This was dangerous ground. "Only it wasn't your voice that got me, it was your face. We've met somewhere, I'm sure of it. Where did you come from?"

"I've been almost everywhere, I guess. Excuse me, I'll fetch a tumbler—you take this in water." He left the room.

McGavock stood up, strolled over to the table. He snapped the catch on the satchel, examined its contents. Other than the customary medical paraphernalia, there were two objects which intensely interested the Memphis detective.

One was a paper sack of chocolate fudge. The other was an old envelope with an annotation penciled on the back. The envelope was addressed to *Miss Judy Tincher, Hetherton, Tennessee.* It was a run-of-the-mill circular from a ladies' apparel shop in Nashville. The notes on the back said, *arsenic—zinc chloride.*

THE DOCTOR CAME into the room so silently that McGavock didn't hear him. A gentle hand appeared from behind McGavock's shoulder, took the paper from his grasp, restored it to the satchel. He said amiably: "There's one thing no doctor can stand—having a layman meddle with his *materia medica.* How did you locate me up here, anyway?"

"I asked the town marshal and he directed me."

"Oh." Dr. Rudd selected a tablet from a vial, dropped it into the water. "A sedative, sir."

McGavock took it down in a gulp. "Ah-h-h! Thanks." He

laid out two dollars. "I feel better already." He returned to his chair. "I think I'll rest a minute before I tackle those stairs. Arsenic and zinc chloride. I'll have to remember that. What's it a prescription for?"

Dr. Rudd dropped onto the wicker sofa, rested his broad shoulders comfortably against the wall. "The layman is always trying to get something for nothing from a physician," he declared good-humoredly. "That's not a prescription, it's not even in my handwriting. Take my advice and don't sample it. You'd be indisposed for some time."

"If it's not a prescription, what is it?" McGavock looked incredulous.

Dr. Rudd said owlishly: "It's an old-time receipt, one of those helpful household hints. This particular formula is a spot-remover. For grass stains, rust, medicine stains—"

"Will it remove bloodstains?"

"Offhand, I'd say no. Why?"

"They tell me in town that you're hell on wheels when it comes to minor ailments, but that you won't touch an emergency?"

Rudd nodded vaguely. "In a general sense, that's true. The townspeople understand and I don't care to discuss it with strangers."

"You graduated from a medical school, you served your internship. That means this embarrassing malady they talk about just came over you recently?"

Dr. Rudd showed no offense. He repeated simply: "I don't care to discuss it."

"I don't see," McGavock argued, "how you get by financially!"

"I've a small independent income. Anything else you'd like to know?"

"I mean no harm," McGavock said pedantically. "Life to me is just a three ring circus—with no admittance fee. I like to ask questions. Asking questions and finding out things is as good as an education. It gives me culture and polish and—"

"Does it really? I hadn't noticed."

"Why, sure." He eyed his host lethargically. "I was talking with Judy Tincher tonight—"

"A sweet girl. How did you meet her?"

"By accident. As you probably heard, her aunt was murdered a couple of hours ago. I wonder if they'd let me take a look at the body?"

Dr. Rudd seemed to be thinking of something else. "The body is at Follett's Undertaking Parlor. It's up to him."

"Is this Follett an old man or a young guy?"

"In his late thirties. Why?"

"I got an embarrassing malady. Old undertakers unnerve me." McGavock meditated a moment. "Judy Tincher said the old lady was sick. That means there must have been someone living with her to take care of her. When the commotion started you'd think they'd have heard the old lady being killed."

"In the first place, I doubt if there was any commotion. Miss Ella was pretty frail. In the second place, the house was empty at the time. Miss Ella liked to live alone under her own roof. She did, however, have a housekeeper, a woman known as Ivy Snowden, who dropped in three times a day to fix her meals. Miss Ella was on a diet, but she was a hearty eater and had impulses to devour anything she could lay her hands on. No food was ever left in the house."

McGavock rose, picked up his hat. "Is there going to be an

autopsy? Miss Judy said something about the possibility of poison."

Dr. Rudd suddenly laughed, a great loud laugh of relief. "Now I've got that voice of yours placed. You're the man who phoned me at the time of the murder. No one's mentioned poison in this affair except you. I certainly didn't. And the idea never occurred to Dr. Caffery, you can be sure." He sobered. "Are you a detective or a murderer?"

McGavock started for the door. "Don't you wish you knew!"

Dr. Rudd went with him out onto the ledge. At the top of the staircase, he made a parting speech. "You're a detective, of course. I'm beginning to get the picture. Let me warn you, sir. This is an unfriendly town, and beastly things may be happening here. Act extremely cautiously, for you are in deadly peril. If things get too bad, and you need assistance, come to me. I may be able to help. Good night—and watch those stairs!"

A gusty wind was whipping up the valley. McGavock plastered his hat to his head with the flat of his hand. "Thanks, friend," he said. He started down the steps. "I may need a little help, at that."

2

The Imitation Westerner

HIS WRISTWATCH SAID sixteen minutes past eight when McGavock returned to Main Street. A drizzle had blanketed the town and now, half rain, half tepid snow, it had glossed the sidewalks and store fronts in an iridescent ebony pall. Normally, this would have been Hetherton's rush hour but because of the weather the pavements were deserted. It was time, he decided, to get his Gladstone from the station where he'd checked it on his arrival. Some of these small-town depots wrapped a long chain around the door at the stroke of nine.

He passed Lace Tincher's drygoods store, Lace Tincher's drugstore, Lace Tincher's grocery, and Lace Tincher's hardware store. A little farther on, he saw a light in the rear of Follett's Undertaking Parlor and after a second's indecision decided to pass it, too, for the moment.

He turned at Market, walked a short block, got his luggage, and headed back for town.

He'd just crossed the tracks when he heard a soft voice in the shadows call out: "Just hold everything, there, Buster. I want to talk to you!"

To his left, indistinct in the murk, was the alley at the rear of Main Street. He could make out the dim outlines of decrepit loading platforms, heaps of refuse, a jumble of packing boxes. He saw no human form or sign of movement. The words had been timed to freeze him in the alleymouth, in the feeble light from the depot. The alley was a good fifteen feet in width, and he was caught dead center. His impulse was to answer—but his instinct was to get gone, and quick.

He took a running step and, *wham!* a gun cut loose.

He kept going, head down, swinging his oversized Gladstone, and reached the shelter of a brick wall.

He paused a moment, boiling in fury. As he got his breath he realized a queer thing. The shot had let go just as he'd got into motion. From then on, for at least seven feet, he'd still been in open range, yet there had been no follow-up. Just that single heavy-calibered report!

That puzzled him. Maybe the shot was just to frighten him. Or maybe it was a case of mistaken identity. Maybe as he passed through the light the gunman realized he'd picked the wrong man.

All at once he grinned. Now he was getting somewhere. That slug had meant business—it had been laid out for him and nobody else. He knew who'd done it, and why there'd been no second and third shots.

The Huston House was on a side street, just back of the courthouse. A square, squat building, one of the oldest in Hetherton, it had been a stage change and tavern in bygone years. McGavock opened the creaking door, stepped inside. The lobby was small and cozy with comfortable leather chairs and plenty of ashtrays. On the beige walls were hung oval-framed crayon portraits of Confederate generals, and, in fairness to any transient Yankees, a dusty photograph of McClellan was stuck ceiling-high behind a pillar. McGavock set down his Gladstone. A short, fat man, with mussed hair and a sleepy, cherubic face came through a doorway and stood behind the desk.

McGavock registered, said: "I'll have my key now, if it's O.K. I'm going out again and maybe I'll be back late. I've got to see a guy, a Dr. Rudd."

The clerk nodded. "Yes, Mr. McGavock. Your room is 116, at the end of the hall. I'll take care of your bag. Glad to have you with us." He didn't look particularly glad. He looked a little strained. "You've been greatly in demand for the last hour. Telegrams and telephone calls."

"Who were the phone calls from?"

"The same party. He didn't leave his name. He had a quavering, sepulchral voice. Down in his chest."

That would be over-cautious, cagy Judy Tincher, McGavock decided. A deep, quavering voice would be her idea of a disguise. He said: "By golly, I bet that was Ivy Snowden. I can't see why she'd be calling me!"

The clerk disagreed. "This party was a man. It wasn't Miss Snowden. I know Mrs. Fannin's voice, and it's quite different."

McGavock blinked. "How's that again, please?"

The clerk looked embarrassed. "Ivy Snowden and Mrs. Fannin are the same person, and who are we to criticise the poor benighted? They're a happy couple and they seem to get along very well." He handed McGavock the telegram.

The clerk left the desk, stepped behind a curtained doorway. McGavock ripped open the envelope, extracted the sheet. It said, HOW ARE THINGS PROGRESSING? NO DAWDLING, PLEASE.

ATHERTON BROWNE.

McGavock crumpled the paper in cold rage. How are things progressing! Been in town two hours, one murder, one attempted murder, and the chief wanted a report on it, wanted it all wrapped up. No dawdling, please!

Gradually, he became aware that the hotel clerk was whispering behind the curtain, talking on a telephone. "... he just came in, Sheriff. He told me he's leaving right now for Dr. Rudd's. You can catch him there."

THE ENTRANCEWAY WAS between a dingy restaurant, The Rosebud Café, and Lace Tincher's hardware store. It was at the squalid end of the business section, in the neighborhood patronized mainly by hillmen with hides and pelts to market, with ginseng and with baskets to barter. The restaurant threw a feeble amber light into the misty night, the sidewalk was lonesome, abandoned.

McGavock entered the narrow foyer, climbed the dark stairs to the second floor. The upper hall was illumined by a hazy, fly-specked bulb. Beneath a window on the landing, there was a battered fire bucket, a pair of large overshoes and a dripping umbrella. The hall extended east, over the hardware store. There were two doors. McGavock approached the first and knocked.

The man who opened the door was old, nearly eighty, McGavock judged. He was dressed in a powder-blue basket weave cheviot and wore a wrinkled black moire tie down the front of his old-style pleated shirt. Skin fell in waxy folds from the hollow under his chin to his scrawny throat. He stared somberly at McGavock through horn-rimmed spectacles. McGavock said: "Don't tell me now that you're Fannin's father!"

"I'm Dr. Caffery." The oldster's voice was muted, reverent. "I'm just sitting up with the corpse. Fannin's inside. Won't you enter?"

McGavock was stunned. "Is Fannin dead? Are you saying that—"

"No, no. Come in, sir." He stepped back, bowed slightly. McGavock entered, and the old man closed the door behind him.

It was an old storeroom, completely bare but for a small white-enameled bed. A blue bandana handkerchief had been gathered about the pendent ceiling light, flooding the cracked walls and splintered floor with eerie, watery cobalt. In the far wall, a connecting door was ajar a few inches, leading into an adjoining room.

There was a dead woman on the enameled bed. She was perhaps forty years old, big-framed. A shoddy tobacco-sack quilt had been pulled up to her shoulders and her head lay on an improvised cushion made from a small heap of cheap feminine garments. Powder and rouge had been inexpertly applied to her cheeks and lips and yet, despite this crude attempt at the mortician's art, she impressed McGavock as having been an attractive woman.

Dr. Caffery said in a hushed voice: "A noble soul, God bless her. She rests in peace."

"Is this Ivy Snowden?"

"It is, sir."

"Was she one of Rudd's patients?"

"She was no one's patient. That is, she was, strictly speaking, mine. I was called in too late. She was gone." The old man's face turned slightly aside. "She was gone, sir. I served her only by making out her death certificate."

"I see. Where's Fannin?"

Dr. Caffery beckoned gracefully, gestured him through the door into the adjoining room.

It was another storeroom, a big one, and the living quarters were sort of clustered down at one end, leaving the far end dark and empty. Here, in one topsy-turvy group were gathered a broken-down wardrobe, a kitchen table, a kerosene range, some dilapidated chairs. Fannin was here, and he didn't look any more pleasing than when McGavock had last seen him in Lace Tincher's "office."

The imitation Westerner was seated on a wooden church pew, by a pink-shaded lamp. His elbows were resting on his knees in a position of weariness as he braided an intricate leather belt. His coarse face was flushed and bloated. He was drunk, but his hands were delicately steady as he worked the thongs into a pattern of rosettes. He gave McGavock a listless, arrogant nod of greeting.

Dr. Caffery said regretfully: "Well, Fannin, I must be leaving. You'll have to take over for the remainder of the night. Brace up, man. Nothing can affect her now, God bless her. Believe me, I hate to go but—"

Fannin said quietly: "You shore spoke true words then, Doc. I mean to tell you, you hate to go."

The old man said coldly: "That's hardly the decent attitude to take, sir. Your wife died, you asked me to assist in the obsequies. Now you mutter in your throat. It is only my friendship for you, a poverty-stricken itinerant, that—"

Fannin gave a nasty grunt. "You hain't foolin' nobuddy, Doc Caffery. You hain't here for no friendship for me. Yo're here because you was in love with Ivy, and you durn well know hit. I heered how you been throwin' sheep's-eyes at her whilst she was alive. You wanted her to leave me an' git married to you, didn't you?"

The old man's jaw moved spasmodically. After a few difficult breaths, he said: "As a matter of fact, I did admire her and could have offered her a comfortable home. However, her loyalty for you was so dominant that I didn't press my affection. You see—"

McGavock coughed politely. "Gentlemen, gentlemen! This'll be the scandal of Mayfair if we don't curb our tongues!" He hesitated, asked: "When did Miss Snowden die? I'd very much like to hear all the details."

Fannin said: "She died last night jest after midnight."

"She was here all day? Then she couldn't have fixed Miss Ella Tincher's supper plate. I don't understand it. I've talked to three persons tonight who all referred to her as being alive."

Fannin showed signs of annoyance. "Folks don't know hit, and why should they? Hit's my business, and Ivy's. Like I say, she died last night. I got Doc Caffery in, knowin' he was sweet on her an' could save her if anybuddy would. But she was on her way out. He claims hit was heart trouble."

Caffery said professionally: "That's it. She had a very bad—"

McGavock said: "Heart trouble doesn't slip up on you all at once. Didn't you suspect it before? Didn't you ever take her to a doctor before?"

Caffery said: "No. Had she been placed under observation—"

"Now that hit's over," Fannin said calmly, "I kin see whur we done wrong. I talked to Doc, here, a couple of times about her misery. Once in court square, once behind the feedstore. I told him how she'd been feelin' an' he wrote me out a little medicine-paper. I fetched up some drops from Lace Tincher's drugstore but hit didn't seem to he'p her none."

Dr. Caffery, offended, said: "So many persons stop me on the street like that. It's difficult to prescribe unless you talk to the patient. I didn't suspect—"

McGavock shook his head. "You people beat me down and I'm not kiddin'. I never heard anything like this in my whole life. Just as a point of curiosity, who embalmed her?"

Fannin flushed. "I don't know."

"You don't know!" McGavock exploded. "What do you mean, you don't know?"

Fannin fought the fog in his brain. "It's a kind of miracle, if you ask me. Here's whut happened. After Ivy dies, I got out on the street with the doc. I'm aimin' to call Follett. The doc leaves me on Main Street. I got a bottle an' before I know hit, I'm loopin' drunk. I wake up at daylight, an' I'm at home, here on the floor. I go into the other room thur, an' Ivy's done been fixed up. I go 'round an' see Follett to tell him I'll pay him when I kin."

Dr. Caffery said: "I guess I left my umbrella in the hall. Well, I'll be going…"

"What," McGavock asked, "did Follett say?"

Fannin looked bewildered. "He said I staggered up to his porch and told him about Ivy about three o'clock in the mornin'. That I waited for him, came back with him, an' when we got here she was already embalmed! He claims he didn't do hit an' they hain't no other undertaker in this part of the country. He said I didn't owe him nothin'."

Dr. Caffery said: "Good night, gentlemen." He stepped out into the hall, closed the door softly behind him.

WHEN THEY WERE alone, McGavock said: "Fannin, stand up!"

The hillman laid down his braided belt, obeyed dazedly.

McGavock's eyes were glazed, and he said in a whisper: "You don't want any trouble do you? I'm talking about big trouble."

"No," the hillman said carefully. "I don't want any trouble, Mr. McGavock."

"You even know my name!" McGavock reached out deftly, laid back the left side of Fannin's baggy blue serge coat. The hillman stood rigid, tensely still. In his armpit was the showy shoulder holster that McGavock had noticed at Tincher's. The holster had been empty when he'd last seen it. Now it held a businesslike, well-oiled Police Special.

McGavock dropped the coat back into position, said: "I figured as much."

Fannin met his gaze squarely. "Figured whut? Whut you mean?"

"You're the dog that tried to shoot me, but you prefer to do it sight unseen. The tip-off was that little scene at Tincher's. Later, when you really got into action, you gave yourself away. You're the man who called to me as I crossed the alleymouth. You were right here, at that window out in the hall. That's why you tried to hold me in target. You snapped a single shot and when I took one step it carried me out of your range of vision! I don't know just what I ought to do to you."

Fannin shook his head. "You got me wrong."

"I got you dead to rights." McGavock was white with quiet fury. "You know who I am. You followed me to Tincher's, went through that rigmarole with Miss Judy about pawning your gun. You said you needed money badly."

"I did need money," the hillman said. "My woman had jest died on me."

"You were building up an alibi in advance, if anything

should go wrong. You're a crack shot—yet you hocked a cheap worthless gun. That was to make me believe that from then on in you were unarmed. *If you had needed cash, you'd have pawned the holster.* That's an expensive holster and you could have got plenty for it. But you couldn't spare that, could you, brother?"

There was a band of perspiration across the hillman's forehead. McGavock asked: "How did you find out my name? How did you know I was a detective working on the Ella Tincher kill?"

Fannin's face wrinkled in diabolic amusement. "Hain't you no revenuer?"

"Hardly."

"Then you'll have to 'scuse me. I jest went an' made a mistake. I hain't been myself all day. Somebuddy's been prankin' me." The hillman frowned. "I don't know nothin' 'bout Miss Ella. Here's the way hit was. I was settin' in the Rosebud Café, 'bout dusk-dark, grievin' over Ivy havin' busted the circle, when I was called to the phone. Some feller, I didn't quite place him, says that a revenuer is in town tryin' to send me to the penitentiary, a man named McGavock. He says I done him a favor once and he's returning hit. He says that yo're out to Miss Ella Tincher's at that minute, pumpin' her 'bout me and Ivy an' all. I'm scared. I pick up yore trail an' foller you to Mr. Lace's. I had the gun, the fake gun, with me. I was aimin' to go later on anyways an' use Mr. Lace or Miss Judy as a witness. With you there in person I thought hit was in the bag."

He walked to the wardrobe, took out a worn canvas hunting jacket. Sewed into the lining were rows of pockets. "For half pints," he explained. "That's why I foller court days. You don't think I make a livin' out'n rope tricks an' fancy shootin', do you? I bootleg."

McGavock asked: "That voice that called you at the café, did it sound sweet and low?"

"Deep like a fiddle string an' sweeter'n a hive o' honey."

That was Rudd, all right But the answer wasn't logical. Whoever had spotted McGavock had been at the death scene, had been listening when he introduced himself to the old lady. That was the only possible way his name could have got out. But Dr. Rudd had been at home at that time. McGavock had phoned him there.

"Well, brother," McGavock said. "I'll be getting along. Accept my sympathy for your bereavement. And don't be touching off any more .38s in my direction."

McGAVOCK HAD A good night's sleep. The sheets in his room at the Huston House were sweetly starched and a small coal fire had been built in the fireplace to mellow the damp chill of the old plaster walls. He'd been on the go for five weeks and he was tired. It seemed to him he'd hardly hit the pillow when daylight was dancing across the cracked mirror on the washstand and his wristwatch said nine-twenty.

He caught a heavy-duty breakfast in the hotel dining room—eggs and sausage and fried potatoes, hot biscuits and blackberry pie and coffee. A little taut around the belt buckle, but contented, he felt ready to go to town.

He ambled into the lobby, slapped his key on the desk, and observed that already things were beginning to churn. There was a man sitting in a poor light, beneath a potted palm, self-consciously reading a newspaper, and another, a big fellow dressed in conservative gray, standing on the curb just outside.

The man in the lobby put aside his paper, walked uncertainly forward. He said: "I'm Lace Tincher. You're Mr. McGavock, aren't you? Welcome to our city." His voice was timid, almost servile, but from his inflection McGavock got the impression that he meant "welcome to *my* city."

McGavock turned slowly, gave him an unfriendly stare. Tincher was white-haired, straight as a ramrod, but his shoddy brown suit fitted him illy, and his shoes were scuffed and patched. He kept nodding his head and grimacing as he stood there. He didn't fool McGavock one bit—he was a small-town financier, the smile and the cordiality were his stock-in-trade. McGavock ignored the outstretched hand, said: "I'm busy this morning, Mr. Tincher. I'll look you up later."

Tincher said slyly: "I want to talk with you, in my office. I'm willing to pay you for your time. If it's the money angle that's holding you back, perhaps you'd like to drop in at the bank and ask about me." He mulled the joke over in his mind, enjoyed it. "I'm not exactly unknown hereabouts."

"You're unknown to me," McGavock said, "and that's—"

Lace Tincher took his elbow between thumb and forefinger and steered him out into the street. With reluctance, McGavock allowed himself to be led.

As they passed the big man on the curb, McGavock said loudly: "Pardon me." The man pivoted his head, pretended to see McGavock for the first time. McGavock asked: "Where can I find the sheriff, sir? Where's his office?"

The man had a heavy, corded neck, the tanned face of an outdoorsman. He seemed mortified and a little angry at the question, and said levelly: "The sheriff's office is in the courthouse. Yonder—" He raised his arm and pointed toward the squat stone building two blocks away.

As Tincher and McGavock continued down the street, the white-haired man chuckled. "I've got a good joke on you, my friend. That was the sheriff, himself, in person."

"Well, bless my heart! Really? Then maybe he was all set to tail me! What a happy accident. Now we can talk in private, just as you wanted."

Lace Tincher gave him a searching glance, started to speak, but refrained.

Two blocks further, and at a gesture from Mr. Tincher, they turned into the square. McGavock showed surprise. "Don't tell me your office is here, in the courthouse?" The white-haired man shook his head, said nothing. They walked through the ground floor of the courthouse, came out into the hitching lot behind.

Tincher said: "Frankly, our goal is not my office. It's the residence of my dear departed Aunt Ella. If the sheriff is following you, as you suggest, perhaps we'd better take precautions."

They started a crisscross journey of back streets. Tincher said: "After you left my home last night, my sister, Judy, told me about your visit. It seems, without my knowledge, she wrote to Memphis and engaged you. She's a minor and in no legal position to retain anyone. As there will be fees to be paid, I think I'd better take over her obligations. Is that satisfactory with you?"

McGavock asked: "Why did she call me in? The whole thing was handled so funny. I was sent around to your aunt's. What's the background to this? When I came there wasn't any murder, was there?"

"Of course not. It was about Aunt Ella's diamond brooch.

Judy somehow got the idea that the thing had been stolen. She wanted you to—"

"Was it stolen? And was it a good one?" McGavock was interested.

"Was it stolen? I doubt it. Aunt Ella was rather forgetful, and she might have mislaid it. Was it a good one? Not too good—worth maybe two thousand dollars. But diamonds have a peculiar quality about them. They're exciting to their owners. Aunt Ella couldn't have treasured it more if its value had been—"

McGavock said thoughtfully: "I'm an outsider. Coming in like this, it's hard to get an honest picture of folks you meet. Judy tells me that Dr. Rudd was Miss Ella's physician. The old lady was mighty sick, yet Rudd tells me that he never administers to serious cases, that he gets buck fever in an emergency. What's the lowdown on that?"

Lace Tincher said amiably: "It sounds strange, doesn't it? Yet I think you're getting the wrong idea. In my opinion, Dr. Rudd is simply resting. I expect him to resume full practice any time now. That's the way everyone in town feels about it. No one censures him. He's just going through a period of nerves. He took Aunt Ella's case before he had his breakdown. He's a topnotch doctor and understands diabetes thoroughly."

"Who's Dr. Caffery?"

"Nobody at all!" Mr. Tincher spoke with scorn. "Between you and me, I deem him a grave danger to the community. He learned his medicine back in the eighties, he sharpens his scalpels on a razor strop and would prescribe morphia for the common cold if the law allowed. When Dr. Rudd cut down on his practice, Dr. Caffery came out of hiding. For twenty years Caffery had been in retirement. Hetherton was short-handed medically and he jumped into the breach. They tell me he's literally coining money."

"Why should you kick? Your drugstore fills his prescriptions, doesn't it?"

"I suppose so. But I'm a man who puts public safety above financial remuneration."

McGavock nodded enthusiastically. "So am I—I hope."

3

Protamine Zinc

AUNT ELLA'S OLD frame house lay back in a grove of funereal cedars, surrounded by a sterile-looking red-clay yard. On his visit of the evening before, in the twilight, McGavock hadn't realized what a melancholy scene it was. The two-story building was as narrow as a match box set on its side. Bricks had fallen from its chimney, here and there across its face the warped boarding had sprung from the joists. Upstairs, in the death room, the rickety green shutters had been closed in solemn reverence to her departure.

Lace Tincher took out his key-ring, opened the front door. They stepped into the musty hall. The white-haired man said: "I'm not so sure that anything's wrong. We won't annoy the law until we're certain. I want you here mainly as a witness. She kept her papers and jewelry and such in a cabinet at the bottom of the sideboard. Let's go into the dining room."

Winter sunlight, harsh and white, beat through the grimy windows across the threadbare carpet Tincher put his hand loosely to his mouth, exclaimed: "What does this mean?"

The sideboard was an old cumbersome affair of heavily carved black wood. A small brass key was in place in the keyhole of the lower left compartment. Lace Tincher bent forward, said nervously: "What's that doing there? This is where she kept—"

"The diamond brooch. I know." McGavock sat on his heels, cupped his hands over his knees. For a good twenty seconds he gazed at the panel. Finally, he reached forward, opened the cabinet door.

There was no brooch. Just some old receipted bills, tied with a string, and several medicine bottles. McGavock asked: "What are these?"

Tincher showed his amazement. "I haven't the slightest idea. She rarely came downstairs. Why should she keep her medicine—"

The bottles were all alike, regulation two-ounce vials, with plastic screw-tops, and filled with a smoky greenish liquid. McGavock took a whiff, got a spicy odor, said: "Digitalis. A mighty mean poison."

"But they're untouched," Tincher insisted. "They're full. I can tell, I've been around a drugstore enough to— I wonder where they came from?"

"That's hard to say. The labels have been soaked off and the bottles themselves are run-of-the-mill." McGavock shut the cabinet door, stood up.

Tincher said dramatically: "So Judy's hunch was right. The brooch has been taken." He leaned forward, his unpleasant breath falling on McGavock's face. "I know just how it was done. Aunt Ella always carried that key in her shoe. When she felt like wearing her diamonds, she'd give someone the key and tell them to run downstairs and get the jewelry for her. Last night she was slain for her key. The murderer then came here and took—"

"She was killed for the key last night, all right," McGavock agreed, "but the killer took no brooch. It was already gone. See these scratches here by the keyhole? These old-time locks can be picked with a piece of baling wire. And that's about what happened. She was killed for the key—but not for the diamonds. The diamonds had already been snitched."

The white-haired man went back on his heels. "That's ridiculous," he shouted. "Why should anyone—"

McGavock looked disgusted. "Your sister, Judy, called me in because she thought the brooch had been stolen. Not because she feared it might be stolen—but because the job had already been pulled. Have you forgotten? The fact is, she got her lowdown from the old lady. My guess is that Miss Ella wanted the brooch to wear and couldn't get it. Without her knowing it, I was called in to recover it. Which is exactly what I intend to do."

DR. MAXIMILIAN RUDD was taking his morning constitutional. Lace Tincher had left McGavock and the detective was headed back to town, for Follett's Undertaking Parlor, when he observed the young doctor sauntering down a side street. McGavock glimpsed him through the black spiderweb branches of the leafless privet hedge. His bald head was uncovered but his chin was thrust into a knitted muffler against the chill penetration of the leaden day. He carried a blackthorn walking stick in his hand as a sign of deliberate gentility.

McGavock called: "Hey!"

Rudd pulled up, broke into a smile of greeting. "Oh, the detective! Glad to see you, sir. You're just in time to join me. I do eight miles every morning. We'll go out to the old mill, turn at the bridge, cut through the pasture, and—"

A great elm grew in the middle of the pavement and the cement sidewalk had been laid in a divided loop about it. A rustic octagonal bench surrounded it. McGavock said tartly:

"Sorry. I've done my eight miles. Sit down."

They sat for a half minute, neither of them saying anything, Rudd turning over the brown leaves with the tip of his walking stick. McGavock said: "Dr. Rudd, I want to ask you some questions. Professional and otherwise. They tell me you're pretty good in your line. Will you give me straight answers?"

The young man composed himself. "Go ahead. Fire away."

"This is hypothetical. Is it possible for an undertaker to kill his customer?"

Rudd smiled tolerantly. "That's strictly a layman's scare. In the old days, I've heard, it sometimes happened but now doctors are on their toes. A slip of that nature is pretty much out of the question. Besides, Miss Ella had her throat cut. I watched Caffery examine her and am perfectly satisfied that she was thoroughly defunct. What killed her was that severed jugular."

"Thanks. By the way, I've just left Lace Tincher. We've just finished searching the old lady's house. There's a diamond brooch missing. He wants me to ask you if you stole it?"

Dr. Rudd said affably: "That Lace Tincher! Penny-pinching, egotistical, small-town bigshot. I've often wondered how he reached maturity untouched by human foot. Maybe I'll have to remedy that!"

"Well, did you?"

"Certainly not!" Dr. Rudd's melodic baritone broke with emotion. "I don't know anything about any damned—"

"Whoa, brother, whoa there, I talked to the old lady, you know, before she died." McGavock looked grave. "She practically accused you of swiping it. She said—"

Rudd purpled. "Never, understand me, never as long as you're in Hetherton must you repeat that scurrilous slander! A man of my spotless professional position accused of petty pilfering! I wouldn't be welcome in any home in town if folks thought I was a thief. Why should I steal? I have a small independent income—"

McGavock stared at the blue hills against the granite sky. "Miss Tincher says you took the key from her shoe one time when you helped her into bed. Then one afternoon when Miss Judy was over she decided to decorate herself and sent her niece downstairs for the pin. It was gone. It had to be you, she figured, because you were the only one with the opportunity to—"

"And they called you in! Called you in for that!" Dr. Rudd sneered. "Ella Tincher was a very sick woman and she managed to garble the actual facts considerably. Here's what really happened. The old lady trusted me every bit as much as she did her niece. Frequently when I was there on a professional visit—"

"Was that often?"

"I gave her her diabetic injection every morning. As I was saying, it wasn't unusual for her to hand me the key and send me downstairs like an errand boy for the brooch. On one of these occasions, about a week ago, it was missing. I stalled her. I was afraid to tell her. I thought she might have simply mislaid it and—"

McGavock cut him off. "You've worked hard and built up a good practice here. Now a doctor's practice is like an insurance agency or a barroom; you catch the customer's good will and keep him coming back for more. Aren't you doing a bad thing when you allow Caffery to poach on your preserves? Sometime you'll want to take up full practice again, and where will you be?"

"I don't care to discuss it."

"When Doc Caffery visits these old-line patients of yours, does he cut you in on the take?"

Rudd looked offended. "Of course not. Why should he? I'm delighted that he so generously gives of his time and energy."

"And Echo answered baloney." McGavock closed his eyes, opened them lazily. "You said something last night that made me wonder. Just as I left you, you said 'this is an unfriendly town, and beastly things might be happening here.' What did you mean?"

"I said they *may* be happening here."

"Don't hedge. I'm ready for a complete explanation to that crack. I hadn't been away from you any time at all when someone took a crack at me with a .38. I'm tired of evasions and feints and sleights. I've been pushed around ever since I hit town. I'm listening."

Dr. Rudd stirred the soggy leaves at his feet with the blackthorn. "Something rather grisly occurred here in Hetherton the night before last. A woman named Ivy Snowden died. Follett, the undertaker, was summoned a few hours later. When he arrived, Miss Snowden was already embalmed. No one has the slightest idea who did it—or why. Somehow that seems pretty ghastly to me."

"It is ghastly," McGavock agreed heartily. "Now it appears that not many persons in Heatherton knew about it. Where and when did you learn—"

"Follett told me yesterday afternoon."

"Yet," McGavock said silkily, "yet last night, while we were chatting in your parlor, you spoke of Ivy Snowden as though she were still alive. If you knew she was dead, that was a deliberate attempt to mislead me. Make a choice, friend. Are you trying to help me, or are you trying to twist me up?"

The courthouse clock clanged eleven. Dr. Rudd listened intently, took a brown paper sack from his coat pocket, the identical bag that McGavock had noticed in his medical kit. "My diet calls for a bit of refreshment at eleven sharp." He produced a square of chocolate fudge, munched it with satisfaction. "You'll pardon me, I'm diabetic."

"Then what are you doing stowing away all that sugar?" McGavock was astounded. Suddenly, he remembered something. His eyes glinted. He said calmly: "What a fool I've been. Protamine zinc, eh, Doc?"

"That's it," Dr. Rudd said frankly. "You've hit the nail on the head. I'm a very sick man."

WHEN McGAVOCK RETURNED to the hotel for lunch, a telegram was waiting for him from the chief. It said, ARE YOU THERE LUTHER? WHY NO WORD FROM YOU? WIRE REPORT OF PROGRESS IF ANY IMMEDIATELY. ATHERTON BROWNE. The Old Man was having himself a tantrum. McGavock, switching swiftly from burning anger to smug satisfaction, wandered into the dining room and lost himself in a dream world of fried chicken and giblet gravy, of mashed potatoes and creamy Sally Lunn. He was a new man, body and soul, when he hit the street again.

Jesse Follett, Hetherton's undertaker, was an anemic, eager young man who affected the gates-ajar collar and thigh-length coat of the long-departed master who had taught him his trade. Mr. Follett led McGavock back through the children's-and-ladies' apparel shop at the front of his establishment which was mainly the bread and butter angle of his business, and ushered him into the workroom at the rear. Miss Ella Tincher reposed in a fine silver-mounted casket in the corner.

"I'm keeping her here," Mr. Follett explained, "until the funeral. All morning her kin have been traipsing in and out of my shop, viewing the remains. What can I do for you, sir?"

McGavock said authoritatively: "I was on my way from Chattanooga to Memphis when we heard about you. They told me I'd better stop by and examine you. It doesn't look too good, Mr. Follett. I want to hear the whole story about Ivy Snowden."

"Who are you?"

"Ha," McGavock said significantly, "that's a question I'll have to pass up. The Lodge doesn't like it when we give our right names. We take an oath, and so on. What about Ivy?"

Follett looked worried, and a little scared. "I don't seem to understand. And who's this *we* you keep talking about? And how did word ever seep through to Chattanooga about Miss Snowden? There are not more than five people in town, right here in Hetherton, who know about the incident!"

"The Lodge is highly interested in corpses, Mr. Follett. We have our ways, our grapevine. Do you care to speak freely or shall we step around to the squire's and have you make a deposition?"

"You people got it all wrong," Follett said earnestly. "I don't know what on earth you're talking about, but I'm here to tell you that I don't want to get mixed up in it! I'm just an innocent bystander in this Ivy Snowden business. Furthermore, as far as I can see, it's perfectly legal. It's just funny, that's all."

McGavock waited with solemn expectancy. Follett continued: "About three o'clock, the night before last, a man named Fannin came to my home in a drunken condition and said that his woman had died. When we got to his room I found that she had already been embalmed."

"Really embalmed? By a professional?"

"Yes. No doubt about it. I examined her. An injection into the femoral artery and into the cavity of the abdomen. An awkward job but done by a professional. Yet there was something different about the whole thing, the smell in the air or something. I can't describe it."

"Any idea who did it?"

"Must have been some outsider. I've been practicing here for years and I have no competitor," Follett paused, "that I know of. It never happened before. And I don't expect it to happen again."

"You're right," McGavock said. "It won't."

Follett looked hopeful. "The Lodge is going to see that it doesn't?"

"The Lodge is going to see that it doesn't. Good day."

McGAVOCK TURNED FROM the pavement, onto the flagstone walk that led to the yellow brick house, when Judy Tincher called him. He raised his head in the direction of her voice. About a hundred feet behind the residence was a small cluster of out-buildings, a dog kennel, a woodshed, an old-fashioned, white-painted stable. The girl was standing in the open door of the stable. She beckoned.

He cut across the dead grass of the lawn, approached her. She was dressed in a short red skirt and checkered woolen blouse. The heavy cosmetics of last evening were gone and in the soft pearl light of the winter sun she looked her age, a high school kid. Wordlessly, she gestured him inside.

He followed her through the cobwebbed entrails of the barn, past stalls and cribs, until they came to the harness room.

The place had been made into a play room. There was a fine, tournament-size billiard table beneath suspended lights, a cue rack, chairs along the wall. McGavock said: "I thought I'd better drop around and tell you. Things are not getting any better. They're getting worse." She gave him a sullen, expressionless scrutiny, said: "Take a stick. We'll run off a little straight rail."

He smiled wanly. "What? And lose my shirt, badge and gun? No, thanks. I'll just sit down over here."

She walked to the rack, selected a cue, and broke the balls on the table with a nice easy stroke that brought all three up into the corner. McGavock said pleasantly: "A billiard table at home is a wonderful thing for growing children. It keeps them from forming sidewalk gangs, from burglarizing cafés and stuff like that. Social workers tell me that—"

She said in a guttural whisper: "To hell with you! You don't get my goat." Quicker than McGavock could count them, she ran three points, and then four more.

He said: "You have access to Lace's safe. Tell me, have you noticed a large unexplained sum of money lately?"

She missed the next shot badly, drove the balls helter-skelter, but followed with a beautiful six-cushion that clustered them again in the corner. "Why don't you ask Lace?"

McGavock clammed up. She perched herself dramatically on the edge of the rail, executed a forced massé, ran off five more. Suddenly, she hung up her cue, slid thirteen markers down the wire, threw herself into a chair beside him. McGavock said rudely: "You only ran seven. And then you missed. Remember?"

"I ran seven and missed and ran seven more. Subtract one from the total of fourteen and you get thirteen. You count the way you like and I'll do the same. What's this about Lace and money?"

"Never mind," McGavock said blandly. "I'll do as you say. I'll ask Lace himself."

She said woodenly: "When I wrote to Memphis and hired a detective I had the silly, girlish hope that maybe I'd draw a gentleman. I didn't expect them to foist off the dregs of the agency on me. However, I'll try to make out the best I can with what I have. Mr. McGavock, I found the money you spoke of, but it wasn't in the safe. It was down at the bottom of the dirty hamper in the upstairs hallway. Fifteen thousand dollars in cash!"

"You mentioned it to him?"

"Of course. There are no secrets between us. He said he was planning on spending a vacation out in Utah. He'd been working too hard, he said, and was considering going away for a rest. He might make up his mind any time, on the spur of the moment, and he wanted the cash where it would be immediately available. I asked him what about me and he hardly heard me. Finally, he told me that he'd keep in touch with me by letter, through one of these remailing agencies. You know, he'd send his letters to them and they'd put them in new envelopes and forward them to me."

"There are no secrets between you, eh?" McGavock shook his head. "That's one for the book. What's he scared of?"

"He's not scared of anything." Doubt crept into her smoky black eyes. "You heard what he told me. He's just tired."

"I was wondering where that kale came from? That's a lot of dough. Could it be possible that he just sold something, a piece of property or—er—anything?"

"It doesn't seem likely, does it?" Her tone was scathing. "That would be quite a coincidence, wouldn't it? Just when he needed money for a trip, presto, a mysterious buyer comes along and hands him fifteen thousand—"

"Is Doc Rudd a personal friend of yours?"

"He's our physician, but not intimate. Why?"

"Did you know he's carrying a letter of yours around in his medical bag?" She flushed, started to shout, but he flagged her down. "I don't mean a letter you wrote him. I'm talking about a letter you received from some female shop in Nashville, a form letter. There's some notes on the back of the envelope—arsenic and so on. He claims it's a formula for a spot remover. What about it?"

She wasn't interested. "I don't know, but I didn't write it. I couldn't even spell arsenic. He must have picked up the envelope from the wastebasket some time when he called on us."

4

Dr. Caffery's Noctuaries

SHERIFF TOL GELSO was sitting alone in the basement corridor of the courthouse, just outside his office. He was the big man in the gray suit that McGavock had seen that morning in front of the hotel. His cane-bottomed chair was canted against the plaster wall, his ankles were hooked into the chair rungs, his knees were spraddled. In the faint light of the overhead globe, he seemed miserably, utterly dejected. McGavock said: "So that's the way it is, Sheriff. I'm duly accredited, and all that. I want to cooperate with the constituted authorities."

Sheriff Gelso said heavily: "—hit's about time. Durn, I hain't shore but I should walk you back to the cells an' lock you up. Whut in hellfire you been up to, anyways? I been tryin' to git to you but you been pepperin' 'round town like a flea in a fryin' pan."

"Well, here I am," McGavock declared. "You want me and I want you. Let's go inside and talk."

Sheriff Gelso's stolid face flinched in self-pity. Stealthily, he got to his feet, opened the office door a couple of inches. Through the crack, McGavock could see three middle-aged women, with dust cloths around their heads, down on all fours, scrubbing the linoleum. They scrubbed rhythmically in circles, the suds flying, and as they worked, they sang a hymn in a gusty, happy tempo. The sheriff closed the door. "The one singin' the lead is Mrs. Gelso. The Baptist Ladies of Thread and Thimble is holdin' a charity meet here this afternoon. We gotta go some'rs else. They won't leave us in. Come with me."

He paused a moment in deep thought, nodded to himself.

He led McGavock down the cold, moist hall, up a narrow staircase at the rear. Unlocking a door at the end of the main floor, he ushered McGavock into a small room, a cubbyhole about eight feet square with two leather-cushioned chairs and an oak table. "Jedge's chamber," he explained proudly. "Set down."

McGavock accepted his invitation. Sheriff Gelso said with honeyed sarcasm: "So yo're Luther McGavock. Mr. Knowy from the big city. You aim to come in an' outsmart the local law. We cain't take care of ourse'ves so, thank you, ma'm, you come in an' he'p us."

McGavock nodded vigorously.

Sheriff Gelso cleared his throat ponderously. "I'm a great scholar of my feller man. I figger this business has got you whipped, so now yo're comin' 'round to me. Am I right?"

"No. Believe it or not, I've come around to give you some information. Do you know how Miss Ella Tincher was killed?"

" 'Course I know how she was kilt. She didn't fall down no cellar steps—her throat was cut." Sheriff Gelso ruminated. "She was a mighty skittish ole lady, afeared of strangers. An' she didn't trust her kin any too much. I wonder if she screamed. Nobuddy heered here."

"She didn't scream, Sheriff."

"How do you know? Was you there?"

"I was."

Sheriff Gelso looked startled. McGavock said: "Don't go off half-cocked. I know you're starving for a suspect but if you salt me away someone else will come out from Memphis to take my place. I didn't kill anybody, and you know it. Lock me up and when this case is cracked, you'll look mighty silly come election time. You want to hear what I have to say, or would you rather have your pound of flesh?"

"Yo're the one that's goin' off half-cocked. We're gettin' along all right, hain't we? Nobuddy's goin' to lock nobuddy up." Sheriff Gelso smiled painfully. "Tell me 'bout what happened, Luther."

"I GOT INTO town about six-twenty, checked my bag, and went out to the house. Those were my orders. The old lady let me in, picked up a tray, her supper tray, from the newelpost, and took me upstairs to her bedroom. While we chatted, she ate. A skimpy piece of chicken breast and a bit of lettuce. She claimed her housekeeper had delayed the meal by an hour and she was plenty hungry. All of a sudden, she rolled from her chair to the floor."

Sheriff Gelso stirred uneasily. "Yo're jest makin' it worse. Now yo're hintin' that she was poisoned, too. That don't make sense."

"When she collapsed, I went downstairs and phoned Dr. Rudd. I returned to her bedroom and found her with her throat cut."

"Will you swear to that, Luther?"

"I certainly will."

"Doggone, I'm beginnin' to wish you hadn't tole me all this. Now, 'y doggies, I guess I'll have to git Dr. Caffery to perform a autopsy."

"No need of that, Sheriff. Here's the answer. It seems complicated but it's really devilishly simple—and brutal. Miss Ella Tincher was killed the *safe* way.

"Miss Ella was diabetic. She was being treated by Dr. Rudd with the new form of insulin treatment, protamine zinc. The patient gets an injection in the morning and it carries through the day. But it's dynamite if you don't handle it just right. The patient has to eat his meals, according to his diet, at specific times. Miss mealtime by an hour, and that brings on calamity. Remember, I told you she was griping because her supper was an hour late!"

Sheriff Gelso folded his hands in his lap. McGavock went on: "This protamine zinc bums up the sugar in the body. If the patient doesn't stoke himself up on carbohydrates at mealtime, bingo, he slips into a coma. That's called insulin shock. Miss Ella complained to me because she couldn't have rice pudding for supper. If she'd had it, she'd have been alive this minute."

Sheriff Gelso said: "But I thought—"

"You thought that diabetics should stay away from sugar. So did I until I remembered. With protamine zinc they have to have it, in the proper dosage. That chicken breast might have been straw for all the good it did. The killer knew that. That's why he set it out for her supper. He planned to wait around until the coma hit her, then to kill her at his leisure. He must have been outside on the balcony waiting. When I left the room, he got in his work. When I came back it was all over."

Sheriff Gelso asked: "Who fixed her meals?"

"Ivy Snowden did. But she's dead, too. You've heard about Ivy?"

"Yes," the sheriff said dryly, "I've heered about Ivy."

"Where does Doc Caffery live, Sheriff?"

"Out on Salem Pike, 'bout a mile from town, jest beyond the bridge. But he's never at home. He spends most of his time 'round town, and takes his calls at Lace Tincher's drugstore. Why?"

"I just wondered."

Sheriff Gelso rolled his eyes at the ceiling, made a little spout of his lips, whistled silently to himself. After a moment, he spoke. "Luther, I gotta admit I had you all wrong. You got a pretty good brain in that noodle o' yours. I'd be mighty proud to have you jine me in this God-awful business. Whut do you say?"

"It would be a pleasure, Sheriff Gelso."

The sheriff took a large pigskin wallet from his coat, extracted an envelope addressed to *Tol Gelso, City.* "You've brought up a couple of names that have been on my mind. Caffery for one, and Ivy Snowden for another. Here's whut come in the mornin's mail. Whut do you make of hit?" He drew out a sheet of thin paper, unfolded it. McGavock picked it up.

The letter had been typewritten with a sticky blue ribbon. It said:

Dear Sheriff,

This is to inform you that Miss Ella Tincher is murder Number Two. Ivy Snowden was murder Number One.

Why doesn't Follett admit he embalmed Ivy?

They say Ivy died of heart trouble. Did old Dr. Caffery pass on her death? Was she really dead when he turned her over to the undertaker? Did the undertaker really kill her? Was this murder? I say *yes.*

(1) Fannin knows something he hasn't told.

(2) Dr. Rudd will soon be back at his regular practice now that Miss Ella is dead. You wait and see.

(3) Lace Tincher was seen coming out of his drugstore late the night that Ivy died.

"Four, Sheriff Tol Gelso has been attending barn dances over in Lunken County with what well-known widow?" McGavock laughed.

"I hain't been attendin' no dances with no one." The sheriff was outraged. "I'm happily married—"

"A typical poison pen letter," McGavock remarked. "Maybe a little more than that. There's an idea, somewhere in there, that he wants to get across. Do you think we can trace the typewriter?"

"I've already did that. The schoolhouse was broke into last night. The principal's machine has a blue ribbon jest like that. He puts machine oil on hit to make hit last longer—"

"Then we'll drop that angle. We're up a blind alley there." McGavock rose. "That business about Fannin knowing something he hasn't told looks like a good tip. I think I'll dig him up."

Sheriff Gelso said anxiously: "A great idee. I'll jest go along an'—"

"We'd better not double up on him; he stampedes easy. You see him now, I'll check later in the afternoon." McGavock hesitated in the doorway. "Oh, yes. Something I wanted to inquire about. I suffer from insomnia, Sheriff. I toss all night. Say I should wake up about one o'clock in the morning, where could I get a drink in this town?"

"I hear tell Sweat Johnson sells lard-can whiskey in that house o' his along the railroad tracks. He's a ex-jailbird an' all-'round bad man. I wouldn't fiddle 'round with him if I was you. An' should you run into him, don't mention me. Hit wouldn't be no recommendation."

The first man McGavock accosted on the courthouse steps gave him directions. He gave him a mighty funny look, too.

HALF AN HOUR later McGavock was following the beaten clay path that led out of town. After a while, the path forked, the wider trail continuing forward, a narrower tine branching to the left. McGavock took this tangent, fought his way through dead pipestem weeds and winter briars. The trail came into the open, began paralleling the tracks which ran along a five-foot embankment at his shoulder. After about a hundred yards, he saw the shack.

It was an ancient log cabin and set back in a hollow, half-hidden by a windbreak of young catalpas. The face of the building was literally plastered with stolen tin tobacco signs, tacked wrong-side out, to keep bad weather out of the gaping chinks. A section of two-by-four had been nailed between two gum trees and the skeleton of a stripped and gutted model-T Ford rusted in the yard. The cabin's one window had been boarded up, giving it a deserted appearance, but a hairy, evil-looking riding mule was tied to the rail hitching rack between the gum trees. McGavock said grimly to himself: "Dear Atherton, wish you were here. Signed, Luther McG."

He put his instep on the soggy cedar log doorstep, rapped sharply. There was no response, and he repeated his thumping. A man came around the corner of the shanty, about three feet from him, and said: "I hear you. I hain't deef. Whut you want?"

He was a big man, barefooted, dressed only in corduroy pants and a dirty undershirt. He had a flat apish face with spread nostrils and ragged uncut black hair. McGavock said coldly: "I want in. What the hell did you think I wanted?"

"Who are you?"

"I'm Inspector Lecoq from the middle of the last century. And I haven't got time to fool."

The man's beetle brow wrinkled. "A dick, eh? I hain't did nothin'." He unlocked the door, McGavock followed him inside.

The cabin was one narrow room with an earthen floor. There was a slab-timber table with a coal oil lamp, a few disreputable chairs. At the rear was a primitive fireplace with a length of railroad tie on a couple of paving bricks, filling the room with the odor of burning creosote. The big man pushed aside a tangle of filthy quilts, perched himself on the edge of his bunk. McGavock swung a chair around, sat astraddle its back. After a moment, he asked: "You Sweat Johnson?"

"I hain't his pappy."

"Well, Sweat, I want you to turn informer. I want you to stool pigeon for me."

The big man began to perspire. Beads of moisture gathered on his cheeks and upper lip, grew to globules, blended into a wet glaze in the firelight. Finally, he got his rage under control, said softly: "Git out'n here. Afore I uncouple you!"

"We'll start with Fannin. He was in here after midnight, the night before last, wasn't he?"

"Who is this Fannin? I don't know him."

McGavock meditated. He took a piece of paper from his vest, pretended to peruse it, put it away. "We'll forget Fannin. We don't want him anyhow, we just want to know about him. You keep Fannin, we'll take the rest."

The big man's face showed confusion, uneasiness. "Whut you mean, you'll take the *rest?*" His apish forehead creased in attention. "Who you talkin' 'bout?"

"You don't know, eh? Well, I'll enlighten you. I want to know about Frederick Henry Seddon, Herbert Armstrong, Dr. Hawley Harvey Crippen, and above all, Landru!"

"Never heered of any of 'em!"

McGavock gave a mocking laugh. "That's very strange. They're all notorious criminals."

"They're wanted, eh? I still say I've never heered of 'em."

"How do you make a living? No need to answer. You've got a nice cozy shack back here in the brush, a stone's throw from the railroad track. Say Crippen or Landru should be coming through, riding the rails. Say they were well-heeled with dough, but hot. A man could drop off, hole up with you in this shanty until things cooled down, and be on his way again. You're playing with dynamite, my boy. Talk, or you're a gone skunkskin!"

The big man's jaw worked but no words came. At last he said hoarsely: "I'm jest a pore farmer. I got a patch o' hilly ground over the ridge an' ride a ole blue mule. My land don't feed me. I run this place an' sell a little whiskey to a few friends. I been in the county jail a couple o' times for shootin' and cuttin' but I hain't got no outlander contacks like yo're a-sayin'. I git along all right an' I don't keer fer no big-city trouble comin' in on me. Why should I stick my neck out for Fannin?"

McGavock looked skeptical. Sweat Johnson said hurriedly: "You ast 'bout him bein' here night afore last. That's true, he was. Met Lace Tincher here, an' left with him."

"Oh, come now. Don't tell me Mr. Tincher frequents your establishment?"

"He comes here now an' then to git tight, if that's whut you mean."

"Was he drunk that night?"

"No. But Fannin was. They was jest the two of 'em here an' they set yonder at the table, Fannin drinkin' an' Lace watchin' him."

"What time was this?"

The barefoot man considered. " 'Bout midnight. I knowed later that Ivy had jest died."

McGavock's voice was casual. "What gave you that idea?"

"The way they talked. Fannin was loaded to the gills. He kep' sayin': 'Ivy's a wonnerful gal, she's gonna get well sometime.' An' then Lace would say: 'She shorely was a wonnerful woman. Hetherton's gonna miss her.' Hit give me goose pimples to listen to 'em. I didn't know at the time whether she was dead or alive—an' they couldn't seem to agree on hit!"

"Then they left together. Is that right?"

"Yep. An' then, some hours later, Fannin come back. You know the way drunks do. He kinda worried me this time. He was outa his head. I declare, he must've drinked a half gallon all told. He was ravin' crazy. Thought I was a game warden that had arrested him when he was eleven years old an' wanted to knife-fight me. Then he thought I was the old preacher that had buried his daddy an' wanted to buy me a side o' bacon an' a sack o' beans to tide me over the winter in pay fer hit. Then to top hit off, he got the idee that I was Shur'f Tol Gelso an' wanted to give hisself up to the law. I had to pertend to take him into custody afore he'd quiet down an' git out."

McGavock scoffed.

"I mean hit," the big man insisted. "He claimed that two

respectable citizens here in Hetherton was kinda feudin' an' that Ivy sorta got inbetwixt 'em—an' got slew. By now he knowed she was dead an' was sayin' she was murdered. He said he'd done hit hisself, unbeknownst to him, by givin' her poison medicine!"

McGavock walked to the door. Sweat Johnson's pig eyes were burning greedily. He said: "Them fellers you mentioned, Crippen an' Landru an' Seddon an' so on. I got their names socked back in my head where I won't never forgit 'em. I want to ast you this, is they any bounty on 'em? Should they drop in, an' I turn 'em over, would hit pay me money?"

"If you can get those very men," McGavock said deliriously, "and can prove it—you can ask your own reward. *Wow!*"

THE BLOCK GILT letters on the plate glass window were in the form of an arch and read, THE HETHERTON NATIONAL BANK. Below, in letters almost as large, was Lace Tincher, Pres. A big boxlike gong was affixed on the clapboard false front, four feet above the door, and another burglar alarm, a strip of thin metal, ran in a circuit around the window pane. Caution, McGavock was beginning to realize, was evidently a Tincher family trait.

He slid his hand along the gas pipe railing, ascended the three flat cement steps, and entered the building. Inside, it was like a miniature fort. The teller's window was shatterproof glass, spaced above and below, from floor to ceiling, with heavy, woven basketlike steel mesh. Behind the cashier were desks, files, volumes of records. The cashier nodded pleasantly. McGavock said: "I want to see Mr. Tincher."

The cashier spoke to a woman at an adding machine. She

disappeared, reappeared, smiled. Someone pressed a button and the electric latch in a small door against the wall began stuttering. The cashier said: "Just go right in, Mr. McGavock. He's expecting you."

McGavock groped his way down an inside corridor, past the directors' room, found himself in a high-ceilinged, oblong office at the rear of the building. Lace Tincher, his hair a silvery halo in the gray afternoon light, sat stiffly behind his desk in his shoddy brown suit. Lace Tincher's suit might have cost eighteen-fifty, but the big mahogany desk with its floral border and carved acanthus leaves legs had set him back about the price of a thoroughbred horse. The desk blotter was spotless and the onyx desk set was as nice and new, except for a treasured film of dust, as when it came out of its wrappings. Mr. Lace Tincher was a man who loved his luxury, and hoarded it. He put on that fixed smile, said: "I thought you'd look me up, sir. It's pretty hard to get anything done in Hetherton without consulting Old Lace. He carries the key that makes the clock run, doesn't he?"

"Does he? That's what I'm here to find out." McGavock gave him a steady, antagonistic stare. "Fannin tells me that you were around to a den of iniquity with him the other night. Out by the railroad tracks at a place run by Sweat Johnson. Is that true?"

Tincher got up hastily, shut the door into the hall. "I've got stomach ulcers. Sometimes I suffer great misery—"

"So you run out to Sweat's for a little relief. Now I wonder how you got those ulcers! I bet it was drinking vile tap-water." McGavock paused, added: "Is Fannin a buddy of yours?"

Tincher got genuinely angry. "Of course not. He rents a room above my hardware store. The night Miss Ivy died—"

"I wish you'd tell me about that."

"I'm attempting to. I'm not unversed in law and I think if you'll allow me, I can answer your question entirely to your satisfaction. I will give it to you just as though I were on a witness stand. A little after twelve the night before last, I was coming down Main Street when Fannin appeared in the entranceway which leads up to his quarters."

"Was there anyone with him?"

"Yes, sir, there was, Dr. Caffery. They stood and talked. As I came up, the doctor departed. I asked Fannin if he was in trouble. He said that Ivy was very ill, that Dr. Caffery had just pronounced her dead but that he didn't believe it. He was slightly drunk, he almost seemed drugged. He insisted that I go up and take a look. I did."

"Was she dead?"

Lace Tincher smiled slowly. "Of course she was dead. Fannin—"

"Someone said they saw you coming out of your drugstore about that time."

"Very true. As I was saying, Fannin asked that I open my drugstore and get some smelling salts or something. He stood on the curb, and I went back into the prescription room. When I came out, he was gone. I began to feel my stomach ulcers about then and strolled out to Sweat Johnson's for a—"

"Then you didn't meet Fannin there?"

"Don't be absurd."

"Listen," McGavock asked, "did Fannin act funny. I mean did he do anything out of line all evening."

"No-o-o." Mr. Tincher pursed his lips. "Nothing out of line. Strange thing though, now you mention it. I had a queer sensation while I was in my drugstore, back in the prescription department, that he'd slipped in from the sidewalk for an instant and was fooling around on the shelves."

McGavock looked disgusted. "You're a liar by the clock, and you know it. Fannin wasn't in your drugstore—now, was he?"

Lace Tincher rose half out of his mahogany chair. He extended a bony finger, shook it in assumed fury. "You can't talk to me like that, I won't sit here and be abused by a smart-alecky—"

"Here's why I looked you up," McGavock changed the subject. "How long have you known Dr. Caffery?"

"All my life. He used to be a great doctor, the old-timers tell me. But everyone agrees now that he's bungling and dangerous. His license should be revoked!"

"You mean on general principles? That's twice today you've said that."

Lace Tincher looked smugly secretive. "I know something about him that the average townsman doesn't know. I know what makes him so sprightly, so energetic. He takes dope."

McGavock listened in silence. Tincher went on: "I just happened to stumble on it and the remarkable thing is that he merely tried to laugh it off—after swearing me to secrecy. Here's how it came about. You know the bank here photographs the checks we handle. I was glancing through the files and came across a check of Dr. Caffery's—made out for eight dollars. Down in the corner, you know, where it says For—he'd filled in *noctuaries.* For noctuaries. Well, I thought of course that he had made a mistake, that he'd meant *electuaries.* I referred to the dictionary, but I couldn't find it and decided there was no such word."

"Your dictionary wasn't large enough."

"I presume now that you must be correct. The next time he came in, I confronted him with it. I asked him politely what noctuaries were. He didn't seem too anxious to discuss it. I pressed him, however, and finally he said: 'Personally, I think it's none of your business but it's an unfortunate habit I picked up years ago. I'd give a hundred dollars if I could break myself of it.' Then he asked me to keep it under my hat and I gave him my solemn promise to do so."

"One thing I like about you, Mr. Tincher, is that you give solemn promises! When will Miss Snowden be buried?"

Mr. Tincher averted his gaze. "I understand she was interred this very morning, poor girl."

"And talking about solemn promises," McGavock said thoughtfully, "I wonder if you'd be good enough to shove one of them in my direction?"

"Anything, my good fellow. Anything, that is, within reason. What did you have in mind?"

"I want you to promise me that you won't take that fifteen thousand dollars and beat it out of town. I wouldn't like it and I don't think Sheriff Gelso would either. If we're going to crack your aunt's murder, we're going to need you around. As you said, if we want to get anything done in Hetherton, we've got to consult Old Lace—he carries the key that makes the clock run!"

Tincher's seraphic face flushed fiery red, paled to dead flabby white. He said furiously: "I'm going to phone your office. I'm going to have you demoted!"

McGavock guffawed. "Well bless your old two-timing double-dealing heart! I'm working now for shoe buttons and beer bottle tops." He lowered his voice intimately. "Would you like to see the agency brand on my back? They got me out of a debtor's prison and I'm theirs to have and to hold for life!"

5

The Abditory by the *Pons Exiguus*

FANNIN WASN'T IN his room above the hardware store. The counterman at the Rosebud Café suggested that he might be found at the cemetery. Time was getting short, but McGavock decided to take a chance.

The cemetery was on the edge of town, just beyond the gin. It was a sterile, ugly place, entirely grassless, enclosed by a sagging cattle fence supported by rotting cedar posts. McGavock sauntered through unsightly, pink boulder gateposts, and looked about him.

The sky, overcast all day, was breaking in the west above the hilltops in a ragged line of brass and the setting sun bathed the barren earth in a harsh, unfriendly light. It was a pitiful layout, yellow clay and tombstones. Big tombstones and small ones, mail order and old homemade jobs, catching the amber sunglow like cubes of loaf sugar. There was no shrubbery whatever, with the exception of a few small evergreens that had withered at the root and stood emaciated in the sunset like X-rays of the human hand. Fannin was seated on a wooden bench, in the cheaper section. Not far from him was a mound of new-turned clay.

He looked up as McGavock approached. If it weren't for the slump of his figure, McGavock would hardly have recognized him. He was neatly shaved and there was even a dusting of talcum beneath his ear. He was dressed in an inexpensive but immaculate black suit and his boots were shined. McGavock sat beside him on the bench, said calmly: "This is no good for a man. They tell me you've been here all day. Get out of here. Drop in on Sweat Johnson."

Fannin turned his head slowly. "You know Sweat?"

"Sure. He's working for me now. Listen, Fannin, we want to clear this up, don't we? Sweat told me that you were talking mighty freely to him the other night. He said that you claimed you killed Ivy Snowden. How about it?"

"That's right. I give her the medicine." He spoke in a monotone. "I kilt her jest like this gun"—he slapped his armpit—"kills. Hit does the work, but somebuddy else has got to pull the trigger."

"Tell me, Fannin—the night Ivy died, did you go into Lace's drugstore with him?"

The hillman looked puzzled. "Not that I remember, no. I went out to Johnson's cabin to wait for him."

"To wait for him? Why?"

"I cain't recall." He furrowed his brow, spoke softly. "But hit'll come to me. An' that's all I'll need."

McGavock said sternly: "No homespun justice, my friend. There's law in town, you know. We won't have any of that!"

"Any of whut?" Fannin sounded weary.

"Any more of that shooting down dark alleys."

Fannin said pointedly: "I didn't have nothin' like that in mind."

McGavock remained silent. Fannin's eye wandered to the new grave. He began to talk. " 'Bout a hour ago, Sheriff Gelso come in here, like yo're doin', an' ast me a lot of sly questions. While he was shootin' off his mouth, I got to thinkin'. Sheriff

Gelso eats three times a day, an' so do you. How do y'all make your livin'? By messin' 'round in other folkses' private affairs."

"So?"

"Well, they's a funny thing 'bout questions. The feller that asts 'em tells a heap more'n he means to. Lots o' people have been astin' me questions, you, an' Lace Tincher, an' Sheriff Gelso. At first hit made me mad, then I settled down to listenin'. With whut I know—an' whut all you folks know—I'm beginnin' to figger out jest what happened to Ivy Snowden an' Miss Ella Tincher."

McGavock beamed. "Fine! I'd like to hear."

"Shore you would. That's yore livin', like I said. I been sittin' here all day, McGavock, an' you know whut's come over me? I 'bout made up my mind to go into the business like you an' Sheriff Gelso. I expec' I'd be purty good at it. An' I don't mean I'm gonna wear no badge!"

"I see," McGavock said affably. "You're taking up blackmail?"

"Somebuddy's got to pay fer Ivy's buryin'—an' if you knowed her like I did, you'd know she wouldn't have been too partickler where the money come from."

"That's a temptation I wouldn't yield to, brother. The only way I can save your hide is to beat you to the draw. Are you a sporting man?"

"I claim to be."

McGavock talked fast. "O.K. Then I'll put it this way. You say you know everything I know, and a little more. That extra bit is like holding an ace up your sleeve. That's cheating and cheating is against the Gospel, and against the law of man and beast. Am I right?" There never was a hillman alive, he knew, who could resist an argument.

Fannin's cheeks were sandstone in the fading light. He said, annoyed: "I guess you got me there. I cain't jest think up no answer on the spur of the moment. O.K., I'll tell you whut I know—but hit won't he'p you none." He chose his words carefully. "After I talked with you last night, somethin' come to me. When Judy Tincher was a kid she was always doin' takeoffs of folks at church an' school. She could imitate a voice to a T. Now Dr. Rudd's voice, gentle an' sweet thataway, should be easy to—"

"You mean it was Miss Judy who called you on the phone and warned you against me?"

"Could be. An' here's somethin' else. Lace Tincher has never charged me an' Ivy one penny rent fer that room above his hardware store. He claims the insurance is cheaper on the store if we're livin' above hit. But I don't believe hit. Money is Lace's life blood. Why should he—"

McGavock got to his feet, stretched. He walked about five paces, stopped, said amiably: "You don't like the Tinchers, do you Fannin?"

The hillman grinned. "No. And I don't think they like me, neither."

AS SHERIFF GELSO had said, Old Doc Caffery's home was a mile out on the Salem Pike. But the good sheriff had neglected to mention that this single, solitary mile was hell on wheels. Just a frog-jump from the corporation line and McGavock found himself in the heart of the swamp country.

The sun had set and in the early dusk the rutted clay road was rough-and-tumble walking to McGavock's city-trained ankles. It was wild, Godforsaken country and the further he walked, the worse it got.

Dr. Caffery's home sat among the boles of giant beeches. To McGavock's amazement, it wasn't a house, it was a mansion. Or rather, it had been at one time. Two stories high, it had three double-deck porches and a stained glass window above the front door. It was an old, sad familiar story—some wealthy man, years ago, had made a bad guess and had backed it with a bankroll. Now, the building was falling to pieces beneath the plucking hand of time. Shingles stuck up from the roof like a chicken caught in a gale, trumpet vines had pried the gingerbread from the veranda railings, its windows were battered, many of them patched with newspaper.

McGavock stepped on the porch from the side, walked half its length, and knocked on the front door. He found the door unlocked, opened it, and called into the gloomy interior: "Hello! I'm breaking and entering! Anybody home? Is there a doctor in the house?"

He entered, shut the door behind him. He flipped on his flashlight and started through the building.

It was like a house from another world, a half-forgotten world of mist and fog. Year after year of seeping moisture had blistered the parlor wallpaper from the plaster until it hung in listless folds, the once fine cherry furniture, the piano, had felt the damp fingers of the swamp until their varnished surfaces were dulled to moldy white.

He left the parlor and walked down the broad hall. The rug beneath his feet had rotted until it felt like moss. All at once, he had the vague sensation that he wasn't alone. He turned, saw no movement, heard nothing.

It was the library that he wanted and he found it at the end of the corridor, by the back stairs. He parted tattered portieres, once fine brocade, now like seaweed, and stepped inside. It was then that his ears caught the sound he'd been sensing, a muted *flip-flip*—like a stocking-footed man, or a fluttering bat.

Dr. Caffery's library showed signs of habitation. The walls were lined with mildewed books, linked each to his neighbor by yeasty fungus, but the circular table in the center of the room, and the easy chair alongside it, testified to occupancy. On the table was a calabash pipe, a humidor of tobacco, an old-fashioned steel pen and a bottle of ink. McGavock struck a match to the wick of a coal oil lamp, placed it on the mantel shelf.

He found three small red books in the table drawer, all alike, each stamped with the word Diary. Two of them were blank, the other had entries on the first dozen pages.

These were Dr. Caffery's noctuaries. Noctuary, McGavock knew, was the old-fashioned word for diary. A diary is actually a journal kept at *night.*

The Memphis detective had heard, too, about the diary habit, how when once it got you in its grip you couldn't shake it off. That was what Caffery had meant when he told Lace Tincher about the eight-dollar check. He'd asked Lace not to make it public. Folks wouldn't much want to retain a doctor who wrote down all about them in a diary. And Lace Tincher, with his slanderous, over-subtle imagination, had thus deduced that the old doctor was taking dope!

THE DIARY, McGAVOCK soon discovered, was disappointingly dull. The entries were mainly speculations about tomorrow's weather or nature notes about wild life the doctor has observed about him in the swamp. The two final items, however, took a surprising twist. The first, dated yesterday, said:

A little snow last night. The seasons must be getting milder. I remember very cold winters as a boy. Saw a female opossum and her young in that hollow red oak by Lester Cullens' peanut patch. I'm afraid I have got myself into a mess. I must be very closemouthed. I feel that I am in great danger.

The second item, dated that day, was short and sweet—and a little confusing.

This afternoon I performed an emergency surgical operation on my pons exiguus. Incised an abditory.

Again, from the general direction of the hall came that furtive *flip-flip*. McGavock ignored it, stared at the diary page in anger. "He can't do this to me!" he muttered. "Pons exiguus, I know, is simply Latin for little bridge. But what the hell is abditory?" He glanced about him. "Ten-to-one he didn't know that one himself. He's being careful. He must have got it out of one of these books of his." He passed up a dictionary as being too obvious, selected a small blue volume entitled, *Our Mother Language, Words Obsolete or Rare.*

Abditory was on page six. Abditory—a secret hiding place.

So that afternoon Dr. Caffery had constructed himself, dug, a secret hiding place by a little bridge. And Dr. Caffery's little bridge must undoubtedly be that pole bridge a few yards down the road. If he had a hiding place, he'd want it in the near vicinity.

McGavock put the diary back in the table drawer as he had found it, replaced the blue book on its shelf, and left the house.

The hiding place, per directions, was back up under the

bridge, all right. It wasn't too hard to locate. You could see where the ground had been disturbed. McGavock pulled aside the earth with his hands, exhumed a tobacco can.

The can appeared to be stuffed with cotton batting. He propped his flashlight on his knee, took out the batting—and the beam of his torch struck a blinding glitter into his palm. He was holding a diamond brooch. Miss Ella Tincher's diamond brooch!

He placed it carefully in his wallet, clambered to the road, and returned to the house. He sat himself quietly on the edge of the sagging porch and waited.

He waited about twenty minutes. The house stayed dark. Finally, so suddenly that it almost took him unawares, the front door opened. He switched on his flash, swung its beam full on the cringing figure startled beneath the impact of the glare. McGavock said genially: "Dr. Caffery! Don't tell me you were home all the time? Did you know I was just inside?"

"I know nothing. I was upstairs, asleep."

McGavock said: "So you were upstairs asleep! Hogwash. You were tiptoeing through the house, following me from room to room."

Dr. Caffery sniffed in prim distaste. "I choose to act the way I please, sir. It's my home so don't tell me how to—"

"I read your diary, Doc. To while away the time. I read about a *pons exiguus* and an abdi-something-or-other."

The old man gave a condescending simper. "Those are pretty big words for you, aren't they, Mr. McGavock?"

"I know what they mean, Professor." Before Caffery could close his gaping mouth, McGavock produced the diamond brooth. "Where did you get this!"

"It is not mine." The old man fidgeted. "I mean I'm keeping it for a friend. You see—"

"Who is this friend? This brooch is stolen property!"

Dr. Caffery gave a weak incredulous laugh. "Surely you must be in error! I'm keeping that brooch for Dr. Maximilian Rudd. He's a very astute man. He wouldn't be victimized into receiving stolen property."

"Thanks," McGavock said blandly. "That's all I want to know." He shut off the flashlight. "How about it? Going to walk back to town with me?"

"I'm afraid I must decline," Dr. Caffery answered hastily. "I feel the need of a glass of sherry. Good night, sir."

ROOM 116 MIGHT not have been the worst that the Huston House had to offer, but it certainly wasn't any bridal chamber. It was clean, though. McGavock opened his Gladstone, took out clean underclothes, a clean shirt. He stripped to the waist, took a quick sponge bath from the bowl, slipped on a worn dressing robe. He had reached in the pocket of his robe for a cigarette when his door opened.

Judy Tincher strolled in, closed the door with her heel.

McGavock said: "Meet me in the lobby. This is no place to—"

"I want to talk to you. The lobby's too public." She was back on the cosmetics again and dressed for a fish-fry. "I hired you. Right?"

"Yep."

"Well, now I'm firing you. Pack up your bag and get out of town. You can send me a bill from Memphis."

He said: "Say that again, I'm fired and all that, only say it as Dr. Rudd would. In his voice." Without a flicker of expression she complied. The imitation was perfect.

He shook his head. "I don't believe it. You're good but not good enough. You could have called Fannin and rattled off a brief warning, but it wasn't you I was talking to the night the old lady was killed. My conversation with Rudd was a long one, full of tricky stuff, questions and answers. You'd have given yourself away some place along the line."

He picked up his clean shirt, stepped out into the empty hall, put it on, and returned to the room. "You were muttering something about my being fired?"

"That's right. You're canned."

He put on his necktie before the cracked mirror. "You're not going to like this, and I hate to disillusion you, but the truth is I'm not working for you. You're a minor. I'm working for Lace. By the way, you were telling me that Brother Lace was once a backwoods storekeeper. Was it a big store?"

"That was before my day. Aunt Ella was living with him at the time. She's told me a little about it. It was down in the wild corner of the county and pretty isolated. He sold groceries and furniture and general farm supplies. He bought cotton, too, I believe." She hesitated, added sullenly: "There's a train for Memphis leaving at ten-thirty. That gives you two hours."

"I know. I'll be on it."

She smiled. "That's better. I thought you said—"

He reached for the doorknob. "I said I wasn't going to drop the case. By ten-thirty, it'll be closed. I know who our killer is, I know the motive and the modus operandi. About all we have to do now is make the arrest."

6

The Amateur Embalmer

McGAVOCK WAS CROSSING the street, heading for the sheriff's office, when a gray coupé pounced out of an alley and slowed to a stop, almost running him down. The driver reached over, opened the door, said: "McGavock! Am I glad to see you! I've had you in mind ever since I left home. Get in." In the faint light of the dash, Dr. Rudd appeared highly excited, haggard.

McGavock climbed in. There was a Colt automatic on the seat cushion beside the doctor.

Rudd launched the car into action, said desperately: "This is it, Mr. McGavock. Believe me, I'm glad you're along."

McGavock gave the doctor a hard inspection. He seemed to have aged ten years. The creases at the corners of his mouth were tense, weary. McGavock asked mildly: "This is what?"

"The end." Dr. Rudd's gentle baritone cracked slightly under some terrific strain. "I'm through with this nonsense. I'm going to face it."

McGavock watched the road. The coupé barreled around a wagon loaded with a farmer and his family, skidded up a side street. Rudd spoke rapidly, almost incoherently.

"It's a queer story and I don't expect you to sympathize with me, especially because I'm not going to tell you the whole thing. This I will say, however. I came to Hetherton, built up a nice practice. I was getting along fine. Then it happened. Not so long ago, tremendous pressure was brought to bear on me. I received orders to continue my work—but to ease out of real emergency cases. I'm revolting!"

"I'm inclined to agree, if you'll pardon the double entendre. Where are we going?"

"To Miss Ella Tincher's tobacco barn. On a lane by the creek back of her house. I just received a telephone call. It seems Joel Taggert is there, badly wounded. The Taggerts and the Gogartys are at it again. There's been some shooting. I'm a doctor, and by God—"

"Who is this Joel Taggert?"

"I never heard of him."

"The Taggerts and the Gogartys. It sounds too good to be true."

"That's what I think. Frankly, I've never heard of any of them."

McGavock thought this over. "And that's why you're bringing a gun along."

"It may be a trap for me. I may need a gun." Dr. Rudd hesitated. "Or it may be true, the boy may be in a bad way. I'm going to find out."

The coupé left the fringes of the town behind it. They turned down a winding lane, Dr. Rudd cut his wheel through an open gate and killed the motor.

They were in a small hollow. Sodden overlapping clouds obliterated the moon and in the stillness of the night McGavock had the sensation of being in a great outdoor cave. He could make out the dim outlines of clumps of brush and tangled saplings. A few yards away was the tobacco barn, a great gaunt structure, twice the size of an ordinary barn, a weird black hulk in the shadows. Rudd said: "It's been abandoned for ten years. You know, of course, what these buildings are like inside. Just one enormous room reaching to the ridgepole. We may have a bit of difficulty with fallen timbers. I've noticed it in the daylight. The rear end of the roof has collapsed. Do you have a gun?"

McGavock didn't answer that. He said instead: "Let's go."

"And one thing more," Rudd cautioned softly. "I wouldn't use a flashlight, not at first. If something's sour, it'll just make us targets." He stepped through the sagging doorway, McGavock followed.

Across the threshold, McGavock took a quick pace to one side, lest his body be silhouetted against the lesser darkness behind him. Rudd had simply vanished in the spongy blackness. He stood for a long moment, listening. There was no sound. It was like being in a grotto lined with black velvet. He took out his gun, said: "Where are you, Rudd? This foolishness has gone on long enough."

Three shots, hand running, split the tomblike darkness. Their deep drumlike reverberations rolled and hammered through the empty barn.

McGavock switched on his flash. Rudd was at the far end of the building, standing midst the wreckage of the fallen roof. His tie was askew and all the buttons had been ripped from his coat. He looked dazed. He held his medical bag in one hand and in the other he had the blue steel automatic.

McGavock wandered up. "What happened?"

"I was attacked," Rudd said helplessly. "I came back here and a man grabbed me and tried to choke me. It was your being along that saved my life. If I'd been alone he doubtless would have shot me. You threw him off, he was afraid of drawing your fire. Yes, by God, he almost strangled me here in the dark without your knowing it. Luckily, I had my gun. I drove him away!"

McGavock listened with interest. Rudd took a deep breath, suddenly exclaimed: "What's that? Why, it's blood!"

There was a red stain, wet and new, on a timber. They followed the sticky train, drop by drop, to the back door which stood open. Rudd looked horrified. "I must have hit him."

McGavock said harshly: "I don't like this, any of it. Our killer is fighting for his life. Let's get back to town. I want you to pick up the sheriff and then well drop in on Lace Tincher. I've a notion he can help us. This business has to be stopped—and I mean now!"

SHERIFF GELSO GOT out of the car rump first, McGavock followed him, and Dr. Rudd came around from the other side. Silently, they took the flagstone walk to the yellow brick house, stepped up onto the porch. The big sheriff was mumbling to himself, uncertain of his position. Rudd seemed docilely bored, but mildly curious. McGavock was about to push the button when Rudd tapped him on the elbow, said warily: "Isn't that my colleague?"

The three men looked through the bay window, into the living room. Caffery was standing by the mantel, laying down the law to Lace Tincher. The old man's face was predatory, excited. He was shaking his bony finger in the air and his aged, loose lips were working furiously in speech the onlookers could not hear.

McGavock rang the bell. Caffery looked wildly about him, as though he were about to fly. Tincher spoke a few sharp words and the three men disappeared around the side of the porch. A moment later the door opened and Lace ushered the old doctor out of the house. He said: "... I take the pink pills on the half hour and the green ones on the hour? I see. Good night, Doctor. My headache's better already. If I need you, I'll phone."

Without a sign of greeting, Caffery pushed through the group on the porch, vanished into the night. Lace Tincher said effusively: "Gentlemen, gentlemen! This is a pleasant surprise." His voice broke regretfully. "I'm going to have to ask you to come back tomorrow, though. I've a splitting headache and—"

McGavock walked past him, into the house. The others followed.

Tincher waved his hand toward the living room archway, said icily: "I must say this is an imposition, but if you insist, at least you shall make yourselves comfortable. My hospitality is beyond reproach. Enter, gentlemen."

McGavock ignored him. He said: "This way, Sheriff." He passed the living room, walked down the hallway to the kitchen. The others trailed along. In the kitchen, he opened the small door to Lace Tincher's annex-office.

"There's your killer," McGavock said coldly. "It's all over. How do you like him?"

Fannin sat in a big overstuffed chair in the center of the room. His sleeve had been cut from his shirt and a gauze dressing had been applied to his shoulder. The big chair had been heaped with pillows. The hillman, sunk in their feathery depths, watched his visitors with angry, vicious eyes. Beside him, on Lace Tincher's desk, lay his fancy holster and his Police Special. Sheriff Gelso said sharply: "Git that pistol! He's armed."

"He wouldn't use it," McGavock remarked, "in public. He's

modest that way. He likes dark alleys and dark barns, eh? Fannin?"

Fannin's lips sneered but his slitted eyes were full of hate. Sheriff Gelso picked up the .38. McGavock said: "There's the man you wounded, Dr. Rudd. What do you think of him?"

Rudd's voice was gentle, melodious. He said: I wish I'd finished him. If you only knew—"

"I know everything." McGavock looked grim. "And it isn't a pretty story. This man, Fannin, had a wife, Ivy Snowden. She had a bad heart and he knew she was going to die. He gave it a lot of thought and finally worked out a scheme whereby he could actually make money from her death! As nasty a bit of business as I've ever run into!"

Sheriff Gelso said: "Made money out of Ivy's death? I don't see how a body could—"

McGavock explained. "The setup here in Hetherton was almost perfect. It had Lace Tincher, here, and Old Doc Caffery. But it had Dr. Rudd, too, and he had to be pushed out of the picture; he was the wrench in the works. Fannin first went to work on Rudd, got him into semi-retirement. I don't know just how he managed it, but it had something to do with the diamond brooch. Would you care to clear that up, Doctor?"

Rudd was white around the lips. "I might as well. You're a little rough but I guess you're trying to help me. You know Ivy Snowden was Miss Ella Tincher's housekeeper. Well, one day Fannin was in the kitchen when I put the old lady's brooch in the sideboard. A couple of days later he told me that he'd picked the lock and stolen it. He said that both he and Ivy would swear that they saw me take the thing, and the old lady knew I had the key. His stipulation was that I should drop out of emergency cases for a few weeks. He scared me to death, I lost my head. I knew of a doctor who was a kleptomaniac and you can guess how the reputation helped his practice! After I got into it, I couldn't get out."

McGavock looked disgusted. "That was one half of the scheme, to involve you, to pressure you into silence. He tried to clinch it by involving you with murder. Later tonight, he tried to eliminate you completely."

Rudd looked bleak. McGavock continued: "I'm speaking of Miss Ella. That was a needless murder, done by a desperate man trying to gild the lily. The cue for action, in Fannin's plan, was the death of Ivy. Remember how he kept her death quiet for an entire day? That was so he could arrange Miss Ella's supper tray—and slay her. I almost upset his plans but he went through with it. The old lady was killed simply to place you in a dangerous situation, Rudd. The key was taken from her shoe and the digitalis bottles were placed in the sideboard. However, I happened to be on the scene and phoned you. That gave you a perfect alibi."

Fannin said hoarsely: "Put this man out o' here, Lace. I shot myself cleanin' my gun. Doc Caffery says I gotta have rest."

"The digitalis, of course," McGavock declared, "was Caffery's prescription for Ivy. Fannin held out his wife's medicine and hastened her death. There were no labels on the bottles but I'll bet that the pharmacist at Lace's drugstore will swear he handed them to Fannin in person. They're on the register, too. You see, Fannin really killed his woman, too."

SHERIFF GELSO LOOKED hard, angry. "I shore hope word of this don't git 'round till we git him behind bars."

Lace Tincher asked: "What became of the diamond brooch?"

McGavock handed it over. "Fannin gave it to Caffery in payment for medical expenses. He had no idea of its value, and neither did Caffery. When Caffery found out its value, he spoke to Fannin. Fannin admitted it was stolen, frightened the old doctor into laying the blame on Rudd if it was caught in his possession."

"But what," Rudd asked, "was the purpose behind this?"

"The purpose was money. It was a scheme built on suspicion but the circumstantial evidence was so tightly woven that it paid dividends." McGavock looked at Lace Tincher. "Your kid sister didn't know what it was all about but she was scared. She brought me in and then tried to get me out of town. She said Miss Ella was killed 'for my brother's money.' She didn't know how right she was!"

McGavock rubbed his jaw, went on: "With Rudd out of the way, an old fumbling doctor was called on the scene. The trap, of course, was laid for Lace who is a kind of amateur undertaker."

The banker flared. "I'm not, sir. I resent—"

"You'd been an undertaker in the old days when you were a ridgeroad storekeeper. Years ago, most storekeepers back in the hills did embalming and sold coffins on the side. Rudd was doing a little detective work of his own. He found some notes of yours on the back of an envelope. He told me it was a recipe for a spot-remover. Hah! That's the old-time formula for homemade embalming fluid—arsenic and zinc chloride. When I found out that Follett was a young man, I knew he wasn't the boy we were after.

"Here's what occurred. Ivy died. Fannin, with Rudd out of

the way, called in old fumbling Dr. Caffery. Caffery examined her, said she was dead. Fannin then contacted Lace and asked him as a favor to embalm her. Lace was maybe proud of his skill, maybe wanted to make a few pennies. He went to his drugstore, got the ingredients, and embalmed her. Later Fannin called Follett—this was to make it bad for Lace."

Fannin lay back in the cushions, yawned.

McGavock said: "Fannin then told Lace that it was his idea that Ivy hadn't actually died, that old Caffery had bungled his diagnosis, that maybe even Lace killed her. Well, Lace is a banker and a bigshot. The prospect of such a scandal knocked him silly. Fannin also wrote a letter to Sheriff Gelso putting out the same idea. This information, in the possession of the law, was a backlog for his blackmail as long as the sheriff didn't know Lace's name. Lace forked over fifteen thousand dollars cash. He told Judy that the money was for a vacation!"

Lace Tincher was trembling. "Did I do anything illegal? I only meant to help—"

"In Memphis, you'd have a little difficulty. In Hetherton, I bet everything comes out all right. You carry the key that makes the clock run, don't you?"

Fannin laughed. "I was too smart for you. You cain't prove a thing!"

"Not about Ivy, no. But here's a case the sheriff might be interested in. You outsmarted yourself when you picked the lock on the cabinet. Sheriff, here's your brief, and it's surefire. Say that he killed Miss Ella for her diamond brooch. Caffery will swear that Fannin gave it to him, if you tighten up on the old doctor. So Fannin just killed Miss Ella, took the key from her shoe, and stole the pin. Simple and clear. Any hill jury can understand it."

Fannin's face contorted in alarm. McGavock said: "I've got a train to make. Good night."

He returned to the hotel for his bag. There was a wire waiting for him at the desk. It said: ARE YOU IN HETHERTON? LET ME KNOW. HAVEN'T HEARD FROM YOU FOR TWO DAYS. ATHERTON BROWNE.

It was ten-fifteen when McGavock got to the depot. He took pencil and paper and onerously wrote three sentences. At the window, he said: "Here are three telegrams. I want them sent at half-hour intervals. Understand?"

The Old Man went to bed early and the wires were addressed to his residence. The first said: ARRIVED HETHERTON, LUTHER. The second said: HAVE DISCOVERED AND SOLVED A MURDER, LUTHER. The third: AM LEAVING HETHERTON FOR MEMPHIS, LUTHER.

McGavock grinned. "That's quick work. I'd like to see his face."

About the Author

I WAS BORN in this little Ohio village where I now live (although I left when I was four). My grandfather was a Methodist minister here in the '80s. Am married, no children; but our 150-pound Newfoundland, Lancelot du Lac, keeps our home and our village fairly active. I've lived a good half of my life in Tennessee and am very fond indeed of the Southern hill country. Have been dragged through four colleges, and assaulted with a M.A. from Vanderbilt. When I was young, I spent a year on coffee freighters in the South American trade. I've been writing full time for about ten years.

I have no hobbies, really, unrelated to my work. My particular interest is in building up a library of early American roguery and vagabondage—the sleights and speech of wandering pack-men, doctors, dentists, fire-eaters and so on (our hinterland highways and wilderness trails were literally jammed with them for many years). There's not too much contemporary record along this line, I'm sorry to say, but now and then you uncover something, and when you add it to what you've already got, the picture grows. And it's a pretty stirring picture.

www.ingramcontent.com/pod-product-compliance
Lightning Source LLC
LaVergne TN
LVHW050929080826
845145LV00001B/260

* 9 7 8 1 6 1 8 2 7 7 3 4 3 *